Gillespie's Gold

Gillespie's Gold

First published in Australia in 2019 by Probert Consulting

Cataloguing in Publication Data is available from the Australian National Library.

ISBN: (trade paperback)   978-0-9874074-8-1

ISBN: (E-publishing version) 978-0-9874074-9-8

Website: www.wurugi.blogspot.com.au
Trade enquiries: probertconsulting@bigpond.com

Cover design: End2End Books
E-mail: admin@end2endbooks.co

Editing: Merlene Fawdry mgfawdry@gmail.com

Printing: IngramSpark

For my friends Fiona Byrnes, Heather and Ron Bence
your smiles and friendship are one of life's treasures.

Gillespie's Gold

Terry L Probert

Cast of Characters

Joe Gillespie	Orroroo farmer married to Laura
Laura Gillespie	Anthropologist
Tilly Gillespie	Daughter
Emily Gillespie	Daughter to Tilly
Les Gillespie	Joe's father
Elspeth Somerton	Laura's cousin
Bill Somerton	Married to Elspeth
Jeff Rankin	Senior Constable
Ted Rankin	Jeff's father
Sam Lewis	RADOR's CEO
Charles Winkler	Sam's boss
Gino Di Massimo	Charles, odd job man
Timothy	Sam's PA
David Wang	Hong Kong investment banker

Orroroo

John O'Rourke	Constable
Fiona O'Rourke	Tilly's friend
Andy McLeod	Friend of Jeff's
Brad Reardon	Garage Owner
Karen Reardon	Married to Brad
Spider Webb	Works for Brad
Spoggy Sparrow	Drifter
Jake	Builder
Rosie	Publican's wife,
Zach	Sharefarmer
Denis	Builder
Uncle Rupert	Adnyamathanha man

Port Augusta Police

Doug Simpson (Sarge)	Senior Sergeant
Darryl Cassidy	Detective Inspector
Rob Ackland	Constable Traffic Division
Angela	Constable
David Builder (Bob)	Constable

Adelaide Police

Salma Akbar	Superintendent
Senior Constable Shannon	
Constable Williams	

Others

Amber Renouf	National Trust
Damian Tao	Works for Amber
Jonathon Smyth-Simms	Gillespie's solicitor
Gavin	Sam's old flame
Sasha	Gavin's fiancé
Matthew Naqvi	Journalist
Enrico	Hotel Concierge
Clive Lewis	Sam's father married to Penny
Penny Lewis	Married to Clive
Simon Lewis	Sam's brother
Chelsea	Married to Simon
Harry Forbes	Retired Detective Inspector
Carol Forbes	Married to Harry
Jack Pendlebury	Politician
Hans Schmidt	Politician
Andreas Pituri:	Politician
Isadora Duncan	American Dancer
Monty	Assassin
Freddie Braithwaite	Aircraft enthusiast

CHAPTER ONE

Bumping his wife's arm, Joe shifted and shuffled the papers on the desk she was working at, he whispered, 'sorry.'

Laura huffed and rolled her eyes, hoping he'd get the message she was busy. His opening of each drawer and rummaging through its contents now causing her to lean away from her work.

'Jeeze Joe, can't you see I'm busy. And what are you looking for anyway?'

'Found 'em,' he said, waving a crumpled packet of paracetamol. He flopped into the armchair opposite, popped two tablets into his hand and tossed the empty packet into the waste bin.

'Joe!'

Ignoring her frown, he reached for her glass of water.

She thrust it at him, 'here...'

'Well you don't want me to dry swallow, do you?'

Leaning back in her chair, Laura combed her fingers through greying hair, fighting against the tide of angry words threatening to erupt. What was wrong with the man? He'd never been anything but supportive of her work before, even protective of her space. Now he was disrupting her for something that could be found in just about every room of the house. Deciding any fight back would be unproductive and cause her to lose even more time, she kept her response short. 'Just go, I need this finished before we fly to England.'

Joe should have noticed the exhaustion in her voice. Last year he would have understood that papers piled on the floor meant she was busy, but today he didn't move. He just sat there rubbing his forehead.

1

Slapping her hands on the desk she said, 'find something to do Joe.'

'Yeah, all right,' he mumbled.

'Joe...'

'On my way,' he said without moving. For not the first time today, he took the faded receipt from the Perth Mint out of his pocket and stared at it.

'Joe if you're just going to sit there you can help. Find me the file marked Arkaroo Rock and when I ask, read each of the reference numbers to me please.'

Her tone penetrated his reverie and he looked up, 'sorry, you're on your own, this headache's got a hell of a hold on me right now.' With that he left the room, still unaware he was rubbing his forehead.

Knowing she'd lost her momentum and deciding a break might clear her head, she called after him, 'better flick the kettle on while you are out there... please.'

Putting the receipt on the bench while he filled the kettle, his mind was still challenging the paper's puzzle. It had troubled him from the very first moment he had seen it in Port Augusta and the rhyme scrawled on the back of it kept nagging at him. He didn't think it possible to despise his father more than he had during his adolescence, but now with this churning gut and all these unanswered questions, it felt as if Les was goading him from the grave and this gave voice to his thoughts.

'Where do you hide one hundred and forty-five ounces of eighteen carat gold, old man? And how did you come by it?'

He remembered the kettle and switching it on said, 'and why keep it from your family?' Reaching for the cups, setting them on a tray continued, 'and why all the secrecy?' He flicked the receipt, 'or did you waste this too?'

These questions crashed around in his mind like the sphere in a pinball machine. He couldn't dismiss it as nonsense. The receipt in his hand was genuine.

The Gillespie family had retained exploration leases over their land, but to his knowledge, no one had ever worked these claims and if his father had ever found gold, where was it now?

Had he hidden it somewhere, wasted it on the ponies, or was the note just another after death trick to play on his only child?

Laura walked into the kitchen and wrapped an arm around him, 'are you still fiddling with that old docket and talking to your ghost?'

Not meaning to shrug her off, he shoved the receipt into his breast pocket and stepped aside. 'Yeah, just can't get it out of my head.'

She took a glass, filled it with water, leaned against the bench and stared at him... 'and the tea?'

'Yeah, I'm on it,' he heard the frustration in her voice and knew she wanted more from him, but existing was all he could manage right now. She didn't understand and he couldn't tell her. Not now anyway, not with everyone thinking their lives had just taken a positive turn?

'It's okay Joe, it really is, but you need to get a grip mate. Whatever the note means it's been there for years. Surely we can make time for a cuppa.'

'Yeah... I know, but my Pop never said anything about any gold, or mines and neither did Mum. It has to be a fake, because there was no mention of it in Dad's will. And then I start chewing everything over in my mind again. Look I don't know... if there is any gold out there, then where would it be? And why he would leave something like this just lying around for me to find, what, almost forty years later,' he paused, remembering their planned trip to Europe. They were due to leave in a few weeks and he didn't want to spend their holiday wondering about the past, 'I know this is going to eat at me while we're away and unless we get to the bottom of it, it'll drive both of us mad. What would you do?' he asked, pulling a chair out from the table and sat down.

'I know what the bloke I married would do. He'd get in touch with the mint to find out if the receipt was genuine. If it's a fake, we'll know it was just another of your father's games and we can get on with the rest of our lives,' she put a hand on the back of his chair and tousled his hair with the other, 'if it is real, then we have a treasure hunt on our hands when we come home.'

She strolled back to their office and after a couple of minutes on Google returned, dropping a page of contact details in front of him and saying, 'there you go, call the Perth Mint and find out what needs to be done to verify it.'

'Gee thanks, maybe I'll give them a call tomorrow.'

'I don't think so, you'll have the lawns done by ten thirty and their offices should be open by then. Just get on the phone and do it. You've been mooning around the house and brooding about your bloody father and his papers since Christmas. I want my husband back,' she pulled his head up so he could see her eyes, 'get this done now Joe. I don't want to spend my holiday walking on eggshells, just because you can't rid yourself of your father's ghost. You hear me Joe? I'm not sharing our holiday with Les bloody Gillespie.'

Forgetting the tea, he stuffed the receipt and the list in his pocket, stormed outside and sat down. Picking up Laura's book, "A Town Like Alice", he thumbed through its pages, reading nothing.

His wife was right. He hadn't been the same since his heart attack three months ago. They did have plenty to look forward to, but there had been changes that had altered his life. Their daughter Tilly, had sold her business and taken

4

over his role of the day to day running of the farm. Her daughter Emily, was growing like a weed and seemed smarter every time she visited. And although Laura was retiring, she had found a new challenge in wanting to restore all the sheds and machinery, suggesting they could build a tourism business around it.

It was hard to believe that only a season ago he had been in charge, managing everything. Had control of his life, kept the farm together, served on the occasional committee, and enjoyed a prominent role within the community. He didn't mean to mope around. He wanted to get back to work and be Laura's Joe Gillespie of old. He wanted his old self back too. His self-confidence was at zero and he worried he was headed for a wasted existence, sponging off the efforts of his family as his father had done before him. Not at all what he wanted.

Now he had two pieces of paper, a peeved wife, a lawn to mow and a stupid rhyme that wouldn't let him rest. He knew that unless he settled this, he'd remain in limbo. Again, the cloud of doubt threatened to close in on him, making him fearful of a future as a nowhere man, with a nowhere farm and nowhere life. He supposed he could just forget everything he'd ever known, walk away from it and become a townie, join the bowls club and die within two years. That's what old farmers did, didn't they? And at the funeral, they would all remember him fondly, toast his memory at the wake, then get in their cars and go on with their lives.

The back door burst open, slamming back against the laundry wall. Turning he saw Laura marching toward him.

'Oh, come on Joe... you're not still out here moping?' Her words, soft with concern masked her anger and rubbing his shoulders she said, 'come on love, cut the grass, do something useful. You can't keep doing nothing all day, it's not like you,' she bent down and lifted his chin to get his full attention, 'Joe, you're the only one who can do anything about your situation. I'm fed up with it. I want the man I married to come back, and I'm not putting up with the cardboard cut-out you've let yourself become. For God's sake Joe, mow the damn lawn and then phone Perth. Remember your motto, *Do it Now*,' her hands were on her hips, 'and there's no time like the present.'

She startled him. This wasn't the first time since the attack that her temper had boiled to the surface and he knew if he didn't do something to bring their relationship back on an even keel, it was only him he'd have to blame. The truth was he didn't feel himself and he had no idea how to come back from this dark place of headaches and confusion. But she was right. He'd mow the lawn, phone Perth, and see where it led him. 'Okay,' he said, 'lawn first then tea.'

Smiling her approval, Laura turned and walked back into the house.

CHAPTER TWO

The mower droned as it spat clippings into the catcher, his thoughts in free fall he hummed to the cadence of the words that had exasperated him as a child.

If Les had hidden gold, was the rhyme a clue?

It had to be, and the measuring of the water level in the wells had to be part of it too.

Miller's Creep was a strange name to call a place. Joe's family used to joke about old man Miller and how he would be forever mending his boundary fences, creeping a line of posts onto the neighbour's property a couple of feet at a time and hoping no-one would notice. The Gillespies had been on the Miller's land since its purchase over sixty years ago, and although forgotten now, old man Miller was a legend for all the wrong reasons.

Joe, reciting the poem in his mind wanted to get it right and have it written down before he phoned the mint. The words formed a song and soon he was singing loudly, feeling his despondency lift with the release. The area finished, he had just shut the mower down when he heard Laura call out to him for morning tea, saying the word as a question.

'Smoko?'

'Yep, I'll put the mower away and wash up while you pour.'

She put the tray on the old patio table under the trees, a long standing ritual in their lives. When he came back, she was smiling, 'you needed that rev-up I gave you earlier, yeah?'

'Maybe, maybe not, but yeah, I guess it didn't hurt.'

'Then why the change? It can't have been the gardening, because it's never done much for you in the past.'

'No, it's definitely not the gardening,' he laughed at the thought, 'and we don't need to call the mint. I've worked it out and,' he paused for effect, 'Laura Gillespie, you and I are going on a treasure hunt.'

'How, what treasure, where?' She laughed with him, 'have you finally lost your grip on reality?'

Joe sipped his tea and leant back in his chair, smug in his new found knowledge, 'it's all in the rhyme. Listen and tell me what you think.'

Little Joe Gillespie
Maybe eights or nines or tens
Has very few companions
Only sheep and cows as friends
But when he's running waters
And the bank its balance low
He has a friend to count on
Does little Gillespie Joe

Laura put her cup down, as if to listen more intently. 'Okay, the first verse is about you, but I don't understand about running water, what's that mean?'

'Well the line, *but when he's running waters*, is what Dad called the windmill run. It tells me that times were tough and we were likely to be in drought, because we're measuring the water tables. The next line is about money, or the lack of it,' he couldn't curb his excitement and recited the next verse.

Cause he has a hole of water
Out there on Miller's Creep
Its 'mill as proud as the tower in Paris
And does Les Gillespies' secret keep
In there, Another well by Harris
Is carved upon the boards

But five below the water line
Joe's dad has left his hoards

Laura could see the eagerness in his face and felt the pull of a treasure hunt too, 'okay smarty, tell me about the second verse. What does that mean?'

He dunked a biscuit in his tea and spoke with his mouth full, 'that might be even more important. Think about it love. The date on the receipt will tell us how far down the water was from the top of the well, then five boards below that is where I reckon he stashed the gold. Why would he mention it on the slip otherwise?'

She shrugged and smiled at him.

'What say we take a look this arvo?' He suggested.

'I'm game, but what about the last verse. What does that mean?'

'Well I think this is the best part. The clues are cryptic, but that makes it all the more exciting.'

And all this gleaming treasure
Mined from the ridge above the creek
In a shaft dank dark and dirty cramped
Well it's no place for the weak
From a seam of Earths' rich bounty camped
Perth's Mint, assayed it gold and true
Wet deep down there my promise lies
And my son, it's waiting just for you

Laura screwed up her nose and asked, 'so?'

Joe looked into the tea in his cup, memories flooding back, 'I thought I'd forgotten it, but now it's back just as if it happened today.' He used his index finger to turn the cup on its saucer. 'the old bastard was hanging onto my ankles and dangling me over the well. He kept chanting that last

9

verse over and over,' he felt cold and a shiver stayed with him. 'it scared me so much I had nightmares for years.'

'Joe, I...'

He cut her off, 'remember I told you that when I was in the glider and when stones were flicking onto the canopy, I said I felt claustrophobic. You know how I get in small spaces. I was thinking about that when I was cutting the lawn and that's when it all came to me,' he looked out toward the Oladdie Hills, as if to bring the past closer, 'I must have been about three or four when Dad took me into this hole, or cave. Thinking back on it now, it must have been a mine. I remember hearing a crashing noise and being covered by dirt. I couldn't breathe,' he put his hand to his chest, gasping at the memory, 'and it seemed to take forever before I felt hands scraping the dirt away and him pulling me out. It's the only time I remember him hugging me. And he was crying too. I was terrified, but even after the well incident, somehow I knew I'd be safe in his arms.'

Laura smiled at him, reaching across the table to squeeze the back of his hand.

Joe always felt lighter whenever she touched him like this and he smiled back at her, 'I think he must have caught hell from Mum when we got home, because she didn't let me go out with him after that. Not until just before she died anyway.'

'So what now? Who's going down the well? Do you want me to do it?'

'Hell no. I'm not having my wife go down a well, if I won't do it myself.'

'I'm glad that's settled then, and just where do you suppose this mine is?'

'That's the funny bit. I have no idea where the mine is, or if it even exists. I don't know if the well is safe, but I do know I don't want to go down it. The last time I was in one of those, I was in my twenties, shit scared of snakes and shaking with fear.

You could ask Jeff, I'm sure he'd help out,' Laura thought for a moment before answering herself, 'no, that's no good. Tilly would crack it. She and Jeff are having their troubles again this week.'

'I can't keep up with those two. What's it about this time?'

'Who knows? I just wish they'd get on with it. I mean, how hard can it be? They're two people who really love each other and yet neither of them can tell the other how they feel.'

With that option squashed, Joe stood up and started to pack the tray.

'It'll be you and me then. I'll pick up the windmill truck and when we get there, we can work out what to do next. If it looks okay you can lower me down in the bucket.' 'Fine by me,' she kissed his cheek, 'I'm just about finished, so you'd better get the truck sorted while I pack a lunch.' truck sorted while I pack a lunch.

CHAPTER THREE

From the window of his Currie Street office, Charles Winkler gazed across to the parklands to King William Street and to the north horizon beyond the suburbs.

'It's time to strike, Gillespie's weak right now and we should be able to roll him without much resistance.' He turned to his personal assistant, 'Sam, find Gino and ask him to come in.'

She stood there.

'Now! Damn you.'

Samantha could keep it up until he said please, but it would only add to his aggression and she thought better of the ploy. Besides she was sure he would want to stay over tonight. His squash partner had phoned earlier and cancelled. She understood their arrangement, Charles would never make husband material and she was using him to further her career. It worked for now, and when she no longer needed him, she would leave.

Gino wasn't hard to find, he never moved too far from his computer, 'Gino, Charlie wants you in his office.'

He snapped his laptop closed as she spoke, but not before she had seen the screen, 'I don't know how that girl does that and don't let Charlie catch you looking at that stuff in his time, you know how he is with security and the company's computers.'

'He's Charles to you Missy and I've got nothing to hide.'

'Good for you Gino,' she loved pushing his buttons, knowing he had a quick temper. She enjoyed the feeling of power his reaction to her teasing gave her, but she knew her limits and curbed her tongue as his face reddened. He was Charles' fix-it man and whatever needed doing he did it without question. Gino Di Massimo was not a man to cross.

12

'Hold your cards close Missy, you won't always be his favourite flavour.' He tidied his desk before leaving the room. His habit of neatness was part of his persona and it extended to his dress. Italian suits for the office, RM Williams his choice of wear for outside work. Once tidied to his satisfaction, he walked the short distance to his boss's to the door and knocked.

'You wanted to see me Charles?'

''We need another plan. You promised me the attack by the Americans would get us onto Gillespie's land failed but, while he's still soft from it, we should do something before he recovers.'

Gino listened, there was no point offering protest or excuses, Charles was right, the last plan was a mess.

Charles continued, 'we need another strategy because, after what's happened, Gillespie's proved he's a match for brute force,' he turned and pointed at his colleague, 'look Gino, it's vital we get onto his place. I know what I want is out there. It's as simple as this, your last plan didn't work and I want their leases. There's gold out there somewhere and I want to mine it.'

Charles stared at the map on the wall, before looking back over his shoulder. 'Fix it.'

Gino knew this wasn't a request, it was an order. He wanted to click his heels and offer a Nazi salute, but resisted, limiting himself to what he knew Charles wanted to hear, that he would take care of it.

Charles turned to look out the window, 'oh and Andreas Pituri, the new Minister for Mines, I need him, or someone connected, in my pocket. We lost the last bloke to the police portfolio, so he's not much use to us right now. Find all the dirt you can on Pituri. You know, the usual stuff, massage parlours, high class escorts, bookies, loan sharks, conflict of interest issues, the lot. And Gino, dig, go

13

deep. I don't want to hear he's squeaky clean. If he is, then fix it so he's not. You know what to do.'

'So rattle the family's rubbish bins, parents, wife, kids, everyone?'

'Go for it, but as always, keep it distant from the firm. Do nothing that can link it back to us, understand. I won't tell you how to do your job. You've done it a hundred times, just don't embarrass me, okay?'

Gino walked over, his face inches from his boss's, 'Charlie boy, you and I both know where we came from, so this is still a two-way street. I can still count on you too, can't I?'

'Charles, damn it Gino. You know to call me Charles in the office, how many times do I need to tell you.'

Gino pointed a finger at Charles nose. 'Yes sir, but the question stands. Can I still count on you?'

"Shit, Gino, it's not something I need to say.'

'Oh yes, it is Charlie. I really do need to hear you say it. What you're asking me to do has risks, big risks.'

'I have your back, Gino. I have your back.'

Both men stared through the plate glass and scanned the suburbs toward Port Adelaide, each wanting to forget their origins but understanding the ties that bind.

***

In Orroroo, Fiona O'Rourke put two coffees on the table outside Maggie's Rendezvous coffee shop and set a couple muffins in front of Tilly. 'You choose which one you want, because I like them both.'

'I'll take the blueberry. After that gym session this morning, I reckon we both deserve a reward,' Tilly looked idly at a passing car of a similar model to the one her father drove, 'you know, I should really go and see Mum sometime today, but I really can't face Dad much at the moment. He's still not himself. I ask him something and he gives me a, *just do whatever you think*, answer,' she used her fingers to indicate quotation marks, 'I swear, at times I wish I'd never agreed with Mum to take on this rebuilding project.'

'Tough then?'

'Not really, the insurers have been great and the various government departments have been helpful. It's just Dad. He hasn't been the same since his heart attack and he's so dammed frustrating. I'd like him to take over again, well maybe not take over completely because I am enjoying it, but I wish he would just show some interest, engage with me a bit.'

'Well by the look of things, your dad has a bit of a spring in his step this morning, see,' Fiona pointed toward Brad's Rescue across the street to where Joe had almost sprinted from the Range Rover to the side door of the workshop.

'What's the old bugger up too? I haven't seen him move like that for months,' Tilly twisted in her chair craning her neck for a better view.

'He must be feeling better.'

'Either that or Mum has given him a rocket. She seemed a bit fed up with all his moping around the last time I was down there. I'll send her a text and find out what's going on.' Her thumbs danced over the keypad on her phone and she didn't notice Fiona's partner, John, until he sat down.

'Jeff?' He spoke the name as a question, nodding toward her mobile.

'God no, he's as exasperating as Dad. I don't know what it is with me and men. They really get up my nose at times and at others, well you can guess, I reckon.'

'What about Jeff?' Fiona asked, 'I thought you guys were starting to make a go of things, come on girl, spill?

15

John can get us more coffee and you can tell me about Jeff.'

'You sure you want coffee, or for me to leave?' John stood up and smiled. There were some things he didn't need to know, 'I'm off to Peterborough for a couple of hours, Fi, and thought I'd say goodbye before I went, that's all.'

'No coffee for me thanks John,' Tilly answered, 'I've had my quota.'

'I'm right too thanks, love,' Fiona stood up to meet his peck on her cheek, 'I'll see you when you get home then?'

Tilly scraped the last dregs of foam from her cappuccino and licked the spoon.

'Righto Tilly, what's going on between you two?' Fiona crossed her eyes and stared at her friend, she wanted answers.

CHAPTER FOUR

Joe wandered into the workshop looking for the owner. Brad Reardon had been in business on the Main Street corner for over forty years, since taking over the garage in the mid-seventies. He had started his apprenticeship there after he left school and, when his employer wanted to retire a few years later, he became a businessman at the age of twenty-two. The drought had almost ruined him, but out of Joe's recent misfortune, he'd been able to re-employ a couple of staff and begin the repairs to most of the Gillespie's equipment.

'G'day Joe, we've still got a fair bit to do,' Brad wiped his hands on the rag that always hung from his pocket, 'the insurance company phoned this morning and gave me the go ahead for the Landcruiser. So I'll get that down to the crash repairer tonight. It'll probably be there for another week or two though and then I'll need to replace a lot of the lines and stuff underneath. All up I reckon you'll still be without it for another three weeks.'

'Yeah, I thought you'd say that. What about the windmill truck, is she right to go?'

'Think so, hang on and I'll find out from Spider. Yesterday he only had to replace that couple of tyres to finish it off. I reckon he'd have it done by now.'

Brad Reardon walked to the corner where an older man was working on the engine of a lawnmower. A few muffled words and a wave of his hand toward the yard seemed to be enough for him.

'Yep, he'll check the tyre pressures and park it out front. It'll be ready in half an hour. That okay with you?'

'Beauty, get him to fill it up with diesel too and we'll call back before lunch.'

Joe felt more like his old self today than any time since his heart attack and if it wasn't for this dull ache in his head he'd feel like singing. Everything seemed to slip when he'd pulled back, letting others make decisions for him. He couldn't remember how or when he'd given up his role of decision maker but, piece by piece he'd lost it. It had probably happened during his recuperation, when others had stepped in to help and now he felt as if his position in life had diminished. It was nothing intentional and no one had robbed it from him, but his self-worth had drifted away with the loss of his former good health.

Tilly had shown she was more than capable of taking charge and had tradesmen lined up repairing the homestead and she had engaged Zack Jones and his new bride to take over the farming operation. Joe had often employed him to help during the school holidays and weekends. Zack had been a townie with a desire for farming and used his part time wages to fund an agricultural college education. They worked out a deal for him to use Joe's machinery with hire costs paid out of the first wheat payments. It would leave Joe and Laura time to enjoy their retirement. Or at least, that was what Tilly and Laura had said to convince him to agree. Sitting around doing nothing had never sat easy with him, but now this treasure hunt fired his imagination and renewed his zest

He and Laura had only been out to Wanooka's Well, their farm, a couple of times since Christmas and watching it decay while they waited for the insurance company to process their claim was heartbreaking. Neglect had crept in everywhere and as time added to the ravage of their home, it appeared even more derelict. They had to wait for the builders to finish before they could return.

Today would be different. Tilly had told them that the new shed doors were in place and lockable. He had never locked a shed in his life and always left the keys in his machinery but, as the past months had proved, times change. Now, knowing his windmill truck could be locked away offered comfort.

Before she finished her muffin, Tilly called her mother.

'Dad wants something to do, love. He's picking up the windmill to take back to the Well,' Laura sounded rushed and evasive.

'Will I see you out home after you take the truck out?' Tilly was doing her best to get her mother to open up about Joe's apparent change of attitude. 'I want to catch up with the builders before they knock off for the weekend and plan on heading out there after I pick up Emily from school.'

'I'm not sure how long we'll be there. We might be though. I think your dad wants to look around a bit before we come home. So yes, we'll see you at the homestead about five or half past, okay?' Laura didn't understand herself why she was being elusive, but it seemed right to hold onto Joe's secret until he was ready to let his daughter in on it.

Laura drove the Range Rover and led Joe toward Miller's Creep, opening the gates and leaving them for him to close as they travelled north west. Dust hung in the late morning air and Joe held back about six hundred meters. He felt good, the day was hot and he had something to do. Even if it turned out to be a wild goose chase, his heart felt lighter. Gip had taken her place on the seat beside him. Laura had urged her to get into the Range Rover, but the old dog knew that with Joe, she could hang her head out of the window as the wind flapped her lips, drool stringing out down the side of the cab.

'A man and his dog eh, girl?' Joe reached across the cab and rubbed his hand along the dog's back. Strands of greying red hair floated around the cabin, 'you've put Laura's nose out a bit, but she'll get over it.'

19

Laura was waiting at Miller's gate, standing with her hands pressed into her back and stretching as she took in the hills and the sky, revelling in the quiet.

'Apart from us the landscape is empty. Hard to imagine there were farms every mile out here once,' she waved her hand across the panorama.

'No time for reminisces now, we've got treasure to find,' his grin spread to his eyes and today she thought he looked younger. Maybe he was back to his old self, 'we can leave the gates open as there's no stock to worry about and we'll shut them when we come back this way tonight.'

'Are you going to tell Tilly why we're here?'

'Not until I've had a look down that hole

Following her, he held the record book against the steering wheel and flipped through its pages. Water table measurements went back to 1946 when his dad had started recording them and this journal had ridden in every windmill truck.

Laura nosed the car into the shade of a pepper tree where hungry cattle had nibbled off the bottom branches to about two metres from the ground, giving it a topiary appearance. She snatched her hat, pulled it down in the front and made her way to the windmill.

'Not that one, we're over here, Darl,' Joe was shuffling around swinging a shovel back and forth in a scything action, 'we'll back the old girl up and swing the boom over the well about there,' he pointed to a mark on some railway sleepers lying among tufts of dry spear grass, 'I'll just get these out of the way first.'

'But the poem says something about a windmill?'

'I know, but we shifted the mill when the water table dropped. The bore went down in the early sixties. Now I understand why he'd measure the level here and not in the bore. He was just a touch cunning, I reckon.'

'Well, while you do that I'll get lunch ready, okay?'

'Give me a hand to line the truck up first then I can set up while you do it.'

She slid behind the steering wheel and eased the vehicle back. Joe could see her in the driver's mirror and with his right thumb indicated which way to turn the wheel, using his left hand to guide her back. This was an understanding they shared and a task they had done many times before except today, water was not their goal.

CHAPTER FIVE

The battered hard hat looked out of place perched on Tilly's head, until she pulled her pony tail through the back strap and it swung from shoulder to shoulder as she jogged past the demolition crew. Oblivious to their admiring glances, her mind was firmly set on the architect's drawings held down by stones scavenged from the rubble of the building. She had not consulted with her parents, preferring instead to clean up the site and get on with restoration. She knew it was probably presumptuous of her, but it was the only way she knew how to help them move forward.

In the kitchen, she noted Jake was using her mother's once treasured kitchen table as a desk. It should have been at the restorers by now and she rubbed her hand over the marks carved into it by the vandals, knowing she would show him her displeasure soon enough. For now she listened to what he had to tell her.

'We found a trap door to a cellar under the carpet in the passage and it's not safe down there. Worse than that though, I think you'll need to get in touch with the National Trust before we can go much further.'

'Why, what makes you say that?' Tilly felt her exasperation building. Everything about this project conspired to challenge her. 'I know Mum and Dad fixed it up a bit in the sixties. That was before they were married and you'd think they'd have said if we couldn't change much of the old parts.'

'Well we knocked a bit of plaster off along the front of the cellar to take care of the salt damp, and there's a foundation stone in there,' he pointed in the general direction and beckoned her to follow.

'Shit no, what's the date on it?'

'Says eighteen sixty-five,' he said, 'and it's not worth the risk getting on the wrong side of the National Trust or they'll have you re-do everything.'

'Damn,' Tilly said, 'who has to tell them?'

'I can, I guess, but we do have to let them know.'

'Bugger it, I wanted to get on top of this and have the place ready for my folks when they returned from their trip to Europe. We couldn't pretend it wasn't there could we?'

'Not with a big city lawyer as my client, if things went belly up? Well, you know what I mean.'

'Yeah, I know, sorry I'm snappy. Ever since Dad got sick it's just one problem after another. I don't know what to expect next.'

'I reckon if someone had been taking pot-shots at me I'd be crook too. Ease up a bit on him Tilly, he'll come good.'

She took her hat off, running a hand through the front of her hair as she looked around the site again, 'we'd better do the progress report then, shall we?'

'Sure. Do you want Emily along?'

'No, I've told her not to bother your men and she's spent most of her life around here anyway. She'll be okay.'

'Righto,' Jake said, 'to start with, the sheds and the tanks are just about done. I'll be finished all of that by the end of the next week but, before we can touch the structure, I'll have to wait until we know what's going on with the Trust.'

'Of course we will.'

He heard sarcasm in her voice and let it go, 'I'll see if I can get onto it now, but being Friday...' he shrugged, 'and the phones don't always work out here either.'

'I knew that,' Tilly, never one to hold her anger for long, laughed at the irony of the situation, 'you see, I told you the bloody place is conspiring against me'

'I'll be right to call them Monday. We're nearly finished here, I'll just give the boys a hand to pack up and then it's off to the pub for us.'

'Lucky you.'

'You could come too?' His wicked smile showed why many a lady had succumbed to his charm.

'It's tempting, but no thanks, besides...' she nodded to where Emily was playing with one of the worker's pups.

'I'll see you next week then.'

'See you then,' Tilly answered, staring as he turned and walked toward the sheds. Tanned, with black curly hair, Jake was every bit a man and the rest of the crew weren't too hard on the eye either. Only one was married and the rest enjoyed a reputation for being, love 'em and leave 'em lads made it difficult to keep her mind on the job at times, but one little thought lapse wouldn't hurt.

Within minutes tools were packed and the site secured, leaving only a trail of dust remaining to indicate they had been there. Emily slipped her hand in her mother's and said, 'you promised to show me where you used to play when you were my age, Mum?'

'Okay young lady, I reckon we've got enough time to climb Wanooka's Hill before your Granny gets here.'

***

At Millers, Joe held the spotlight and peered into the well. Cobwebs glistened among the boards. Insects and grubs sought sanctuary as they scurried from the light. Laura put her hand on his shoulder to steady herself and said, 'I'm glad it's you going into that. Just looking down there gives me the shivers.'

A cricket ball sized stone dropped from his hand. 'Listen,' he shushed her and counted, 'one, two, three, and there we go. It sounds about one hundred and fifty feet deep, or forty-five metres in new money as Pop used to say.'

'So what now? I've helped pull pipes before, but what do we do next?'

'I'm going to let a lantern down on a string and check if it's okay down there first and then it's into the bucket for me,' he had a lilt in his voice for the first time in months.

'But what if there's a build-up of coal gas down there? You know survey teams have crawled all over the district for the last two years searching for suitable fracking sites. If that lantern flame hits gas while you're leaning over the hole it'll do more than scorch your eyebrows.'

'You worry too much. I'll soak a rag in diesel and drop it down first. If there is gas down there, it will light up like the bikie's camp did.' He grinned at the memory of Dante's camp filling with flames and explosions in the Horseshoe.

'Okay, but stand back, I don't want to nurse you with third degree burns.'

He moved the truck a distance away and cleaned an area around the well with a shovel. Laura had a point, if there was gas down there, the timbers could catch fire and cause the well to collapse. He dipped a rag into the truck's fuel tank, taking it back to the well before setting it alight. 'Are you ready?'

'Let it go.' Laura tingled all over. They hadn't enjoyed time together in this way for a long time. Joe had shaken off the moodiness that had clouded their lives and was doing what he did best, his happiness showing in his customary smile as the rag dropped into the well. She held her hands over her ears, turned from the well and closed her eyes in anticipation of an explosion.

'Bang!' Joe roared and grabbed her hips.

She spun around in fright to see him doubled over laughing at his prank. She slapped his arm, 'you bugger, Joe, you nearly gave me a heart attack.'

The well was silent and Joe peered over the rim to see the flicker from the rag drowning on the water. Ebony and gold, it was a pretty light show, even if short lived. Diesel fumes wafted out of the hole, as cold air rushed into the well.

'All set to go girl,' he was still laughing, 'seriously, you should have seen your face.'

'You'll keep, Joe Gillespie, believe me you'll keep,' Laura pretended a huffiness she knew he wanted to see as she climbed into the truck to back it into position.

CHAPTER SIX

On the Hammond Road on the outskirts of Wilmington, Jeff Rankin sat at his father's table staring at the papers in front of him, rolling a ballpoint pen between his fingers in concentration. If he signed this, he would be saying goodbye to a career he had started in his teens and he questioned whether he could make a living outside the police force. All his savings had been invested in his glider and he didn't want to have to sell it to survive.

'Are you going sign the bloody thing or just stare at it all afternoon?' Ted Rankin hated procrastination and, knowing his son shared this trait, he thought a little prod would do no harm.

'It's all I've known, Dad. It's natural to worry because what happens if I can't find another job?'

'You've got plenty of things you can do and you've got twelve weeks or so of long service leave plus a couple of week's holiday pay and some super if you really need to touch it. That's a whole heap more than your Mum and I had at your age. Get on the computer and check out if there's anything coming up with the National Parks, or you could give Joe a hand or fly a mail run. Just don't sit about the place moping.'

'I know you're right,' Jeff's hand dashed across the bottom of the paper. He looked at his father and smiled, 'done'

'Good, another door is waiting for you to open and begin a new chapter of your life,' his father was satisfied. Jeff had been mulling over quitting the police force since Christmas and had become lost in indecision, 'now you said something about us going out to meet Tilly at Joe's place. Do you want to take your car or mine?'

'We'll take mine Dad, you're still better sitting on a horse than behind a steering wheel.'

Ted took a hat from the rack in the hall and looked back, 'c'mon Son, you shouldn't keep a lady waiting.'

***

At Millers, Joe double checked the journal. The water was now about three metres lower than the level his father had last recorded so he knew the board would be well above the water. He climbed into the bucket confident he'd stay dry and switched on his headband light, which seemed incongruous on such a sunny afternoon.

Laura laughed at his appearance as he stood holding onto the bucket issuing instructions.

'Now, ease me down slowly, when the cable changes colour to greasy at about thirty metres, slow it right down and I'll give you a shout when to stop.'

The bucket rocked back and forth as he settled into position. Fashioned from a forty-four-gallon drum in the fifties, it was only slightly smaller in diameter than the well, but it gave him room to move. Laura pulled the control lever back and he disappeared into the gloom. On the eastern wall and three boards from the top were the words that Harris had carved there decades before, just as the rhyme had said. Joe figured Les would have stashed his hoard on this side and all he had to do was find the loose board.

Fear of confinement forgotten in the quest for adventure, he dropped lower into the well, his light reflected in the eyes of tiny creatures living between the boards. At different levels, the species of insect and spiders changed and he became caught in the wonder of it all. Occasionally a cobweb would waft across his face and his arms flailed to release it and all around him the coolness of the well and the fading smell of burnt diesel offered a strange comfort.

The cable stopped and he searched the boards.

'Are you going okay, Joe?' Laura's voice seemed a mile away.

'Yep, just let me down about another two metres, I can see the bottom of our sounding string just below the bucket.'

She let the winch run out another two metres of cable. He tapped the boards with the hammer he'd tucked in his belt, listening for a hollow sound as he worked his way around the timbers. Nothing.

'Drop me down another metre.' He called up to the top.

'Manners, Joe'

'Please.'

As the bucket slid another length, he kept tapping. 'Whoa! Hold it there, love... please.'

'Have you got it?'

'I've found a loose board, now to see if I can get it out.' He wedged a pry bar into the end board, but it had no effect. He tried the other end, and again it refused to move. He tapped the other boards until, at the edge of the light, he noticed a small indentation or a slot, like a keyhole but larger. The hammer was too big to slide into it and the pinch bar was too wide.

'What's going on down there?' Laura leant over edge, holding onto the cable to get a better look.

He looked up and spoke to her silhouette, 'I need a screwdriver from the tool box. The big one with the blue handle will do... please.' After a moment's silence, he heard the muted sound of her rattling through the box at the back of the truck, then another space before she was back at the top of the well.

'Here, do you want me to drop it down to you?'

'No way, if I don't catch it, you could kill me,' he was becoming more excited, 'the best way is to haul up the string, tie it to that and let it down gently.'

She was pleased to hear the old enthusiasm in his voice and commented, 'it's a good job you've bucked up a bit, mate, because the way you've been lately, I'd have been happy to throw it at you.'

Even if he could feel the bite in her words, the lightness in her tone took the edge off it and her words rippled down the well. He smiled, thinking even if there was nothing down here, they were enjoying themselves. The tool swung on the string and, standing on tip toes to reach it, he felt the bottom of the bucket creak. One edge had rusted over the years and the shift in his weight caused it to open slightly. He reached up and grabbed the cable's clevis.

'What was that?' Laura shouted.

'The bottom's falling out of the bloody bucket.'

'Hang on. I'll wind you out.'

'No way, I'm down here now. Look, you'll find some rope and a harness under the passenger seat. Take one end of the rope and tie a loose loop around the cable then, using the string, lower it all down to me like you did with the screwdriver.'

'We had a harness and you didn't use it...' her words trailed as she sprinted to the truck. There was a time and place for nagging and this was neither. As he waited, he could hear Laura's muffled movements as before, but an eternity seemed to pass as he trod air while he waited for the harness, then Laura was back passing the safety gear down to him.

She felt the string loosen and asked, 'how's that?' then watched as the cable bucked a few times before she heard his grunting echo up the well and his delayed reply.

'Yep, it's all good. I have the harness on and the rope is holding me to the clevis. I reckon I'll be right,' he slid the blade of the screw driver into the slot, but it fouled on the side of the bucket. He jiggled and still couldn't manage to move it, 'I need to go down about another two feet love so I can get at it properly.'

The bucket bounced on the stretching cable and the crack opened wider. Spreading his feet and shifting his weight away from the opening he pushed on the screwdriver, heard a click and watched the board spring towards him.

'You clever old bugger Les.'

Laura cupped her hands and shouted down to him, 'did you say something, Joe?'

'Just talking to myself, sort of. I've done it, but I still need to go down another foot so I can see in the hole.'

Laura let the cable play out until she heard him yell stop. He shone his light into the opening. Spiders had taken residence and it was evident that generations of web builders had claimed their piece of underground real estate. He wiped around the sides with the screwdriver collecting a mass of silvery filaments on its blade.

'Anything?' Laura's own excitement was building and she wanted to know what was in there.

'Hang on, I can see an old wooden box. I'll try to lift it out.' He prised at the bottom of it. The nails had rusted through and its sides fell away. He reached in and brushed them to one side, the debris splashing into the water below. Three rectangular bars lay behind the rotting timber, cool and heavy to his touch. Although small, he didn't trust the bottom of the bucket to hold the extra weight they would bring.

'We have a problem.' His voice slid off the walls on its way upward.

'What kind of problem?'

'The best kind and I need you to find something to put it into.'

'So it's down there after all?'

'Only three little ingots, but I think it's what the poem was about,' he resisted an urge to jump up and down, knowing the bucket wouldn't hold if he did, 'I have a tool bag in the back, empty it out and send it down to me. If you hang on a minute, I'll send the hammer and stuff up on the string.'

Laura fed the bag down to him, 'is that the one?'

'Yep that's the one thanks love.'

He tied the tool bag to the clevis and lifted each bar into it. Bending down for a last check of the cavity, he noticed a piece of slate with words scratched onto its surface. Stretching to reach it caused the bottom of the bucket let go completely taking the slack of the harness rope as he dropped, jamming his arm in the crevice. Laura heard him cry out,

'What happened? Joe?'

'The bottom's gone and I'm stuck,' his words were laboured, 'take me up about a foot.'

She responded to the anguish in his voice and eased the cable up.

'Got it,' he shouted, 'now get me out of here.'

Laura changed the winch gears and the engine revs built as the cable wound onto the drum. She was anxious to know what had happened, but stayed at her post until the bucket was clear of the well.

Joe was a sight and as he hung in mid-air. The bucket now looked like a rusty half open jam tin with a pair of legs dangling out of it. She swung the gantry to one side, lowered the bucket until it was lying on its side and dumped its contents onto the dry grass. She saw immediately what was wrong, his ashen face and his loose right arm told her it was his shoulder.

'Shit, Joe. What happened, are you okay?'

'I reckon it's dislocated, but I got this too,' he took the slate tablet from his damaged hand and passed it to her, 'now I reckon you'd better help me out of this lot.'

CHAPTER SEVEN

Emily and Tilly had seen dust rising from the road and made it back to the homestead in time to meet Jeff as he emerged from his car parked by the sheds.

'G'day,' he pecked Tilly on the cheek in greeting then stepped back as his father walked around and held his hand out to her. The older man smiled and took in the surroundings as if drinking in the peace of the homestead's setting.

'Jeff tells me you're trying to get all of this working again. I can't imagine what Laura must be going through at the moment, Joe neither. How's he doing?' He asked.

'He hasn't been himself since before Christmas, just mopes around most of the time. I've had to take over the work around here because he can't seem to motivate himself to do anything,' the weight of the day showed in her words, 'I'm trying to not let it get to me, because I know this is normal after all that's happened, but it peeves me off a bit at the moment. Mum won't say anything to him, but I can see his moods are wearing her down too.'

'I wouldn't let it get you down too much, he just needs some time that's all,' Ted loved offering advice, 'and if you've taken on his load, maybe he feels it's diminished his self-worth in some way. He'll get back to it as soon as he can.'

Tilly felt her hackles rise and suppressed it. This wasn't advice she wanted to hear and suspected this was where Jeff got the know-it-all attitude he sometimes displayed. 'I suppose,' she offered a weak smile and turned toward the sound of vehicles coming through the creek, cupping her hand over her eyes for a better view, 'now that's strange, why would Mum be driving the truck? Jeeze, Dad doesn't look too good, he's slumped over the wheel of the car.'

Laura brought the truck to a stop, flew out the door and rushed back to the Range Rover without acknowledging the watchers. Joe was in agony. The adrenalin from the initial shock was wearing off and the pain in his shoulder sapping his consciousness.

Jeff was at Laura's side ready to help. 'Come on Joe let's get you out of there.'

'It's my shoulder, mate. I think it's dislocated,' he lay on the ground calling for Jeff to put his foot against his ribs and grab him by the upper arm, 'not the wrist, I think that's broken and Tilly, no Ted, you hold my neck and arm and on the count of three, pull as hard as you can,' he saw Emily's pale face looking at him with concern, 'wait, Laura get Emily out of here first.'

Tilly held her hand over her mouth and heard Joe do the count. The bones slipped into place and colour started to return to her father's face as he resumed control of the situation, 'now all you have to do is get a couple of sticks on the wrist and it'll be as good as new, well almost,' he tried to laugh, but the pain cut it short.

Laura's placed her hand on Emily's back, steering her away from the sight of her grandfather on the ground, but the child resisted, craning her neck over her shoulder to see the action, 'I wanted to watch Granny, what did they do?'

'They helped put Pop's shoulder back in place. He had a bit of an accident but he'll be okay now.'

Tilly was caught between anger and admiration, unable to see that while her father had a short leash on his moods lately, hers wasn't much longer, 'Jeeze Dad, what the hell just happened?' She looked at her mother and back again to her father, 'where have you two been, and how did this happen?'

'Well, happy to see you too,' Joe was still sore, but the pain had dissipated to a dull ache and the relief was welcome, 'I thought as we were bringing the truck out, I'd see if I'd gotten over my fear of claustrophobia.'

'And?'

'And things went a bit belly-up, that's all.'

Jeff, never comfortable with the Gillespie bickering, waited for an opportunity to break in, 'how's your shoulder now Joe?'

'Much better, thanks to you and Ted. Laura and I tried, but we couldn't get it back in on our own.

'It's a good job you were both here,' Laura said, 'I don't think Tilly and I would have been able to manage it by ourselves either.'

'You were out at Miller's, weren't you?' Tilly was still agitated, but her anger was draining away, 'bloody gold fever I suppose. Did you find it?'

'Gold fever? Did you find anything? Am I missing something?' Ted was curious. He had heard of a lost mine in the Flinders that contained a legendary gold reef, but always thought it was just a story the old blokes exaggerated around a campfire, 'I've heard stories, but I never believed the Chinaman's Curse existed.'

'It's all clap-trap. Dad has this rhyme his father used to sing and I'll bet that's what you two were doing, wasn't it, trying to see if there was any truth in it? That's why you needed the windmill rig. Well come on, may as well fess up, did you find anything?'

Laura could see the interest in Ted's eyes, but didn't want to give the story away. She thought she could trust him, but this was a gold find and the yellow metal did strange things to people, 'we found the bucket was rusty and the bottom fell out it before we could do much, then Dad hurt his shoulder and it was all I could do to get him out of the well.'

Tilly thought the story sounded unconvincing. Unable to understand her mother's reluctance to speak openly, she pushed, 'Jeff and Ted are as good as family, Mum. If you and Dad want your secret kept, we'll all keep it. That's right isn't it, Ted?'

'Yeah, sure it is, of course,' Ted loved a story, true or otherwise, but he was a man of his word.

'Jeff?'

'You shouldn't have to ask, you know you can,' Jeff knew Tilly wasn't questioning his loyalty but wanted to put her mother's fears to rest.

Emily, who had re-joined the group from her exile near the creek, slipped behind Laura and reached for her hand.

'It's okay Em,' she drew her into her side, 'we were all a bit worried about Pop that's all. I think if your Mum goes to the back of the car, she'll find a bit of a surprise she can show us all.'

'Just bring the pretty ones, love,' Joe said.

CHAPTER EIGHT

Sam Lewis completed binding the dossier Gino had asked her to collate. She wanted to read it, but that would have compromised her position with Charles and, where Gino was concerned, it was better not to know. She bound the sealed packages in the order he had given them to her and knocked before entering Charles' office. He was packing his briefcase, everything strategically placed. He, too, liked order.

'Will I see you tonight?' she asked.

'I don't think so, Babe. I've got to go through this lot over the weekend,' he indicated the large folder on the desk with a nod of his head, 'and I'm off to Sydney on Monday. Maybe Tuesday we can go to your place early then, after you've made me my favourite dinner, who knows, you might even get lucky.'

'Or I could come to Sydney with you and we could both get lucky.

'Look Sam, I've told you a hundred times we're never going to have that kind of relationship. You need to realise I'm the one doing the favour here. I don't want, or need you with me in Sydney. So, when I think you deserve some of my time, I'll tell you. You work for me, Sam, that's all.'

Sam understood her place in Charles' life. It hadn't always been that way, not in the beginning, when he'd showered her with gifts and flowers and compliments, when his powers of seduction had been full throttle, but she soon learnt everything hid did was to advance him and his ambitions. His was complete control, but she handled his callousness by watching the way he operated, to learn and be ready to apply those hard-fought lessons and when the time was right, she would advance to a corner office on the top floor of a large corporation. It might even be this one.

'I probably won't come in until Wednesday then. I might slip back to Mundulla and catch up with Gavin.'

'Go for it. I'm sure that country hick won't offer you much and I'm damn sure he doesn't think of you as marriage material. If he does, I've got some stories that would see him run a mile. Just remember Sam, for as long as you continue to work for me, I own you.' As if driving home his point, he picked up his briefcase, pushed past her and walked out the door without another word.

In the underground carpark, Gino pulled on his seat belt and turned to Charles in the front passenger seat, 'do you want to know what isn't in Joe Gillespie's file.'

'What?'

'Dirt. We can't find any on him. Jack Pendlebury says he's still connected to ASIO, and I'm not sure that's the kind of wasp nest we want to kick. I think we'll have to find another way.'

'ASIO, the spy mob?' Charles thought their research would have uncovered this link years ago. 'What's the connection there?'

'Jack only found out when he was Minister for Police. They'd looked at Gillespie with criminal damage when building their case against Dante's Disciples, the bikie gang. Harry Forbes, the DI running the case, told him that they had no idea of the breadth of Joe's influence when he threatened to charge him.'

'Great, you invest all that time and money into finding that disgraced US Marine with a grudge against him. And for what, now he's dead and Joe fucking Gillespie is still alive and kicking. What a cock up. Is ASIO the reason why your American friend didn't get the job done?' Charles punched the dashboard in frustration, 'we need to regroup, go over everything and plan your next move carefully.'

'I thought Monty and his boys would have taken care of him. Shit, he was angry enough at the time.'

'You didn't tell him directly to kill Joe Gillespie, did you?'

'I didn't have to. I just put enough things together to put him in touch with Jimmy Symes and let it develop from there. Oh, but that chance meeting with the Disciples. Yeah, I made it so they bumped into each other, but there's nothing linking it back our way,' Gino smiled at his own cleverness, 'we've got nothing to worry about. All the players are dead.'

'All but Gillespie, let's keep it that way,' Charles leant back into his seat, 'what about now?

Gino pointed to the folder as he pulled into the Friday peak hour traffic, 'you'll find some interesting stuff in there and most of it damaging to our friends with influence, but there's not enough to really squeeze them.'

'So, if we can't get to Gillespie this way, we'll need another strategy. We need to trigger some kind of interference, you know, something to disrupt the State Government. Jesus Gino, we need to get Jack Pendlebury back to the Mines Portfolio. Get onto someone with confidential access to their latest survey information, buy the bastards if possible, we need to know what's happening before the market does. You know what to do, just get on with it,' he tossed the file he'd been holding onto the backseat, 'I've heard whispers they've found something in the mid-north, but no-one in the department has enough info to put everything together,' Charles drummed his fingers on the console as he thought.

'So you're giving me open slather, an off the books budget and none of that little bitch Sam looking over my shoulder?'

'Open slather it is.'

'Starting when?'

'From tonight. I'll organise a transfer to the usual account.'

'I'm on it already.'

Charles flipped down the sun-visor and checked his image in the mirror. He straightened his tie and smirked, 'find out if there are any of more of Gillespie's neighbours who have property for sale at the moment. Shit, the old bastard has a drought on his hands, his home is trashed, and his equipment is ruined, plus the man's had a heart attack into the bargain. He's got to be ready to sell. Get someone to make them an offer, someone who can't be traced back to us and use an accountant firm in...' he paused, searching for a name, found nothing and continued, 'oh, I don't know, somewhere interstate. Set up a management fund, create a new company and use an offshore account. Hong Kong would be good.'

'How long have I got?'

'Do it yesterday, you know how we work. Don't make any mistakes, but keep our arse covered. Start tonight, Geneva is still open.'

'I could use some help?' Gino was scheming as he drove.

'Call Sam, she's got plenty of time on her hands,' Charles smiled to himself, showing Gino he was still the boss and foiling Sam's planned weekend to see Gavin, was just another spoil of war.

CHAPTER NINE

Joe and Ted looked on as Tilly and Laura inspected the building site that now consumed the family home.

'I reckon it must be tough to see the place all knocked about like this,' Ted stared at the holes in the walls where the windows had been. The frames stacked on one side of the garage made the house appear even more forlorn, 'do you know how long the rebuilding will take?'

'I've left it in Tilly's hands. She's capable and the place will be hers one day, so she might as well have it rebuilt the way she wants it now.'

'You're not interested in coming back here then?'

'Well I would be, but I reckon Laura deserves some time too. She's had to fit in around what I've done all these years, and now we're that little bit older we need to ease up a bit and the cottage is easier to manage.'

'I guess, but this is a beautiful spot. Just sitting here now listening to the birds and watching the sunset is so peaceful, even with the wreckage before us.'

'It is and we have a lot to be thankful for, but I think we should do things differently out here and I want to take some time and think about it all,' he passed Ted one of the gold bars he'd been holding, 'I don't know where this stuff came from, the old man might have won it or pinched it, but it will pay for a grand holiday. What do you think?'

'You know me. I've never seen as much wealth. Worked all my life and little to show for it, even with the wife's pay packet we couldn't put much aside.'

'Yeah, but you raised a good kid, both of you. Look at him, top job, good bloke and easy to like too.'

'He does make me proud and I wish his mother could have seen just how well he's done.'

'Hey, don't go getting all soppy on me.'

'Not me, but what about you? Tilly says you haven't been yourself since everything went belly up last year'

'I've let things slip a bit and then, after putting her in charge of everything, it all just sort of slipped away,' he looked at the other man, 'you know how it goes. But I found something today that will help me get back on my feet. If only I'd checked the bottom of the bucket, then I wouldn't have fallen through,' his laughter interrupted the flow of words and his caution returned, 'and I'm still not convinced everything's over. And I'm damned sure it didn't finish in Port Augusta,' he looked at the shadows in the creek and placed an arm around Laura as she returned to his side, 'still today was a good one, wasn't it, love?'

Tilly, Jeff and Emily headed to unlock the shed and put the windmill truck away and Laura linked her arm with his around him and squeezed, 'you should have seen him though, Ted,' she laughed aloud, 'here's Joe, the bottom of the bucket open like a rusty tin and his legs dangling out of it. If it hadn't been for the harness, he'd have dropped into the well and had to climb out on his own,' they were all laughing now, Joe breaking into a belly laugh, the first Laura had heard for a long time.

Ted was turning the gold bar over in his hand when the others returned, catching Emily's attention, 'what's that Mr Rankin?' she asked.

'Well your Pop found it and one day he might share his secret and show you where. It's pretty heavy too,' Ted wasn't sure how to answer and became evasive, 'do you want to hold it?'

'Sure,' she looked at Joe, 'can I Pop?'

'No worries kiddo, but don't drop it. It might break.'

'Do you really think...?' Tilly's words trailed and she watched her daughter turn the bar over in her hands, studying every mark or blemish.

'I think it's the gold from the poem,' Emily said, 'and see here, there's something written on it.'

Tilly took the bar and passed it to Laura, 'well, all of that can wait for now, young lady. We promised Jeff and his Dad a barbeque tonight, so we'd better make tracks, okay? What about you and Dad,' she looked at her mother, 'do you think he's up to it?'

'Dad and I'll give it a miss tonight, love. I want to get his arm looked at, so we'll see you tomorrow.

CHAPTER TEN

The doctor snapped the X-ray film from the light panel,' you're lucky, Joe. That wrist has a nasty sprain and you'll be sore in the shoulder for a while. Putting it back when you did saved me a lot of trouble, but you'll need to take things easy for a week or two.'

'Thanks Doc, but I'll be right I reckon.'

'I'll make sure he does,' Laura added.

'You'll need to rest it though. I'm not telling you to withdraw from life, just give it time to heal that's all.'

'Will do, and thanks again doc.'

'Come on Joe, I'd better get you fed.'

***

Ted had taken Jeff's car home after the barbeque and once Emily was in bed, Tilly and Jeff used the time alone to reflect on their relationship, which seemed to have become bogged down in recent months. She knew neither of them wanted to have this conversation, but there were things that needed thrashing out if they were ever going to move forward.

'You want to go first?' Jeff wasn't being polite. He wanted to put this off.

'No, but I will anyway,' frustration clipped her words, causing her to veer off the subject, 'what's with your father lecturing me on how I should treat my Dad? He pissed me off today with his bloody know everything attitude.'

'Ouch, I didn't see that coming, I thought we were going to talk about us but...' he weighed up the wisdom of answering her question then decided to push through anyway, 'well you have to admit you've been charging in and taking control, making decisions on your own with no consultation with anyone and I don't think that has helped your dad.'

'Oh, and now you're jumping on the lecture bandwagon. These days I feel I just can't win whatever I do. There's work to be done and someone has to do it and all I am doing is what he wanted, that's all, doing what he asked me to do.'

'I dunno, it seems you've been spoiling for a fight for the last couple of weeks and I can't do anything right so I know exactly how you feel. What's going on, don't you want me around anymore?' This hadn't been the direction either wanted to take yet neither seemed to know the way back.

'Well if that's what you think, that's entirely up to you, Jeff Rankin. I just want your support, that's all' Tilly was close to tears, 'or is that too much to ask?'

'Be fair Tilly, I do support what you're doing, well I try to anyway, but it seems as if I can't have an opinion on anything. If I do and try to share it with you...' he turned away, not wanting her to see how upset he was by the tone of the conversation, 'jeez Tilly, I just can't stand by and be mute. If we're going to make this work, our partnership has to be equal and not one where either of us feels they have to hold their tongue. You agree with that, don't you?'

'Of course, I do, but you have no idea what I'm going through.'

'Well let me help, confide in me a bit. Shit, Tilly, share the load with me. That's what relationships are all about - partnership. I might only be a copper, but I'm not altogether dumb. Ask me something sometime, use me as a sounding board and it might surprise you how I can help,' he reached out, but Tilly wasn't ready to end this yet and slapped his hand away, 'and take no notice of Dad, he's really just trying to help.'

'What do you want Jeff? You say to ask for your help, yet how can I be sure you're going to be around to see it through? For the last month you've been nothing but evasive. I can't get a straight answer from you if I ask about us. Just say if you don't want us in your life. Let me know now, I can handle it. What I can't or won't take is being jerked around like a worm on a string. Or is it Emily? Because she's part of me and I've made it clear from the start that we come as a package, a two for one deal?'

'No, it's not you and it's certainly not Emily. I'm fine.'

'You're not fine, Jeff. What's going on? Is there someone else?'

'Someone else, no... shit, Tilly no.'

'Then why the change, what's got into you?'

'I haven't meant to change and, if anything I love you more than ever and this is...' he searched for the right words, 'well, it's hard to put into words without sounding petty, but when I look around and see all your family has, I can't compete. Look around you, the land, the houses and everything. Tilly, I have nothing, and I've probably wasted my money chasing some crazy boyhood dream.'

'Is that what all this is about, money?'

'No, it's not about money. It's about my feelings of worthiness and how I can provide for you and Emily the way I think you both deserve. You knew I was going to quit the coppers and I haven't got anything lined up. Even if I did, it would never bring in the kind of money you're used to.'

'Is that all?'

'It's not a small thing, Tilly. A man should be able to provide for his family. It bothers me.'

'You're an idiot, Jeff Rankin. Do you think I'm worried about that? I don't care about how much money I make, or what Mum and Dad have either. I didn't go into the law to make a fortune. Like you, I just wanted to make a difference. The fact that we took avenues that reward

47

differently is irrelevant. God, do you really think I'm that one dimensional?'

'Look, it's not you.'

'Don't give me that old cliché,' she tried to look cross, but her earlier anger has evaporated with his words and a smile formed on her lips, 'I know that... how could it be?'

'Yeah, but ever since I was a little kid I believed in the man bringing home enough money to feed his family.'

'And you will,' she held his hand, 'I won't have you sitting around the house waiting for me to come home. Anyway, how do you think my parents accumulated all they have?'

'Joe's a pretty good farmer and the place has been in the family for years.'

'Yeah, that's part of it, but Mum has always worked as a lecturer and author. They did it together. Look, when Dad came home after Vietnam the place was a mess and drowning in debt. Sure, they had a few assets and a good share portfolio thanks to his grandfather, but when his own father died, probate and death duties nearly cleaned them out. They have what they have, because they worked together and we can do that too. We don't have to, but it's what I'd like to do,' when he didn't answer, she continued, 'so, what I'm saying is, I want you to follow your dream, but I just want to be sure that you can find some space for me and Emily while you do it, that's all.'

Jeff took some time to reply and Tilly could feel the silence crushing them. She wanted to say more, but needed him to answer her. He rubbed at his eyes and dropped onto his knee, 'Tilly Gillespie, I want to ask you to be my wife and I've been trying to build up the courage for weeks. It's just that lately, probably since deciding to quit the coppers, I haven't felt worthy,' he took her hands and kissed them, 'you can't know how much I love you. I promise I'll do my best for both of you for as long as I live. Hey...' he cracked a smile, 'and you know I won't always agree with you and I'll probably piss you off more often than I should, but I can't imagine life without you. I need you in my life and I'd like to grow old with you.' Without being conscious of what to say or do next, he asked, 'Tilly Gillespie, will you marry me?'

Tilly turned away from him and peered through the corner of the curtains, staring at the empty street for a long time before turning back to him, her eyes were misted.

'Jeff Rankin, you can be so bloody exasperating,' she pulled a tissue from her sleeve and dabbed at her eyes, 'of course, I will, just don't expect me to become one of those annoying little housewives who always says yes.'

'So what, that's a yes?'

'Of course, it's a yes,' he saw a wicked twinkle in her eye, 'I've always wanted to be Mrs Jeff Gillespie.'

'Mrs Gillespie?'

'Well, you'll change your name, won't you?' Tilly was still laughing at her own joke when they heard a car in the driveway.

'If it's your parents, are you going to say something?'

'No, I'd rather tell Emily first. Let's see if we can get rid of whoever it is and then you and I can celebrate.

'No regrets then, the future Mrs Rankin?'

'None at all, the future Mr Gillespie, none at all.'

CHAPTER ELEVEN

Three gold bars sat on the kitchen bench. Laura had weighed them separately. These weren't minted ingots; their shape was rough and irregular.

'You know, I don't think this is the same gold your Dad talked about in his poem, Joe. If it came from the mint it would have some sort of official mark on it,' she looked up at him, waiting for his reply, 'wouldn't it?'

'Pardon?' He was studying the slate and turning it over in his hands, 'what's the weight?'

'You didn't listen to me, did you?' she looked back at the scale, 'the scales say sixteen hundred and eighty-five grams, but these aren't exactly accurate.'

'Yeah, I don't think this is the gold he meant either, but it's not bad for one day's work, eh?'

'So, you did hear me. You just chose to ignore me.'

'I always hear you love, it's only sometimes that I don't listen,' he knew a flick with a tea-towel was coming his way and pushed back on his chair as he stood, 'just stay away from the shoulder, okay?'

'I'll give you stay away from the shoulder, Joe Gillespie.' Soon they were standing at each end of the table, when she moved to her right, he did too, circling the table and rattling the chairs, one seeking to catch, the other to avoid. Laughter loosened their spirits and it was only when he clattered onto his chair and cowered did she flick him. His shoulder hurt, but they were laughing and it felt good.

Laura regained her composure and pointing to the gold asked, 'what are we going to do with them?'

'I dunno, I reckon we should get them assayed and work it out from there,' he passed the slate to her, 'and I think this holds the clue to where the gold's from. After dinner, we'll have a look through that old case of letters again. You know, to see if anything in there helps this message make sense,' he shook his head, 'we might only have a few bars of brass, love.'

'It's too heavy and not green enough for brass,' she passed the slate to him and turned to put her scales away.

'Yeah, I reckon it's gold real enough,' he rubbed his thumbnail against the scratching, 'but these marks that Emily found, I'll need my glasses to see what it says.'

'Here,' she interrupted her preparation of tea to push his glasses on for him and he screwed up his nose and stretched his face trying to get them into their usual position, 'you can be a silly bugger at times Joe Gillespie, and grumpy into the bargain, but I do love you.'

'How could you not?' The microwave beeped to let her know the beans were ready.

'Egg on the toast and beans on top, okay?' Laura knew which way he liked his eggs, but she sometimes played this game.

'No, God woman, I don't know how many times I have to tell you. Eggs on top, I like the yolk to seep into the beans,' he realised she was having him on, 'you said that just to wind me up, didn't you?'

'Gets you every time, Joe, it gets you every time,' she put the plate in front of him, 'oh, and I cut the toast up into bite size bits too.'

'Thanks, this sling's going to be a bit of a nuisance and there'll be a few things I'll need help some with,' he said as the reality of his situation began to take hold.

'Oh, and you don't go thinking you'll get out of the dishes either, you can stack the dishwasher with one hand.'

He pretended not to hear, 'you want to know what I think about those ingots?'

'You think we should spend it on me.'

'That's not quite what I had in mind, but tell me what you think about this? We throw one of them at our holiday, you use the other for restoring the barn and whatever you find in it, and the other we put aside for unexpected nuptials.'

'You bloody old romantic Joe Gillespie. The way those two are behaving at the moment though I think Emily will beat her mother to the altar.'

'Nothing worth having ever came easy.' He sipped his tea while Laura cleared the table, placing a bowl of ice-cream in front of him before sitting back down

'Now if Jeff's getting that old plane out of the barn tomorrow, how are you going to help him with one arm?'

'Andy's coming over from Port Augusta. Jeff said he'll bring a trailer, a truck, or something they can take it back on. They've organised a forklift too, so if you want to get anything moved, here's your opportunity.'

'Where's he going to keep it?'

'Dunno, you'll have to ask him tomorrow,' he smiled at her, 'you're going to be covered in dirt and dust all day, and because of this,' he lifted his arm, 'I get to sit and watch.'

'Okay, now that you have your treasure, and Jeff gets his tomorrow, when do we go to Wilsons to get my old Model T?'

'Fair go. Bloody Hell, how many things can you do at once?'

'I'm a woman Joe, we delegate. We multi-task,' she poured a second cup of tea as she spoke, underscoring her remark.

'I'm taking this in to watch the football and, as you're so good at multitasking, I'll leave you with this lot,' he laughed as he picked up his tea by the saucer and headed to the TV room, 'and bring me some bikkies when you come. There's a good girl.'

'There's a good girl my arse,' she dropped one shoulder, tucked her hand into her shirt and rubbed her forearm in exaggerated mimicry, 'my arm is so sore, sob,

sob. Jeeze my shoulder hurts,' crossing the room with an exaggerated limp, she kissed his forehead and gave an evil cackle as he stood to leave the table, 'you can have tonight off, but tomorrow, I'll recast my spell and you'll be under my control once more.'

'You can't cast a spell on an injured man. That's the rule.'

'Off with you now, are you sure I can't tempt you to watch Better Homes and Gardens?'

'Yep.'

CHAPTER TWELVE

There was nothing on television to capture her interest and Sam looked at the clock again. If she didn't know better she could think it was broken. It seemed like hours had passed since she'd gotten rid of Gino. Charles would be swanning it in Sydney by now and she would love to call him just to get under his skin, but that would be inviting trouble when he returned.

Deciding physical activity to be a better option she made her way to the bedroom, disrobing and dumping her work clothes into the laundry hamper on the way, before putting on sweat pants and top. She had considered using the gym in the basement of the building, but the evening was pleasant outside and a couple of circuits around the park would tire her enough, she hoped, to take her mind off Charles and her grubby relationship with him.

Normally she'd run with her iPod feeding a beat into her subconscious, but tonight the sights and sounds of the city seemed a better choice. Traffic was sparse now that most of the city's workers had made it home and it would be a while before the clubbers crowded their way into pubs. She loved to run the city square, it kept her in shape and her spirits rose as she anticipated the burning in her legs that came from a good run. Adelaide was safe if she avoided known trouble spots and, while she'd never had to use her martial arts training, it added to her sense of security.

After loosening up with some stretches in the kitchen, she bounded down the front steps of her building and almost crashed into a pedestrian as she turned onto the footpath, the last person she expected or wanted to see, Gino.

'Well what have we here?' Still in his suit from work, he loped along beside her at an easy gait.

'Piss off.'

She stepped up her speed but his was still cruising, running lightly to the soft slap of his leather soled shoes against the concrete. He turned around and ran backwards, keeping eye contact and speaking effortlessly, 'the boss wants us to do a bit of overtime.'

She ran faster, noting Gino didn't even raise a sweat as he kept pace. He was doing this easy.

'I told you to piss off, I'm on my weekend. You can both go to buggery until Wednesday.'

'Can't do that. We have to form another company and we have do it tonight.'

'Do it yourself, I sure as hell don't want to spend my time off with a prick like you.'

'Now that's not nice. Go home and I'll wait for you to change, or you can come now. I like my women all sweaty and worked up.'

'Piss off.' She was sounding repetitious and she knew it.

'Ring Charles, he told me to take you to the office and get things in place tonight. He wants to transfer money into new accounts as soon as we're done. You know we have to do this so don't be such a snotty nosed bitch and do as you're told.'

'Fuck you, Gino.'

'Only if you insist, but we have a lot work to do first. Now stop jerking about and let's get on with it,' in one fluid movement he stopped, turned and ran back toward her street, 'I'll race you. If I win, you buy dinner.'

She turned and sprinted after him, but he kept an easy speed five steps ahead of her. His breathing was easy when she caught up with him at her door and she was sucking hard for air, 'you had a head start,' she panted.

'I like to run.' He was mocking her and it hurt.

Sam opened her front door and he followed her in. 'I'll change and be right with you,' she called from the

55

bathroom, 'I thought you put everything he needed in the file.'

'Something's come up and he needs us to move now. Look, I don't want to spend any more time with you than you do with me. Let's just get this done and I can go back to my life.'

'Jesus Gino, I didn't think you had a life.'

***

Charles expected the knock on his hotel door. The caller said they would be there at nine thirty and it was now that time. Dealing with Asian banking syndicates was always difficult. Thankfully David Wang spoke fluent English, but it didn't make him a pleasant man. Charles admired that he was all business, but he knew how ruthless men like Wang could be.

Black label whiskey made a musical noise as it splashed over the ice in the two crystal tumblers Charles had prepared. He passed one to his guest. 'Would the others...?'

David Wang raised a hand, 'no thank you, I need them to stay sharp. They can wait in the lobby and I'll call them when we're done.'

There was coldness in the man's tone and it unsettled Charles. He'd be glad when the meeting was over. 'To many bigger deals to come, cheers,' the Asian raised his glass and almost sipped. Charles couldn't be sure.

'Good flight?' Charles made small talk to mask his uneasiness.

'You've stuffed up, Charles, and my directors don't like that. Our company has invested heavily in you and we need assurances that you'll come through for us. Our policy is to carry no passengers, you knew that when you asked us to invest. There'll be heavy penalties for over-runs and you know that, too.'

'I can explain. I thought I'd have secured the leases, the land and everything, but I overestimated the ability of the people I had negotiating the settlement.'

'Bullshit. You were trying to be too clever. You're a cheap bastard, Winkler. Now everything at our end is ready to go and your delays are costing us money. The fracking plants are costed and ready for production. Without your promise showing fruit, I'm in an untenable position. I don't enjoy negotiating terms of trade with your government without a sound platform. You promised to secure rights to the extensive coal gas fields in this area,' he pulled a map from his pocket and pointed to the Walloway Plain, his index finger jabbing the location of the Gillespie land, 'this area held the best prospect for more than just gas you said, so you will secure those rights before the fiscal year ends, understand?' He folded the paper and slipped it back into his pocket, 'my people are becoming anxious, we have a lot of money tied up in this already, and not all of my fellow investors are as tolerant as I am,' he hit the call button on his phone.

'I have Gino....'

Wang cut him off, 'you agreed to our terms. We want returns not excuses. Bring your part in on time.'

There was a knock on the apartment door and Wang rose, holding out his hand to Charles, knowing this handshake to be as binding as any written contract.

'I want our friendship to blossom Charles. It would be foolish to do anything to cause it to wilt. I expect a full report by Wednesday.' He opened the door and disappeared into Sydney's night life.

Not many people in the finance business could intimidate Charles Winkler, but David Wang wasn't just any business man, he fronted for a Hong Kong investment bank and Charles knew any slip up on his part and it could become ugly.

The office block was empty, apart from the security personnel doing their rounds and the two people starting a new exploration and development company. Charles had transferred start-up money from his personal account in the Cayman Islands to a holding account in Switzerland and then into a new account in Hong Kong. Sam and Charles had done this before, but she had never worked this routine with Gino. She had always thought of him as muscle and realised now she had underestimated his intelligence.

At three o'clock in the morning RADOR Exploration Company registered in Hong Kong. They still had more work to do before Charles met with the Minister for Mines and the head of his department.

While on his way to his Sydney meetings, Charles watched the screen on his phone as Twitter lit up with tweets about a group of politicians and business men investing in a new coalfield in the Hunter Valley. This offered promise and he wanted in before it went to the market. There were questions about the Minister for Mines and Energy and people connected to his department, but none of that concerned Charles. He wanted in.

If, as the rumours suggested, most of the key players had a price, then Charles needed background information on all of them. More importantly, he had to confirm just who had raised the initial capital for the project. He called Gino and told him to ask Sam to dig up everything she could by the end of the weekend.

Satisfied, he poured himself another scotch and peered at the skyline. Everything was in motion and he could relax for a few hours.

CHAPTER THIRTEEN

Joe stood at the kitchen window and smiled as he watched the dawn chase the shadows of morning across the plain. He breathed deeply the fresh air blended with the aroma of coffee and toast coming through the open window. It was good to be alive, people would be arriving soon and he and Laura had a treasure hunt ahead of them. He hadn't felt this good in ages.

As if reading his thoughts, Laura came up behind him, sliding her arms around him and into the pockets of his windcheater, her squeeze tender and loving. It made him realise just how much he had missed this closeness. She had been supportive while he recovered, yet he had closed her out and now realised he'd been a fool for doing so.

'You smell nice.'

'It's baby shampoo,' she put her head against his good shoulder, 'I thought I had a new bottle in my sponge bag, but I must have left it somewhere. Anyway, this was still in the cupboard from when Emily was small.'

'Well I like it fine.' He closed his arms around hers, it may have hurt, but it felt good to have her close.

'What did you use?' Laura asked.

'Soap, no conditioner, it's what we do.'

'If you keep that up you'll lose all this lovely grey hair,' her hand came out of his pocket and she tousled his hair, grateful to have her husband back again.

'I think we'd better get those bars into the bank on Monday,' he said, 'times are still tough around here and I'd hate to think anyone might be tempted. As it is, we'd better prepare for a few people asking us for a hand out if the news gets out.'

'I was thinking the same. If we just gave it to any Tom, Dick, or Harry it would be gone in an instant. It'd never satisfy enough people, but I have a proposal for you.'

'Am I going to like it?'

'I think so.'

'Well?

'Well, I think you need a challenge right now and there are a couple of things I want to do too, so between us...'she started to take the dogeared copy of Neville Shute's *A Town Like Alice* from her jacket pocket, but the banging of the back-door interrupted them and Laura slipped it back.

Emily, pulling out a chair and sliding onto it in one fluid action asked, 'got anything to eat, Granny?'

'Didn't Mum feed you?'

'Yeah, but I'm still hungry and Jeff says we have a big day. So can I have some toast and milo, please?'

Tilly was on Emily's heels, 'what have I told you young lady?' she stared at her daughter.

'Not to ask for food.'

'People must think I never feed you. I hope you don't do this at other people's houses.'

'Nope, just Pop and Granny's.'

Joe stood up to greet them. Laura slipped two frozen slices into the toaster, 'anyone else, there's plenty of bread?'

Joe filled the kettle and reached for three cups, 'tea or coffee, Jeff?'

Tilly flashed her stare from Emily to Jeff. They'd had bacon and eggs only half an hour before. They couldn't be hungry.

Jeff shrugged at her and smiled, 'tea for me thanks, Joe,' he leant in and kissed Laura on the cheek, 'good morning Mum.'

Laura smiled at his greeting and turned to her daughter. She shrugged, turned her palms up and let a bemused look shape her face. Tilly walked close to Jeff and when no one could see, jabbed an elbow into his ribs. She wasn't ready to tell the world about their engagement and wanted Jeff to ask Joe first. It was the old-fashioned way and probably the only wedding tradition she thought necessary.

They could hear cars pulling up in the street and the curiosity of doors closing was too much for Emily. She slid from her chair, crashed her plate onto the sink, poured the remaining milo down the drain, and darted to the front door to see who had arrived.

'I'd better get them organised,' Jeff said, shoving the last of his toast in to his mouth and swishing it down with tea far too hot to swallow, 'are you coming out Tilly?'

'I'll be out after I've helped Mum clean up after you lot.'

'You go with him love,' Laura said, 'he's got a big day ahead of him and I reckon you'll get a kick out of it too.'

'I swear Mum, he's like a big kid today. He and Emily have been up gabbing since five o'clock. It feels like I've got two kids in my life where once there was one.'

'Go on, you go out and play too. I know you've had plenty on your plate lately. Enjoy today with Jeff and your friends. Let your inner child free.'

'But I...'

'Later, go. Dad will help me here and then we'll be out too. Go and welcome your friends. How many are we feeding for lunch?'

'Who knows, probably the gliding club and every copper and their kids for a hundred miles. All I know is Jeff and Andy have been planning and talking about getting the old plane out ever since you told him about it. If you want anything weeded, cleaned up or sorted out, today is the day.' The sense of adventure was gripping her too.

'I'll think of something.'

'Dad there's an army of blokes to direct, are you up to it? You know with your arm in a sling and all. Hang on... where's your sling?

Laura had her hands on Tilly's shoulders steering her toward the door, 'you know your father, he knows better than the doctor. You'll be fine, won't you Joe? He's as tough as old boots.'

Laura had forgotten about the sling, but knew he'd resist wearing it today. 'Once the dishes are done we'll be out there, sling and all.'

Joe waited until he saw Tilly in the yard and well out of earshot. 'What did Jeff call you?'

'He kissed me and called me Mum,' she screwed the tea towel between her hands and held it to her mouth, 'Joe do you think...'

'Nope, he's just messing with you and Tilly. He has to ask our permission before he asks her. I told him that once.'

'When?'

'You know, before, when we were in the glider.'

'He asked you about it back then?'

'No, no, nothing like that. It was just before...' he turned away from her and thought about the pain in his chest, flashing back to the moment again he had nearly caused them to crash.

'Sorry,' Laura rubbed his back.

'We were just talking about things that's all, and I said if anyone wanted to marry my daughter, they'd have to speak to me first, you know, us, you and me together.'

'You only just saved it old man, but I'd stop digging if I were you,' she looked at him and watched the crowd milling around the machinery, 'can we dream, or should we plan,' she reached around him and squeezed.

'Dream now, plan later when we know more, I reckon.'

'I'll dream now, but if she's holding out I'll kill her.'

'They'll tell us when they're ready, love,' he said, 'now I'd better get out there.'

'Put that sling on and give orders.'

'Yes boss,' he slung it over his head and wriggled his elbow until he was comfortable, 'are you coming?'

'Soon, there are a couple of things I need to do first.'

By morning tea time, the volunteers had cleared the debris and rubbish to reveal the front of the stables. The red brick driveway was clear of weeds and bore deep scratches where the blade of the bobcat had scored them. Joe saw the bricks had come from Zanker's kiln, one of many discoveries they would make this day.

'Do you want us to keep the old yards or just clear it all away?' Jeff looked to Joe for advice.

'Hang on I'll check with Laura,' he walked to where she was laying a table with cake, scones, and savouries. Disposable cups stood in straight lines beside the electric urn, tea and coffee waited beside buckets of sugar. Umbrella style covers hid sandwiches from flies that were trying to steal anything with moisture, 'should we clear the yards or do you want to save them?'

'Let the timber ones go. I've got photos I can use to put them back, but the stone ones should stay I think. They add a nice bit of character to the old girl.'

Joe screwed his nose up at her. 'Old girl? Are you going soft woman, it's just a building.'

'Oh, it's she's more than that and I think it deserves a lot care and attention,' she winked at him, 'besides I have plans.'

His attention was diverted as Jeff approached asking for more directions.

'Cart the timber away and keep the stone yards, all the feral trees and weeds can go too. Sort the steel and stuff into different piles ready for the swimming club's midyear scrap sale.'

Laura looked at her watch and put her hand on Tilly's arm, 'better call them for a break, the cuppa's ready,' she moved to distribute tea bags into some of the cups, but stopped and turned back to her daughter, 'and, I want to talk to you alone later. You've avoided me since breakfast and I'd like to know what you're up to.'

'Sure, I'll get their attention now,' she took out an air horn and pressed the button. Its shriek caused Laura to jump. Tilly knew her mother wanted to know what was going on with her and Jeff and she had thought about telling her, but it was more fun to watch her mother struggling with her curiosity, 'I'll tell you later, Mum, much later.'

About twenty-five helpers and their families had turned up, some were Jeff's flying friends and colleagues from the force. Doug Simpson, his Senior Sergeant, had proved good on his promise and roped in his new son in law. A team of locals promised to drop in over the day to help, there were people everywhere.

Boys combed through the yards for treasure, while Emily and her friends had marked out a hopscotch patch and were taking turns to throw the stone and hop. A bonfire at one end of the house paddock flared and smouldered with each feast of fuel from old timber and sticks that kept it burning and a sense of community returned life to the place.

'I didn't expect to see you here today?' Tilly said to Angela.

'Me either,' Fiona chimed in, 'I thought you'd gone back to the city?'

'Well, I have gone back but...'

'But what?' Tilly asked.

'It's funny, but you see that gawky, geeky, good looking bloke over there? He asked me to come today and I couldn't say no.'

'Which bloke over where?' Fiona asked.

'Andy, I've been out with him a few times since you introduced us at my farewell.'

'I should've had a farewell, too,' Tilly said, 'seems like a good tactic if that's all it took. How often have you seen him?'

'Most weekends he comes down. On my days off I drive up to see him.'

'Well, at least you're taking it slowly,' Fiona responded, 'how have you managed to hide it from everyone and why hide him anyway?'

'We haven't, just stayed out of the limelight that's all.'

'Well, looking at him now I can see you've taken charge of his appearance. I thought he looked a bit different,' Tilly said.

'Yeah well, I went through his wardrobe and had a good throw out. He's better for it, that's what I told him anyway.'

'Does Jeff know?' Tilly asked.

'No, today is our first day out with friends,' Angela, eager to stop further interrogation, put her hands on the table and asked, 'so, what do you want me to do first? I'm here to help.'

Now Tilly had something to discuss with Jeff and she was as curious about Andy and Angela as her mother was about her. It was something she would corner Jeff with later. She gave Angela a hug, 'I reckon that's the best news I've had in days.'

'Do you want to help make salads?' Fiona asked.

'Sure,'

Tilly wanted to show countrywomen inclusion, 'just grab a knife and start dicing and welcome to the wives and girlfriends club.'

Two truckloads of dirt and rubbish had gone to the tip by lunch time. The building was emerging from the neglect and Laura and Joe walked to the bottom of the paddock where they could view the barn from its old approach.

'She looks better with her faced washed don't you think?' Laura asked.

'There' still a pile of work to do before we can get anything out of there though. Just after lunch we'll have the old hardstand cleared, then we can pull the wagons out and line them up outside. Jeff and Andy should be able to get to the crates after that.' Joe was about to ask Laura about her plans, when Jeff gave the call to lunch

Joe had set up an old cement wash trough for the men to wash their hands and before long, shiny faces and wet hands formed a line for food and Ted took his place alongside Joe to turn snags and flip patties.

Tilly stood by her mother and nodded toward the burger boys. 'They can't help it can they, why do men have to be so competitive? They're going at that grill so hard, that' anyone would think they'd wagered a sheep station on it.'

As if on cue Joe cursed his sling Laura had insisted he wear, flipped his arm out of it and tossed the tongs into his right hand, flicking the offender over his shoulder. 'Okay Ted let's flip some burgers and get this lot fed.'

'You okay, old man, or do you want to sit down and rest up a bit. I've got this.'

'Old man be buggered. Anyway, I reckon you're a good bit older than me, Teddy boy. So, let's see if you can keep up.'

'You're on old fella, now this lot's sizzling, let's load the hotplate and make a start. I'll take care of the onions you do the bacon... deal?' Ted grinned, like Joe he was enjoying himself.

'Deal.'

Jeff and Andy were so close to getting the old Avro out of the barn that they were prepared to go without lunch to finish the job. Now there were only a few things to drag out and the boxes would see daylight for the first time in almost a century. Joe had promised Jeff the Avro after his heart attack had caused him to jam the controls of the glider they were flying, when it had only been Jeff's presence of mind and flying skill that pulled them out of a death spiral.

'We gunna open the boxes today?' Andy asked.

'What do you think? It's probably all turned to junk by now anyway, but it'll be interesting to see just what sort of junk it once was. Besides, we owe it to everyone to show them what they've worked for,' Jeff said, 'really, we're only doing it for the interest of others.'

'Yeah, sure we are, it's not like we're interested in it much. More of a favour for the Gillespies, right?'

'Right, we're only helping them to clean the shed out. Probably should've organised a garage sale,' Jeff mocked himself, but he couldn't wait to see what lay inside those boxes.

Andy felt a hand on his arm. 'You blokes really ought to get something to eat, I just saw Joe and he told me to come and get you,' Spider Webb had brought the forklift from the garage, 'I'll get some of the little stuff out of the way first, and then you can tell me how you want these crates handled. Brad said he'd be here after lunch, I reckon he's busting a gut to see what's in here too.'

'Thanks,' Jeff said, 'we'll be back soon.'

Spider grabbed the straw broom from behind the forklift seat and swept the area he was going to work in. 'No need for a puncture is there, Gip?' he reached down and patted the kelpie, 'jeez dog, they've got some stuff buried in here.'

For the next twenty minutes Spider moved boxes, machinery, old windmill parts and a dray. He was getting closer to accessing to the biplane, tugging at an old drop sheet as Jeff and his army of supporters filed back in.

Spider was a sight. His trademark red and white polka dot neckerchief covered his nose, the part of his face that was exposed was covered with dust and sweat beaded and fell in tracks down his forehead.

He pulled his makeshift mask down to talk, 'I got a fair bit moved,' crooked and yellow teeth contrasted against the reddish pink of his mouth when he grinned at them, 'what do you say we get her out into the light for a proper look?' He flicked the sheet up and down to dislodge one corner and showered everyone in grime, 'and there we go, one box of what used to be an aeroplane.'

'Christ, Spider, you've covered us all in dirt and spoggy shit,' a voice boomed from the back, 'just because you love rolling around in the dirt, doesn't mean everyone else does... shit, shit, shit,' he brushed at the dirt and pushed to the front, 'out the way, Webby, I can take it from here. How do you want me to do this, Jeff?'

'Pass me the broom,' Andy said to Spider, 'I'll brush the box down a bit.'

'There should be some sling marks on it somewhere, son,' Ted Rankin offered, 'but I reckon you'd better ask Joe.'

Jeff studied the crate and determined they could carry it with the forks if they were careful. It would take a few lifts, but it should come out easily.

'How'd they get it in here?' He turned to Joe, who was now standing beside him.

Joe pointed up to where a gantry with a block and tackle lazed high in the roof. 'I wouldn't trust it now though.'

With the forklift in place to take the strain, the old crate creaked its displeasure before falling silent once off the ground. The forklift moved back, lifted, and swung the box around several times until it greeted the sunlight. 'One down, two to go and the rest are easy so, let's get to it,' the driver gunned the fork lift and went back inside.

Jeff picked up a pry bar and a hammer and passed them to Andy, 'careful as you go, partner.'

'Partner?'

'Yep, I got a plan, mate. I'll tell you about it later.' He followed the fork lift into the barn and soon all three crates were lined up on the hard-stand outside.

Steel clanged against steel as Andy and his friends worked, taking care not to damage the pine lid of the crate marked: *FUSELAGE*. If they removed it in one piece, then it could go back on when needed. In a few minutes the contents stood before them. Wrapped in tar paper, the original consignors had made it difficult to reveal the old aircraft.

Helpers now surrounded each side, jostling for the best view of Andy at one end and Jeff at the other peeling the paper back. The plane looked fragile, the spruce frame pushing against the fabric covering. The leather on the narrow seats still held a shine, but some of the stitching had pulled away. Two propellers secured by woven straps for safety lay along the rear of the crate.

'Paint looks like new, partner.'

'Canvas is as tight as a drum too,' Andy said.

'But it can't be an Avro,' Jeff turned to Joe, 'these markings are German.'

CHAPTER FOURTEEN

Joe and Laura waited until the last car left, before they walked inside where Joe flopped onto the couch. 'Big day, love?'

'Indeed it was,' Laura said, 'I'm off for a shower and you, off the couch, you're covered in dust. Brush yourself off outside and then you can come back in… and leave those dirty boots out there too.'

The waning sunset made the barn shine. Colours of evening picked out the red of the brick and contrasted with lines of grey mortar. He had never noticed it before but, in this light, he could see a logo cast in plaster above the front entrance. Even in its crumbling state, there was no mistaking the date, 1887. Construction provided a lot of work for the town's builders in the past, something that Orroroo could use again today. Walking back inside, Laura called from the bathroom, 'you've been a while, what've you been doing?'

'Just looking at your old barn, on the front there's a crest with a date on it. When do you think, the place was built?'

'Eighteen, eighty-seven.'

'You knew it was there?'

'Did you want to jump in the spa and soak your shoulder for a while?'

'I think the shower will do the job tonight,' he unbuttoned his shirt, wincing as he slid it over his shoulder, 'I'm beat, love, I can't keep up with those young blokes anymore.'

'You're not supposed to. It's not a competition. It's their time to take on more of the load and it's our obligation to let them.'

'Bloody hard to let go.' He looked in the mirror at his grey hair and rubbed the wrinkles around his eyes.

'Think of it more as having more time to go treasure hunting.'

'With everything we had going on today, I'd forgotten about that. Is it still there?'

'Yep.'

'Where?'

'It's safe enough. I put them into three of those old margarine containers stacked on the bench in the porch. Don't worry they're still there, I kept an eye on them. Besides we had coppers all over the place today. It was safe enough.'

'Coppers are the last people you want to trust.'

'Okay,' she poked her head around the door, 'I'll be in the kitchen, poached eggs do you for tea tonight?'

'With bacon?'

'Not likely, remember we still have to get your cholesterol down. I'm not even buttering the toast.' She left him and he moved his shoulder, feeling the water's heat relax the tension in his upper body.

In the street outside Tilly's home, Jeff and Andy checked the straps on Simmo's truck one more time. They knew they had a piece of history, but would the old girl fly again, the task was daunting and exciting at the same time.

'Well I'd better grab Angela and head home mate. What's all this partner stuff anyway?' Andy asked. 'You said it earlier and I thought you were just mucking about, what's going on in that ex copper's head of yours?'

'I'll tell you more when I've discussed it with Tilly, but for now I want you to come in with me on the restoration of this old girl,' he tapped the crate, 'I can't do it all on my own and you have the skills to get her airworthy. Think about it, it won't make you rich, but we could barnstorm the country like the pilots of old,' Jeff laughed, 'and you could even do wing walks.'

'Not likely mate, I remember what happened with Joe. You gave him a bloody heart attack. For the life of me, I don't know why he gave you an aeroplane for that, but I'm glad he did. And yes mate, I'd love to be your partner, but I'd have helped out anyway, you know that.'

They shook hands and a partnership seeded.

Andy opened the cabin door for Angela and waited for her to climb in before shutting the door. He sprinted to the driver's side and lunged up behind the wheel. Smiling came easy for Andy, but today he felt renewed and it showed. He reached across and squeezed Angela's hand. He'd always had a positive frame of mind but now, with a girlfriend and half a share in a rare plane, he had many things to be thankful for.

'Come over again soon,' Tilly called as they drove off, 'it'll be Jeff's turn to cook.'

'I've had a great time,' Angela called back over the starting of the engine, 'I'll phone you.' She made the gesture with her hand to her ear and then waved.

Back in the kitchen, with Emily watching television in another room, Jeff folded his arms around Tilly and kissed her neck, but she pulled away playfully, saying, 'we've got some people to tell about our plans and I think we'd better start with Em first. How about you slip down and ask Dad, while I tell her we're getting married?'

'What, you want me to ask him on my own? You're not coming down?'

'It's tradition. You know that. Besides the man just gave you an aeroplane, he won't say no. If he does, tell him it's a shottie,' Tilly grinned at him.

Jeff gawped at her, 'you're not pregnant... are you?'

'Would it bother you?'

'No, course not, I'd be rapt, but,' he watched to see if her face gave her away, but nothing showed, 'you're just winding me up, I know it.'

'You reckon?' Tilly almost allowed a smile. 'Go on get down there, tell them we'll all go to the pub for tea, then come back and get me. I don't think Mum wants to cook tonight.'

Jeff reached lower, feeling her waist and she slapped his hand away, 'just checking,' he said, 'just checking.'

'Get off me. No, I'm not pregnant. Now go and see Dad, while I talk to Em. She'll probably ask when she can have a baby brother and then I'll be neck deep in questions. Remember to tell them about dinner at the Commercial.'

Laura looked up and saw Tilly's car in the driveway and Jeff was heading toward their open front door. She hadn't expected to see anyone and now panic set in as she wondered if something was wrong.

Jeff launched into his request as soon as Joe opened the door 'Joe, I want to ask you something.'

'If it's about ownership of the old plane, I'll get Tilly to do some documents and pass the title to you, fair and square. I've got to say though we had a great time today and I can't tell you what it means to us for all your mates came over and tidy the place up. We're extremely grateful.'

'Joe.'

'You can't know how much it means to us, that you've helped out like you have...'

'Joe,' Jeff raised his voice to stop him babbling, 'Joe, it's nothing to do with that. I have something much bigger to ask you.'

Laura crept along the passage wall. She knew Joe could see her, but stayed back enough to be out of Jeff's vision, gesturing to Joe for him shut up, but he misunderstood and started babbling again. Fixing his eyes on Jeff he tried not to look at Laura.

'Look mate I know you've given the coppers away, but things are still a bit tight around the place at the moment. I'd like to help, but with the finances...'

'Joe, I don't want a job. I just want you to listen and not say anything until I'm finished. Jeez, I'm nervous enough as it is,' he shuffled from one foot to the other.

Joe tried to hold his gaze, but Laura's gesticulations. 'Sorry mate, I don't mean to make you nervous.'

Laura mimed banging her head against the wall. When Joe still didn't understand and opened his mouth to speak again, it was too much for her and she burst in the room, 'oh, for Pete's sake Joe, shut up and let Jeff say something.

'Joe, I just want your permission to ask Tilly for her hand in marriage.'

'Bloody Hell, Laura...' Joe held out his hand and clasped Jeff's with affection, looking to his wife for confirmation, 'sure, I'd like nothing more, what do you say Laura?'

'Jeff, you come over here and give your mum-in-law a big hug. I couldn't be happier unless...' Laura put a finger to her lips, 'is she pregnant?'

'No!' Jeff was astonished. Did they all think the same things, these Gillespie women.

'Oh well, plenty of time for that. Well what are you waiting for, go man go. Go and ask her properly. Should I ring and let her know you're coming?'

'Don't you bloody dare?'

'Go, go on now, scoot,' Laura ushered him out the door and turned to go inside when he pushed back through the door, 'I nearly forgot, Tilly said to ask you to come to the Commercial for dinner with us. We will pick you up around seven, okay?'

Laura watched him leave and went to find Joe. 'Good job I never started on those eggs, now you'd better get spruced up, they'll be back down here soon.'

'How would you know that?'

'It's what we did. He'll have enough time to phone Ted and then they will be down here, Tilly bursting to tell me all about it. Think about it Joe, a wedding to plan for, it's exciting. Then more little ones,' she fell into emotional dreaming, but Joe brought her back to earth before she got too far ahead of herself.

'England and the continent are off then, is that what you're saying?'

'No... It'll be just another thing to add to the list, that's all.' She rubbed her hands together and smiled broadly.

CHAPTER FIFTEEN

Brad Reardon pushed at a few lazy peas with his fork, making swirls in the gravy on his plate. The kids had gone to the city for work and there was nothing to hold them in Orroroo anymore. The bank had helped him with spot loans to get Joe's machinery back on the road but, even if it rained, the money wouldn't start to flow until the district's farmers were sure of a crop.

'You're miles away tonight, love. What's wrong?' Karen Reardon had watched her husband wilt under the drought's intensity only to have his hopes rise when it rained. With their savings gone and their garage mortgaged, she understood his feelings of failure. Not only did she understand them, but knew the real danger was how those thoughts could turn into depression, 'I thought with the work coming in from Joe and Laura's repairs we were getting on top of things,' she waited for his answer.

'Nah, I'm not worried at all Darl, just the opposite really. Today, working with everyone gave me an idea and I was thinking about how we might say goodbye to our troubles that's all.'

'How?'

'I was talking to Laura and she said she wanted to restore a lot of the old machines and other stuff in the barn, but when I looked around I could see the whole place needs restoring first, so I'd like to talk to them about taking over our place if you were agreeable.'

'What, sell your workshop? I thought I'd only get you out of there in a box.'

'Me too love, but enough is enough. I've had a gutful of begging the bank. I hate chasing the poor buggers who can't pay and I'm sick of dodging creditors because I'm late. Time to let it go I reckon.'

'What'll you do and where will we live?' She wondered how far the business had slipped and if he was holding anything back from her. 'Is there money owing I don't know about?' She could feel heat inside her building to anger. They'd had an offer on the place just before the drought started, an offer that could have set them up for life, but he wouldn't take it. 'Well?' she pushed her chair back with her legs and leaned on the table, 'is there?'

'No, you do the books,' he'd thought she'd be happy with his change of mind, 'look I was stubborn and missed a golden opportunity when it came along and I've kicked myself about almost every day since but, if we could sell, what would you want to do?'

She started to clear the dishes, buying thinking time, 'I don't know. I'd need to mull it over for a bit. Anyway, what do you think you'd want to do?'

'Not sure, I guess I'd need to chew on it a bit too,' he pointed to the dishes, 'come on then, let's get this lot cleared away.'

"And then what?'

'Then my girl, we can talk about all the dreams we might realise if we can sell before the bank taps me on the shoulder and asks for the keys,' he slipped his arm around her companionably, 'I'd like to leave town with my dignity intact if possible.'

She shrugged in his embrace, 'leave town, why, what did you have in mind.'

'Well I've always thought about having a place near the beach, maybe Glenelg, or Brighton. Some place the kids can get to more easily.'

'Better make it a small unit then.'

'Why?'

'Well, you'll be going on your own and you won't want to look after anything too big.'

'You'd come too though, wouldn't you?'

'No bloody way, I'm staying here. This is my home. I'm sorry Brad, but if you go it will have to be on your own.'

'I always thought... you always said you hated it here.'

'I don't hate the place or the people, just the grind. Think about it, no debts, no staff, no wage bill, no call outs. Orroroo is wonderful without the worry,' she was laughing at him now, 'I love you, dummy. I only hate the problems and without the business we won't have any problems.'

'Well, all I have to do is approach Joe. I want to work through some stuff first and then see what he says,' he kissed her on the top of her head, 'and you'd better get those grey roots fixed.' He jumped back, dodging her elbow.

'Get those dishes in the sink spanner boy, before I connect next time,' she turned and hugged him, 'a debt free dream. I like the promise of that.'

Emily heard the car roll into the drive and burst out of the front door to meet Jeff, Tilly was three steps behind her as he got out of the car.

'Is it true Jeff? Are you going to be my dad?'

'That's up to you Poppet, is it okay with you if your mum and I get married?'

'Do I get to be in the wedding, Mum?'

'Yep, I wouldn't have it any other way.'

'But what do I call Jeff?'

'You can call me anything you want Em, anything.'

'Careful, she has a great imagination. What do you want to call him?'

'Is it okay to call you Jeff still? I mean, till I get used to having a dad?'

'Jeff's good, I'm kind of used to that anyway,' he bobbed down to look her in the eyes, 'so, you reckon we make this work as a family, you, me and your Mum?'

Emily turned to her mother, 'I'll be like most of the other kids at school, now. I'll have a dad.'

Jeff's phone interrupted the discussion, looked at Tilly and shrugged. Reading the caller, he held the screen out so she could see who was calling.

'Jeff, it's Laura, did she say yes? Of course, she did, she wouldn't have let you come down here without...'

Joe's voice came over Laura's drowning his wife's out. 'I told her not to phone, but I couldn't help it she picked up my phone and hit the speed dial.'

He could hear Joe and Laura laughing, arguing and grappling for control of the mobile. 'Joe, Laura, settle down for a minute, give me time to ask her.' He beckoned Tilly to come closer and put the phone on speaker.

'What's he doing now?' Laura asked.

'I don't know, I told you not to phone yet. Leave them alone woman, I'm hanging up.'

Jeff held the phone so all three could hear and knelt onto one knee. Tilly listened to the phone to hear if Laura and Joe were still there. Jeff began, 'Tilly Gillespie will you do me the honour of becoming Mrs Jeff Rankin?'

'No way Jeff Rankin, we've discussed this,' she winked at him and Emily, 'you either change your name to Gillespie, or it's all off.' She put her finger to her lips and shushed Emily with a smile and a wink. Sure that Em had caught on, she raised her voice, 'switch that off until you're ready to be a real Gillespie, Jeff. Otherwise, I'm not sure I can entertain living with you.'

Jeff knew his cue and pressed the off button.

'Just couldn't help herself the old girl, I'll bet they're up here in a few minutes. Oh, and just in case you were wondering, I'd be honoured to be Mrs Jeff Rankin. You'd better phone your Dad.'

'So, we're still going to be a family, right?' Emily needed to be sure.

'We certainly are going to be a family, young lady. You, me and your mum. The Three Incredibles. Okay?'

'Yep but does that mean I'll be...'

'No need to worry about that now missy, are you happy?'

'Will there be cake?'

'Yes, Emily there'll be cake.'

'Okay, I'm happy then.'

Tilly was keen to divert any of Emily's questions until she and Jeff had more time to work things through, wondering briefly if she had time for this with everything else that was happening now?

'How do you want to play this? Your olds will be here any minute now?'

'You talk to Ted while I take Em inside and help her get ready for dinner. Dad will settle Mum down, but she won't wait for us to pick them up, she'll be on her way,' Tilly hugged him, 'just wave them inside and I'll take it from there. It's not like her to be an old busybody, but now I want to see the look on her face, we both do, don't we Em? It will be good to play a joke on Granny.'

Emily didn't seem so sure, but knew to say nothing until her mother had told her grandparents what was happening.

Ted was delighted with the news and welled up thinking back to his own wedding day, the birth of their son and the tragedy of knowing they would only have the one child. The two men laughed and cried together when talking about how proud Jeff's mum would have been. Hanging up after the call, Ted took the photo of his wife from the mantle and traced the outline of her face. She was everything his world needed and every day he ached at losing her. Ice tinkled in a cut-glass tumbler they'd received as a wedding present, he sniffed the cap of the black label Glenfiddich he saved for special occasions and the ice cracked in celebration as the honey coloured liquid splashed into the glass.

'To Jeff and Tilly love. We got Emily as a bonus and let's hope they give us a grandchild one day.'

He stared at the photo, looking deep into his wife's eyes, happiness and grief combined to wrack his emotions and soon his tears fell on her endless smile.

Tonight he would dream in the sleep of a happy man.

CHAPTER SIXTEEN

Tilly finished brushing her daughter's hair and was tying it into a plait when she heard a car in the driveway.

'It's them,' Jeff called, 'are you sure about this?'

'She should have waited. It'll serve her right if she gets all worked up for a bit. I'll let her down soon enough. Watch and learn fella, watch and learn,' she kissed his cheek and turned to Emily, 'not a word young lady, okay? This is something I need to tell Granny and Pop. Can you do that, it's my surprise, okay?'

Emily dropped her lip as disgust and hurt painted her face. She crossed her arms and stomped to the couch landing on it with a thump.

'Okay Em?'

'I wouldn't have told them anyway,' the look she gave her mother could sour milk, 'I know it's your surprise.'

Jeff raised an eyebrow and tried to keep from smiling, 'well, that's a side of her I haven't seen before.'

'Don't you dare go and comfort her. She has to learn that some things are not hers to share.'

'I could explain...' he wanted to reassure his soon to be step-daughter that he would always be there for her.

'Don't you bloody dare. She's a good kid, but she's getting a bit of attitude lately and I want to nip that in the bud now. Are you okay with that? I can't be telling her one thing, only to have her run to you and have you saying yes, when I've told her no. Can we make sure of that?' Tilly felt as if she was in the middle of a training session for the whole Gillespie family.

'Sure, I understand a chain of command,' his smirk gave him away as he struggled to regain his composure.

'What's that supposed to mean?'

'Nothing, I was being flippant, just trying to break the tension. Look it's always going to be okay with me. I'll always check with you if she's trying to play one of us against the other and she won't always like what I have to say. Nobody can break the bond the two of you share. I know that and I wouldn't want to.'

The doorbell chimed for a second time. Laura found waiting difficult. She shuffled and straightened his collar for the third or fourth time, while Joe fumbled in his pocket and hitched at the back of his jeans. He'd lost weight since the heart attack, living on what he described as bird food. This was embarrassing and he was sure his face was burning. Jeff had said to wait, but no, Laura couldn't help herself.

'Come on, Tilly. What can be keeping them, Joe? Why won't they answer the door, usually Emily is out here before the car stops.'

'He said they'd ring us. What's the hurry? They might have other commitments right now,' Joe was uncomfortable and this urgency was out of character for his wife, 'she won't want a fuss, you know Tilly.'

'Sssh, go around the back and look in the window.'

'No, I will not. Come on Laura, cut it out. How would you have liked someone peering through our windows?' He was frustrated and embarrassed by her behaviour but she wasn't hearing him.

'Give the door a try, we'll just walk in.'

'No way, come on, Jeff's probably still asking her to marry him and Tilly will be doing what she always does. She'll have him on the end of a string and he'll be waiting while she says nothing. She'll walk around the room, turn to him as if she's going to answer, then she'll close her mouth and shake her head. Next thing she'll do is nod and walk away again.' He grabbed her hand and pulled her toward the car.

'Wow, so you think that's how it'll play out, do you?'

'It's what you did to me, and Tilly is very much her mother's daughter.'

'Who's her mother's daughter?' Tilly said, as the door opened. She and Jeff had been listening to Joe and Laura through the closed door. 'Mum, Jeff told Dad we'd call you when we were ready, and Dad, I don't walk around the room making Jeff wait.'

'Well are we having a wedding and when?' Laura threw her arms around Tilly and squeezed her.

'Nope, there'll be no wedding, not for us anyway,' Jeff shrugged and turned away to join Emily on the couch, 'she told me no.'

'Tilly, why? I thought this was something you wanted?' Laura pushed her to arm's length, looked into the sad face of her only child and stroked her cheek.

'I'm not sure I can share my life with someone just now. I've got you and Dad to think about. Then there's the rebuilding. Jeff wants to start a new business and there's Emily to consider,' she pushed out a tear, letting it fill in her lower eyelid, willing it to fall on her mother. She hadn't deceived her like this since she was a kid, 'it's all too much,' she turned away and applied more pressure, 'you and Dad will be away for months and I'll be worried about you all the time.'

'Darling if that's it, we'll stay home. We'll do more to help. The trip's not important is it, Joe?' Laura couldn't see Tilly's face so she didn't catch the wink her daughter gave Joe. He knew to play along now.

'I can manage girl. I'll get back into things again soon, you'll see,' Joe helped Tilly reel her mother in, 'we could even have Emily stay with us for a while.'

'Gotcha!' Tilly said, turning to look at her mother. 'Didn't you think I would want you to be the first to know after I'd told Em? Of course, I said yes. Em, you can come out now.'

'Congratulations Jeff, are you sure about this? These Gillespie women can be a bit of a handful,' they shook hands for the second time that night and Jeff surprised Joe by stepping in close and hugging him, shocking him further when he kissed him on the cheek and whispered a drawn out, 'thanks Dad,' in his ear.

'Get off, you silly bugger, you're as mad as the women are,' Joe was uncomfortable with displays of affection between men, but Tilly and Jeff were happy and, tonight that was enough for him.

'Joe, have you forgotten why we hurried up here?'

'No, we came up here because they asked us out for tea.'

'He is truly the most exasperating man I ever married,' Laura said, 'we came up to congratulate you both and to give Tilly something... something special. In your pocket, Joe. You know, old and shiny. Something borrowed, something old, something blue.'

'Alright, alright,' he reached in and drew out a ring box covered in purple-blue baize that showed signs of wear. The brass clasp was twisted and loose and the gold leaf of the jeweller's name was long gone with only the indentation of where the lettering had once been, 'it's up to you, but this belonged to my great, great grandmother and I...' he looked at Laura and held out the box to Jeff, 'we'd like you both to have it. That's if you want it? It doesn't need to be your engagement ring, just a keepsake.'

'Oh, thanks Dad, Mum. I've always loved this but I'm not sure what Jeff has done in the ring department so we'll talk about it how we'll use it, okay?' Tilly hugged them both.

Jeff had opened the box and passed it to his fiancé, 'thanks Joe, Laura,' he looked from one to the other, 'like Tilly said, we'll need to talk about it,' he leant over and kissed Laura's cheek,' now, how about that tea at the pub?

Come on Em, tonight we celebrate the occasion of you and me and mum planning to become a family.'

***

Andy looked at the bedside clock and grabbed his phone. It was unusual for anyone to call this late, especially as he'd seen most of his friends this afternoon. Angela only woke enough to rub her hand over his thigh and let it drop again.

'Yeah that's okay, after lunch then. Oh, and congratulations by the way.' He rolled over and snuggled into Angela's back, resuming his slumber.

'Who was on the phone?' she mumbled, 'and why did you congratulate them?'

'It was just Jeff, said they'd got engaged and they won't be here until after lunch tomorrow. That's all.' Satisfied he'd delivered the information, he buried his face in the pillow and hunted for sleep.

Angela lay there for a minute before the news sank in, siting bolt upright and fluffing a couple of pillows behind her back, no longer tired, 'come on tell me everything. I want to know what Jeff said, every detail.'

'I dunno, what time is it?'

'Eleven thirty-five.'

'Go to sleep, he said they'd be late, we could sleep in.'

'No, there was more, what about their engagement? What did he say about that?'

'Just that they were engaged.'

'When did he propose, or did she ask him?'

'God, I don't know, does it matter?'

'No, it doesn't matter, but what did he say? Did he go down on one knee when he proposed? I suppose Jeff proposed, I mean Tilly is a lady, and she'd wait to be asked?' Angela bounced on the bed until Andy gave her more of his attention, 'she's pretty independent though, I could see her putting the question to him,' she prodded her companion. He rolled away taking the sheet with him. She shook him again, 'did you ask when they are getting married?'

'No. He just said they got engaged, that was enough for me, they'll be here tomorrow, you can ask Tilly everything then.'

'Urrgh men. Now I'm wide awake.'

'You'll get back to sleep soon enough, just put your mind to it.'

She lay awake listening to his regular breathing, happy and excited for her friend as she waited for a return of sleep.

CHAPTER SEVENTEEN

Joe stood at the sink, staring across the plain toward Black Rock Peak and this early part of the day was one of the things he enjoyed most. The town was quiet with only the occasional rooster calling for the sunrise. With the scent of coffee to accompany him, he went out the back door of the cottage, drew out a chair from the picnic set, put his mug on the table and sat down. Light dew had settled overnight and a golden orb spider was dismantling the last remnants of her web. He wondered if she had she been successful in netting her prey. He watched as dewdrops slowly filled with light from the dawning sun, appearing like gold baubles dripping from the sultana vine his grandmother had planted on the patio half a century before.

He felt for the gold bar in his pocket and laid it on the table. Warm from the heat of his body, he played his fingers along its surface and tantalised by texture, grew confident in its value.

The shadows cast by the old horse drawn vehicles they had dragged from the barn yesterday became more distinct as the sun rose. Today was the first time the machinery had welcomed the morning for decades and he felt reassured, seeing this as a symbol of a new beginning, the changing of generational responsibility. He wasn't sure he was ready to let everything go right now, but knew he was ready for a shift in direction. Before they had left the pub, Tilly had asked Joe and Laura if Emily could stay with them overnight and now, almost unnoticed, the child had squeezed between him and the table, cuddling into him for warmth. She was growing up fast and he held her tight, wanting to imprint the moment in her memory as much as his own.

Gillespie's Gold

In Wilmington, Ted Rankin looked at his mob of yearlings as he made his way from the horse yards to the house, only stopping to shift the water on his pumpkins before he went inside. He felt fresh eggs in his pocket and smiled. He didn't often have a cooked breakfast, but today was different.

The arthritis wasn't bothering him as much and he felt lighter, younger, and he began to hum before breaking into, *Oh What a Beautiful Morning,* in a rich baritone. The kettle steamed and strips of bacon wrinkled and twisted as they sizzled to a crisp. He sniffed the pan, just the way he liked it. Morning sunlight streamed through the small window, falling over where he sat. Sunbeams glittered and faded as they danced in and out of the light and he knew today should be good and filled with joy. His only son would be there for lunch with his new fiancée and, with a bit of luck, the Rankin line would continue with Jeff and Tilly.

He reached down and scratched his dog's ears. 'I think I'll take 'em to the pub for lunch Red, so, you'll have to look after the place, but I'll be back after two. Then we'll walk that mob of cattle around the outskirts of town,' he knew the dog couldn't answer with words, but a tail wag let him know he understood, 'well, I'd better get spruced up, they'll be here soon.'

Ted laid out his best moleskins and flicked a clothes brush over the soft cream fabric. A crease, pressed as sharp as folded paper had been his preference for years, and no matter what the fashion was these days, this was his look. Mother of pearl buttons stood sharp against the deep claret coloured satin of his preferred western style shirt and he smiled as he checked his image in the mirror. Twenty years ago, she'd have loved it, but twenty years ago, his wife would have shared today with him.

His eyes dropped to the picture on the dressing table and a tear splashed the glass. Jeanie should be here. He shook his head and took the shirt off. It was a bit loud for today. The light olive one would do, with the shoestring tie he saved for special occasions. Jeanie had given it to him to wear on their second date, and he'd worn it on the day they were married three years later. Maybe he couldn't share today with her, but he did have something of hers to give them, a treasured memento the next generations of Rankins could carry into the future. He reached into the back of the drawer and without looking at it, put the object in his pocket. For him it had always been a tangible reminder of his wife. He didn't have much to give the couple as an engagement present, but he did have this. It had considerable value, but more than that, it carried traditional significance.

CHAPTER EIGHTEEN

Joe found Laura at the kitchen table downloading the photos Tilly had taken of yesterday's working bee.

'What are you doing love?' He said.

'Tilly said to download any of the photos we wanted from yesterday. There were a lot of people there I don't know,' she opened a new folder in the computer and dragged the pictures across, arranged them into a slideshow then copied to a USB stick, 'we'll check it on the flat screen later,' she set the stick aside, 'but right now you can show me around my projects.'

Joe grunted and turned to put his boots on, 'you're revelling in all this, aren't you?'

'Yep, come on, last one to the barn buys dinner,' she kicked a boot out of reach and disappeared at a half run down the path.

***

In Adelaide, Gino settled the weight bar onto its rest and, without moving off the bench, picked up his phone. He stared at the picture on his screen of two men were working a barbeque.

He read the accompanying text, *Quarry winged, big rumour here, gold bars found.*

He smiled at Spoggy's message and typed, *Job's right.* Then forwarded the photo to Charles and went back to lifting weights.

***

Lunch with Ted had ended with Tilly's head in a spin and the last thing she wanted to do was offend him. She was still rolling things over in her mind when they met Andy at the airfield where Jeff and Andy set about pulling bits out of boxes and laying them on the hangar floor, Emily was helping with the smaller items, while she and Angela watched.

'What do you mean you have two rings?' Angela said, 'you sure you're not being a bit greedy there, girl?'

'Ah, it's not that. I wanted us to find a jeweller and choose the one we liked, that's all. I don't want to seem ungrateful and I can't favour one family over the other, but if I'm truthful, neither of these is for me. Do you know what I'm getting at, or am I just being ungrateful?'

'If I ever get the chance,' Angela nodded her head toward Andy and rolled her eyes, 'if ever I get asked, I'd want to pick my ring too. Either that or...'

Tilly took a ring from her pocket and dropped it into Angela's open hand.

'...my god girl, look at those stones? Your problem is one I'd like to have,' she slipped a ring onto her finger and stretched her arm out, 'um, no not really my style either.'

Tilly passed her the other ring and said, 'I know, after lunch Jeff asked Em if she wanted to look at Ted's cattle, chooks and horses,' Tilly looked around to make sure Jeff couldn't hear her and whispered, 'Ted and I were in his kitchen talking, getting to know each other better and he said he'd spent almost three month's wages on this ring. Imagine that, sitting on a horse tailing along behind cattle for all that time and knowing when you got home, you'd blow all your wages on an engagement ring.'

'Wow, a fair bit to put into a ring?'

'That's why it's so hard. There were tears in his eyes when he gave it to me. God, I don't want to hurt him or Jeff either, but I'd prefer to start out fresh, with my own ring.'

Angela was rotating Ted's ring around in her fingers, letting the light catch the diamond. She gave it back and Tilly passed her the other one. This was older and made of rose gold. A smaller diamond, mounted high on white gold and ringed with rubies, its style came from another era.

'They are beautiful though, aren't they?' Tilly said.

'They're gorgeous, but I can see your problem. What does Jeff say?'

'I haven't had a chance to talk to him. When Mum sprang Grandma's ring on him last night, he was as ambushed as I am,' she put her head in her hands, 'it's not a great start to our engagement and I don't like having to choose.'

'You could always have a jeweller make the two rings into one of your own design. You'd probably have enough left over for wedding and eternity rings too.'

'I don't know. Ted was fairly adamant this was the most beautiful thing he'd ever seen, and Mum was mighty forceful too,' Tilly felt her shoulders slump and stared at Emily helping the boys dig through boxes.

'You could tell them by restyling the rings you are melding the families. You know propose it as a symbol of unity between,' Angela made quotation signs with her fingers, 'the House of Rankin, and the House of Gillespie,' she put her arm around Tilly and laughed.

'That sounds like a good idea. We'll have to be sensitive about it though, we don't want to upset any of them. I'll talk to Jeff and see what he thinks and then we probably need to all sit down and come to a decision,' Tilly dropped the rings back into her pocket, 'it gets hard when there's so much emotion involved.'

They watched Jeff and Andy rest the wings against the bi-plane's fuselage. The hangar floor resembled a life-size model aeroplane kit. The men prised the wing stands from the crate and set them along the wall.

'A few grunts and the wings can rest there until we need them.' Jeff said.

'You sure about this, I mean, this is a very rare machine?' Andy asked.

'Mate, Joe gave her to me hoping she might fly again. I reckon it'll take a lot of hours to make her airworthy and I don't have the skills. A fifty-fifty partnership sounds like a good deal to me, but I'll understand if you want to back away too.'

'Not on your life, partner. We share the work and the cost though. I can't wait to get started,' Andy said, 'I know you've got a bit on this week, so tomorrow I'll come in make an inventory of everything. Then I'll see if I can find someone who can tell us where to start.'

'I'd better run. I can see Tilly's anxious to make a move. Talk to you during the week.'

'Later then,' Andy, seeing Angela was ready to leave too, pulled the hangar door closed.

Swinging the car into Ted's driveway Jeff said, 'you two can go and see Gidget while I talk to Dad and, I reckon like me, he'll be more than happy with Angela's idea.'

'God I hope so, the last thing I want is to get off on the wrong foot as his daughter in law.'

'You're making too much out of it,' he leant across the console and kissed her, 'and besides, your parents said to use that ring anyway you wanted. I'll talk to Dad, you two can talk to Gidget and everything will be hunky dory, you'll see.'

'Are you upset about your wedding, Mum?' Emily said as they looked into the pony's stall.

'I don't know, Em,' she ran her hand down her daughter's hair, 'it's not like me to worry about this sort of stuff.'

'It's just because it's new and you don't want to hurt people's feelings.'

Tilly felt Ted putting his arm on her shoulder as he leaned against the rail and stood beside her.

'Sorry about the mix up. When I was telling you about the ring and what it meant to me, I didn't for one minute want you to think I was attaching strings. Jeff said you were worried that I'd be hurt if you used both rings to make a new one as a symbol of family commitment,' he gave a little squeeze and dropped his arm, 'I knew I should have expressed myself better and I'm sorry it's worried you. Like him, I reckon it's a great idea.'

She turned to face him, 'so it'll be okay?'

'What's an old man like me going to do with it?' he stretched his hand out, 'look a bit outta place on one of my fingers.'

CHAPTER NINETEEN

Sam admired the gold leaf lettering on the door to her new office. She had bargained hard with Charles to give her this role and it had been conditional on her investing in the new company. It had taken all of her savings, but she now held a quarter of the shareholding, Gino had ten percent and Charles the balance.

Not yet thirty, she was the CEO of RADOR Exploration. It was something she had prepared for all her life.

Although there were exceptions that had been born into it, she knew the odds were against a woman setting the mining world on fire from scratch, but she was ready for it. RADOR needed cash and plenty of it and the first challenge was to build a nucleus of people she could trust. Sam argued with Charles over key personnel, but within a week she had the people she wanted and agreed to an accountant of his choice. RADOR was ready.

It had taken a lot of late nights to prepare documents, build a prospectus, and prepare the company to launch onto the Australian Stock Exchange. The only obstacle was the geology reports. She needed access to the Gillespie property and the family holding the leases was resistant, denying the drilling contractors permission to enter their land. She stormed into Gino's office and slammed the latest letter from Pictinco Mining on his desk.

'Have you any idea who these people are?' She felt her blood running hot. Several attempts to meet with the principals of Pictinco had been denied, 'I don't know anything more than the solicitor's name on the bottom of their page. The company's owned by the Gillespie Family Trust. I know the property's called Wanooka's Well and it's Joe Gillespie's land, but just who manages Pictinco?'

Gino pointed to the signature. 'You wanted this job, you work it out. Charles wants a meeting on Friday and I suggest you have something positive to tell him,' he smiled at her, 'there's a lot of money riding on you, don't stuff up.'

She slammed his door on the way out, angry with herself for allowing him to bring out the worst in her. It was time for a different strategy and she decided to take a more direct route. Brushing past Timothy's desk on the way through to her own office, she dropped Tilly's letter in front of him, telling him to try every Gillespie in the book if he had to, 'but start with those in Orroroo first. Tell her I'll meet her wherever. Just get me an appointment,' she stopped at the door to her office, 'and I want a meeting with the Minister of Mines and Energy ASAP. I don't want to know how difficult it is. Just get me a lunch date, anything. Today is fine.'

As her personal assistant, Timothy was used to her moods and understood the strain his boss was under. He scrolled through the government directory and picked up the phone.

Gino heard her barking orders and leaned back in his chair. He knew she would fail. If Charles had taken his advice, Sam would be working for him and all of this would be in place by now. Time was on his side. He would watch her stumble through the process and then he would ride to the company's rescue again.

At noon Sam walked into Penfold's Magill Estate Restaurant and the waiter showed her to her table. Minister Pituri stood and shook her hand. Over lunch, they talked about her desire to begin testing on the Gillespie land and of her frustration coming from the family's refusal to discuss the project.

'I'm not sure I can assist you, Miss Lewis. The Gillespies have complied with the act. I've had one of my people speak with Ms Gillespie and she was most adamant that the family was solid in their position.' He folded his napkin and stood up. He held her chair while she stood and walked with her to the counter. Their meeting was over.

'I'll get mine.' He said and passed his credit card to the waiter.

Sam paid and folded the receipt into her wallet. The minister walked with her to the car and held the door open for her. 'I'm sorry I can't help, maybe you could take a drive north and meet with Ms Gillespie,' he suggested, 'see her face to face, you never know, it might make your case stronger.'

'She won't take our calls. My PA has pleaded, but...' she shrugged, 'he says she's adamant.'

'If you want some simple advice, forget you're a CEO and try a softer approach, woman to woman. Take the drive, who knows what you'll achieve when you see her on her own.'

'Thanks, I'm not sure I'm convinced, but it's probably worth a try.' She slipped behind the wheel and he closed the door. Checking her mirror as she turned into the traffic, she saw the Minister for Mines step onto a city bound bus. There was no chauffeured car for Minister Pituri and she wondered why.

Gino put the phone down. His snitch in the minister's office had told him what Pituri would advise Sam. He could wait, everything was in place for when the time came to make his move.

'How did it go?' he called to Sam as she breezed past his door.

'Yeah good.'

'Anything I should know, or do to help?'

'No thanks. I'll be out of the office for a few days, so give everything to Timothy until I get back. If it's urgent, I'll handle it from there.'

'So where are you off to?'

'I'm going to have a look at our leases in the Flinders, check on progress with our drilling teams and stuff,' she smiled at him. She knew just how well Gino read people and didn't want him to see she was panicking inside, 'do you want to come?'

'Nah, I have plenty to do here, I'm at the end of the phone if you need me though.'

'Yeah, I'll remember that. Thanks.'

Timothy was waiting in her office. 'I made contact with Ms Gillespie and she told me the family weren't interested in meeting anyone from RADOR. Their position remains the same as when she wrote the letter you received this morning.'

'What's wrong with these people? Until a couple of years ago, their neighbours were begging us to drill on their land. The Gillespies aren't hanging onto those leases for nothing. Charles has to be right. That old yarn about Les Gillespie's gold mine must be true, because what other reason could they have to stop exploration?'

Timothy shrugged and passed her a list of messages. She wrote instructions alongside each item and instructed him to handle it before walking to the wall where a geological survey map showed their leases. Colours depicted areas where diamonds, precious stones, copper, tin, manganese and other metals were likely to be found. To the east, deep coal seams were evident and Charles had secured a prime for the parent company. One area stood out, devoid of test holes, and she wondered if it might be easier to drill on the moon than gain access to Wanooka's Well.

'Get me a list of our people in the area and let them know I'll be calling. Organise accommodation until Saturday and a four-wheel-drive wagon. I'll e-mail you a list of maps and geo-survey reports I need. Have someone drop the car off at my unit at four o'clock. I'll bring them back to work on my way out. Oh, and for the accommodation, see if you can get me into an Airbnb or a nice little bed and breakfast place in Orroroo.'

Sam stowed her laptop into her satchel, grabbed her hi-vis vest and hard hat and marched out. It was time to let the Gillespies know she meant business.

Gino heard the lift doors close and walked to Timothy's desk. 'How do you think she'll go?'

'Yeah, she'll make it happen.' Timothy said.

'And if she doesn't?'

'Then, I hope I'll be working for you.'

CHAPTER TWENTY

Gino had influence and this Kent Town restaurant was one of the more exclusive places to dine. His guest, Hans Schmidt, the Minister for Agriculture, was already waiting when he arrived. Gino sat down and picking up his glass, tasted the red and looked at the bottle. He knew Schmidt was never one to hold back when others were paying. 'Nice choice, 2004 Shiraz from Witchmount Estate, won an award some years back too, he said.

'You know your wine. It took out the 2008 Syrah Du-Monde in France, too.' Schmidt liked to share his knowledge.

Gino raised his eyebrows. 'I thought you'd be supporting the local product.'

'One has a duty to his office, a duty that he must understand the competition and to sample the best produce at every opportunity.'

'And your constituents might say you have your snout in the trough, but what they don't know won't hurt them, yeah?'

'I think you and I understand each other and I also believe you have something for me?'

Gino passed a brown envelope under the table. The minister took it and sliding it into his inside coat pocket. 'Good.'

'Kind of bulky, even for hundreds.' Gino said, 'Now what I need in return is access to test the soil and ground water in these areas,' he showed the minister the selected locations on his phone screen, 'we know the owner has had his bores and wells poisoned and we know your department has called for tenders to survey and develop a plan to repatriate the ground,' he winked and the minister nodded, 'our offer is already on your table and I'd like to think we are the best company to win the business. We want to

101

begin testing as soon as we can,' he bent forward and motioned for the minister to do the same, 'maybe some preliminary testing, you know, to help your department formulate an action plan, is what I'm thinking.' He nodded to a young man at a far table, who acknowledged with a smile and brought a briefcase to them. Gino thanked him and watched as he returned to his table.

From the case Gino removed a manila folder and placed it in front of the minister. 'Here are my thoughts of how you should frame and judge each tender. I've included a summary of how we'll carry out our survey. I trust you will make sure it gets to the right people.'

'Sounds like a solid idea.'

'One more thing,' Gino said, 'you asked me to let you in on anything we find that might make the stock market bounce'

'Yes'

'You'll know a few days before we announce it.'

'Just as we discussed last year.'

'Just as we agreed last year.' Gino said.

'To RADOR,' Minister Schmidt proposed, 'long may you prosper.

Gino thought the gesture was over the top, but joined the toast. 'RADOR.'.

The two men folded their napkins, making small talk while they waited for the ministerial limousine to arrive. They discussed the football draft and the Adelaide Crows chances for making into the eight this year. Gino asked about other ministers and their sporting allegiances. It might have been small talk for the minister, but for Gino it was research. It was how he and Charles operated.

Schmidt beckoned to the waiter. 'Bring another bottle, but leave the cork in this time,' he knew how to milk any situation, 'I'll take it as a traveller, thank you.'

The waiter was back and Gino asked for the account, afraid that if they stayed much longer, Schmidt might order the whole carton.

Gino paid the waiter in cash, including a fifty-dollar tip, and the two men stood and shook hands. He passed Schmidt the briefcase, which now held the folder and the wine, the Minister had always been expensive, but it was beneficial to have him secured as a friend to the company.

Schmidt waited for his driver to open the door, settled into the rear seat of the government car and as the chauffer closed his door, the politician disappeared behind tinted glass.

Gino took the recording pen from his pocket, tapped the stop record button and slid it back from where it came. He thought about Sam as he walked home, she might have the corner office now, but in time she would find the unpalatable stuff too hard to deal with and step aside. If she didn't, she would be pushed. He could see the inner softness that even she appeared unaware of.

***

Sam had rejected the first four-wheel-drive, hired by Timothy from a company specialising in mine rentals. She wanted something more discreet and a burgundy RAV 4 suited her needs better. Her accommodation was a bed and breakfast overlooking the Orroroo Golf Course. Timothy had paid by credit card, there would be enough food for the week and she could pick up the key from the Commercial Hotel.

It was dark when she arrived in town and the locals turned on their barstools as she pushed through the corner door. It didn't feel much different to the pub in Mundulla. Even in casual clothes, she saw she was still overdressed and could feel the eyes of everyone on her as trying to work out who she was, the universal look from people too used to seeing the same faces day after day. The barman looked away from the seven o'clock news, lifted his eyebrows and looked at the taps and back at her, a communication technique that took minimum effort.

She showed him her driver's licence. 'I was told I could pick up the key to Miss Carter's Cottage here.'

He took a bunch of the keys from the hook above the till and passed it to her, nodding toward the taps again as he did so, his eyes never leaving the television.

'Thanks, but no.' She walked out and smiled at the whistles that followed her. There were still red-blooded boys in the north country where political correctness had yet to reach, she thought.

Even before Sam reached the cottage, Gino received a text and a photo telling him a new species of bird had been spotted in town. He smiled, his spy was still working.

***

Tilly wondered about the four-wheel-drive parked outside her house when she returned from the school run. As she opened the door of her own car a woman in her twenties greeted her.

'Ms Gillespie, Tilly Gillespie?'

'Yes,' Tilly looked at the woman and thought she must have been a journalist or someone looking for work at her old firm, 'I'm Tilly, how can I help you?'

'Hi, sorry to doorstep you like this, but I've wanted to talk to you for a while and haven't been able to get through.'

'Sorry about that, you know, a child at school and I have a lot on my plate at the moment. Sometimes I wonder where all the time goes,' she held out her hand, 'you didn't say your name.'

'Samantha Lewis, my friends call me Sam.'

'Samantha Lewis, from RADOR?'

'That's me.'

'I don't think I can help you Samantha, I've made our position clear. Our family is opposed to any mining or exploration on our properties. I thought I'd detailed that in my last letter. Now if you'll excuse me, I have things to do.'

'How about we go to that little coffee shop in the main street and have a chat about it. You haven't even heard my offer yet.'

'I don't need too. We're not interested. For over fifty years, different companies have tried to buy our leases and we've refused, today isn't any different. Miners aren't welcome on Gillespie land.'

'I understand what your position has been in the past, but I'm not willing to let this rest. My Company needs access and we'll go to the government if necessary.'

'And do what? I took a call from Andreas Pituri last night telling me he'd met with you and he asked if we would change our position. I told him what I've just told you. It's not going to happen.'

'Do the rest of the trustees agree with that?'

Tilly didn't answer as she lifted a couple of shopping bags from the back seat of the car, 'I think we're done here, Samantha, don't you?'

'Not by a long shot, Ms Gillespie. I'm prepared to take this through the courts and do whatever it takes to get access to your land.'

'You'd better have a lot of firepower to match your threats then. Take your pretty, little four-wheel-drive and go back to the city and your pretty little office, where you can bother someone else.'

'What, you think you can scare me off with a few cheap jibes? I hope you've got a fortune to waste defending your position. Our legal team will be in touch. I'd hoped we could reach an agreement without any unpleasantness, but if you want a fight, I'm your girl. Down and dirty farmer's daughter style. There's a fair bit of South East sheila in me, so don't think your outback routine puts you at an advantage. I can take you and the whole Gillespie family anywhere, anytime,' Sam walked to the hire car, 'see you in court.'

'Come back and see me when you grow up.' Tilly wanted to swear at her, a good slanging match might relieve some of the tension she'd been feeling.

Sam slammed her door and jammed the Rav4 into drive. Its front wheels scrabbled for traction and chirped as the caught the bitumen. This hadn't gone the way she had planned and she blamed herself for losing control. She'd envisaged sitting in the sun with Tilly, having coffee and discussing the exploration plans she had for Wanooka's Well. She would drive out to one of the drill teams today and rethink her plans overnight. Nobody and nothing could stop her. Tilly Gillespie may have had the last word today but it wasn't over yet, not by a long shot.

Once inside, Tilly phoned Jonathon, leaving a message for him to return her call when he didn't answer. If there was going to be a court battle it was best to be prepared. With Laura and Joe still holidaying in England, she wouldn't be able to let them know until tonight and Jeff was taking an Outreach Flinders tour and wouldn't be back until Friday. She called Fiona to see if she wanted a coffee, a friend to talk to was what she needed.

Tilly heard the front door open and flicked the switch on the kettle. Fiona swept through into the kitchen, dropped her bag on the floor and perched on a stool. 'C'mon, tell me all about it and don't leave anything out. What did she look like?'

'Rav4, hired I reckon. Moleskins, RM Williams boots, belt and pink check top. She was about a size eight and looked like someone off the set of McLeod's Daughters, all she needed was the hat.'

'So, you're friends then?'

'Not bloody likely,' Tilly knew she had to control her thoughts and not let too much out, 'she wants access to drill test holes on our place. We've had a no drill policy for longer than Dad's been around so I told her no and she threatened to take us to court over it,' she passed her friend her cup, 'sorry, I just needed to let off a bit of steam.'

'What are you going to do?'

'Fight fire with fire. I used to be pretty good at this kind of stuff. I won't go down without a fight.'

Feeling better for getting some of her concerns off her chest, their talk relaxed into everyday events until the ringing of Tilly's phone acted as a prompt for Fiona to leave.

Tilly waved a silent goodbye to her friend as she took the call.

'G'day Tilly, it's Jonathon, you called earlier.'

'Yes hello, Jonathon, and thanks for calling back. I might need some help with a mining firm trying to get access to drill on the Well. I haven't been able to contact my folks yet, but I thought I should get something in place if we do end up in a fight over it.'

'The company, is it RADOR?'

'That's them.'

'No can do, they're our clients now too. Charles Winkler signed with us this morning.'

'Who's Charles Winkler?'

'Some hotshot mining exec, the major shareholder in RADOR. Sorry, I can't tell you more.'

'So, all you have at the moment is an agreement to represent them.'

'Yes, that's all.'

'And our relationship? Isn't there a conflict of interest?'

'Not if we sever.'

'You wouldn't?'

'I wouldn't, that's why I resigned at lunch time.'

'But the firm is your heritage, you can't just resign.'

'No choice. I raised my objections, but the other partners saw a cash cow and sold us out. I packed my desk this morning. Father's retiring from chambers next month, so there's nothing but my name on the door to hold me.'

'You're really leaving then?'

'Yep, Alice has wanted to move back to Adelaide for a while now. I need to talk to her, but I'll hang my shingle on a wall over there somewhere. I'd like nothing more than a legal fight with my former partners, that is of course, if you want me to represent you'

'Well yes, I don't know what to say other than I'll have to do a fair bit of leg work for you, as things are tight at present.'

'Yeah, I thought you might be up against it a bit, but don't worry, you know how slow things move in this job. I think it's best to wait and see what they come up with first. When we come over house hunting we'll come and see you. In the meantime, you'll know what we'll need to defend your case.'

'You sure you want to risk it?'

'Yep, I remember talking to that spook from ASIO, Colin Buchanan. He said he hadn't felt as alive as he did when he worked on your Dad's case. Tilly, I felt the same and this is another chance to feel the old buzz again.'

'Thanks, I hope you're sure about this though.'

'The change will be good for us. Expect a visit soon. Oh, and now the kids are at uni, she says she'll step into the secretarial role again. So, you get the two of us on the one bill.'

Tilly could hear relief in his voice. He'd finally broken free of the old firm as he always yearned to do. 'I'm looking forward to seeing you both again. Let me know where you put your shingle, and thanks. I'll sever our contract with your old firm today.'

CHAPTER TWENTY ONE

Gino signed the last of the tender documents and slid them into an envelope, placing it alongside five bundles of one hundred dollar notes in a green carry bag and picked up the phone.

'Same place?'

'I'll need to buy bait, say five thirty. We can wait for the snapper to come on the bite.' Gino said.

'Sometime after five thirty, then.'

After leaving the office Gino stopped to buy fuel for the boat and get bait before he left his Patawalonga mooring. He called Charles from the car to tell him it was all set to go.

'Good, has Sam made any progress with the Gillespies?'

'She hasn't said, but my sources say no.'

'Let me know what develops. This thing in the Hunter smells a bit fishy and I reckon a lot of politicians are going to be embarrassed someday soon. We can't afford the same thing over there. I want no loose ends, no paper trail. I want nothing that could lead back to us if things go belly up. Understand?'

'From what I read, the Hunter thing was all a bit clumsy.'

'Make sure everything we do is on the money. We can probably make more out of this mess in New South Wales than chasing the Gillespies, but we're in for the long haul now.' Charles sounded weary.

'You losing your appetite for the chase, Charlie?'

'Nah, late night that's all. Be bloody careful with Schmidt, he's as slippery as a greased turd.'

'I know. It's why I wear gloves. Enjoy gladhanding all those politicians out there in the Hunter. Just think of me sitting out here in the gulf hauling in big snapper.'

'Save one for me. See ya.'

At four o'clock Gino was anchored in the middle of Saint Vincent's Gulf at the pre-arranged coordinates. He threw handfuls of burly over the side and lowered a basket of crab shells, all he had to do now was wait.

At four twenty five, a sport fishing boat drew alongside. No surprises here, Gino had heard the aluminium hull crashing against the waves for the last fifteen minutes. They might be fast, but boats like that were loud.

'Any bites?' the driver asked.

'Not yet, maybe after sundown,' Gino replied.

'You're a long way out for that old girl.'

'She's been solid for over thirty years and I reckon she'll work for another fifty.'

'Hope you bag out then, see ya.' The driver pushed the throttles forward and the twin Hondas lifted the hull as if it was a leaf. Gino watched it until it became a black dot in front of a white line of foam.

'Oh, I intend to, I'm planning to bag me a big one.' He spoke his thoughts aloud as he baited a handline with a small trumpeter he'd caught earlier. This line was a contrast to the new rods and reels that had festooned his visitor's boat and he baited another and tossed it a few meters closer than the first. In five minutes he had five lines out and sat with his back against the stern feeling the rudder move the tiller as the carvel hull rolled at anchor. This boat had been his father's only toy, an escape from the drudgery of the Holden assembly line. He had worked two jobs to pay for Gino's education and pay off the family home, only go to the grave in his fifties. He remembered how proud his father had been when he had finished painting the words, Messina-Maria, the blue script contrasting with the white hull. They were the names of his father's hometown and his only love, Gino's mother. Gino could afford a new boat, but it wouldn't hold the memories of this one. A slow drag on a line telling him a crab was trying to steal his bait put an end to his reminisces.

Hans Schmidt was late, but Gino had made it his business to know the politician's habits and Schmidt had often bragged that it had always amazed him how many of Adelaide's good and great were prepared to wait for hours while he powdered his nose. The hum of a diesel trawler beyond the horizon was replaced by the sloshing of a pleasure boat wallowing alongside the Messina-Maria. Hans was alone and Gino had his pen pressed to record again.

'I thought you'd have brought the Fisheries launch,' Gino said, as he lashed a line from the stern of Schmidt's boat.

'Can't be too careful, besides my boat's better for these meetings.'

'I understand.'

'You got it?'

'I couriered the documents to your office earlier. What you want is in the light box at pier twelve on the Patawalonga Marina,' his gloved hand passed the minister a key, 'toss it into the harbour when you're finished.'

'What the fuck? You arsehole. Don't tell me I've come all the way out here just for you to give me a key?'

Gino tried to hide his grin, 'I thought you enjoyed boating?'

'Not to pick up a pissy little key.' He was already casting off.

'You won't stay till after sundown, I can promise snapper,' Gino was laughing.

'Christ Gino, I have stuff to do.'

'Yeah, me too,' Gino pushed the cruiser away, 'like I said, half now and the rest when I have the tender in my hand.'

'No guarantees.'

'Yes, there are,' there was menace in the voice behind his smile, 'and you know it.'

'Good luck with the fishing.' The minister spoke with an insincere sneer.

'The fishing's always good here,' Gino waved his hand at the horizon, 'want me to save you a big one.'

'Not for me, I only eat fish in restaurants.'

'If you're sure?'

'I'll check this out.' Schmidt held up the key.

'I'm sure you will.'

Gino pressed the small pen as he watched the boat cruise away and pulled in the line the crab had been gnawing at. The bait had gone. He held his arm outstretched and measured the distance between the horizon and the sun. Five fingers, he had an hour and a half before the snapper would bite. He rebaited all of his hooks set a couple of crab nets and dozed.

He was woken by his phone message alert and looked at the text, a photo of Hans Schmidt taking a green shopping bag from the light box. Even if he had nothing on the line he had bagged himself a politician.

Tilly Gillespie needed someone to talk to, not to discuss the business, or the problems with the farm, she felt like dinner and a friendly chat. A call to Fiona had her husband John agreeing to feed their children and Emily too.

'Be back by nine,' was all he asked of them. He wanted to check the pubs just to tell anyone who was thinking of driving home with a gutful of grog to make other plans.

The Commercial Hotel offered a fair menu, it wasn't five star, but for a country pub the standard was high. Being diagonally across from the police station meant that if John was called out, Fiona could be home in a flash.

Tilly's was seated with her back to the door when Fiona asked, 'what did that woman who got you fired up this morning look like?'

'I told you, size eight, confident, around thirty. Prissy little bitch.'

'Don't look now, but I think she's just walked in.'

Tilly sculled her Vodka in response.

Fiona downed hers and passed the glass over, 'what are you going to do?'

'I'm going to ask her to join us.'

'What, why?'

'She's in our town and I want her to know we don't fear or favour anyone. Plus, it might work to my advantage to know why she's so desperate to get access to the farm,' Tilly winked, 'now give me your glass.'

Perched on one of the stools as she waited for the barman, who was busy pulling a beer for one of the locals in the main bar, she turned to Sam Lewis, 'waiting for someone, or are you here on your own?'

'Oh, hi,' Sam had hoped to have a meal and get back to the cottage to study the drilling team's reports, 'I didn't feel like cooking in a strange kitchen so I thought I'd just grab and go.'

'Nonsense,' Tilly said, 'we can't have you eating alone, come and meet Fiona,' she thought Fiona could eat this city chick for breakfast and still be hungry, 'what can I get you to drink?'

'Oh, I'm just on Light Ice.'

'I'll get it, how about a whisky chaser?'

'Vodka?'

'I like your style.' She ushered Sam back to the table where the three of them waited, masking the strangeness of the situation in small talk, until Rosie, the publican's wife, called their meal number.

Sam pushed at the coleslaw on her plate, uncomfortable to be sitting there when all she wanted was to ask Tilly about the mining and exploration leases. Whenever she had managed this type of meeting for Charles, it had been as the messenger, now she was both.

Tilly sensed her frustration. 'Fi and I have to go soon, but if you like, we can talk about what it is your company does. I'm not prepared to go into offers for our leases or anything but I am interested in you, so tell us about yourself.'

'Not too much to tell. I was pretty good at school, studied geology and business management. Signed up with Wagmin Resources as a PA, we created RADOR, I applied for the CEO's role, and here I am.'

Fiona was curious. 'Why geology?'

'Dad spent a fair bit of time as a driller before he bought the farm at Mundulla. He probably dropped a few holes down out north of here too. He worked for a company called Australian Diamond Drillers in the early seventies.'

'Yeah?' Tilly said.

'Mum once told me they stayed in the caravan park, while the boss was camped in a house around here somewhere. Big old place on a hill looking over the town. I think they had a speedboat and upset the locals by water skiing on the reservoir. So, I guess the family's been here before, even if I can't remember it.'

'Well before our time, I reckon.'

'And anyone special?' Tilly asked.

'You first.' Sam had spent so much time working, she had forgotten how to relax with her own gender, reminding herself to keep her guard up not to talk about her company's ambitions.

Tilly was proud of her relationship with Jeff and only too happy to talk about it. 'Well, I found this was a good fit,

115

a few months ago,' she pushed her left hand forward and showed off her engagement ring, 'and I love it.'

Sam whistled, 'well someone's found a diamond mine around here by the look of that stone.'

'And your fiancé, what's he like?'

'Don't get her started on action man,' Fiona laughed, 'we don't have enough time.'

'Action man?' Sam asked, 'how much action?'

'More than she expected twelve months ago,' Fiona answered for Tilly, 'much more.'

'Jeff's a retired police officer who likes gliding and who takes troubled kids into the outback with Outreach Flinders. When he's not working, he spends his time gliding over the Flinders Ranges in his championship sailplane named Lynda,' Tilly let it roll off her tongue as if she were introducing him on Perfect Match, 'and when he's away, like he is at the moment, I miss him.'

Sam and Fiona let out a sigh in unison and then laughed, clinking their glasses, 'to Jeff and Tilly.'

The moment was interrupted when John phoned Fiona she was needed at home as he'd been called out to attend a scuffle at the top pub. She made her apologies and left and Tilly looked at her watch, 'I'd better pick Emily up too, she has school in the morning.'

'How about tomorrow, can you give me some time? I'd like to talk something over with you. Explain what it is we want to achieve by getting access to your property,' Sam made the most of this relaxed, more mellow Tilly, 'mining isn't just big holes in the ground, there's a lot to do before we get to that stage.'

'I'm not sure,' Tilly thought for a moment, 'look, come down and see me after nine. I won't change my position, but if you want to come for a ride while I have a look at a few of our paddocks, you're more than welcome. I need to see how the place has fared after the rain and we can talk in the car.'

'I appreciate that, thanks,' she shook Tilly's hand, 'see you at nine.'

'Good I'll pack a tucker box for two.' Getting to know your adversary was one of the first things her father had taught her and more time with Sam may reveal a weakness.

***

Gino's phone buzzed and he set down his filleting knife, leant over the side of his boat and washed his hands in the sea, wiping them on a towel he always kept tucked into his fishing shorts. The screen showed a picture of the Gillespie's daughter, Sam and another woman in her late thirties. He smiled. Spoggy was doing well, but it would not be long before he knew too much and Gino would have to take him fishing when this was over, just to be on the safe side.

He looked at his catch. Three nice snapper, a dozen King George whiting and a ten Blue Swimmer crabs, he had bagged out. He thought about the calamari he used for bait and wondered if he should have put them aside to eat. What thrilled him most though, was the politician, most were not as easy to land as this one had been. The moon was still bright and, with the filleting done, he scooped seawater in a bucket and washed away the mess, then felt for the pins in the flywheel and wrapped the leather belt around it. He rocked the Blackstone engine over compression and pulled. A put-put boat she may be, but the Messina Maria could be trusted in deep water, he liked that.

By midnight he was home.

CHAPTER TWENTY TWO

Joe wondered if there was a castle, a ruin, or a building of significance that they hadn't seen as Laura dragged him through all the tourist spots in England and Wales. Scotland was next, a week in Ireland and then a few days in Paris before they headed home.

She sensed his restlessness and asked if he was ready to go home.

'Nah, but a change of pace would be good. I've been thinking about all these tourist traps and how often we have had our hand in our pockets. I reckon we could learn a bit from the Poms if we were to go a bit further with your idea for a second income.'

'So restoring that stuff in the barn isn't such a silly idea after all?'

'Not if we plan it properly,' he brushed at a piece of fluff on the cuff of his jacket, 'and I'll be pleased to get home to some decent weather too.'

'But that business with the gold bars and the last few stanzas of your dad's poem that's still got you puzzled, yes?'

He rubbed at his temple, 'yeah, I reckon we need to work that out soon too,' he looked out the window, mid spring and England had delivered another grey day, 'heard from Tilly?'

'Just a text, a picture of Emily in her netball outfit. She's growing up fast.' She showed him the phone.

'It's gunna be good to feel those arms around me again,' he said, 'we've been away too long.'

Laura stroked his back and stared into the drizzle. 'Well, not long now. C'mon, let's go and see Elspeth and Bill. She said he had something he wanted to show you after lunch.' Laura liked Elspeth's company, they were second cousins, but it was more than that. Elspeth was a self-appointed custodian of family history and from the moment they had met, Laura felt a connection. It helped too, that Joe and Bill could talk for ages without any awkward silence and they had become mates in the short time they had known each other.

Bill and Elspeth planned to visit Australia for a holiday. Ten years ago, their daughter and her husband had moved out there and now they had grandchildren to visit. The family lived on Queensland's Gold Coast and, although it was a long way from Wanooka's Well, they would make sure a few weeks with Laura and Joe was in the itinerary.

'Are you all right?' Laura asked, 'you seem a bit down at the moment.'

'I'm okay, just missing Tilly and Em I guess. That, this persistent headache and those bloody gold bars. I try to keep busy and push it to the back of my mind, but the questions always return. Where the hell did he get them? Or, where did he find enough gold to smelt them, there has to be an answer somewhere.'

'You can ponder that on the plane trip home. C'mon there's a home cooked roast waiting and Elspeth said there'd be Yorkshire pudding too.'

'We'll give Tilly a ring later and talk to Emily, too. That'll cheer you up.'

**

Sam unlocked the front door, searched for her phone and threw her hand bag on the bed. In the kitchen, she opened her lap top, dropping a capsule into the coffee machine as she waited for the computer to boot up. A stack of reports sat in front of her, as foreboding as the ramparts of a medieval castle. They would wait until morning. After spending time with Tilly and Fiona, she had begun to think of them more as friends than adversaries and felt the stirrings of the old Sam, the person she had once been before ambition had won out. Crashing through the cares of people she didn't know had been easy in the past and she had crushed them without emotion. It was business. She thought about her life as it had once been in Mundulla, another small town where she thought of the people and their lives as small, too, all farming and football. Some of her friends from school went teaching, or nursing, others went to the meatworks in Bordertown and the boys either went onto farms, or worked in town. Blokes like Gavin, who could only see himself on the family farm living his days out in a small town, playing small town football and raising small town kids.

That had never been for her. She had ambition and the girls who had teased her for being frumpy and laughed at the braces on her teeth, had her vowing to not go home until she could march back into town as a person of wealth and power, her riches on show for everyone to see. But tonight, after seeing Tilly's happiness, she questioned whether this is what she really wanted. Suddenly she could hear the ticking of her biological clock gaining speed. She shut it off, reminding herself she had a job to do.

The screen on her computer opened with a picture of her family. Sam knew she should ring home and check in. How long had it been now? She thought it may have been her brother's birthday, and then remembered he had rung her and she felt a pang of guilt. She had not spoken to her mother since Christmas and knew she wasn't holding her place in the family commitment deal. Maybe she would call them sometime next week, she would have time then, or later, after this whole Gillespie thing was over. She had business to look after and small town stuff could wait.

***

Tilly settled Emily and picked up the mail on the sideboard but couldn't find the interest to open it. All she wanted was to hear Jeff's voice and talk about her day, but he was out of phone range. She checked the home phone for messages, only to hear the click of a caller hanging up, probably a telemarketer. With no one to talk to, she turned the lights off and went to shower before going to bed.

She missed her parents, but she felt herself aching for Jeff more. A couple of years ago, a man had been the last thing she wanted in her life. The beating from Rocky had seen to that. Even now there were times when she woke up from a nightmare, clutching herself and shivering, thinking he was in the room with her and that maybe she should return to counselling. She hadn't spoken to Jeff about it and felt undefinable guilt over hiding this secret, deciding to tell him about it on the weekend. A resolve that left her feeling lighter thinking about how it would be to lay in his arms again.

Tilly undressed and ran a brush through her hair, continuing her daydream until the blue light of the telephone reflected in the mirror, strobing the blackness, demanding her attention. She was sure she had cleared the messages earlier, but maybe not. The light was insistent and she pressed play and waited.

'G'day,' she knew the voice, but couldn't place it, 'it's Sarge here, Jeff's old boss,' her first thought was that something has happened to Jeff and her heart beat harder and her chest tightened, 'I think the bugger's got me playing cupid, but he asked me to phone tonight and tell you to look under the tray in the cutlery drawer. Anyway, sorry it's late. I did try earlier but you didn't answer and thought I'd better leave a message. I hope everything's okay and don't forget to drop over and see us sometime.'

Tilly was in the kitchen almost before the message ended, the cutlery rattling as her fingers grappled with the drawer insert. Why couldn't he just leave a note under the seat in the car or somewhere easier than this? She lifted the liner and its contents spilled onto the bench when she dropped it.

Emily suddenly morphed alongside her. 'What's all the noise Mum? Why are you in the kitchen?'

Tilly jumped. 'What are you doing out of bed young lady?'

'I heard something crash and wondered if you were okay?'

'I'm fine, now go back to bed.'

'But what are you looking for?'

'Never mind. Go back to bed.'

'Tell me why first.'

'I think Jeff left me a letter.' Tilly smiled at her as she pulled herself up and sat on the bench alongside the drawer insert, pretending to sort until her mother found the envelope.

'Uh-oh,' Emily said and jumped down from the bench, she disappeared into her room and came back brandishing another envelope, 'Jeff asked me to give you this before he left. He said to wait until after tea last night. Sorry... I forgot.'

Tilly didn't know whether to be cross or not, 'I think it's late and good girls should be in bed. Now off you go.'

'Is it a love letter?'

'How do I know, I haven't opened it yet,' she narrowed her eyes and fixed them on her daughter, 'now bed.'

Emily hugged her mother and turned toward the bedroom when she stopped and looked over her shoulder, 'you could use a happy mood I think. Read the one I gave you first. That way if Jeff asks, I can say I gave it to you before you opened the second one. Night mum.'

'Go to bed, or you'll have one cranky mum for a month, young lady.' Tilly settled into her bed and slid her finger along the fold of the first envelope, sniffing the envelope to find a trace of him. She thought it funny that he still used, Old Spice, something her father used and probably his own father had too, but a bottle of Calvin Klein would be in this year's Christmas stocking.

The paper was soft to touch and written in pen. Dated Sunday, she wondered when he'd found time to write it. She pictured him sitting somewhere quiet putting the words together and her loneliness grew.

Dear Tilly,

Just a short note to tell you I love you and my body will ache for you until I get home. Tonight, look up at the stars in the southern sky. I'll be in my swag looking at them too, wishing we were together.
Love you heaps,
Jeff.

She kissed the signature and set it aside then ran a finger under the lip of the envelope from the drawer. He had written poem, or a love song, for her, called *Adnyamathanha Stars*. The rhythm of the words played to a tune in her mind as she turned off the light and she stared into the night. Her eyes picked out the constellations and she pictured him in her mind. The features of his face lit by the campfire, orange and yellow light dancing across his lips, his back against his swag as he strummed his dad's guitar.

She imagined him singing it tonight and felt his love in every line.

CHAPTER TWENTY THREE

Bill had gone to his study to recover some photocopies of aircraft material he thought Joe could pass onto Jeff. Elspeth and Laura were clearing away the lunch dishes and Joe took advantage of the time alone to move into their reception room and take a piece of paper from his pocket. He felt guilty taking these sneak peeks, but he didn't want to spoil her holiday and tried to keep it out of sight. He unfolded it and studied the image he had copied from the slate they found inside Les's hiding place in the well before they left Australia. He stared hard at it, looking for clues, but the more he looked the less he saw. The image was familiar, but he couldn't work out where it was. He recognised the creek, hills and roads, and yet, exactly where it was remained a mystery. What he did see was a stack of yellow bricks inside what looked like a set of stock yards. There was a compass in the bottom left corner to help him orientate the sketch, but nothing to help with the scale. Hearing Bill returning, he shoved the paper in his pocket.

'Found it,' Bill said, 'I knew someone might have some use for it one day,' he handed a tattered leather satchel to Joe, 'my Grandad had a mate who flew in the First World War and this was his stuff. He gave it to my father before he died and I wasn't much more than ten when he passed it on to me. It gave me hours of fun, dreaming I was an air ace battling with the Red Baron. When I look back it was probably the thing that influenced my decision to go into aircraft engineering. That, and my interest in mathematics. Anyway, I didn't have any boys to pass it down to so your prospective son in law is welcome to it,' he dug into the bag and drew out a book that he passed to Joe, 'you might find some clue about the young bloke's old plane in there.'

'You sure you want him to have it?' Joe asked.

'Yes, it's not much use to anybody around here now. I've retired and it'd be good to think that someone will get some pleasure out of the books again.'

'I'm sure he'll appreciate it, ta,' Joe rubbed a hand across the leather, 'you never bought a plane yourself?'

'Too busy and I had too many demands on my salary to indulge in a hobby like flying. Besides, if I'd gotten hooked, I'd have never been able to get enough of it, so I made a little promise to myself and denied the temptation.'

'I'll see he takes good care of them.'

'You know I might be able to unravel the mystery of those Hun markings too. That may not be a German plane in your photos.'

'It looked German to me.'

'Next time you're talking to Jeff tell him I'll look into it for him if he wants. I can discuss it with a few aircraft history contacts I have and, with some luck, I'll have something before we come out next year. Hell, if I get onto it soon, I might even dig something up before you go home. Love a bit of trouble shooting, I do.'

'I like things plain and simple these days. Mysteries can wait for others to solve.' Joe felt the paper in his pocket, knowing the conundrum would play on his mind until they were home.

'Sounds like Laura's making ready to leave,' Joe said, hearing her approach, 'better shift my stumps I suppose.'

'She does it too?' Bill asked, 'women are all the same I reckon. Run a man to rum at times'

'We need to head off anyway, I haven't spoken to Emily in ages and it'll be good to hear her voice again.'

The two men shook hands and Bill surprised Joe by pulling him into a hug. 'It was good to have met you Joe...' Bill held the embrace for a minute, 'God it's been good having you around. I'm going to miss this.'

'Yeah... thanks, I've had a good time too,' Joe said, calling to Laura as he patted the other man's shoulder in parting, 'ready to go?'

'What now? What's the rush?' Laura said.

'I want to call Emily before she goes to bed.'

Minutes later they were in the car and winding through another evening mist, wipers sweeping across the screen. 'It got a bit emotional back there, is Bill okay?'

'Elspeth told me that while he knows a lot of people, he doesn't have any close mates and he just clicked with you,' she shifted in her seat, 'he worked for a life time with a long commute so he didn't make any lasting friendships. She says he's really done it tough over the past eighteen months.'

'Why eighteen months, he seems fit enough, is he sick?'

'Nope, she thinks he's lonely after being retrenched.'

'Retrenched, the bloke's older than me by ten years. He should've been retired for years.'

'I'll remind you of that, and one day soon I'll wager.'

'Of what?'

'Joe Gillespie, you know you won't retire, without the Well you'd shrivel up and cark it after a couple of years,' she smiled at him, her hand comforting on his thigh, 'you're a good man, Joe. Just as soon as Bill has found a friend he can talk to and share a joke with, he's looking at losing you. Sure, he's sad right now, but I reckon you two will call and e-mail each other. We'll need that high-speed broadband the government's bleating on about.'

'He's got mates, though?'

'Yeah, well he has one now.'

Joe wondered how much of herself was in her description of Bill, but now was not the time to discuss it. The paper in his pocket still stoked the fires of his quandary.

The tucker box was heavy with freezer blocks, bread, meat for a barbeque and the rest of the day's needs when Sam knocked on the door.

'Just about ready, I thought we might make a day of it so I packed a picnic.' Tilly said.

'I like a girl who's prepared. Looks nice, I haven't been on a picnic since I was a kid, and billy tea, are we doing that?'

'I thought we might. Can you carry this out to the Landcruiser? I'll lock up, grab the dog and we'll be out of here?'

'You want it in the back?'

'Nah, just leave it by the wheel, it's heavy and I'll toss it up there when I tie Gip in.'

Sam said nothing, but hoisted the box over the side of the tray and pushed it against the headboard. Things might be congenial now, but she didn't want Tilly thinking she was a pushover city chick. She might look it, but Sam Lewis knew her way around the bush. 'All done,' she said, as the dog sniffed her legs.

'This is Gip, Dad's dog. She'll howl and moan all day if she heard the Dad's car start and she wasn't in it,' she ruffled the dog's ears, 'this old girl has outlived more of Dad's farm utes than I can remember, but I guess the day will come when he'll have to go without her.'

'So, which way are we headed?' Sam clicked the seat belt home as Tilly fired the Cruiser into life and reversed out of the drive. She noticed everything Tilly did was fluid and purposeful, no nonsense, similar to herself.

'I thought we'd go out the back way, through Coomoroo, past Poverty Corner and across the hills to Wilson's, it's about forty kilometres northwest from here. The place is starting to green up after the summer rains and I want to get a good look at things to decide what crops to put in. If I stray from our normal rotation, I'll have to buy seed and that'd be a bit of a risk out there.'

'When I drove around yesterday I saw heaps of old stone dwellings. I guess that's what they were, just a fireplace and crumbling walls most of them.'

'Which way did you go?'

'North from here, Johnburgh road area, where our drillers have found coal deposits, then I cut across to Yalpara Station. I remember Dad talking about taking me to a Diprotodon site out there when I was a kid. It looks like heartbreak country, nothing like the South East where I grew up.'

'You'd be familiar with Goyder's Line and the predictions he made about farming outside the ten-inch rainfall line then?'

'I've heard about it, but being a geologist I spent more time looking into mineral deposits in the Nackara Arc.'

'That's around here, isn't it?'

'Yeah, covers a big stretch out to the Nackara Fault, but enough about work, I'll make you a deal for today, okay?'

'What's the deal?'

'I won't bring up your leases or the land and we can have a day of getting to know each other, after that, the gloves are off when I get back to the city.'

'Get to know your adversary, eh? I can work with that.'

'Good, now let's see some of this country you people are so passionate about.'

'Deal, but I warn you I can be tough if I'm crossed.'

'Me too.'

The road behind Morchard was rough. Tilly would normally take the highway, but this was a good test of Sam's resilience. The Toyota was a strong workhorse and offered more carrying capacity than passenger comfort. Tilly looked across to see how her companion was taking it. 'The council needs to run a grader through here.' She said.

'Yeah but I'm kind of used to it, we go into some pretty, rugged country too.

They travelled in silence for a while. The CB crackled with a couple of truckies discussing the location of a police car hidden in the trees at Morchard.

'Use the CB much?' Sam asked.

'Not me. Dad has it to communicate with the carriers at harvest and Mum likes to know where he is too. Most of the time it's there in case of fires, or if a neighbour wanted to catch up etcetera. It's handy when the tractor's working and that, but most of the time mobile phones are the go now. More privacy.'

'I can understand that,' Sam looked out the window, the grass that shot after the summer rains was showing signs of withering, 'I can see how tough it would have been in the early years. Imagine trying to keep workhorses fed when things are like this.'

'That's why there are so many abandoned homes out here. The government of the day told the settlers that rain would follow the plough. Not bloody likely,' Tilly looked out the open driver's window, 'want the air-conditioner on?'

'No, I'm okay, it's good to get some honest dust in my hair again.'

They continued to travel in silence until they reached the well paddock gate, where Tilly stopped and grabbed for the brass ring packed with an assortment of multi coloured keys that hung over the four-wheel-drive lever.

'If I do one thing to make life easier out here, it'll be to get a set of master locks made. Dad's just kept adding another padlock and winding on another key. He knows which is which, but I have to go through them all until I find the one I want.'

'And with your plan, if you lose the master, you'll lose the lot?'

'Yeah, that's what he says, but I'm willing to give it a try before he gets home.'

'Keep a few copies of the master.'

'Mum says it makes sense too. We'll just have to wait and see.'

Tilly eased out of the seat and as she did a piece of paper slid out of her pocket. Sam thought she should leave it on the seat, but then no-one had ever accused her of not being curious. She watched Tilly working through the keys, her actions betraying her desire to hide her frustration.

Sam grabbed the paper and unfolded it, read a line and looked up. So, action man was romantic too, she felt envy and voyeuristic at the same time, but read on. She spotted Tilly coming back before she finished reading, folding the poem and wedging it into the back of the driver's seat. Tilly had a man who wrote poetry while her own world was full of men who would rather drink acid than write a letter, let alone one that said how he felt in rhyme.

'Okay, when I drive through can you lock it again?' Tilly passed Sam an open padlock. It was heavy in her hand, probably brass, and older than anything she had seen before. Joe Gillespie didn't throw anything away if it still worked and she surmised that was why they had prospered in hard country. 'Do you want me to tighten the chain, or do you leave it a bit loose?'

'Just firm will do.' Tilly said and dropped the keys back into place.

Sam looked at her. 'Something slid from your pocket when you got out before, you're probably sitting on it.'

'What was it?'

'Looked like a receipt or something. I just thought you might want to put it somewhere before it dropped though the gap in the seat.'

'Thanks.' Tilly recovered the paper and slid it into the front pocket of her jeans.

Sam closed the door and waited at the gate as the big vehicle waddled through the ruts and stopped. As she clicked the lock closed Sam looked around, the place had a familiar feel, as if she had been here before. She took in the location, the windmill, the scrubby bushes around the tank, the red dirt. It all felt familiar but she didn't know why, she had no memory of visiting the place.

'Was a film ever set around here?' she asked as she climbed into the four-wheel-drive.

'I don't think so, not in my time anyway,' Tilly said, 'Why?'

'I don't know, but for some reason I think I've seen a photo of the windmill before. Probably one from a Facebook friend or something, you know how it is, we see so much stuff online and think we have been there.

'Yeah, I'm trying to keep Emily from becoming addicted to watching a screen all day but it's hard when all her friends have the latest technology. She's asking for her own iPod for her birthday. She's only eight, but stands there and tells me she'll be a social outcast if she doesn't have one.'

'What do you say?'

'I tell her to toughen up, there are plenty of kids with a lot less than she has. She needs to learn the value of things and giving her what she wants when she wants it won't teach her that.'

'You sound like my mother. I hope if I have kids I can be just as strong.'

'You'll be right, just ask yourself what your own Mum would do,' Tilly said, 'that's what I do'

'I'll remember that.'

The four-wheel drive was up to speed now and dust billowed behind them. 'I noticed the windmill back there is out of gear and you didn't check the tank,' Sam said, 'no stock here?'

'No, we had a few dramas last year. Dad found a beast clay-panned just inside the gate, a few weeks later someone poisoned the tank and the bore. We lost most of the cattle that had survived the drought and he had to shoot the mob to stop them suffering. Those that weren't already dead before he got to them anyway. Dad hasn't been able to come back here since.'

'That's awful, how is he now?'

'Not good, it's one of the reasons Mum has him in England.'

'It makes you wonder what kind of sick bastard would want to poison defenceless animals.' Sam kept seeing the photo of the windmill in her mind.

'I don't think it was the animals they were targeting. They were after my Dad and until the inquest is over, that's all I can tell you.' Tilly wanted to talk to someone about last year's events, but realised Sam was not the one she should share with.

Sam decided to let it go, something in her mind kept dragging her back to what she had seen on Gino's computer. 'With all this new growth, I thought I'd see more wildlife, you know kangaroos and stuff.'

'The EPA recommended we turn the water off and I guess the roos and emus have moved on.'

'Okay, where to now?' Sam said, casting her eye over the country, searching for different reef outcrops and sedimentary strata in the escarpments. She hadn't seen anything that would excite the geologist in her yet.

'I want to go to Wilson's next and have a look at the rain gauges. Dad says it's a bit of a sad story out there and the house has been boarded up from way before he was born. I don't think he's even bothered to look around it.'

'You're not curious?'

'Nah, I think it's like a lot of old houses people walked away from, just dust and cobwebs. The people who'd worked there would all be dead now anyway. You'll see when we get there, it was a big settlement in the old days.'

Tilly noticed Sam's interest in the rock formations, 'taking a look at how the land was formed, eh?'

'It's hard not to, considering what I do for a living.'

'I suppose we see different things. To me the place will look great with grass up around the cow's knees and straight lines of crop emerging from the earth. Signs of new life as the ewes drop lambs in late winter. You're able to live with the seasons on the farm. I couldn't do that in the city.'

'I guess not, my dad has always had a romantic view of the bush. It's probably why he bought our small farm at Mundulla. Mum said she wouldn't raise his kids if she had to follow him while he travelled around the country drilling holes. He loved the outdoors and the money would have been good too, but she insisted my brother and I went to school in town.'

'And after that geology called, eh?'

'Yeah, Dad talked about how the bosses made the big money and I thought I'm up for that. So, I completed a degree in business. I'm a bit of a nerd and the study was enjoyable. Got the job as PA to Charles Winkler and in a short few years, here I am CEO of an exploration company. What about you?'

'A bit of the same, only I went into law. I was going to right the wrongs of the world. Make sure the oppressed were heard, fight for justice and look after the little bloke. I fell for all that guff they spewed at us in uni. Then I got a job with a high-profile firm in Sydney, one thing led to another and soon I was a hotshot defence lawyer. Fell for a client and, well I don't need to go on about that. Suffice to say I'd had enough of that life and decided to come home and regenerate. So here I am, a capable woman in her late thirties looking after my family's farm.'

'And an engaged woman.'

'Yeah... and he's lucky to have me, or so he keeps saying.'

'Tell me a bit about him?'

'Oh, not much to tell, he probably fell for Emily as much as he did for me. Instant family us,' Tilly rolled her hand around the steering wheel and looked at her engagement ring, 'I'd thought it would always be just the two of us, you know. Who wants a woman with a seven-year-old child?'

'Seven?'

'Well she's turned eight now, but going on twenty-eight if you listen to her.'

CHAPTER TWENTY FOUR

Tilly eased the Toyota into Wilson's house yard and took the track through to the creek. 'You up for a cuppa?' she asked, 'we'll boil the billy here.'

'Sounds good to me, where do you want me to get a fire started?'

'There should be a circle of stones over under that big tree. You could set it up there.'

Sam dragged twigs and leaves, stacking them into the hearth. 'I'm always amazed at how big these gums grow. When I was a kid, Dad would get me to estimate their age. I'd never get close and he'd say one like this would have been half this size when Captain Cook landed. He has an appreciation for nature and the way of things, my Dad.'

'He sounds like a good bloke.' Tilly dropped the tucker box by the wheel and lifted Gip down from the tray.

'I think so.'

'See him much?'

'Nope, I'm always too busy. He is too.'

'How about the phone?'

'No, God, am I a bad daughter?' Sam looked at the small flame trying to lick the twigs and add to its energy, 'I haven't talked to him or Mum since Christmas. They call and leave messages, but I haven't spoken to them for a couple of months, just a text from time to time.'

'What about you?'

'Yeah, that was me too. It all changed after...' Tilly looked at the top of their tree, surprised by the emotion in her voice, 'well enough about that,' she placed a few heavier logs on the fire and whistled for the dog, 'let's take a walk while the fire drops to coals. I want to show you something.'

They walked about five hundred metres along the creek and came to a spring, where there were tracks made by roos and emus when they had come to drink. A frog croaked from under a rock ledge behind the reeds and small birds flitted in and out of the acacias. The women followed the track along the edge of the creek until it narrowed to where a slab of rusty coloured granite angled up toward the overhanging ridge.

'See those circles etched into the slab?' Tilly asked.

'Where am I looking?'

'On the slab about a metre from the bottom and a couple of metres in from the edge, they're about the size of a side plate.'

'Yeah, I've got them now.' Sam moved in to get a closer look and ran her hand over them, the texture smooth and warm to touch.

'This is just one of the reasons we don't want mining on our land.' Tilly climbed onto the slab and sat there looking at the pool. She reached out and helped Sam swing up beside her. 'Just think of how many generations have sat here like we are doing now. The local Aboriginals don't really know for sure who chiselled these marks. They believe they appeared during the Dreamtime.'

'But Australian laws prevent companies like ours disturbing these areas.'

'The act may say that, but as a lawyer I know everything can be challenged if you have enough money and influence. We prefer doing it our way.'

'There are other sites like this too. I know when I flicked through the information at the cottage, there was something about marks like these in the creek that runs to the west of the town. Also a piece on a poem, if I remember right.'

'Look I'm sorry to bring you here. We agreed not to discuss our differences.'

'No probs, I was scanning the country for interesting geology, too.' Sam crossed her hands behind her head and lay back on the rock. She closed her eyes and imagined a family of Aboriginals playing in the water and feasting here for over a thousand years. 'Do you ever wonder how they did it?'

'Did what, who's they?' Tilly said without lifting the hat she had slipped over her eyes.

'The Aboriginals, nothing like the life we have now. No fashion, no hot running water. I don't know if I'd be tough enough.'

'No coffee shops.'

'Exactly.' The warmth reminded her of the waterholes she and her brother played in as kids.

'The men would be of hunting, leaving the women to do all the hard slog,' Tilly laughed at the image in her head, 'then they'd come back all smelly and want to have sex.'

'That's a downside?'

'It would be if the chosen man is one of the elders and you're only fifteen.'

'I get what you're saying now.'

Tilly worked her way off the slab, 'c'mon those coals should be right by now, I should bring Jeff and Em out here one day to have a swim, run around and catch yabbies.'

'I take it he's not too old for that then.' Sam had the picture of an elder and a young girl in her mind, 'of course, you'd have to run just fast enough for him to catch you.'

They laughed companionably and joked and talked of nothing important on the way back to the fire until Sam spotted something carved in the large gum tree on the house side of the track.

'What's carved on the tree?' She walked over and craned her neck for a better look. 'It's some kind of memorial.'

'Yeah, Dad's grandfather carved it back in the depression. He was friends with the old bloke who owned the place and did it as a tribute. The family story goes that

Mr Wilson was quite progressive and treated his workers and their families well. However, when the depression hit and the droughts came he kept his people employed for too long and the farm went bankrupt. Before the banks foreclosed he sold the assets to my great grandfather for what he could afford to pay. The banks were happy to take the money and the place was his free and clear.'

'So, in a way your family benefitted from the troubles of another.'

'I suppose when you look at it in a narrow way, but the bank would have sold it anyway and with the debt the Wilsons owed to Great Grandad and the cash he had, he bought the place. It would have made sense at the time.'

'What happened to everyone?'

'Not sure, the sad thing is though, Mr Wilson put his family on the train in Hammond and kissed them all goodbye. He rode out here for one last look around. At some stage, he took the saddle from his horse, tied a noose to that limb, stood on the horse's back and jumped off. A swaggie found the horse standing nearby. By the time the police and the undertaker got here, crows and eagles had made a mess of him. There's a small cemetery over on the hill and they buried him there.'

Sam looked around, 'and that's why the tribute was carved?'

'Dad says that his Pop couldn't bring himself to go through the house or sheds. He just covered everything up and only cropped the land. He allowed no-one to go through the place while he was alive and we more or less forgot about it. Mum says there are beautiful murals on the walls. Some of the furniture has gone and some of the sheds have old machinery in them, but I've never seen any of it. I guess Dad's respecting his Pop's wishes too.'

'My curiosity would tease me too much and I'd want to explore it all.'

'I get that, but all I had growing up was old stuff. Mum's an anthropologist. She dragged me to the ends of the earth looking at middens and ancient campsites. When I was in my teens I'd have loved her to focus on Egypt, or somewhere. I found what she did boring, but now that I'm older, I have a better appreciation of our own Aboriginal culture.' She raked at the coals and set the billy on one side and a steel plate on the other.

'Time for a chop picnic, I reckon.'

'Not a barbeque?'

'Mum always called it a chop picnic, I don't know why. I just remember thick chops and bread slathered with lashings of butter and grease running down my chin,' Tilly smiled and looked back toward the water hole, 'simple times back when I was a kid.'

'I remember them too. We didn't have to worry what we looked like, or what we did, Mum and Dad made it safe for us.'

'And then we grew up.'

The girls lazed with their backs resting against the warm rocks. 'I might have to bring a man back here one day, if I ever find a keeper.' Sam smiled. Her thoughts turned to Gavin and Charles and she couldn't see either of them enjoying this place. She looked at Tilly and asked, 'do you know any men, eligible, and hot enough to boil water?'

'Shit, shit, shit. I forgot about Jake. Come on, we'd better get moving.'

'Why, what did I say?'

'I'm supposed to meet the builder, Jake, over at Mum and Dad's place before he knocks off. I only remembered him when you mentioned hot and men in the one sentence. I'll put the chops on and get a move on.'

When Sam stood up a piece of paper fluttered past her and caught on a clump of grass. She picked it up and unfolded it. It had come from Tilly's pocket. This time she didn't have to look at it, she folded it and held it until she reached the fire.

'Are you trying to lose this?' She passed the paper to Tilly.

'Thanks, I've got to be more careful.'

'What is it?'

'Oh, just Jeff being romantic,' Tilly opened the paper and scanned it again, 'it's a poem. He wrote it for me before he left to go bush, the cunning bugger hid it under the knife and fork drawer and asked a friend to wait a couple of days before phoning to tell me where he'd left it.' She passed it over.

Sam felt a little guilt wash over her, but she couldn't say about reading part of it before. 'Thanks, but are you sure, I don't want to intrude.'

'I don't think Jeff will mind.'

Sam took the paper and heard the chops sizzle as they hit the plate, soon the smell of grilled lamb mixed with the eucalypt. A magpie warbled and other birds chattered at once and, with the smoke from the fire wafting around her, she realised it had been a long time since she had felt as relaxed.

She passed the poem back without opening it. 'I'd sooner you kept it for yourself, today we're friends and I'd like to keep it that way. I wouldn't want to see anything I'd be tempted to use in a fight. Just so you know.'

'Thanks, I appreciate your honesty,' she pushed the paper more deeply into her pocket, 'do you want to make the tea?'

'Sure, it's been a while for that too.'

After lunch, I'll take you to see Jake and heartbreakers, deal?'

'Shirtless I hope.'

'Last time I was there,' Tilly scrolled through the images on her phone, 'here's a sampling.'

'Look out fellas, here comes, Sam Lewis. God, listen to me, I sound desperate,' Sam was laughing at herself, 'did anyone ever tell you you're good company?'

'Once or twice, I recall, once or twice.' Tilly found a suitable gum leaf, tossed in a handful of tea and swung the billy before pouring it into the pannikins. 'Do you take milk? There's some in the Esky.'

'Today I'll have it sweet and black with two sugars thanks.'

'Hmm, that sounds good, me too.'

The women sat there, a mug of tea beside them and a leg chop stashed between two slices of buttered bread, juice oozing between their fingers.

'Here's to poets and all other red blooded men,' Tilly raised her mug and it clacked on Sam's.

'May, I find one soon,' Sam laughed, 'sweet and... well sweet and strong anyway. Take me too your builder, girlfriend.'

'As soon as we finish here, but I have to check the mill first.'

Sam cleaned the cups, poured the remaining billy tea on the fire and covered the coals with dirt. Tilly could tell this woman was not city raised, but someone at ease in the bush. She moved Jeff's poem to her breast pocket and buttoned it, keeping it close to her. She could remember every word and as she checked the windmill tank his words warmed her and she recited them over in the head. He had called it: *Adnyamathanha Stars*.

Throw open your curtains and turn out the light
Fear not the shadows, for I'm near you tonight
Look out from your window and up to the stars
My kisses I'm sending on light waves from Mars

And all alone on my swag I'll stare at the night

141

Terry L Probert

Longing to touch you and hold you so tight
With each little moon beam, that falls on your face
I'm sending my love song, from this ancient place

Tonight I sleep in a place where my ancestors slept
A place where stories of wisdom and secrets are kept
I see far above me a constellation of stars
And know if I lost you, on my heart there'd be scars

Two more nights 'til I see you and my days will just
drag
Two slow days of more listening, to young fellas brag
Two more days of them bitching their unending moan
And at the end of all this, my darling, I'm home

So, sleep well tonight in our love nest of latex and foam
Think of me lying here on a bed of red clay and loam
Take these kisses from moon beams that land on your
cheek
And store in a glass, my candle of love, 'til the end of
the week

Throw open your curtains and turn out the light
And fear not the shadows, I'm with you tonight
Out of your window look to these old Adnyamathanha
stars
And know I'm sending you my kisses on light waves
from Mars

He'd be home on Friday and she would arrange a sleep over
for   Emily.

CHAPTER TWENTY FIVE

Laura was weary and tugging at her seatbelt leant her head against the window, wondering how people lived here among the hedgerow lanes and putting up with weather that closed in on you. The drizzle that never seemed to end was beginning to make her feel homesick but she hid this from Joe. She looked over and saw he seemed to be lost in his thoughts of his own. Her eyes closed and she drifted into the netherworld of half sleep.

She was brought back to alertness by the sound of Joe's phone ringing in the console. 'Grab that will you love?' Joe said, 'I've got a bit on my plate with this slippery bloody road.'

Laura picked up the phone and looked at the caller identifier. 'It's Bill and Elspeth's number.'

'You'd better answer it on speaker then.'

'Hello, Laura speaking.'

'It's Bill here, Joe still driving, is he?'

'We're about twenty miles from home. Do you want me to get him to call you back?'

'No, I can call back later, just ask him if he'd like to go to an aircraft restorer's meeting with me on Thursday. I thought he might find it interesting.'

'Hang on, Joe's nodding so, that's a yes,' Laura lied.

'Sometime after breakfast then?'

'He's looking forward to it,' Joe went to grab the phone from her hand. He had to get out of this, the last thing he wanted to do was sit in a room with a bunch of old boffins, talking about stuff he knew nothing about but Laura was too quick for him, 'see ya,' she said and stopped the call.

'There is no-way I nodded just then. I never intended to nod, or even thought about nodding. Why did you tell him that?'

'Look getting out without me will do you good. You know it will and besides, Bill's a bit short on male company so you'll both benefit.'

'And what are you going to do?'

'Me? Elspeth and I will take the train to London and shop for a few days. I'm sure she won't mind.'

'I'll bet she won't, but I will. This trip is costing us a bloody fortune. I'll have to hunt up more lost gold to pay for it.'

'That might mean going down a hole again.'

'Or you could ease up on the outings.'

'I could, but I won't. I could always dip into my super.'

'Or, we could do that.'

'Come on, you'll enjoy yourself, you know you want to.' She knew he'd enjoy some male company and she could do with a bit of a respite from his whinging about the weather for a while too.

Joe said nothing more. Laura closed her eyes and searched for a few minutes more sleep.

***

Arriving at the Wanooka's Well homestead, Tilly could see Jake had been pushing his men to get the smaller jobs done while they waited on the National Trust's decisions.

'He's finished the entrance. Mum's going to love that,' she said to Sam.' Stopping the Toyota they walked to where the stone pillars had been smashed in last year's attack. Jake's mason was good and she ran her hand over his work where newly hewn stones stood out among the originals. 'What do you reckon, should I get him to paint these white again or just have them sealed?'

'I'm not the one you should ask about colours. I'm a geologist remember.' Sam took in the whole site. 'What happened here? It looks like a warzone.'

'Pretty close. Someone either wanted to scare Dad, or kill him. They almost succeeded too, but he's a tough old bastard. Now jump in and we'll go up to find Jake.'

Sam looked in the side mirror. 'God, my hair's a mess and I've got dust all over me,' she raked her fingers through her hair trying to get some order into it. Joe had always slipped rubber bands from his newspaper over the four-wheel-drive lever, 'do you mind?' She asked.

'Go for it, but let me tell you, they won't notice your hair.'

'Shit, look at me. Sam fizzed and fussed, rubbing at the dust around her neck and ears.

'Don't worry their eyes will go straight to your boobs, bum, and legs. These blokes have worked through the weekend and haven't seen a woman in ten days. If I ask them your eye colour tomorrow, they won't remember.'

Tilly found Jake talking to a woman in her mid-fifties dressed in a tailored suit and heels, a male companion standing behind. The discussion was animated as Jake was pointed at the mortise joining the roof purloins to the veranda post timbers. Jake saw Tilly and winked as he threw his pencil on the ground and stormed over to them. He ushered them around the corner before speaking. 'She wants me to save those old posts or replace them with new cut timber. I told her because the posts are a mishmash of water pipe, native pine and whatever was at hand, we should use milled timber. I know we both agreed to go native pine and keep the place as it was, but I want her to win this battle, so I get my way with the next one.'

'Well what's she holding up now?'

'The cellar, our architect says we can extend it as you wanted, but because of that foundation stone, she doesn't want to change it. So, I'll bitch and moan for a bit and give in to her on the posts, if she'll allow me to enlarge the cellar. You can mediate if you like.'

'What do you mean?'

'You know, come in over the top and overrule me. Suggest we make a feature of that foundation stone if she lets us extend the cellar. I'll introduce you.'

'What? No way. You do it, I haven't prepared or anything.'

'Just wing it,' he flashed a smile, 'you're a big, city, legal hotshot. I trust you.'

'Okay, let's do it.'

He took her arm and escorted her to the government officials. 'Tilly Gillespie, meet Ms Amber Renouf from the National Trust and Damian Tao, her assistant. Amber, Miss Gillespie is my client and this is? Sorry I didn't get your name,' he held his hand out to Sam looking at her questioningly as she accepted the shake.

'Samantha Lewis, Sam will do.'

'This is Sam, Miss Gillespie's...' he waited for Sam to speak.

'Geological Advisor. I'm a geologist,' she pointed to the dust on her arms, 'we're looking into the therapeutic properties of the soil out here.' Tilly stood on Sam's foot, but she held her composure.

With the introductions taken care of Jake asked if Tilly could help settle the dispute Amber was having with him over the posts.

'Look it's a simple thing really,' Amber said, 'I want to keep the cellar the same as it was. That date stone is a beautiful piece of history that records the early part of the homestead's evolution. If you enlarge the cellar, all that heritage will be gone.'

'It's just a stone. For crying out loud, there are hundreds of stones just as important and they'll end up covered with plaster anyway.' Jake made a show of protesting.

'I agree we must keep the heritage, but no one will ever see it down there unless we enlarge the cellar to make it useful,' Tilly said, 'my folks and I would like to make a feature of it, so we can use the space. I wonder if we could somehow incorporate the stone into one of the new walls and put glass over it, maybe.'

'Let me talk to Damian.' Amber and her silent sidekick went to the corner of the house and peered through a window. She gesticulated as she spoke, he nodding in agreement. She turned and walked back to where Jake and Tilly were, 'I wonder, Jake, if you could do what Tilly suggested?' She asked.

'Certainly could,' he scratched his head as if in thought, 'my blokes are good with stone, it's what we do.'

'Well that's settled, then,' Tilly said, 'it was nice meeting you Amber, Damian.'

Damian, keen to confirm the agreement, held his hand out but Amber brushed it aside.

'Hang on, I haven't agreed to it yet and I need to know about your plans for the veranda posts.' She said.

'I'll tell you what? If I agree with what you want for the posts, how about you let us put the date stone behind glass in the wall of cellar where people can see it, as Tilly suggested,' Jake waved his arm around, pointing to different areas of the site, 'Amber, the National Trust isn't footing the bill for any of this besides, if I hadn't reported it, you'd have never known it existed,' he led Amber toward the drawing board, 'look, you get the posts, we get the cellar extensions and I get to finish the job without them,' he nodded toward Tilly, 'dragging you into court. Tilly is a bit of a hotshot in Sydney legal circles and I reckon the Trust can do without the grief. Me, I just want to do the job right and get out of here,' he patted her shoulder, 'come on, a woman as beautiful and powerful as you can make it happen,' he held out a ball point pen, look all you have to do is note the changes and sign the docs, I'll get Tilly to do the same and the job's as good as done,' he teased the pen away as she went to take it, 'come on Amber, we've done this dance before and it's always worked out better for the sites we've worked on.'

She took the pen and made the necessary comments. 'You owe me, now I'd better hurry up my architect and head back to the city.'

She called Damian to the car and Jake watched him open the door for her. She wound down the driver's window and waved.

'Woof, woof,' Jake yelled as she drove toward the gate.

Tilly looked at Sam and they both turned to Jake. 'Woof-woof?'

'Just a bit of a joke, Amber and I have worked our way around this National Trust stuff for about twenty years now. She always brings a pup, this time it's Damian who's following at her heels. The blokes reckon she picks them up from a puppy farm on the trip out of Adelaide. The kid knows his stuff though I'll give him that.'

'That's awful,' Tilly said, 'you should be a bit more respectful.'

'C'mon Tilly, he needs to toughen up. This country is no place for wimps who trot around going, yes ma-am, no ma-am all the time. Give him to me for a week and I'll toughen him up. Make a man outa him in a month,' Jake was ready to let his frustration out, but knew to hold it in check. His eyes fell on Sam, 'tell me Sam, just exactly what is a geological advisor and what would she do in her spare time?'

'Oh, in my line of business I look at the strata of rocks, try to figure out how the land was formed and what minerals it may contain,' she felt his eyes drinking her in and his interest excited her too, 'in my spare time, I skinny-dip in rock pools and, I try to get a swim in before lunch, whenever I can.'

This last was so unexpected he burst out laughing, lost for words.

'You'd better show me how much you've done since I was here last week,' Tilly could see Sam's interest in Jake and she knew his reputation as a womaniser too. They were probably a good match, but this was neither, time nor place, 'and how long, before the windows go back in?'

Jake took Tilly's arm and ushered her toward a workman reglazing a window.

Sam had her chance now, everyone was at least ten paces away. She walked to the other side of the Toyota and opened the door to find a little privacy. She looked in the side mirror, dragged at her hair, and smoothed her jeans. Should she slip another blouse button to expose some cleavage, why not? She bent forward, pushed up her boobs and tousled her hair again. She knew she was preening, but couldn't help it. Jake was a hunk, not only him but his whole team. Only the glazier seemed older than forty. Before she was ready, she felt a hand on her shoulder trying to turn her around. She jumped up and backwards nearly knocking him off balance. It was Jake, He steadied them both.

'C'mon, would you like to have a look around?'

His hands were rough and she felt his eyes drop to her chest. Well that was easy, she thought

'Maybe I'll just wait in the Toyota.'

'Nah, you'll be right. I'll get Dennis to show you the place while I talk to Tilly.'

Jake introduced them and as they walked around the homestead, Sam began to quiz him about the renovations. She wanted to know more about Jake too, but that could wait.

'This is an insurance job as much as a reno,' Dennis said, 'seems someone tried to kill Tilly's old man and not quick either, people say the bloke wanted him to suffer. They say it was over something that happened during the Vietnam War. And they had a couple of goes at him too,' he pointed toward the hills beyond the creek, 'coppers reckon they killed one of Joe's cows over in one of the east paddocks, just to draw him away from the house.'

'Really?' Sam stared back toward the track they had taken to get here.

'Yeah, well Joe and Laura spent the weekend in town to get away from that, but then came home to find this place all smashed up. Someone trashed it big time and tried to make it look like bikies had done it too.'

'Yeah?'

'Yep, made a real mess of the place, look here in the passage,' he offered his hand, 'don't slip, these boards are a bit loose and it's about three metres to the floor of that cellar,' he ran his hand over the plaster, 'if you look close you can see a stain where they used poo to make an insignia.'

'When you say, poo?'

'Yep when I say poo,' he wiped his hand on his shirt, 'I mean human excrement, shit. I just didn't want to say it in front of a lady, that's all.'

'You won't offend me, Dennis,' Sam smiled at him. She liked being called a lady, 'I work with exploration teams and my dad was a driller. I can't think of a word that I haven't heard yet, not one that would shock me, anyway.'

His voice had the quality of a practiced story teller and she could hear a bit of Steve Irwin in the way he spoke. 'Well, Joe and Laura find these bikies camped in the Horseshoe. The bastards have got a girl tied up to bloody big motorbike and she wasn't volunteering either,' eyes wide, he had gone into a crouch and had his hands forming the shape of binoculars, 'I hear they'd done terrible things to her too. Well from what people say, all hell breaks loose. The whole camp is hit by lighting and everything explodes. In the meantime, Joe slips in, rescues the girl and he and Laura get her to hospital. By lunch next day, Adelaide coppers are everywhere and all the bikies are locked up.'

'I remember seeing that on the news.'

He led her outside again, 'yeah, reckon you could have,' he smiled at her, 'would've been good to see, too. Just like watching a Hugh Jackman movie, I reckon.'

They walked back into the motor shed alongside the house. Sam saw Laura's table and traced her finger around the insignia carved into its top. She had seen it before, but couldn't place where. Maybe she would remember later. 'This is the same as on the wall, it spoils a grand old table.'

'Yeah, Tilly's not sure what to do with it yet. It upset her mother something awful, I'm told.'

'So, what happened to the girl?'

'Poor little bugger died in Adelaide and before her mum and dad could get there too. Bloody sad for everyone, being from a farm and all that.'

'And the bikies, they did all this?' She tried to take it all in.

'No, as it turns out it was this bloke from America. It seems Joe had caught him and his platoon wiping out a village in Cambodia. Somehow his squad stopped it and later they convicted the bastard of war crimes. Gaoled him for life, but life's not life is it, can't be, because somehow he got out and twenty years or more later, came looking for Joe.'

'Really?'

'Yep, come and look at this. He put his hand on the corrugated iron of the shed. 'See these holes here and those little pock marks on the stone wall. They're bullet holes. Joe was pinned down here,' he lifted his arms as if sighting a rifle, 'pow, zing, bullets were flying and Tilly's Dad, well he had to decide to run, or fight. They say he checked his ammo and not having enough, decided to run. That Toyota you're in took a hammering that day. Joe smashed her down through the scrub,' he pointed to a line of scrub along the creek, 'right along the old coach track, driving like a madman he was. Dirt and stones was squirting up from the tyres, bullets whippin' around everywhere, brush slapping at the windscreen and Joe just going for it.'

'He got away though, yeah?'

'Well... he did for a while, but then they come for him again. First, a bloke on a bike tried using a shot gun and then a couple of blokes in an old Ford pick-up, they had a rifle.'

'Shit, but he's okay. I mean, Tilly says her parents are overseas?'

'Yeah, the coppers found three dead blokes on the Hammond road. Two had their face and hands blown off and the third one was burnt to death in the old Ford. Bloody grizzly, if you ask me. They found the other one dead at a picnic table in Hammond. He was the one who was after Joe. The others helping him were his stepsons.'

'Who killed him, them?'

'Old people round here reckoned the Adnyamathanha sung them to death, pointed the bone, or something. I'm not so sure about that stuff though. The inquest will settle it I reckon.'

Sam felt a shiver pass over her as he described it. In the back of her mind his story and the marks niggled at her. That and the windmill paddock. She just couldn't think what it was. 'You don't believe in the Aboriginal tales and myths then?'

'If I can't touch it, or see it... let's just say, for me, it's easier to make sense of something I can see and feel.'

'I get that,' Sam said, 'thanks anyway, now I'd better let you get back to work. I'll just take a walk along the creek, if you let Tilly know to blow the horn when she's ready to go, I'll come back.'

'Yeah, good-o then,' he held his hand out, 'nice meeting you Sam, you take care now,' her hand felt small in his and he liked it, all smooth and warm, 'see you again somewhere, eh?'

'Yeah, that'd be good.' She turned and headed for the creek.

Tilly had watched Sam walk away and noticed Jake's eyes follow her. 'She might be too much woman even for you, mate.'

He didn't flinch. He just watched each movement Sam made and took it all in. 'You reckon?'

'Are you still seeing that doctor's wife when he's not about?'

'Now and then, but she's starting to get clingy. I tried to cut her loose last time I was home, but...'

'But you didn't have the guts, that's it isn't it. That's why the blokes had to work all weekend.' Tilly slapped him on the shoulder.

'Ouch,' he rubbed the top of his arm, 'come on I need to talk to you about the size of this cellar,' he led her into the dugout under the house and turned on a lantern, 'now, if you can get your architect bloke to draw up some new plans for this extension, incorporating that bloody stone, I'll get the blokes started on clearing this out,' he pointed at the loose mortar in the freestone walls, 'we can start putting a floor down and rebuilding the stone work.'

'So, I...'

'Take a few photos and e-mail him. I'll send you the dimensions and other stuff in an attachment tonight. Give us another six weeks and the place should be at lock up I reckon. Then you'd better start thinking about the second fix. I'll need to know what wiring and plumbing is needed a couple of weeks before I get those trades in.'

'God, I didn't realise there would be so much to do when I agreed with Mum and Dad to keep an eye on this.' she looked up and caught her breath, 'but they'll be home before then, so I'd better wait.'

'I wouldn't leave it that long. You've got switches and stuff to pick out. The fridges, kitchen sink, everything. We have to know where it's all got to go. In a new build the architect has it on the drawings, but these places are more of an organic process. I'm going to need you here every day, once we start on the second fix.'

'Jesus, Jake, you're more demanding than a fishwife.'

'Yep that's me, Jake the fishwife.'

'Tell you what,' he pointed in the direction where they had last seen Sam walking, 'you send Sam out here to do it if you can't find the time.'

'Oh yeah, you'd get a lot done with her roaming around the place. I don't think so. Anyway, it looks like we'll have a bit of a stoush coming with her and her company soon.'

'I thought you two were friends?'

'Not really, she wants to put a mine on our country and I don't want her to. Things could get ugly.'

'Looks pretty harmless to me?'

'Not to me Jake, not to me,' Tilly looked around for Sam, but couldn't see her, 'she'll be studying the rocks in the creek. She also has a satellite phone with her, so I bet she's gathering the coordinates and taking photos of specimens. I don't trust her a bit.'

'Why?' Jake raised his eyebrows.

'Because she reminds me of the person I used to be.'

'And it frightens you?'

'Yes, I think I'm going to have to revert back to being a callous and ruthless hard-heart just to beat her. I don't

154

want to, but if that's the way it has to be, it's the way it's going to be.'

'Well why the hell are you dragging her around with you then?'

'Get to know your enemy Jake,' Tilly tapped her nose, 'find out all you can.'

'And she gets to know you too, bit risky, isn't it?'

'Got to gather everything I can. I'm betting my charm and hospitality won't get her to change her mind, but I've found out some stuff in her personal life that'd embarrass her though, at least I hope it will.'

'High stakes?'

'Yep,' she kissed his cheek, 'stay with the doctor's wife until Sam and I have had our little bust up. She'll need a strong shoulder after I've dragged her skinny little arse in and out of the courts.'

'I thought I'd ask for her number,' he put his palms out.

'You would... I'll give her yours, but one word to her about what I've just said and you're off this job, okay.'

'Righto Ralph,' it was his catch phrase to finalise an agreement, 'works for me.'

'I'd better go and pick up Em. Remember what I said, e-mail me those dimensions and stuff. I don't want to hold anything up. Nice job on the entrance, by the way. Mum'll be pleased,' Tilly drove off, tooting the horn at the creek and waiting until Sam got back. She was carrying a small stone and Tilly could see she was pleased with her find.

The door opened and Sam slipped up onto her seat. 'Take a look at this,' she passed the stone over, 'you don't see them down this far in the Flinders, but just look at it. It's beautiful, it's an Ediacaran fossil. Most of the time you only find these further up. I could only find the one, but it's exciting though. I wonder how it got here.'

'I've seen something similar before, Mum was always looking at rocks and stuff, she could have dropped it there,' Tilly put the Toyota in gear and started to head for home, 'I'd better get back to Em, if I don't lift my game, Fiona will get sick of me dumping her there all the time.'

'Yeah, I'll have an inbox full of stuff to attend to as well,' Sam turned the fossil over in her hand, touching the striations in the stone, 'would Emily like this?'

'She would, but she won't appreciate it the way you will. No, you keep it as a memento of today. Mind you, that's the only thing I'll let you take off the place.'

'You know, I thought today would be awkward. I didn't know what to expect, but you're good company and I've had a nice day.'

'Would it be better if I told you Jake wants to catch up?'

'Yeah?'

'I said if it was okay with you I'd give him your number,' she fidgeted in a side pocket, 'here, sort through these, his card's in there somewhere.'

'Wouldn't it be better if he rang me?'

'Are you woman or wuss?' Tilly reached over and pushed her shoulder. 'Wait for a while, if he doesn't call in a few days, you ring him.'

Sam knew they would test each other soon and was prepared for the fight, 'I've had fun today, thank you.'

'Me too, I wasn't sure how we'd get on, but I think it went okay. I'm beginning to like you Sam.'

'We should try to make that the priority you think?'

Tilly dropped her hand from the wheel, reached between the seat and the door panel. She crossed her fingers. 'Yes, I think we should.'

CHAPTER TWENTY SIX

Tilly knew John was working, his police car was in the shed where the old cells once stood and the highway patrol had parked theirs at the front of the station. She turned into yard at the back of the police station, noting the area behind the police house held a trampoline packed with kids of all sizes, wondering where Fiona got the energy to look after her four and at least five other kids she counted. Fiona was sitting at the outdoor table, the two coffee mugs on the table telling Tilly she was expected. A light breeze ruffled the fringe on the cafe umbrella John set up every summer, although at this time of the day it was always in the shade offered by one of the many gums that lined Orroroo's streets.

'You must be psychic,' Tilly said.

'You can smell fresh coffee, that's all it is,' Fiona pushed a mug toward her friend, 'well, is she still the same size eight, jumped up little bitch you thought she was yesterday?'

'Well she's still a size eight,' she laughed at her own joke, 'but no, not really.'

'Okay?'

'You know if it weren't for her pushing me to let them drill on the place, I reckon I could come to like her.'

'Saw a few similarities with the younger you, did you?"'

'Yeah, I suppose a few, but no, she's nice enough. A bit lonely though.'

'Are you going soft?'

'Hell no, and I'm not sure my charm offensive will work either?' Tilly looked around for Emily, 'my secret weapon is Jake I reckon, he was taken with her.'

'Jake, your builder?'

'Yes, but I told him I'd neuter him if he stuffed things up for me.'

'How could he stuff things up?'

'I don't know, but it felt necessary to warn him off. However, I reckon he'll call her the moment I send him her number.'

'Well aren't you the little matchmaker, doing cupid out of a job are you?'

'Anything I can do to help love along. Besides I'd like to see him settled down and her looking the size of a house. She'll run to mud after carrying his kids.'

'Good, I thought you'd softened for a minute,' Fiona said.

'Talking of soft,' Tilly waved in the direction of the tribe on the trampoline, 'can I ask another favour?'

Fiona waved the suggestion off as if she were brushing away a fly. 'I know what you're going to ask, but our kids enjoy their friends so why not and it's not like I have a job to go to. So yes, you know you can ask.'

'I wondered if you can have Em to sleep over Friday night.'

Arrangements made she said goodbye to Fiona, extracted Emily from the mob and left for home. Ushering Emily to the car she could hear Fiona calling out to the other children to pick up their toys and make tracks for home and for her own mob to get bathed before dinner.

Kids scurried everywhere and Tilly had to wait as two of them dodged ahead of her while she backed around to face the driveway. 'Now, it's straight into the shower when you get home too, young lady. I have a lot to do tonight.'

***

Sam couldn't wait to get rid of the grime of the day, kicking her boots off outside as she worked her key in the cottage door. By the time she reached the bathroom, she was naked. Carrying her clothes over an arm, she hadn't seen Gino sitting on a stool in the kitchen. He bided his time, waiting until he heard the shower running then poured himself another scotch, dropped ice into another glass, poured in two fingers of Vodka and pushed a wedge of lime onto the rim for Sam. He could hear her humming and smiled. He had her right where he wanted her. After waiting a few minutes, he sauntered into the bathroom and put the drinks on the basin, closed the toilet lid, covered it with a towel and sat down. Face in her hands, Sam had her back to him and he supposed the running water had prevented her from hearing him. He loved to liken himself to a cat, stealthy and composed and he reached across, picked up the Vodka and held it toward the shower, smirking at his own inventiveness, 'drink?' he asked.

Sam knew his voice and bit down on her fear, screaming would do her no good. She felt vulnerable and yet she knew her nakedness gave her power too. Men were weak, and Sam needed control of this situation. If she managed it right he would leave. Gino, however, was not like other men and she knew that too, if she got it wrong there could be real danger.

She took shampoo from the shelf and lathered it in her hands, then turned to face him, her feet apart. She felt his eyes take in every inch of her. Her hands worked the shampoo into her hair, suds washed from her hair onto her shoulders and she watched his eyes track it all the way to the drain. He was a creep and it took all her composure to say, 'the drink will be nice, just let me finish in here and I'll see you in the kitchen.'

Gino put the glass back on the basin, stood up and smoothed the towel back onto the rack. Ice rattled when he lifted both tumblers and without looking at her again he walked to the kitchen, telling her to take her time.

Sam felt dirty and tried to scrub his eyes off her skin. She knew he was dangerous, but this was super scary and she needed to eliminate his influence before he harmed her.

Hair wrapped in a towel, she pulled on a bathrobe, picked up a steel nailfile and slipped it into a pocket. No, that wouldn't do, the bathrobe offered little protection; she needed more time.

'Phone the middle pub and book us in for dinner, I'll shout you a good old, country pub meal tonight.'

Gino looked at the directory, a pub meal wasn't what he'd planned, but if she was paying, what he wanted could wait. 'Which one is the middle?'

'The Commercial,' she could hear him on the phone as she planned ahead, jeans and boots for tonight and plenty of people around too, 'give me a few minutes, yeah?'

'Take your time, then after dinner, I want you to tell me what you've learnt today.'

At the hotel, he drew her chair out and waited for her to sit before taking his place opposite. She ordered a T-bone steak, while he chose the Surf and Turf. To onlookers he could have been her boyfriend. Chatting with the locals and flirting with the waitress, he could out charm anyone when he wanted to and he knew it.

Tonight he was a picture of calm and it gave her the chills. She hadn't asked where he was staying, fearing he planned to share the cottage with her. She only knew she would have to set him straight before it got out of hand.

'You took a ride with Tilly Gillespie today.' He said this as a statement rather than a question.

'I did and it was a nice day too, I enjoyed her company.'

'That's great, but how will you feel when her lawyer is grilling you about your reasons for being there today?'

Leaning toward him Sam whispered, 'I don't know who your spy is, but stay out of what I'm doing. Until I ask for your help, you can piss off. Got it? I'm still the boss,' she leant back in her chair and stared hard to emphasise the point, 'now if you want, I can tell you what I saw from the window of Tilly's car. But I want some answers from you too. I want to know why you're here Gino. Just what is it you want? But, before you answer that, don't even think about pulling another stunt like you did today. There's laws against that form of trespass.'

'Jeeze, Sweet-cheeks, keep your hair on. I only came to see if I could help in anyway. I also needed to check how the drilling's going on the Walloway Plain. I want to know if the team has found anything other than coal. It's not just RADOR I have an interest in, I work for Wagmin too.'

'Yeah, right, like I'm going to swallow that. Charles is so fixed on exploring the Gillespie's place, but why?' She increased her stare, 'look, I've studied the geophysical data for this region in detail and there is nothing commercial out there. Why waste good money chasing barren leases.'

'Listen, our job is to do what we're told and not ask why. If Charles says there's something there, then it's our job to find it,' he returned her direct gaze, 'it's simple, just do your job, short and sweet.'

'Yes, but a host of companies before us have spent millions out here, only to find nothing. I know we're better off spending our resources where there's more than a better chance of finding something. Why go out and put a huge pit in good farming land on a whim?' She straightened her shoulders. 'Look, see for yourself, you can't drive around out here without finding the remains of miner's dreams littering the countryside. Diamonds, coal, copper, gold, manganese, the list is endless. Everyone, as far back as first settlement, everyone, has failed to find sustainable quantities of anything. Why should the Gillespie's land be different?'

'Those bloody Gillespies are hiding something and Charles knows it. Ask yourself why they won't let us in to look around? They know there's something there, there has to be and I'm with Charles on that. I reckon it's big. I reckon it's heavy and I'm prepared to bet it's yellow.'

'Bullshit, Gino. The rocks I saw today tell me different. I don't need to waste a fortune on drillers to know that. All I found to interest me was this,' she took the fossil from her pocket and pushed it across the table, 'it shouldn't be where it was either, so I'm not sure it's even from the Gillespie place originally. Probably dropped there by someone thousands of years ago. I say we cut and run. Let's look somewhere where we have at least half a chance of getting some return on investment.'

'That's your opinion, is it?'

'My professional opinion... yes.'

'Charlie won't be pleased.'

'He'll be less pleased if we toss ten mill down the drain, because that's what it might take and I don't want to put the parent company at risk either.'

'You can tell him.'

'I'll have no problem with that.' Dinner came and Sam stabbed her steak and savoured the first bite. Gino could stew as far as she was concerned. All her savings were tied up in this project and she wasn't ready to lose them.

CHAPTER TWENTY SEVEN

Bill and Elspeth arrived at nine. There was certainness about Bill that Joe found reassuring. He never appeared stressed or in a hurry, everything was always in order and Joe admired that. Even though there was dew on the morning air, Bill chose to drive his MG TD. He had bought it as a lad, restoring it over the past ten years.

Laura looked out the window and chuckled, 'how are you going to fit in that? It'll be like watching a snake get in and out of a beer bottle.' She imagined Joe contorting himself into the seat and laughed again at the thought of her husband, the Aussie bushman, in a little English car, knees pressed up against the dash.

'You'd be surprised. I tried it out last time we were there, and I fit in it quite well,' he tapped his nose, 'now Jeeves, where are my cap and scarf?'

They didn't wait for the doorbell to ring. Joe pulled his jacket on, kissed Laura, opened the door and led her outside. The top was up on the little square rigger and it shone black like patent leather. The passenger door was hinged from the back and Laura greeted Elspeth as she extricated herself from the car, noting the Harris tweed she wore and the MG suited her style. 'Well just look at you two,' she said, spreading her arms to welcome her cousin, 'the car and the clothes, you both look splendid.'

Joe went to slide into the seat Elspeth had vacated.

'Mind if I use your loo first?' Bill asked, 'bumpy ride, weak prostrate, old age and all that, makes things a bit urgent.' He pushed past the three of them.

'Men,' Elspeth rolled her eyes, 'too much information, Bill, Laura doesn't need to know all that.'

Bill just waved them off and headed inside.

'Joe, do you trust us to go to London for a few nights?' Elspeth asked as her husband emerged from the front door.

'Did you know about, this?' Joe said and pointed to him.

'Yeah, it's a bit of a setup but what can you do?'

***

Sam remained silent while Gino finished his dinner and then let him have it in a barrage of questions. 'What are you doing here? Is Charles checking up on me, or are you just being your usual nosey self?'

She was sure he wasn't sharing everything and it made her uneasy.

He held his hands out in an unconvincing gesture. 'Now that's unfair, I came here to see how you're doing and offer my support.'

'Gino, you do nothing without purpose and you sure as hell don't want to help me. What is it you want?'

'Well, a little birdie told me you were driving around with the Gillespie woman today and I was interested to find out just what you'd learned.'

'I've told you there is nothing to learn. This place is barren of anything commercial. You only have to read reports from everyone who's drilled, surveyed or searched for anything around the Gillespie's land. It's not worth the investment. I'm not going to waste any more money here. I'm going to look for a new site that will have some chance of success.'

'Charles isn't going to be happy to learn that she's got to you.'

Sam could feel her anger rising, but didn't want to make a scene. She leaned across the table and whispered to him, 'piss off back to the city and let me do my job. Go home, Gino, just go home.'

'I thought I'd stay in your cottage tonight, you know save the company a quid.'

'You're a sleazy bastard. That little trick in the bathroom did nothing for me. I just want you gone.'

He grabbed her wrist and twisted, 'don't piss me around, Sam. I could snap your arm, it'd be that easy,' he snapped the fingers of his other hand, 'I just want to know what you know.' He twisted harder and she slid down in her chair. 'Get up,' his voice was low and she felt another chill run through her, 'don't make a scene.' He relaxed his hand and Sam returned to sitting position.

The barman noticed what was happening and sent one of the patrons to fetch Constable O'Rourke just as a weasel featured man bumped Gino's chair and kept walking. He stopped at the Gents toilet door, looked back and then stepped inside.

Gino stood up, nodded toward the street and said loud enough for the people around him to hear, 'I'll see you back at the cottage in about ten minutes then, Darling?' He bent to kiss her cheek, she turned away and he whispered, 'just walk out now and wait for me, don't try anything sassy. I'll follow you in a few minutes.'

'Get lost, Gino. If I make a scene, that local copper will be all over you and neither of us wants that. Get in your car and go back to the city. I'll see you in the office Friday if not then, Monday. And you can let your spy know he can crawl back into whatever hole he came from,' she slung her bag over her shoulder, 'you don't need to check-up on me. My report will be comprehensive and accurate. Now piss off'

'Everything okay here?' Constable John O'Rourke asked as he arrived on the scene.

Sam's eyes adjusted to the dark and she saw his shape standing by the door to the bar. 'Sure, just a bit of a misunderstanding, that's all.'

'Good, around here, we come down fairly hard on blokes who harass women.'

John passed her his card. 'Anyone bothers you call me on the station number. If I'm not here it'll go through to another station. No point being a hero, especially when the bloke's bigger than you.'

'No, it's nothing, just a colleague flexing his muscle, nothing I can't handle – but thanks anyway.'

'You were out with Tilly today, weren't you?'

'Yeah, how did you know?'

'Nothing gets past a small-town copper. Besides, you had dinner with my wife Fiona last night.'

'Yeah Fiona, say hello to her for me, we had a good night.'

John looked at her. 'Just call me if you need any help, okay? The last thing I want is to complete the reams of paperwork that comes from an assault. Save me the report, eh.'

'Okay, but I'm fine though really,' she twisted his card into the light to read the print, 'goodnight John.'

'Goodnight Sam.'

She hadn't told him her name, concluding that Fiona must have mentioned her. Orroroo and Mundulla were more similar than she first thought.

It wasn't far to the cottage and Gino's car was in the street. He was still around and she flinched at every sound, her heart pounding when a cat scaled a brush fence in front of her and dropped at her feet. Snapped into a reflex karate stance, she relaxed as the cat rubbed against her ankles.

Gino was leaving as she reached the cottage. 'Friday, sweet-cheeks, Charles will want a full report and an action plan. You know he needs access to the Gillespies land, like yesterday. If he says there's gold there somewhere, I'm not going to argue. You know he'll stop at nothing to get what he wants, so I suggest you concentrate on doing just that,' he drew a finger across his throat, 'I've told him, if you can't get the job done, I can. So, watch your back.'

'You're a creep, Gino. My report will be on his desk Friday. Now, as I've told you more than once tonight, you can piss off.'

***

Bill and Joe had lunch at the Old Warden Restaurant, part of the Historic Aircraft Association. The car park was a show of restored cars, Jaguars and MGs seemed most popular, while a couple of American classics broke the array of everything British. Before lunch, Joe had met several of Bill's colleagues, soon gathering a pocket full of business cards to remember them by. During lunch, there was a lecture on air safety and Joe found himself scribbling notes on a napkin. The afternoon was spent among new friends talking about old aircraft, restored cars and interesting farm machinery. Joe thought he had a lot in common with these people and enjoyed being around them.

During a lull in the program, he studied the photocopy again. The resolution was poor and he should have found a colour copier, but didn't want to anyone to see it. Colour would help. Les would have known if the levels in the well rose, the water could wash chalk or pencil away and so he would have etched it, using different coloured crayons to fill the indentations. There were also traces of a varnish, but it had taken away some of the colour as it deteriorated. It remained a mystery. He folded the paper and returned it to his pocket. It would have to wait another week or two, but it didn't mean he could let it rest and he knew his father's secret would agitate him for a good while yet.

His phone vibrated in his pocket and he took it out to see a text showing Emily holding a Merit Card for mathematics. This reminder from home led to thoughts of his heart attack, about the bloke who had tried to kill him, and the grip of everything that had happened last year that left him teetering on the edge of depression. He looked at his granddaughter again and knew he didn't have to slide into fear. Emily could brighten his mood any day.

The group broke up and began moving toward the door, like a mob of sheep pressing their way through a set of yards as home called his mind again. He missed the place and wanted to get back to work. The season was about open and he wondered if Tilly had the machinery ready for an early start, but it was no longer up to him, their sharefarmer was in control now. He mumbled to himself his words catching Bill's ear.

'You say something, Mate?'

'Just thinking out loud, that's all.'

'Anything you want to talk about?'

'Probably not the time or place, I was thinking about seeding, but we should be home in time to see the start.'

'Getting a bit homesick, are we?'

'Yeah, a bit I guess, but enough of that. Haven't we got a few old aeroplanes to see?'

'Sure, I'll just get a few goodbyes out of the way and then we'll be off. I'll meet you at the car if you like.'

As Joe walked through the display of vehicles he stopped at a series one Land Rover, a short wheel base version almost identical to the car he learnt to drive in. He pictured himself as a kid learning the gears in Pop's old bomb and the day he drove it and met Laura. It was still in one of the sheds at Wanooka's Well. He could drag it out one day and see if it still ran, maybe take Emily for a drive.

'Interested in old Landys, are we?' The voice was cultured a man with a David Niven moustache and a tweed coat, complete with leather elbow patches completed the picture.

'I learnt to drive in one. Nothing like this one though, mine's pretty old and battered now.'

'You're the Aussie I missed earlier. Pity that, yes this is one I found in Gibraltar. Cost a bomb to bring back to this condition, but it's worth it to me. Although the good wife wasn't too happy to find out I'd used over twenty thousand of our nest egg, especially after I'd told her it'd be cheap to do, no sense of humour my Phyllis,' he stood, hands on hips, admiring his Land Rover, 'I hear on the jungle drums that you've unearthed a mystery bi-plane. I'd love to know what it is.'

Joe offered his hand to the stranger, 'Joe, Joe Gillespie.'

He took it. 'Fred Braithwaite, but call me Freddie, everyone does.'

'Nice to meet you Freddie,' the handshake was different to what Joe expected. The other man's hands were strong and calloused, much like his own, 'play a bit of polo?' Joe asked.

'No way, rich man's game that. I work the horses for a few riders, keep them fit and all that. Don't let the accent put you off, I come from common stock,' he looked at the cityscape on the horizon as if lost in thought before continuing, 'now the wife, well she's different. Her folks had position, power and no money. When the old people died, we took over the house and now I'm a retired British Airways long-haul pilot, rebuilding her family's country house one stone at a time. What I wouldn't give for a small house in the town. All the mod-cons and no upkeep would do me. That's just a dream though when you marry into the McMahons.'

'My soon to be son-in-law is trying to work out what the plane is. A bit of a mystery though, because the family thought it was an Avro of some sort, but the markings on it are German, so we don't know.'

'Here's my card and e-mail address, send some photos after you get home. I still have a few old chums in the air ministry who pull the strings. Why not use the McMahon name to help a fellow out at times eh?'

Joe watched him open the car door and climb in.

'It was nice meeting you Freddie. I'll send those photos through.'

'It was a pleasure Joe. Don't let that old Rover rot, fix her up, or sell her to me. They're on trend now and worth a bomb, too,' he pressed the starter button on the firewall, 'you send those pictures through. I'd like a look at them.'

Joe watched until the wisp of oil smoke blended with the dust on the driveway. There was something about the Land Rover that warmed him inside and he smiled at the feeling. He saw Bill shaking hands and making his way out of the gathering and waited for him to catch up. Bill pointed to the MG. 'Righto let's find these old planes then onto our digs, get some dinner and then onto the TED Talk tonight, okay?'

'You're the driver, mate. I'm ready whenever you are.' They walked to the where the car was parked.

'I saw that Freddie had you bailed up. You know that car is the only thing he has left out of his Air Force Pension and British Airways superannuation. Everything else has gone into that bloody house they live in, if you can call it living. Never marry into aristocracy I say, the bludgers are debt ridden wasters, all of them. His wife's always on his back to do more, outings like today are the only escape he has. Once he was flying long haul 747s across the world to supply her with cash, now he's doing masonry work on the house. Blow that for a joke, I'm glad Elspeth's folks were as common as mine.' He laughed at his own joke, and Joe thought of Laura and how much he valued her.

CHAPTER TWENTY EIGHT

Sam had not slept well, thoughts of Gino standing in the bathroom while she showered were still troubling her. She could go to the police, but that would show a weakness and Charles didn't keep weak people. She had begun to like Tilly too, however, in her position, she couldn't afford the friendship. John O'Rourke had made her feel safer, but she couldn't tap into those feelings either. Sam packed her things and took them to the car. All this trip north had done was confuse her and it was time to focus so she could write her report.

Something made the hair on her neck stand up as she loaded her cases, but she told herself it was her imagination. However, she could not let it go, looking each way along the street to the golf course over the road where a man leaned on the front of a battered Falcon utility, the same man who had bumped Gino last night. She stared back at him, willing him to turn away. He didn't, instead he raised his right hand and with two fingers, touched his eyes, pointed back at her. He was watching her and wanted her to know it. She wondered should she challenge him or invite him over. She needed a plan.

One last look around the cottage to make sure nothing had been left, she closed the door and headed to the pub to return the key.

'Called back to the office early,' she said to Rosie by way of explanation, 'pity though, it's a lovely town.'

'Can't offer a refund I'm afraid,' the older woman lifted her shoulders and shrugged, the action reminded Sam of a turtle retracting its head.

'I didn't expect one. You could have the extra nights on me, treat yourself to the spa, you know chill out for a while.'

'God no, Darlin', my husband would think we were teenagers again and want to get all lovey-dovey. These days he'd get lost in all this.' She looked around to make sure no one was in the bar, cupped her hands under her boobs, pushed up and jiggled them. Sam thought they were about to spill out of her dress. The woman laughed at her own joke.

'I used to be your size once, now look at me, more than twice the woman you are.' Rosie said and the deep belly laugh made her body shake and bounce under the loose fabric of her frock.

The action caused Sam to think of her dad and how he would have said Rosie looked like a blancmange in a nightdress. Rosie touched her hand and Sam's mind snapped back to the present.

'Run along now, lovey, when you come back again, you ask for Rosie and I'll make sure you get a couple nights for free, okay.'

Her laugh subsided to a chuckle as the door closed and Sam knew the vision of Rosie's mirth and her dad's description would dance around in her head for days, a reminder she would have to phone home this week.

The terrain to the north of the town offered no indication of gold deposits, but Sam thought a drive through the Pekina hills might offer a chance of finding a quartz reef along a ridge. She would walk up a few creeks with her kit and see what they revealed.

A check of the map showed a cave system to the south of the town with easy access and a deep creek system ran from the range of hills to the east and emptied into the reservoir. Being mid-autumn, she knew the creek bed would be dry and she would be able to collect samples from the gravel above the road crossing.

The Rav4 rocked up onto two wheels as Sam left the road and wound her way along the creek bed downstream, from the ford where road workers may have disturbed something that had washed into crevices. She opened her prospecting kit and took out a pry-bar, slipped on a pair of gloves and grabbed a miner's hammer, snap-lock bags and a few cable ties, stowing everything but the bar into a shopping bag. Sliding her handbag under the front seat, she checked her phone was in her pocket, locked the car and set off downstream.

Gravel had built up in front of an outcrop of bedrock that crossed the creek at an angle. She thought anyone who was interested would have picked this over before, but decided to look anyway. One of the stones was split and she could see where gravel and sand had washed into the crack and looked back up the creek to assess recent water flow. If anything heavy had washed this way the crack should have trapped it.

Using the pry-bar and hammer to dislodge the stone, she realised prising it from the reef was going to be harder than she first thought. She decided to allow half an hour to try and, if it hadn't released by then, she would give it a miss.

Sweat ran into her eyes and she could feel her shirt sticking to her back, but by using the bar as a lever she had almost moved the stone enough to expose the sand under it. Her pulse raced with the same excitement she had felt as a child at Christmas. Was it the chase, or the promise of riches that drove prospectors, she wondered, deciding it had to be the chase, for most often they found nothing. She looked around for a bigger lever and spotted a guide post tangled among the debris from a flood. If she could get that out, it would do.

Straining to dislodge the marker and carry it back, the shadows had moved and the rock was now in the shade.

She drove the post in under the stone and heaved, moving it almost halfway before it fell back. She kicked a stone under one side and wedged it before giving it another shove to expose whatever had washed there over eons. Gym work built muscle, but this was hard work and she strained to roll the rock out of the reef, then sat and stared at the small grains in the bottom of the hole the stone once occupied.

She couldn't see the road from her position, and had taken no notice when she heard a car rattle through the ford, now she sat panting, going over in her mind what to do next when she felt a presence behind her. She didn't need to look around, knowing instinctively it was the man she had dubbed weasel-face. The odour of the man frightened her.

'What-cha got there?' The voice matched his face, gravelly, rasping like fingernails against a blackboard and she shivered. He pushed on her shoulders making her fall forward. 'You're not wanted here and you're not safe here, Bitch. Piss off back to the city where you belong.'

As he moved forward and put his knee in her back, Sam twisted away, snatching the pry-bar as he lost his balance. Once on her feet, she smashed the iron rod across the side of his left knee and he crashed forward, his head buried face first into the pile of gravel she'd moved earlier. Taking advantage of his incapacity, she jumped into his back with both knees and knocked out any breath he still had in him. Springing back and onto her feet, she pushed the chisel end of the bar into the small of his neck and watched a line of blood form, poised to smash the bar into him again if he moved.

Her attacker was wheezing, sucking hard to gain his breath as she dragged him back by his collar until he was in a seated position.

'Don't ever sneak up on any woman ever again. You're damn lucky I don't smash you with the bar and drop your body down the cave over there,' she was panting too, but her recovery was faster, 'who are you?' The bar was now at the back of his head.

'Piss off.'

'I'll ask the questions thank you. Starting what do you want, why are you following me and what's your name?' She tapped the bar on the base of his skull to emphasise each question.

'People call me Spoggy.'

'And who do you work for Spoggy?'

'No-one.'

'C'mon, even an arsehole like you doesn't follow someone and threaten them just for fun.' She dug the blade of the pry-bar in between his shoulders and he bent forward to ease the pressure. She kept pushing and watched a line of red start to soak into his shirt. 'I'll ask you again. Who are you working for? Come on, you don't want to make me madder than I am already.' She moved the bar over another vertebra as he squeezed forward and still he said nothing. 'I'm betting no-one knows you're here and they couldn't care less if you didn't show up for a couple of weeks.' She moved her knee into the back of his neck and swung the bar around so she was pulling it against his throat.

He gargled something and she eased the pressure. He was quick and gripped the bar, pulling it away from his throat. Pushing up with his legs, he bent further forward and threw her over his shoulders. Now she was on her back, watching as he tried to wrench the bar from her grip. She rolled to her right, where the creek bed was sandy. The force of her twisting ripped the bar from his hands and she sprung to her feet, cracking the bar down on his right shoulder and he fell to his knees again.

'I've had enough of this, scumbag, who the fuck, do you work for?' Sam yelled, holding the bar in a baseball stance, ready to smash it down again even if he so much as flinched.

Spoggy knew if he gave up Gino's name he would have to hide somewhere where nobody could find him. However, as his mind raced he thought how this could work to his advantage and drive a wedge between her friendship with the Gillespie woman at the same time.

'Joe Gillespie, your new bestie's dad. He's paying me to look out for her while he's away.' He shuffled and tried to stand, Sam prepared to hit him again, raising her weapon.

'Where's your phone?'

'I don't have a phone.'

'Bullshit.' She prodded his pockets. If he did have a phone it had to be in his car. 'Come on,' she said, 'we're going back to your ute. It'll be there, I bet?'

Spoggy limped and shuffled his way back to the vehicle. She noticed he was limping on the wrong leg. 'Stop and sit down.'

'What?'

'I said to stop and sit down. Do it now and kick your boots off.'

'What?'

She tapped his sore shoulder with her bar. 'Are you deaf too, or do you want me to bust the other collarbone?'

'Shit woman, I'm doing it alright.'

'Faster and you won't get hurt.' He worked the boots off with his alternate toes. 'Now kick them away. Just as I thought, you do have a phone. If you're lucky, scumbag, I'll post it back to Ms Gillespie next week.'

'Fuck off, bitch.'

'C'mon, on your feet and you can piss off home now, too.' She held her bar between his shoulders prodding him to hurry up until they reached his vehicle. He reached for the door handle. 'Not so fast,' she reached through the window and snatched the keys from the ignition switch, 'now get in and put on your seat belt.'

'And if I say no?'

'As I said, I'll drop your body into that cave over there. Do it.' Her patience was thinning, but she knew he was still dangerous.

He opened the door and shuffled into his seat, wincing as he moved. Spoggy was sore in a lot of places.

'Happy now?' he asked.

'Put your hands on either side of the spoke on my side of the wheel,' she held the bar against his jugular while he gripped the wheel, 'tighter.' His knuckles whitened and she slipped a cable-tie around each of his wrists binding him to the car.

'You think I won't come after you?' He more spat the words than said them.

She grabbed his hair and pushed his head toward the centre of the car, with her other hand, she put the column shift into first gear. 'Now put your foot on the clutch.' She was screaming at him now, shock was setting in and she knew she needed to get away from him.

'What, I can't drive like this, I'll prang it.'

'Not my problem. Tell Tilly I said, hello.' She reached in and turned the key. He lunged forward and tried to bite her, but the car started. She dragged her hand away before his mouth reached her.

Sam watched the Falcon utility wandering along at a crawl. Spoggy was out of view when she heard a horn toot and old bloke in a farm ute went past. She had only a few minutes to scrape some gravel into a bag and get out of there before someone reported an erratic driver and the copper   showed   up.

CHAPTER TWENTY NINE

The screen identifier on Tilly's phone showed Sam's number calling. The background road noise when she answered the call told her Sam was driving and she raised her voice to be heard, 'Hello, are you okay? I hear you had a bit of bother last night.'

Sam wanted to let Tilly know she knew about her connection to Spoggy, but if working with Charles had taught her anything, it was to keep your competitor from knowing what you knew and for as long as possible. 'Nothing I couldn't handle, but I wanted to ask you about a weasel faced bloke, calls himself Spoggy. He bumped Gino at the pub last night and today I found him watching the cottage. Someone said he works for your Dad?'

'What? Is he from around here?' Tilly waited and as Sam continued describing him, she could tell something, or someone had frightened her.

'I think the man you're talking about drifted in a couple of years ago and people call him Spoggy. I don't know what he does, or where he works, but I know John has always kept an eye on him.'

'That's nice to know.' Sam found Tilly and Spoggy's statement were at odds and, as much as she wanted to tell Tilly to keep him away from her, something in the back of her mind demanded caution because Tilly may not have known about her Dad employing him. On the other hand, she had complete control over the family company and hiding someone like Spoggy from her would be difficult. Either that or the weasel was lying.

Tilly broke the gap in conversation, 'I gave Jake your details, you know, just in case he calls,' all she could hear was road noise, 'are you still there Sam?'

'Yeah, sorry, I lost myself there for a minute.'

'When I talked to him last night, all he wanted to talk about was you.'

'That's good,' her voice sounded distant, 'look, sorry, reception's bad here, I've gotta go.' Sam switched off.

Tilly thought Sam seemed abrupt and wondered why, but she understood poor mobile coverage and the vibrations of gravel roads, after all that was her life too.

Sam cut down through Appila and across to Jamestown, stopping in front of the Commercial Hotel to look through Spoggy's phone. She scrolled through the call list. One number kept coming up on incoming calls and it unsettled her, it was vaguely familiar, a number she knew from somewhere. She scrolled back to the menu and found a number of texts with pictures attached, all to that same number. Then she remembered, it was Gino's private mobile phone.

Spoggy was Gino's man in Orroroo, but why would he need a spy out there? The town had welcomed other exploration teams and why this bloke? He didn't look like part of either world. It was a mystery only a volatile meeting with Gino could solve. She wondered if Charles knew, then decided he had to because Gino didn't do anything without Charles knowing. It was time for her to reassess her next move, Gino was becoming more dangerous.

She opened her laptop and downloaded all the photo files and contact lists from Spoggy's phone onto two memory sticks, dropping one of the flash-drives in a postbag addressed to her mother, with a scribbled a few words on the back of a supermarket receipt. The note would do until she phoned home on Sunday. The other drive she slipped into the pocket of her wallet. Placing the phone in a plastic bag she wedged this behind the front wheel and reversed then drove forward again. The sound of the screen shattering as the stone was forced into it empowered her. The pieces of shattered and twisted phone rattled as she picked up the plastic bag before dropping it into a postbag and walking around the corner to the post office and dropping both packages through the slot. All done and dusted with enough time for a coffee before she took to the road again.

Sam's time management skills meant she never wasted a second of her day and before reaching Gawler, her voice recorder was full of items to prioritise for her report and another file for the connection between Gino and Spoggy. She wasn't due until Friday and with the weekend added to that, meant she had until Monday to attend the office. Staying away for a couple of days would give her a chance to prepare without interference from Gino and she would break all communication until Charles was back to keep herself safe.

Suspicion played games in her mind and made her worry about the ease with which Charles and Gino could find her. If she stayed in her town house, they had access to her at any time. She had bought the flat from Charles and, given recent events, she couldn't be sure if the place was bugged. She would stay in a hotel in the city until Monday and still be able to access the company files through her private log in, but first she needed to phone and make peace with Tilly. Spoggy was wounded and nasty with it.

Tilly's phone went unanswered so she left a message, 'Hi Tilly, it's Sam again. I thought I'd give you a quick update. I've found out that Spoggy works as a free agent for one of our directors. He's also dangerous, so take care. I'm going to ground until Monday. Thanks for yesterday and we'll talk soon.'

***

It took Spoggy almost an hour to get back to the main road and as he approached the hospital entrance he had a choice to make. Should he try to get over the ramped entrance, go to the pub or go home? Each probability had its own complication. The bindings on his hands were cutting off the circulation and his left hand had gone numb. He knew the doctor would report his condition to the police and the last thing he needed was John O'Rourke looking into his history. That left the pub. Combined with that bitch smashing a steel bar into it and the crouched position over the steering wheel, his shoulder was troubling him even more now. He needed medical treatment but the hospital was not an option that appealed whereas, if he stopped at the Orroroo Hotel, someone would have to help.

The Falcon was beginning to overheat as well and he could smell the oil and grime melting from around its engine. In better times he would have turned the motor off at the top of each hill and coast down, but he couldn't reach the ignition key. He stretched his fingers, it was no use, several times he got close to the keys, but he almost steered off the road with the effort. Then he remembered that if the engine stopped, the brakes and power steering wouldn't work so he gave up this plan, lifted his foot off the accelerator and crawled toward the pub. He'd have to suffer the embarrassment and, once free, he planned to bolt and disappear to somewhere where Gino would never find him.

CHAPTER THIRTY

Spoggy looked at the ceiling, trying to lose himself in its expanse of white. He hadn't planned to be here. If only Trigger had cut the ties on the wheel like he had asked, it was all he wanted, but no. Trigger, the oaf, had to get everyone out of the pub to laugh at him. The more they laughed the longer he stayed trapped to the wheel, when all he wanted to do was bolt.

Now here he was in hospital waiting for the doctor to come. Debating whether to go or stay, he unwrapped a stick of chewing gum and settled back on the pillow, the swelling in his ankle pulsed with pain. The throbbing from his shoulder almost had him in tears. God, he hated that bitch Lewis.

He had to wait for the doctor to read the x-rays. His head pounded and he couldn't lift his arm. She had hit him that hard, he was sure his collar bone had broken. If he was in trouble now, it was only going to get worse when Gino discovered the bitch had snatched his phone. It didn't bear thinking about. He closed his eyes and focussed on the story he had told the blokes at the pub. He needed to remember it, to practice it until it was a truth in his mind. He had done this before and he could do it again. For an hour, the story repeated by rote in his mind until he knew it without falter. He was almost asleep when he heard.

'G'day, mind if I sit down?'

Spoggy turned on his side and opened his eyes to find the local copper facing him. Could things any worse, he wondered, as he waited for John O'Rourke to settle.

'Want to tell me what happened? I've had a yarn with the blokes at the pub and they've told me what you told them, but I need to hear your version of the story'.

Spoggy was tired of the gum and reached for a tissue to put it in. 'Damn, I can't reach it.'

'Here let me,' John grabbed the tissue and Spoggy dropped the offending item into his hand. The policeman walked to the bin and stepped on the pedal, letting the lid crash down and hoping Spoggy didn't notice he had slipped the gum into his pocket. Resuming his seat, the other man began to tell his tale.

'Nothing to tell. I don't want to charge anyone, even if I knew who they were anyway.'

'I won't chase it up if you don't want me to, but I can probably charge you with several traffic offences anyway,' John turned his chair so he was facing him, 'I'm thinking that, by now, your mates have probably posted a hundred photos of you all over social media. It's not every day they come to the rescue of someone in your situation,' John leaned closer, 'I've checked and you don't need grief like this. Tell me what's going on here and I'll leave it alone.'

'Yeah?'

'Look, off the record, I really don't give a shit about you, but,' he raised his voice to an authoritative level, 'I do care about the people and what happens in this town. So just give me a description of the blokes who jumped you and I'll leave you alone.'

'Promise?'

'My word's as good as I can do.'

Spoggy shifted in the bed and crooked up on his good arm, looking around the room in his customary shiftiness to check if anyone was listening. 'It's like I told everyone. I was out on the Pekina road, having a bit of a fossick around in Brambrick's Creek and a couple of Asian guys jumped me from behind. I didn't get a look at them though.'

John listened until Spoggy finished his story and asked, 'how do you know they were Asian?

'They sounded Asian, big Asian blokes too. One said something in Chinese.'

'What kind of big guys, same size? You know, how big?'

'Mate, everyone's big to me.'

'And you're sure they spoke Chinese?'

'Yeah.'

'And do you speak Chinese?'

'No, I dunno, sounded like Chinese to me.'

'So, you can't be sure.'

'No, as I said, I didn't see them.'

'And you say you don't speak Chinese?'

'Look, I can say yum-cha, kung-fu, Kawasaki and fuck you, and that's about it. Think about it, they're probably miles away by now, just let it go. I'm not pressing charges, so what does it matter,' he waved his good arm along his body, 'I'm the one who's hurt here.'

John ignored him, made a couple of notes in his book and said nothing, knowing silence would force cracks into Spoggy's story if it were a fabrication. He watched the man swallow and squirm as he tried to find a more comfortable position in the bed, waiting until he was unable to stand the silence and asked, 'well?'

'And you say there was no reason for the attack, they just came at you from behind and belted you with a bar. Then they took your boots, marched you barefoot to your ute, tied your hands to the steering wheel and set you on your way.'

'Yep.'

John's smile turned to a grin, 'even you'd have to admit it sounds a bit thin.'

'It's what happened, okay? Look, I just want to get out of here. I don't want any fuss. The bastards got me from behind and now they're gone. End of story.'

'Alright, say I believe you. What's your full name, no alias, just the name your mother gave you?'

'Kane, Kane Steven Sparrow.'

'So why Spoggy?'

'I don't know. Probably because around here, it's slang for sparrow.'

'Who owns the Falcon ute?'

'I do.'

'Not by the name on the rego certificate.'

'Yeah, well I do, alright. I bought it from a mate in the city.'

'Is it your address on the paperwork?'

'I get the renewals sent here,' a sneer began to form, 'don't want to drive around unregistered, do I?'

'Know what I think, Kane Steven Sparrow? I think your story's all bullshit and within a few hours, I reckon I'll know more about you than your mother does. Don't go anywhere without letting me know.'

'There's nothing more to me than I've told you. Dig all you like you won't find much.'

Back at the station John searched every data base he could access. Spoggy had never had as much as a parking fine. His former address in Brahma Lodge was the vehicle's garage before moving to Orroroo. The original owner, Liam Le-Strange, still lived there. From his office in the front of the station house, he could hear Fiona calling the kids for dinner. For now, Spoggy would wait.

***

Sam left the Rav4 at the fast drop-off at the airport and took the shuttle back to the city. Settled into her accommodation, she gazed out over the park as the town hall bells chimed six o'clock. She would need more clothes before Monday but the risk of going home, knowing Charles and Gino would be watching out for her, meant that was not an option. She chose instead to order online, from one of the boutiques in the lobby, and have them delivered to her room.

Everything ached from the beating she had taken from Spoggy but knowing she had humiliated him took away some of the pain and her first concern was what Gino was up to. It was times like these she wished she had someone to offer words of comfort but her lifestyle hadn't left room for social contacts outside of work. As if on cue a text message beeped its arrival, Tilly had passed on her details to Jake and he was asking if he could call. She wanted nothing more than a friendly voice but she didn't trust the security of her phone or any other at that moment. There was too much at stake.

She set up an office in a corner of the room that overlooked the park, arranged a printer for her suite, ordered paper and organised a temp for the following day. Only once this had been completed to her satisfaction did she peruse the menu and wine list and ordered room service. She wanted to open the picture files from Spoggy's phone, but she had too much to do first. Her own phone kept beeping with messages so she set the phone to silent and promised herself she would look at Spoggy's file once she had studied the samples she'd collected from the Brambrick's Creek.

Taking a pair of pantyhose from her bag to use as a sieve, she sluiced the samples by pouring water from a glass and using the water jug from the fridge as the repository to catch anything that washed through the sieve. She didn't know what to expect, semiprecious stones would be great, diamonds a possibility, but gold would be even better. Stretching the stocking over the jug and securing it with a rubber band, she used a finger to create a depression and poured in half of her sample, sealing the remainder in the bag and dropping it back into her briefcase.

Room service arrived and she slammed the briefcase shut, closed the screen on her laptop and washed her hands as the waiter steered in a food trolley.

'An experiment,' she said when the waiter looked at the contraption on the sink, 'for my thesis. Prof says it's easy, but I'm not so sure.'

'Better you than me, I was too interested in girls to put much stock in study. Now look at me, nearly fifty and still waiting tables. It's a good job that one of those girls said yes and made me get a steady job,' he laughed at his own joke, 'would you like me to set out, or are you right to manage it.'

'Thank you, I'm fine, I can do it.'

'Thank you, Miss and,' he pointed to the phone, 'give the desk a ring and I'll come back for the tray, or you can leave it outside the door if you don't wish to be disturbed.'

'I'll do that, thank you,' she looked at his lapel badge, 'Enrico.' She noticed the softness of his touch when she shook his hand. He lifted it to his lips and bowed.

'Until we meet again...' he smiled and was gone.

Sam washed the sample before she ate and set the tap to a slow run, placing the jug on a side plate and putting it under the stream where it would fill and overflow. The large heavier specimens would remain in the stocking while the litter could overflow into the sink. Her rig was crude, but should work well enough.

She had missed lunch and only now realised how hungry she was. She bit into the bruschetta and lifted the cover off the main course. It was no way to treat a silver service dinner, but she was hungry and manners could wait for another day.

***

Tilly had Emily in bed and had finished washing the dishes. All she wanted to do was sit and relax, maybe watch something on TV, however, the e-mails and correspondence from the National Trust required her attention. She also needed to call their sharefarmer and discuss his plans. It was easy to feel swamped by the enormity of everything that relied on her for a decision. At least in her old life she could delegate and someone in the office would handle the simpler phone calls.

The computer flashed on and she waited to as e-mails made a pinging entry and a red flag caught her eye. A message from her father,

Mum's been nominated in Queen's Birthday honours, landing in Adelaide on Saturday at 1.10pm, Qantas International. See you there.

Love, Dad.

'That stuffs that then,' she said to the computer. 'Jeeze Dad, you couldn't time things better.' Her plans for Friday's night would have to wait.

***

Gino collected his paper from the news stand while he waited for his coffee. He scanned the headlines, turned to the back page and checked on what was happening in the world of sport. Nothing needed reading immediately, so he paid the bill and took his coffee upstairs, throwing the paper onto his desk and opening the blinds. The morning sun streamed in. He knocked on Sam's door and opened it. The room was dark and that surprised him. He knew she had checked out of her accommodation yesterday and expected her to be here. He could hear her PA opening the office and stepped back, closing door after him.

In his own office he unfolded the paper, turned to the business section, and considered his next move as he sipped his coffee.

'Where's Sam?' Charles had walked in while Gino was lost in thought, 'I tried her phone this morning, she's not answering.

'I thought you might know. I've been calling her since lunchtime yesterday and she's still not responding. You said you'd had a bit of a set-to with her up in the bush and now I can't raise her. It's not good enough Gino, I expected you to keep an eye on her, not frighten her into doing something stupid.'

'Keep your hair on, Charlie.'

Charles held his hand up to silence Gino, walked back and moved to close the door, but not before he turned to Gino and hissed, 'Charles, it's Charles. And it would pay you to remember that around the office.'

'Charles...' Gino drew the word out, 'I can't shadow her every moment of the day. She's competent and strong willed with it. Yes, she went out driving with that Gillespie woman, but that doesn't mean she spilled her guts or anything,' Gino couldn't believe his own words, the last thing he wanted to do was defend Sam, 'or did she?'

Charles sat in the visitor chair at Gino's desk. Gino turned away and looked out the window. He found the silence pressing, turned back put his palms on his desk and looked Charles in the eye. 'I wonder.'

'Wonder all you like, but I want this back on track today. If Sam can't do the job, I'll find someone who can.'

Gino watched Charles' face redden with every word and waited. He thought for a minute and said, 'however, if I was to come up with a different strategy, one that achieved the same outcome, then Sam and I could put each proposal forward leaving you two options to choose from. Would that help?'

'Yeah,' Charles scratched his chin while he thought, 'but I promised she could run this one, as long as she kept me in the loop. Christ, where is she? she knows I can't have my CEO off the grid, find her and we'll discuss it.'

'I'll find her, but in the meantime, how about I run a few ideas past you?'

'Like?'

'Like getting onto that land without having to deal with the Gillespies. Have you got a couple of minutes for that?'

'No shit, how?'

Gino outlined his ruse for testing the Gillespie's land for contamination. He glossed over how he had made sure RADOR would win the tender process, but Charles was smiling.

'I'll have us on there in a week, two at the latest. I promise, but do you really want to know how?'

'How are we with legal?'

Gino lifted an eyebrow. 'Why, of course it's okay with legal. We're only testing for contaminates. Anything we find outside that will be a bonus and we'll quarantine the samples.'

'And you can get us on in a couple of weeks?'

'Say the word and I'll send the teams out. I'm only waiting on confirmation, which should be through any day now.

'Do it.'

'And Sam? What about her?' Gino suppressed his smile, contorting his face to one of concern instead.

'She's gone the day you get the permit to drill.'

'And the corner office?'

'Goes with the job,' Charles put his hand on Gino's shoulder, 'now get it started. I've got to gladhand prospective investors this morning. Find Sam and get busy on a glowing prospectus,' he made quotation marks with his fingers. Gino knew what was required, 'I want to float RADOR as soon as we have ASIC approval.'

Gino had what he wanted, now it was time to put the second   part   of   his   plan   into   action.

CHAPTER THIRTY ONE

Changing their travel plans had been easy and Joe and Laura queued to check their baggage for the flight home. Bill and Elspeth had come to see them off, waiting with Laura while Joe paid an excess baggage fee for the extra cases that Laura had filled during their stay.

It was while shopping in London with Elspeth that Laura had taken a call from someone in the Prime Minister's Office advising her she was to receive an award in the Queen's Birthday Honours for her work in Aboriginal language and culture. The caller questioned if she would be back in Australia in time to attend the reception at Government House.

Laura had never sought recognition for her work and the idea of accepting an award for doing something she enjoyed perplexed her while Joe, on the other hand, was excited for her. He'd known about the nomination before they left Australia, but stayed quiet to allow Laura to break the news. Laura had said nothing about the reason for the call to Elspeth, instead saying it was from one of her colleagues writing a paper on the effects of white settlement on Aboriginal families.

When they did reveal they were going home early, Elspeth was disappointed, but her spirits lifted when Laura promised they would come back to finish their trip next year.

***

Fiona met Tilly at Maggie's after the school morning drop off where she had to drag her friend away from the number of parents gossiping about the Spoggy incident and pumping her for John's account of it. Tilly could see Fiona was flustered and found it hard to understand why these people pressured her when everyone knew Fiona never discussed police business.

'Thanks,' Fiona said and dragged her chair into the sun. She cupped her hands around the coffee and drew in its aroma.

'It gets a bit rough some days, eh?' Tilly asked.

'It pisses me off because they know I won't say anything. It's more than just John's job, he has his pride and the last thing I want to do is undermine that. Sometimes I want to shift back to the city just to get away from it all, but then you'd have to come with me... and besides, John and the kids would hate it,' she looked across at her friend, 'you keep me sane Tilly, do you know that?'

'Ditto Fi.' She wondered if she should tell her about Sam's message, but decided to call John later. 'Oh, and I won't need to leave Em with you tomorrow, after all.'

Fiona's focus shifted to her friend, 'why, what's happened? Is Jeff okay?'

'Yeah, everything's fine, well I suppose it is. I haven't heard from him. It's just that Mum and Dad have cut their trip short and are coming home Saturday. God I'm booked in to get my legs waxed this afternoon, hair and nails tomorrow. I wanted to make it special.'

'You can still make it special, just not in your own home. Book a suite in the city, set Em up with her own room complete with TV etc. Improvise, girl. How do you think John and I ended up with four kids? It didn't always happen when we were home alone.'

'You reckon?' Tilly looked past her friend to the road leading into town, hoping to see Jeff's car come around the bend.

'What are you two talking about,' John asked as he came around the corner of the building, posing the question but not expecting an answer, 'I was just on my way to the hospital when I saw you two out here, sunning yourselves and drinking coffee,' he kissed his wife, 'just thought I'd let you know I won't be home for lunch, love. After this I'm off to Port Augusta, should be home a bit after six.'

Joe fidgeted, he had plenty of room and the seat was comfortable, but he felt uneasiness wash through him. Since his heart-attack in the glider last year, flying was different. He worked hard to suppress his fear, speaking little. Logic told him he had nothing to worry about, but that was little comfort.

'God Joe, you nearly elbowed me then, what are you doing?'

'Looking for my iPad, I want to watch a few of those TED talks Bill up-loaded for me.'

'You can't use it until we're airborne. Just settle down will you? I don't want us thrown off the flight before we've even started.'

'Got it.' He dragged his bag onto his knees and after scrambling around, waved the device so she could see it.

'Kick that bag back under the seat, Christ Joe, just relax. I know flying makes you jumpy,' she rummaged around in her handbag, 'here take a Valium,' she went to pass him the tablet when he leant down to fish around under the seat again, 'what are you looking for now?'

'My water bottle.'

'Here, have mine,' she reached forward, grabbed the bottle from her seat pocket and thrust it at him, 'seriously Joe, how can a tough, sensible man like you get so agitated when you have to fly? You have to pull it together, because we've got a few more take offs and landings before we get home.'

'I know, but doesn't mean I like it.'

'It damn well better be. Everyone's looking at us.'

'Let them.' He swallowed the pill, handed back the water bottle and lay back with his eyes closed.

'Just sit there and count to ten thousand, and Joe, do it by ones, believe me, we'll all be better for it.'

He pulled a face and slumped deeper in his seat. Laura may be right, but she had no idea of the demons that hid among the caves of his memory. Sometimes sleep only made them more real. He prayed the Valium would help.

Laura opened her book and began to read and five minutes later the plane began to move. She looked across to her husband, his head leaning to one side, mouth open and breathing in a soft snore.

'Sleep well my love.'

CHAPTER THIRTY TWO

Gino paced his office. Twenty-four hours had passed and neither Sam nor Spoggy had answered any of his calls. He dialled Spoggy's landline and was halfway through before remembering it had been disconnected months before. He wondered where his spy could be. He had asked him to give Sam a scare and nothing more, but now he thought of it, the idiot had probably gone too far. Gino's mind wondered just how much he had hurt her? Or was it worse and Spoggy had fled the scene? A million possibilities went through his mind as he fought to bring his confusion under control.

He told one of the secretaries to keep trying Sam's phone and only disturb him if either she or Timothy found their missing CEO. He needed a clear mind to put everything into a logical order and shut his office door, closed the blinds and meditated.

Timothy finished answering e-mails and began entering the day's data, not a job he enjoyed, but he knew everything needed to be up to date when Sam came into the office. He had tried her phone several times, but it diverted to message on each occasion. He clicked into office diary of the company's internal e-mail system to find her journal hadn't changed. Deciding she might still be in the bush with her phone either flat or out of range, he didn't understand Gino's urgency to find her. She had often been away from the office for extended periods. He sent another email and followed it with a text message to her phone, knowing it paid to keep Gino on side. His curiosity increased and he wondered if she had accessed her files and put in a call to the systems technician. Someone had used her access code and been online for most of last night and there been another entry for an hour that morning. He left his desk and knocked on Gino's now open door.

Gino stood at the walked to window looking down on the traffic struggling along King William Street. He spoke without turning around. 'Well?'

Timothy hated talking to anybody's back, but sometimes with Gino, it was preferable. 'Sam has accessed the database.

'And you checked that the IP address was hers?'

'Yes, or someone using her password.'

Gino remained silent.

Timothy expected an explosion but there was no reaction. 'I'll keep a copy of everything she's looking at then?'

Gino still said nothing.

'And I'll check for any patterns, you know, try to analyse her research and keep you updated on my progress, will I?'

Gino remained quiet. Timothy bowed, an unconscious gesture and berated himself under his breath for it. Then backed out of the door closing it behind him.

Gino smiled, Sam was working on something and soon, eager to please, Timothy would find out what it was and why.

***

Sam had left the tap running through her sample for most of the night and in the morning, spread it onto a wad of tissue paper to dry. Unable to keep her curiosity in check, she pored over the fine gravel for traces of gold or gemstones. It looked like dolomite, agate and dirt. Maybe one of the bigger mud stones held a secret, but she needed something heavy to pulverise it. Phoning room service she had the kitchen deliver a mortar and pestle to her door. It could handle the mudstones, but the quartz would need to wait.

An hour of pounding and grinding yielded a small sample of hard stones and dirt. She washed it out as before, spread it on tissue and left it to dry near the window. However, the sparkle coming from a red stone was enough to make her reconsider the need of a temp, and picking up the phone Sam cancelled. This was a task only she could do.

Back at her laptop, she saw the data she had downloaded provided a complete history of her company's exploration of the area around the Gillespie land. Her next task was to research old mining records and newspaper cuttings from the area's first settlement,

Before making a start, the clothes she had ordered from one of the hotel's boutiques last night arrived. Soon she had changed into a crisp shirt and slacks, ready to get down to business

Picking up and scanning a report, she wondered why Charles was so determined to search for gold in what everyone considered a mineral wasteland, crossing to the window to study the stones. A red shaft of light reflected along the tissue's edge. At least one stone had promise, but it was smaller than a poppy seed, the rest of it was plain dirt.

For the next hour, she gathered data to support her findings and set them into separate files, each of which would need an executive summary and bibliography. The summary she could dictate, but the tedium of supporting documents was hers to create. She set a target to complete them with the promised reward of a good lunch if she achieved it. A tomato sandwich would do if she missed.

***

Timothy tried Sam's mobile phone every twenty minutes, with no success. He didn't care much for his boss, but her absence worried him so he phoned all of the drill teams. They reported seeing her earlier in the week, when she had gone out to the farm with the Gillespie woman. He prompted them for any small-town gossip that could connect to her disappearance, but the only rumour in the town was about a couple of Asians beating up a bloke while he was fossicking.

Not wanting to disturb Gino without something concrete to report, he opened his private phone and trawled social media for anything unusual that might have been posted by someone in Orroroo. Plenty of chat about the fossicker, sport and other gossip, but there was nothing about Sam. He was about to give up when he caught sight of a picture taken inside a pub. One of the locals had taken a selfie, the foreground was grainy, but in the background, he could see Gino and Sam and neither looked happy.

He traced the post back to local woman who owned the account and the bloke with the woman in the picture was tagged to Liam Le-Strange. Strange was right, the photo was way out of focus, but the background clear, almost as if the foreground had been unimportant. He copied the photo, sent it to his home computer, deleted the file and wondered why Gino hadn't mentioned he had seen Sam that night.

The Facebook photo nagged at Timothy and his curiosity drove him back to it. He opened the profile page, noting the woman was full of chat but that Le-Strange had no social media sites. While Timothy searched, he checked Sam's Facebook and Twitter accounts. She had posted nothing all week.

He struggled with his conscience for the rest of the day. He understood Gino's ambitions and how determined the man was to achieve them. Would it be wise to tell him about the photo? He decided it might be more prudent to wait for Gino to let everyone know he had been with Sam in Orroroo that night.

An internal memo from Gino flashed on his screen. He was concerned about the company's security in case someone had stolen Sam's computer and had instructed the data technicians to disable her access until she called in. It reinforced Timothy's decision to hide what he knew. Gino knew more about Sam's disappearance than he was letting on.

A check of his missing CEO's company credit card showed a petrol purchase two days ago in Orroroo, a meal for two and the accommodation account. Nothing since. He checked with the car hire company who told him the vehicle had been returned to the airport over twenty-four hours, ago. Had she gone interstate or somewhere else? He now became concerned for her, but still didn't dare ask Gino and knew he couldn't go to Charles. Gino would not like that.

Timothy didn't notice Gino standing at the front of his desk until the man coughed just loud enough to startle him and he pushed his chair back and sprung to his feet in reflex.

'Zip around to the Department of Ag, they have an envelope waiting and drop this one into a letterbox on your way.' Gino said.

'Sure, I'll just close down,' he was sure Gino had something planned and felt disloyal to Sam, but this was business and he had to put his own career first, 'I checked with the rental company and someone returned her hire car yesterday afternoon.'

'Did they say if it was her?'

'They couldn't say. It had been left in the express return park. No-one saw it come back, but it checked it in at...' he looked at his desk pad, 'four o'clock.'

'She must be somewhere. If she's not in by morning, we'd better report it to the police. Anything on her credit cards?'

'I checked the statement at three o'clock and there's nothing. I've been trying her phone all day and it just says it's off or out of range. So, I figure it's flat. Have you tried her at all?' Timothy ran a hand over his head, sure Gino would see perspiration beading on his polished scalp.

'No, here,' he handed him an envelope, 'slip out and get that package and on your way, I want you post this into a box on the street. Don't just put into our system, got me?' Gino tapped his nose in a gesture Timothy understood, 'I'll update Charles on the car.'

'Nice afternoon for a walk,' Timothy took the post, 'I'll see you when I get back.'

'Don't dawdle, that's all, I need that package like yesterday.'

CHAPTER THIRTY THREE

At six thirty on the second day of her self-imposed exile, Sam woke as room service knocked at her door and dragged herself from bed. Feeling gluggy without her regular exercise she avoided a heavy breakfast, picking at a poached egg and half a piece of toast. Her mother would have chastised her for wasting food and she wondered why she couldn't have been the daughter they wanted. She could have married a local farm boy and had a tribe of kids by now, but it was a thought that sent a shudder through her. She had wanted to prove she was every bit as good as those girls who had teased her at school. They might have come from old money, but none of them had made it out of the sticks into the land of big business.

Still groggy from spending most of the night working on her presentation, she showered to sharpen her focus and was ready to start the day when the alarm buzzed at seven.

Less than three blocks away, Gino looked at his watch. It was seven thirty and Charles was already moving about his office. He thought about going in when Charles walked through the door and sat in a chair across from him. 'Problems in the Parliament'

'You sound pleased?' Gino held a straight face.

Charles threw the Advertiser onto the desk. Gino read the headline. MINISTER DENIES EVERYTHING and a photo of Andreas Pituri with what appeared to be a naked woman in his arms filled the front page.

'The pedantic little prick will have to go now. I wonder how deep someone had to dig to find this little lot,' he winked at Gino. It was hard to suppress his joy,' have you read it?'

Gino shook his head.

In a rare moment, Charles let the shabby status of his upbringing show. 'Boom, adios and goodbye to the bible bashing bastard, I say. I'm tipping his colleagues will skin him alive today,' he pushed his chair back, walked around to the other side of the desk and clapped Gino on the shoulder, 'shit, I wish I could be fly on the wall in there today, mate. The party room will be all over him.'

Gino noticed his change of tone, but let Charles revel in the minister's problems for a few minutes. He turned the paper to study the headline and smiled. Charles, almost dancing, paced the room.

'Wait for question time, the opposition will be all over this once they smell blood on the floor,' Gino said.

'As long as the government pushes him out of the mines portfolio, I don't care. I haven't even thought about who I'd like to see them shuffle into the job though. I hope it's someone we can rely on,' Charles said, 'what about you? Have you any thoughts about a suitable candidate?'

Gino stared at the paper and tapped the headline with his finger, 'I'd like to see the Police Minister take it.' There was no emotion in his voice.

Charles spun from the window, put an arm around Gino's shoulders and shook him. 'Jack Pendlebury,' he laughed, 'not your mate from agriculture?'

He shook his head, took the paper and passed it back to Charles. 'He's too much of a loose cannon, can't be trusted. Pendlebury is my pick,' he made a folding motion with his hands, 'and we do know he's ambitious.'

'You're a bloody legend,' Charles bent closer, 'can we make it a project?'

'Wheels are turning.' Gino waved for Charles to sit down again and waited for his boss to finish gloating before pushing a file in front of him.

'What's this?' Charles sat it on top of the newspaper and flicked through the paperwork.

Gino waited until he finished reading. 'As I promised, today we have a contract to establish contamination levels on the affected areas of the Gillespie property,' he let the statement hang between them, 'of course, it'll require a lot of drilling to understand just how deep that poison has reached,' he looked at his boss knowingly, 'lots and lots of test holes and, if we find something else, it would be a tragedy to discard anything without full and proper investigation.' He fought to keep his smirk from showing.

'And irresponsible, too,' Charles was excited, 'how soon before you can get us out there?'

'I've authorised a couple of our drilling teams to be ready to move by Monday. Once papers have been served on the Gillespies, it's hello Joe and off to work we go.'

Charles had no doubt that Gino had paid someone off, his man Gino had a penchant for dirty tricks

'Right, well I'd better get organised to meet with our investors in Sydney,' he stopped in the doorway and looked toward Sam's office, 'have you heard from her?'

'I half expected she'd come in with you,' Gino needed to think, what if Spoggy had gone a bit too far. Sure, he had told him to frighten her, but as neither had replied to his calls there were too many loose ends. He was beginning to wonder if Spoggy dropped Sam's hire car off as a cover up. A million different scenarios had played in his mind, but he was not about to share them. 'I asked Timothy to follow it up and he said he'd checked with the rental company, all they could tell him was that her car was in the fast-return bay at the airport, somewhere around mid-afternoon yesterday.'

'Keep looking. She can't be far away. I suppose you've checked the security at her unit.'

Gino nodded.

'And she didn't book a flight anywhere?' Charles asked, staring out onto the street as if to conjure her appearance.

'Not on the company account.'

Charles heard Gino's dismissive tone, but said nothing. 'Try her mother, she could've gone home. And check to see if her Mazda's parked at the unit.'

'Gino tapped an icon on his phone. 'The Mazda's still where it's been for the last month.'

Charles looked at the screen and waved it away. 'I don't know why she bought the bloody thing when she never uses it.'

Gino nodded again and turned to face his boss, 'I'll get Timothy onto it again later,' he pushed the folder into Charles' hand, 'now that I've delivered what Sam couldn't. How soon before I start my new role?' He stepped back and watched blood pressure turn Charles' face red.

'Jesus Gino, just let me enjoy today's headlines will you. If Sam hasn't made contact with the office by this afternoon, let the police know she's missing, but for Christ's sake, be discreet. I don't want the world to know we don't know where our CEO is.'

'Okay, I've already put a few contingencies into place in case she doesn't show up.'

'You're a callous bastard, Gino.' He pictured them as kids, Gino tying strings of fireworks onto the tail of neighbourhood cats, before lighting them.

'Look if she hasn't reported in by this afternoon, you'd better assume her role,' Charles said, 'and before you ask, if she's not here before Monday, you can change the sign on her door. If you don't want to keep Timothy, let him go and find another PA for the position.'

Charles strolled through to his office, reached his desk, turned and walked back Gino's office again. 'You don't have any idea how that headline hit the paper today I suppose?'

Gino turned his palms up, 'sorry boss, I know nothing.'

'Yeah, of course you don't.'

'About the PA,' Gino pointed to the outer offices and toward Timothy's desk, 'I'll keep Timothy. He's got a good handle on what Sam was up too, but it still surprises me that you haven't heard from her?'

'Check the gossip among the drillers, they'll have had a blowout at one or both of the Orroroo pubs last night. Find out if they've seen her, or maybe she told them what she was up to. I'm in Sydney tonight, so I'll leave you a message on the internal mail with the time to call me. If you haven't heard from her by tonight, phone the local copper and get him onto it. I'm not ready for us to call in any favours from this end just yet.'

'So if or when she turns up, you'll let her know she's finished?'

'Just find her.'

***

Joe stretched, his hand knocking Laura as he did. 'Sorry old girl, I forgot where we were for a minute.'

'Mmm, I must have dropped off too,' she looked at her watch, 'we've been in the air for over six hours. How did you sleep?'

'Not bad.'

'So the Valium helped?'

'Must have. I slept better than I have for a long time,' he raised the blind, saw the darkness outside and pulled it down again 'tell you what though, I did have a dream.'

'Okay Martin Luther King... what kind of dream?'

'Oh, you know, one where the sun shines all day and it only rains at night.'

'That's Camelot, you idiot. No, come on what do you mean you had a dream?' She shuffled around to face him.

'Just before you woke up, I had enough time to go over a few things in my mind. Before we left, Brad Reardon bailed me up and asked if we'd be interested in taking the garage on.'

'What, buy him out, why?'

'Hold on... anyway, I asked him why and how much he'd want. The price seems fair for both the business and the buildings. He said we could pay off the stock as we sold it. Brad reckoned he and Karen were tired and looking for a change.'

'Why didn't you tell me at the time?'

'I thought nothing of it at the time and besides, we'd planned this trip,' he pulled the flight magazine from the seat pocket and thumbed through it. He knew it would annoy her, but it gave him time to organise his thoughts. He put it back and faced her again, 'anyway, I said I wouldn't discuss it with you until we came home. Look, after spending the last few days with Bill I've been thinking about the prices these Poms are paying for gear like that old stuff we've got in the barn. That and other bits and pieces stashed about the place. I reckon we should look into it a bit more. There might be a dollar or two to be made.'

'When I suggested cleaning the barn out, you said it was all rubbish and ready for the tip. Now you're turning everything around, why?' Laura saw the flight attendant coming, sat back in her seat and dropped her tray table, 'and taking on Reardon's clapped out business too. Joe, what the hell are you thinking?'

'Steady on Love, I haven't committed to anything yet.'

'Well if Brad can't make it work, what makes you think we can?' She grabbed his shoulder to turn him back so he could see her.

'We'd do things differently. Brad said carrying staff and bad debtors through the drought has cleaned them out, financially and emotionally. They just want a change. Think about it, Love. He's worked his arse off for all those years and they've got nothing much to show for it. Said he'd never been able to put away the superannuation his accountant advised. Apart from the business, the house is all they have.'

'So, tell me how would it be any different for us?'

'We'd change the business model. Focus more on restoration than repair. Be a new challenge for us, Love.'

His eyes had a spark she hadn't seen for a while.

'Yeah, and I can just see you working as a blacksmith too. What about Tilly?'

'Easy, Tilly can take over the farm, it's her time now.'

'Have you stopped to think about what she might want, have you even asked her?'

'Well, she's stepped in with the farming and the renovations and all, I just thought...'

'Don't just expect her just to do what you want, Joe Gillespie. There's Jeff to consider too,' she thought of her daughter's joy when Jeff had proposed, 'and now a wedding to plan for.'

'Yeah, I know, love, but...' Joe was confused, lately Laura was always telling him to be more positive, now she was reining him in, 'how about, we think it over for a while and run it past Tilly when we get home.'

'Yes... and if she doesn't want the farm we'll sell it,' she ignored his look of dismay and continued, 'then we could move into town and take on Brad's place. Lot of work though?'

'Yeah, and there's this too.' He fished around in his shirt pocket for the piece of paper that was beginning to fall apart from over-handling, 'it's all I've thought about while we've been over here.'

'Tell me about it.' Laura looked up at the flight attendant. 'You've been miles away at times. If I didn't know better, I'd think it was another woman.'

'Another woman,' Joe screwed his face up, 'One's enough for me.'

She smiled at the double meaning, leaning back for the attendant to reach his cup. 'You keep this up and I might get to like this new, non-brooding Joe.'

'Aah, just drink your coffee.' He wanted to tell her about fainting and his trip to accident and emergency, but that was a discussion too difficult to face at thirty eight thousand feet.

CHAPTER THIRTY FOUR

Jeff walked in from the balcony of their hotel suite, turned and looked back over the Adelaide skyline. He thought about the contrast it had to the skies he had seen during his last week sleeping in the outback, yet even here, he felt the pull of his ancestral stars. Tilly had set two wine glasses on the counter while he took the chilled wine from the fridge and with Emily settled and asleep in her own room the night was theirs. Romance and family life made an amazing fit.

The digital display on the bedside clock glowed 2.45 am. Jeff turned and patted the bedclothes searching for Tilly, but he was alone in the bed. He rolled up onto his elbow and looked toward the balcony window to see her silhouetted against the glow from the city lights. Sensing his eyes on her, she turned and came back to him, crawling along the foot of the bed and into his arms.

What were you doing?' He asked.

'Thinking.'

'About what?'

'About another time, another city and how I thought nothing like this would happen for me.'

'Nothing like what?'

'This,' she stroked her fingers through his chest hair, 'having someone to love me.'

He pulled her toward him and kissed her. 'You have me forever, Tilly. Forever, understand?' He felt her head on his shoulder and the warmth of her breath against his ear. 'I'd do anything for you, all you have to do is ask, okay?

'Okay.'

It was barely daylight when Emily loomed at her mother's side. Tugging at the blankets and reminding her she had promised they would go to the Pancake Parlour for breakfast. 'It's almost seven o'clock and you haven't even had a shower yet. Granny and Pop will be here soon and Pop said they had presents.'

'Okay miss, you go into the other room and watch TV while we get ready. Have you packed everything?'

Emily nodded.

'Cleaned your teeth?'

'After breakfast, you always say.'

'That's at home, now go into your bathroom and clean your teeth, we'll be as fast as we can, okay?'

'Okay.'

Tilly closed the door behind her and dragged Jeff out of bed. 'Come on, it's family time,'

***

Sam stretched in bed and looked at the clock. The big push yesterday had the presentation completed by ten o'clock last night. All she had to do today was get it printed at the Officeworks down the road and she was done.

She had been in the suite for nearly forty-eight hours and was desperate for fresh air and exercise. After a shower and running a couple of circuits of the parklands, she was beginning to feel like her old self again and, dawdling over a late breakfast, her thoughts drifted to Gino. If he wanted to intimidate her out of the job, let him try. This report showed the only likely area for a commercial gold find was along the Nackara Fault and the most probable site was around the old mining town of Waukaringa where prospectors had been picking over the place for years. Even then it would be expensive.

She proposed RADOR shift its focus to the Northern Territory, where it had a better chance for success and her research demonstrated willingness by the Territory's government to offer subsidies and funding for both exploration and mine development. A call to the Chief Minister indicated there were employment subsidies available for local and indigenous workers. Because the population was already there, her budget forecasts proved this model was more efficient than employing Fly-in Fly-out labour.

The budget allowed for a contract drilling team to test the area around an old platinum mine at Rum Jungle. RADOR's parent company, Wagmin Resources already owned the leases, but more work was needed to determine if a new mine was viable. Sam proposed a modern open cut process using large machinery but, before she could make it profitable, a thorough geological survey was required. Everything was cross-referenced in her forecasts. She had identified a market for fine by-products from the crushing plant for use as road-base. There was enough dolomite in the overburden that, once separated out, would be diverted to a cement plant. Wagmin already owned a cement plant it had inherited as part of a mining deal less than a year ago, only to mothball it months later. Transferring the plant to the mine precinct made sense, and government subsidies for rail freight and harbour charges to carry the excess south made it extremely profitable. Everything was in there and, apart from the lack of sales rhetoric, this report was a prospectus.

She knew Charles would have to go for it, the proposal was a winner. As she squared the edges of three hundred and fifty-seven pages into a neat pile, she felt her confidence rise another notch.

***

Gino had ignored Charles' directive to advise the Orroroo police about Sam's disappearance. After the altercation with her in the pub and Spoggy not answering his phone, it could wait a few days. He always liked to know the answer to every question he asked and with this, he needed to do a bit more digging first.

Most Saturdays the smell of coffee and croissants drew him to Cafe Caparezza. Today was no different, and he took his usual table near the window where he could watch the passing parade and read the paper without being disturbed. The headline above the picture of the Minister for Agriculture taking a briefcase from a man with his back turned pleased him. Just looking at the picture would make any reader question if the minister was on the take. His plan to move Jack Pendlebury into the mines portfolio was working. First it was Andreas Pituri in trouble and now Hans Schmidt. The Premier would have to announce a new cabinet soon and if the lobbyists on Gino's payroll did their job over the weekend, by Monday night his plan would be complete. Gino knew the thrust of the story he had leaked, but read the article anyway. His plans to usurp Charles were progressing and he only had a few more tricks to pull before his ambition would be realised. He sipped his coffee and watched Adelaide's morning drift past.

***

Spoggy, unhappy with John O'Rourke's directive to remain in town, had other plans. He knew the policeman coached the Orroroo Junior Colts football team and that they were playing in Jamestown today so time was on his side. Once out of hospital, he grabbed only the things he needed from the farmhouse and started on his plans to disappear.

Taking the Jamestown road would be too big of a risk, so he hoped the engine in his old ute would hold up until he could change to the Commodore he kept at Brahma Lodge. However, once he was on the move, the ute's engine felt strong and he need not have worried. Closer to Adelaide the Falcon could blend in to the traffic, but until then he would backtrack to Crystal Brook where he could pick up Highway One. The timing was right for Liam Le-Strange to come back to life again.

Near Snowtown he saw a dead pig on the side of the road and it gave him an idea and Spoggy could disappear for good. At Port Wakefield, he bought a bus ticket to Adelaide. It might take a day or two longer than he intended, but the time was right for Spoggy to die. He thought about relationships, the casual friends he had made using this identity. Would they miss him? He supposed not, he had destroyed most relationships out of fear of attachment and as Liam Le-Strange, he could begin a new life.

***

Sam stood at the print counter at Officeworks looking at the freshly bound report as she held her hand out for the flash-drive, pleased with the result. Sitting at a table in the coffee shop next door she flicked through the proposal. It covered every detail and although it looked good, something wasn't right and she couldn't pinpoint what it was. She had a strong urge to split the report into two, to hold onto the Rum Jungle proposal until Charles had time to study the Gillespie report.

She walked back to the hotel and started rewriting everything. It was pure folly pursuing the Gillespie's for the exploration and mining rights to their land when there was nothing   there.

CHAPTER THIRTY FIVE

Joe and Laura landed in Sydney to find their connection to Adelaide delayed by twenty minutes. Grateful for the delay, Laura took time to freshen up and change her clothes while Joe had a shave. She emerged from the ladies' room as their flight was called.

'God woman I don't know how you do it, you went in there with one bag and come out with four. How did that happen?'

'Talent Joe, talent,' she held two bags out, 'you take these. One's Tilly's and the other one's for Jeff.'

'And you get to spoil Emily.'

'That's the plan.'

They were home and pleased to be here.

**

Emily's agitation was beginning to wear her mother's patience. Tilly had shown her the signs displaying arrival times and flight numbers and Emily kept walking between the terminal gate window and the arrival time's screen and asking what the time was now.

'Em, you can tell time. Try and work it out for yourself.'

'C'mon kiddo, how about I get you a donut and your mum and me a coffee. That should make the time go a bit quicker,' Jeff sensed Emily's excitement was tiresome and, putting his hand out for her to take, they walked toward Hudson's Coffee. Tilly watched them go. Emily sounded like a machine gun, firing questions at him as they went. Jeff liked this new-found role as a father and felt warmed by the trust Emily showed in him. Two flight attendants strolled past and heard them whisper something about it being

215

lovely to see a dad with his daughter. He smiled, his day complete.

Emily sat behind her hot chocolate and iced donut, eyes darting between the gate lounge door and the window. Traces of chocolate icing ringed her mouth and a few wipes of her tongue were required to remove a frothy moustache. She had pressed against the window, watching the airport staff position the aerobridge against the fuselage. Soon people began filling the area to wait for the arrivals and now back with her mother, then seeing the doors open yelled, 'they're here.' As she burst out of her chair, Jeff caught her plastic cup as it rocked a couple of times, when he looked up she was at the barrier.

All Tilly could see was a bit of chocolate remaining on Emily's lip. She pulled a couple of wet-wipes from her bag and walking over to her daughter said, 'what am I going to do with you Em, and what will Pop and Granny think if they see you like this?'

'Granny'll be so happy to see us she won't notice and Pop, he'll touch it with his finger, lick it, and ask me where he can get some,' she screwed her face up as Tilly scrubbed at the offending substance, 'anyway, they'll be too busy telling us about their trip to worry about a bit of chocolate.'

'Come on Em, stop babbling and let me look at you,' she held her daughter at arm's length, bending down to look at her, 'and... you've got a spot on your new dress too,' she pulled at the hem and did her best to remove the stain, searching for another clean wipe before giving up, 'okay, that'll have to do.'

Jeff winked, 'can't see anything, can you, Em?'

'God, don't encourage her, it was your big idea to get her a donut.'

Jeff held his hand out, when Tilly took it he pulled her toward him, his other arm was around Emily. They were watching the line of passengers filing into the lounge. He saw Joe in the crowd and nodded, while Emily, who hadn't seen them yet stared into a hundred strange faces, searching the line of people disembarking to find them.

'Well who have we got here then?' Emily spun out of Jeff's grip, 'Granny.'

Laura's arms extended with a bag in each hand, but Emily ignored them, launching herself at her grandmother and melting into her hug.

Jeff stepped back as Tilly hugged her father. She felt strength in his embrace, as every time before. He was good old reliable Dad.

Laura walked over and embraced Jeff, holding him for longer than he expected, evoking memories of his mother holding him in a similar way. Then Joe grabbed his hand and shaking it drew him into a hug too, his feeling of family was now complete.

'Let's go somewhere to sit down so I can watch you open your presents,' Laura said and shook a large carrier bag in front of Emily, 'then after we've picked up our luggage, you can tell me about everything that's happened while we were gone.'

'There's a McDonalds here. I vote for Macca's,' Emily said, 'we can have lunch there too.'

'Me too,' said Joe. 'I'm famished.'

Emily prattled, firing questions at her grandparents until they reached McDonalds where they watched Emily fill the space with wrapping paper and sucked in a few deep breaths. It was good to be home.

Once out of the airport and on their way, Laura sat in the back of the car with Emily between her and Tilly. Joe took the passenger seat while Jeff drove. Tilly understood her parents would be feeling drained from their flight and brushed away their questions about the farm. Instead she asked her mother about Elspeth and Bill, while Joe told Jeff about the different aircraft Bill had shown him. The trip had energised him and he felt more alive now than he had since the trouble of past year. It felt good to have Jeff around too, to have someone in the family with whom he could share bloke's stuff.

Thirty minutes into the drive home Joe leaned back almost mid-sentence and began to snore. The girls in the back didn't last much longer and Jeff was on his own, surrounded by family. He fell into contentment as the big car gathered up the miles.

CHAPTER THIRTY SIX

Scrolling through the list of callers on her phone. Sam hoped for anything other than company related calls, but the bulk of them were from Timothy. She dialled the voicemail on her home phone, nobody had called or left a message other than the people she worked with. Everyone wanted the same thing, where was she and when would she be in the office. Every call was work related, there were no personal calls.

What was wrong with her? She was witty, sociable and loved a party but couldn't remember the last time she went out for fun. For the last seven years, all she had done was work, climbing the rungs of the corporate ladder had taken up all her time. She had put aside parties, wedding invitations, or chances for a girl's night out in her quest for success and the cost had been her personal life. Even Charles had only left business related messages, his last one in an angry tone. Something had to change. Yes, she was running an exploration and mining company and yes, she was important, but there had to be someone who liked her for more than just her business skills.

The more she thought about it the more she wanted to call Jake. He was funny and didn't seem to take himself too seriously. She needed to buy a phone Gino and Charles would not know about. This would fill in some time and she could copy over any numbers she wanted from the contact list in the company iPad. Even that was a sad reflection as the only numbers she had were those of her family and Jake's.

She found a phone shop in the Mall and made her choice, it took another half an hour to organise the settings and enter the contacts then she called Jake's number, only to hear a message from his end. 'You've called Mr Jake. If it's to do with work leave your number. If it's personal, leave a message, either way I'll get back to you as soon as I can.'

Sam pressed the stop key, deciding to try again later. She was so desperate for company she was even tempted to call Charles. He might be a self-centred arse, but he could be great company when he wanted to be. But all he ever wanted was her body and thought he owned her.

Thinking about Charles and the way he manipulated her made her feel dirty, the plaything of a powerful man, forgetting for the moment she had allowed the situation to develop. She changed into her gym clothes and went down to the basement gym, running on the treadmill and a few reps on the gym equipment would stop her feeling sorry for herself.

She enjoyed the wine that came with her room service dinner so much that she ordered another bottle. The effect of the alcohol was beginning to numb her senses and she wanted the feeling to last. Halfway into the second bottle she decided to call her mother to tell her about the new phone number, to have a chat about everything and nothing, the discussion she never had time for. She tapped in the farm's number onto the screen and waited.

'Hi you've called the Lewis's, we can't come to the phone right now, so if you leave your name, number and a brief message and we'll call back.'

Her mother's voice was always cheery and full of life. This, and the wine she had drunk loosened her emotions and she thought the family would be together at the pub or football clubrooms. Everyone would be there, except her. It had been so long since she had joined them for a Saturday night out they probably didn't even miss her, maybe they no longer even thought of her. She flopped onto her pillow and let self-pity dominate

Not wanting to disturb her parents after their long flight, Tilly suggested she and Jeff should distract Emily and spend Sunday away from town. They could call on Jeff's dad, take him out for lunch and drive across to Port Augusta. It would be an opportunity to catch up with Jeff's friends from the gliding club and if the club's two-seater was free, maybe Jeff could take Emily for a few circuits.

'That sounds like a plan. I'll call Andy and see if I can book the old Cirrus for the afternoon,' he smiled with his voice, 'Dad might even come over with us, would that be okay with you?'

'Yeah why not, we can make a day of it. Would he be interested in a picnic? We can stop off the road somewhere, boil the billy and all that.'

'He'd be in it in a flash,' Jeff looked at Emily, 'we might not be able to go gliding though?'

'That's okay, I can fly yours when I'm older,' she said.

Tilly put her arm around Emily's shoulders. 'I suppose we need to think about what you're going to call Jeff's dad, Em. I think he'll get sick of hearing you say Mr Rankin all the time.'

'What do you think I should I call him, Jeff?'

'Well I think he already sees you as his granddaughter so if Joe's Pop, how about Grandpa?'

'Yeah, but I like Pa better. It's easier to say.'

'Okay, we'll try Pa out on him tomorrow, he'll soon let us know if he doesn't like it,' Jeff kissed Tilly on the cheek, 'I'll leave you two with the dinner dishes and give Andy and Dad a call.'

'A woman's work is never done, is it Em?'

Emily looked at Jeff and rolled her eyes. 'Never...'

Ted Rankin was waiting at his gate when the family arrived, his grin as broad as the brim on his old Akubra. He opened the back door for Emily. 'I've got a surprise to show you, Squirt.'

'G'day Dad,' Jeff reached out a hand.

Ted took his hand and drew him into a hug, 'good to see you son.'

Tilly stood to one side and waited. Ted patted his son's shoulder a couple of times then broke his embrace to greet Tilly, 'nice to see you, Tilly,' he put his arms out and she took the offer of his hug, surprised at the ease of it, 'Joe and Laura get home okay?'

'Yeah, they're probably a bit weary from the flight, but they'll be fine and Dad looked happy to be home. I'm a bit surprised Mum managed to keep him away this long.'

'I'll bet he is. It'd be too far away for me.'

Emily tugged at his arm, 'you said you had a surprise Pa?'

Ted's eyes seemed to sparkle more and he looked at Jeff, who mouthed the words, 'her idea...'

Ted tipped his hat, 'well come this way,' he said and led them toward the stable.

Jeff dragged a roll of wire a bit further away from the path and stood it against the wall. A cat rubbed against Tilly's boot and began to purr, she noticed it was lactating. A kitten was the last thing she wanted Ted to give Emily and wondered how to tell him her daughter couldn't take one home.

She was relieved when they walked past the cat toward the stables and Ted took Emily's hand and put an apple into her palm saying, 'come and meet Gidget, and if you hold your hand flat she'll take the apple with her lips.'

Tilly breathed a sigh of relief, cats didn't eat apples.

'Because if I hold it in my fingers, she could bite them,' Emily said.

'Too right, she can smell the apple, but can't see your fingers very well, this way she'll feel for the apple with her lips.'

'New horse, Dad, but a bit on the small side for you, I reckon.'

'She's lovely,' Tilly said, 'looks nice and quiet too.'

'I thought, seeing as I have a granddaughter now, maybe I could take her riding sometimes,' he looked at Tilly, 'that's if your mum says it's okay, young lady.'

'Dad, you should have asked Tilly first,' Jeff said.

Ted shrugged, 'sorry, Tilly, I'm just so thrilled to share a grandchild.'

'It's fine, for a moment there, I thought you might have been giving her a kitten. That might have been a problem.' She laughed to soften her words, not thinking for the moment of the responsibility that came with a horse. She squatted and looked her daughter's eyes, 'what do you think, Em? Do you want to learn to ride?

'Yes please...' she continued to stroke the horse's head as she answered, enthralled.

Jeff had moved into Gidget's stall and was running his hand over her coat, he lifted a hoof and saw she was freshly shod. 'Can I lead her out into the sun so we can get a better look at her, Dad?'

'Sure.' Ted swung the stall door back and ushered the girls outside.

'You're a lovely girl,' Jeff said, as he slipped a bridle over her muzzle.

'How about we put a saddle on her, Emily?' Ted looked at Tilly, 'and if Mum says it's okay maybe we can lead her around the yard a couple of times?'

'What do you think Em?' she asked and without thinking Tilly reached down stroking the cat as it brushed against her leg.

Ted looked at Tilly and winked as he smiled, 'you can have a kitten too, if you want.'

Tilly looked at and mouthed, 'Oh, no you don't.'

'Well Em, should we find my old saddle? I'll bet Dad has it here somewhere,' Jeff walked the horse over to the stump Emily was standing on.

Gidget bent down and nuzzled the child looking for another apple.

'I'll get the saddle,' Ted offered.

'Don't go to any trouble, Ted,' Tilly said.

'I can do it bareback,' Emily said, 'like kids do on TV.'

'No trouble, Squirt. No trouble at all.'

Jeff tied the reins to the rail and left Emily talking to the horse. He put his arm around Tilly and kissed her cheek. 'I'll bet he's been keeping an eye out for a pony for Em from the moment we told him we were getting married. Look I know he can get under your skin, but he probably never thought I'd ever give him a grandchild and you've got to know he'll spoil her whenever he can.'

'I know, but look at Em, Jeff. She's fallen in love with Gidget already, damn it, I'm in love with Gidget,' Tilly said.

Ted carried a western saddle that looked new. 'Here we go, Squirt, now watch what I do, because one day you'll have to saddle her on your own.'

'New saddle, Dad?'

'I had some leather I'd been working years ago, found the makings for a saddle amongst some of my old droving gear and thought of Emily here,' he put an arm around her, 'it took a while, but I finished it last week. It should do until she's in her teens.' He put it on a rail for Emily to inspect.

'What do you say Em?' Tilly said.

'Thanks, Pa,' she picked up the billet strap and traced her finger around the embossing, then put it to her nose, 'it smells nice, just like Granny's car when it was new.'

'This all seems too much Ted,' Tilly rubbed Ted's shoulder, 'are you sure it's okay?'

Ted grinned and talked to Gidget, telling her what he was doing as he lifted the saddle onto her back. In a few quick moves he had everything secure. He turned to Tilly, 'I went over to Burra to look at some heifers the other day and the bloke selling them told me about his daughter going off to college. He didn't want to keep feeding a horse that wouldn't be ridden. Said he was thinking about sending her to the meatworks at Peterborough,' Ted looked at Emily and shortened the stirrup length, 'he told me if I took the cattle at his price, I could have the horse too. Well, as Jeff knows. I'm a bit of a softy when it comes to ponies and I knew a young lady who I reckoned would love her.'

He tapped the stirrup strap and Emily reached for the saddle horn and lifted her foot into the stirrup. Ted boosted her up onto the saddle. 'Now, if it's okay with Mum. I can keep Gidget here and whenever she can spare you we'll go riding. But not until you've groomed her and cleaned out the stall. Deal?' He put his hand up.

Emily bent completed the hi five, 'deal.'

'You shouldn't spoil her,' Tilly said, 'she'll expect it all the time.'

'Squirt, or the horse?' Ted looked at Jeff.

Tilly smiled at her future father in law, 'both I guess.'

After Jeff had led Gidget and Emily for a few of circuits around the horse yard, Tilly suggested they get moving. Emily wanted to stay with the horse and Ted, but after a few pouts she agreed.

'See ya Gidget,' Emily said, laying along the horse's mane to hug her. 'And thanks Pa, I love her.'

'She seems to like you too,' he smiled at Tilly, 'come over again soon okay?'

'We'll be back before you know it,' Tilly said.

Deciding the little family could benefit from time spent together, he told them he had too much on to take time out to picnic and led Gidget with Emily still in the saddle to the car, where she let go the reins with reluctance. Watching the car go, he patted the horse's flank absentmindedly wondering how he'd ever got this lucky.

CHAPTER THIRTY SEVEN

Gino called Timothy into work on Saturday and by Sunday night they had drafted a new prospectus for Charles' approval. By scrolling through company archives, Timothy had found an executive summary Charles had drafted for an earlier document and never used. Financial statements and projections came the same way. He and Gino sourced data from thousands of draft proposals that failed to make it to the boardroom. Between them, they plundered whatever they needed from wherever they could. It might be bogus, but the result was a prospectus good enough to list RAYDOR on the stock exchange.

Charles would want to move within a few days. The only thing stopping him was the Gillespies, and Gino had a plan for getting past them too. If everything fell into place, drilling could start on the Gillespie's land as early as Monday. Even emails containing test site locations were in readiness to send to the teams. Gino set the report on Timothy's desk and tapped the cover with his index finger.

'We did it,' Gino placed his arm around his companion's shoulder, 'good work mate. That idea of yours, to use core sample reports from other explorations sites, was pure genius. I'll be sure to remind Charles how you cut and pasted them into the Gillespie's Pictinco leases. The document appears authentic.'

'Well, it was your idea, I just did as you suggested.'

'Credit where credit's due, that's why I insisted on naming you as author. Play your cards right and you could take over this place one day. Not even Charles wants to work forever,' he counted out ten bundles of fifty-dollar notes, 'there you go mate, should be enough for a day and a half's work. Now how about a selfie to record the beginning of the project?'

'Yeah, why not?' Timothy held the prospectus to his chest and Gino's rested an arm on his shoulder. They smiled at the screen and waited for the flash.

'Now jump behind the desk and fan the money out and hold up the prospectus, it'll be a fun shot. I take one of you and you do the same for me. When you retire, you'll look back on today as the start of your minerals fortune,' Gino assured him.

'Are you sure? What we've done is a bit suss?'

'Look everyone in our game does it. It's how you raise the capital to find the stuff you're looking for. Charlie knows there's gold there, anyway after a month this'll be superseded by a new prospectus and no-one'll be any the wiser,' he pointed to the money, 'you should stick that into shares. Ours or others, doesn't matter. Analysts will tell you it's better in the stock market than the bank.' Gino poked him in the ribs and laughed. 'Tell you what. After news gets out that we've fired Sam, the company share price will drop. Find a broker and put that cash into our company. You'll make up to ten percent in the next morning's trade.'

'You reckon ASIC won't twig?'

'Nah, get it in and out, become a trader raider,' Gino was upbeat and Timothy fell for his charm, 'now jump behind there, go on.'

Timothy sat in Gino's chair and piled the money in front of the document.

'The shot's not good enough. Hold the book up again with one hand and maybe, fan some of the money out with the other,' Gino took the photo and looked at the screen, 'what's your mobile number?' His office phone rang. 'I'll have to take this.' Gino pushed a pen in front of Timothy and tapped the desk pad before walking to his office.

Timothy scrawled his number on the pad and waited. Gino mouthed the words, 'go home,' pointing to the money and the door. The PA picked it up and left and he could hear Gino talking as he took the lift. By the time he reached his flat, a message pinged its arrival, an image file of him with Gino taken earlier but sent from a number he didn't know. He didn't give it much thought. Gino was always buying new gadgets. The money felt heavy in his pocket and he knew he would never have made this much money working with Sam. Nope, he was sure Gino was a better boss, someone who appreciated his staff and wasn't frightened to show it.

Monday morning Sam Lewis sashayed through the revolving glass door and made her way to the lifts. She pressed the up button and waited. The thought of Gino breaking in on her while she showered added to her determination to do something about him. Today was as good as any to sack him. She smiled, knowing his departure would be the only way RADOR could function with integrity.

Exiting the lift, she crossed the foyer of the top floor, touched the fingerprint reader and waited for the click of the unlocking door, nothing. She touched the screen again but it remained red. She would deal with Gino right after she gave security a piece of her mind, storming to the intercom to call reception, said. 'This is Sam Lewis, I'm in the foyer and the door is jammed. Get someone over here to let me in ASAP. Then tell security to meet me in my office now.'

'Yes, Ms Lewis.' The intercom went silent.

Sam paced, what was taking so long? It was 7.30am and she wanted an early start. Charles expected a report when he returned from Sydney and she needed to attend to the mail from last week. This is a complete cock up she thought and stabbed the finger pad again. She wanted to kick the door, but remembered her shoes were new and expensive, so held back.

'Ms Lewis,' a security guard appeared from the lift behind her, 'Mr Winkler asked to give you this if you returned.' He passed her a manila envelope. Sam took it.

'Just open the door. I'll read this later.'

'Sorry I can't. Orders.'

'What do you mean you can't? Can't what?'

He looked at his feet. 'I can't let you in, Ms Lewis. We have orders to escort you from the premises. It's nothing personal.' He looked helpless, but Sam wanted to shout at him.

'Bullshit, I run this place.'

He held his hands wide. 'What can I do, we have to go now. You have to leave, Miss'

'Not bloody likely,' she looked at his name plate, 'Michael, let me through the door now and that's an order.'

He put a hand on her shoulder in an attempt to turn her away. She grabbed his wrist, twisted, pulled down, spun in under him and lifted. The guard crashed onto the floor and the noise of his gear smashing into the tiles drew people from their offices. With noses pressed against the glass panels they saw Michael sprawled face down, Sam Lewis with her foot on his shoulder pulling at his wrist.

Gino opened the glass door. He was grinning and started to slow-clap her. Sam dropped the guard's arm and watched Gino as he pointed to the envelope. Seeing Timothy standing at his left shoulder added to her anger, she had thought him to be better than this.

Gino stared at her, speaking through clenched teeth, 'Miss Lewis, your services have been terminated as of last Friday.'

His words hissed with venom-laced syrup.

'Time to go Samantha,' these words were loud and said with clarity, 'now, Ms Lewis, apologise to the security officer and leave the premises and there'll be no further action taken.'

'Fuck you, Gino.'

'Look bitch, Charles has made you a more than generous offer, I suggest you take it. Everything is explained in this statement of separation,' he turned to the crowd, his voice smooth and clear, 'back to your desks everyone. The show's over, Ms Lewis isn't with us anymore.'

Michael picked up the package and passed it to Sam, 'c'mon, Miss Lewis, I'm sorry, but we have to go.'

'Yeah sure.' Sam knew when she was beaten. Conspiracy thoughts swam round her head and she needed somewhere quiet to think. The lift doors opened and he guided her inside with his hand against the small of her back.

Without looking, he pressed the button for the lobby and said, 'no one has ever put me on the floor as quick as that. I saw stars for a minute.'

'Are you okay?'

'Yeah, I'm fine. You'll be better off without them Miss. I can't say I've ever liked your old bosses much, there's always a shiftiness about them.'

Sam wanted to press him to clarify this, but decided against it. She knew where she could find him again. They rode the lift in silence.

He walked her into the sunshine, where she stopped on the street looking up at her old office while Michael hailed a cab and passed her his card, his home phone number scrawled on the back.

'Phone the desk later and tell me where to send your stuff. If you need anything, anytime, contact me at home. My wife will answer, she runs a private security service. I'll let her know you might call, okay?'

Sam didn't think she would ever need protection, but agreed anyway. The taxi arrived and he held the door, passing her the envelope.

'Thanks Mike,' she said.

Opening the front door of her unit, Sam could see someone had been there. They had cleared her letter box and junk mail sat in neat piles alongside the letters. There was a card from her mother, an invitation to the thirtieth birthday of a friend from Mundulla and a letter from Gavin. Sam loved his letters, always telling her she was special and pleading for her to come home and marry him. She could use a little loving right now and thought about her parents and friends from school. She and Gavin had been so close once, sharing thoughts and dreams but, in the end, they both wanted different things.

Charles' letter of separation could wait. This time Gavin had front running, she slid her fingers along the top and prised the soft stationary from its envelope. Enclosed in the letter was a card inviting her to keep her Saturdays in December free. He and Sasha would announce their engagement as soon as they settled the day. She screwed the letter up and threw it in the bin. Gavin told her he'd wait, he just hadn't told her for how long.

'Go right ahead, Gav,' rejection added another element of bitterness to her day and her lip curled in a sneer as she thought of what she would say to him if he'd been here, 'marry little Miss Sasha pretty boots, cuddle up with her daddy and all of his acres. Buckle to old country traditions, because that's what it's all about, Gavin, family land and bloodlines.' She snatched the letter from the bin and slapped it on the bench, trying to smooth the paper with her fingers. Tears stained the page and the ink ran.

She told herself to get a grip. She hadn't loved him for years and something else was driving her rage and disappointment. She should go back home to the family, talk to her father about geology and bastards and take her mother out for a coffee and gossip and if she saw Sasha, to congratulate her and smile, because she will always know she'd been his first love.

Single minded in her decision, she knew she should look at the letter from Charles, but it could wait. It would refer to her contract with all the usual clauses about confidentiality, telling her she couldn't work for a competitor for at least twelve months. She would keep her salary until then and he would have offered a generous compensation. Sam knew the frame of the letter. She had drafted many similar.

Seeing the mail in neat piles bothered her, the cleaner had been in the day before she left for Orroroo, Charles was away so that only left someone who had access to his key to enter her unit. She felt a tremor run up her spine, knowing it was Gino who had Charles' key. There were many things to change starting with the locks.

She tried Charles' phone, but it went to message. He was avoiding her like the coward she knew him to be. She checked the time. He was probably still in the air, she could make a scene when he landed, but it wouldn't do any good. She had seen other executives vent their frustrations on Charles and sue for wrongful dismissal, only to find the industry considered them untouchable. Today was not one for anger, but one to plan revenge.

***

It took two days for Joe and Laura to sleep off the jetlag, before they felt ready to catch up on the progress of the homestead. Laura called Tilly and arranged to have coffee with her and Fiona, while Jeff and Joe toured the farm, before meeting their men at Wanooka's Well. They would meet at the creek below the house for a picnic lunch.

Waiting for Jeff to arrive, Joe wandered about the cottage, peering in cupboards opening and closing drawers.

'For Pete's sake, Joe, he'll be here soon. Tilly said he had to fuel the Cruiser first,' another drawer slid shut, 'what are you looking for?'

'Keys to Wilson's, they have to be here somewhere.'

'Joe it's been years since anyone went inside that place. Why do you want them now?'

'I just do.'

'What are you up to?' His voice sounded sheepish and she wanted to know why.

'I wanted to show Jeff over the place, maybe tidy it up a bit so we can show him and Tilly the murals. I thought we could all go there on the way home.'

'You could borrow Brad's car trailer and get the model T while you're at it.'

'Jeeze you don't forget anything, do you?'

'I made room for it in the shed yesterday although it will mean leaving the cruiser outside for a few weeks. The car is better here than out there where someone can pinch it.'

'No-one's seen it in seventy years. It'll still be there in another twenty.'

'Humour me, Joe. Every girl wants her very own Tin Lizzie. I'll phone Ron about the trailer now.'

Joe went into the laundry and rummaged through the drawers in the linen cupboard, but the keys remained elusive. He thought about the set of keys hanging on the gear lever of the Cruiser and knew they weren't on that. If he were at home at Wanooka's Well, he could go straight to the set on the nail behind the door in the shed, but after the damage, they'd probably be gone. He wandered out to the stone and iron shed where his grandfather once had his office, another place piled with remnants from an era long past. He twisted the handle and leaned his shoulder against the door, it twisted and the timbers shrieked as he pushed. He stood back and looked at it. The planks had dried and warped with time, the chain and padlock that once looped through the door and the frame had worn both holes smooth. He closed his eyes and pictured his Pop at his desk, sitting in the round back swivel chair. The door to the big safe was open and invoice books and ledgers stood like regiments of toy soldiers along the shelves. A row of cup hooks held the keys to his Ford Zodiac and other vehicles, a label with the registration plate numbers above each. He remembered seeing Wilson's label above the second hook on the right and thought it was probably still there.

This time he took the weight of the door by lifting the door knob, the brass felt loose and the dents spoke of its history. The hinges squeaked and Joe made a mental note to oil them as he felt instinctively for the light switch. It, too, was brass and hissed as he pushed it down. The yellow from the light bulb filled the room with sepia tones and he found the keys under the label, just as he had pictured. He imagined hearing his grandfather on the phone, the safe door open and a cheque book, fountain pens and rubber ended pencils sharpened down so far one would find it hard to hold them. If he closed his eyes he could still smell it all.

'Here you are?' Laura was behind him, 'I'm just off to Tilly's now. Did you find what you were looking for?'

'Yeah sorry, I was lost in my thoughts there for a minute,' he stepped over a carton of old invoices and took the keys from the hook, 'Pop kept it tidy, Dad was the slob.'

'Yeah, well you've got plenty of time to clean it out over the next few days. If we move into Orroroo for good, I'll want a permanent office and this one looks promising.'

Joe sighed and turned to leave, Laura didn't move.

She saw his eyes were damp with unshed tears, asking him, 'after all this time and things are still a bit raw?'

Joe nodded, kissed her, wiped the back of his hand over his eyes and pushed past. He waited until she stepped out and pulled the door on a memory he had tried hard to forget. The sound of the Landcruiser was the distraction he needed. Jeff was here. He slipped the key ring over his little finger and called, 'See you for lunch at the Well, love.'

CHAPTER THIRTY EIGHT

Sam was surprised at the hesitation in her mother's voice, on the few occasions when she did call, Penny Lewis had pleaded with her daughter to come home more often. Today she sounded as if it would be better for Sam to stay in Adelaide.

'What's wrong, Mum? You sound apprehensive.

'It's nothing really, look come home we'd love to see you and your room is always here for you. Your Dad'll be beside himself when I tell him you'll be home tonight.

Sam heard her mother's enthusiasm begin to rise, but needed to be sure, 'I had a letter from Gavin today.'

'Oh, that's nice, what did he say.' The uncertainty returned to her mother's tone.

'That he was engaged and to hold all my Saturdays in December free.'

'There's an engagement party this week end.'

'Don't worry, Mum,' Sam took a deep breath, so that was why her mother was tentative, 'I'm not going to make trouble for them.'

'Of course.'

The tension faded from her mother's voice and Sam smiled, picturing her in the homestead kitchen, leaning against the sink twirling an old-fashioned telephone cord through her fingers as she talked. 'Jeeze, Mum. I hope they end up with a football team of kids and in bloody quick succession too,' she tried to hide the sneer, feeling petty for revealing her jealousy to her mother.

'You sure you're not just coming home to cause trouble, like you did at Gavin's twenty first, when you pushed Sasha into the cattle trough,' Penny suppressed a laugh, knowing Sasha probably deserved it.

'Seriously?' Sam just let the word hand there. Sam knew Sasha had it coming after the way she had gone after

Gavin. Running her hands up inside his shirt and grinding against him on the dance floor. She pushed the picture from her mind, 'no... of course not. Mum, a lot of water's flowed under the bridge since then.'

'Well as long as you keep it together. Dad and I don't want any trouble. Funny though,' her mother sighed, 'there was a time when we thought you and Gavin might have made a nice family, but you had other ideas.'

'Mum, it wouldn't be fair to Gav if he'd married me. I wanted to make it in the real world and he only wanted to make circles with a tractor,' she shuddered at the thought, 'I'd have been like a dog on chain, always straining to get off...'

Penny waited for her daughter to finish the sentence, but the line was silent, 'are you still there, Samantha?'

'I'm still here Mum...' she brought the subject back to the present, 'I know Sasha would have insisted Gavin write to me just to show she'd won him at last, and good luck to her. I reckon they deserve each other. Look,' she changed the subject again, 'I've had a shitty few days and this morning my contract was terminated. I could use a catch up, that's all, Mum,' Penny detected a weariness she hadn't heard before in her daughter, 'I know I've put the job first and neglected you guys, but Mum, I feel like a broken doll, one that only you and Dad can mend. Do you think you can help me with that?'

Choked with emotion, her mother nodded wordlessly.

Sam heard her mother's tears and dabbed her own eyes and blew her nose, 'I've got a few things to take care of first and then I'm on my way. I should be there before six.' She heard her mother pull a tissue from the box on the shelf below the phone and pictured her wiping her eyes, pushing her hair back and checking her reflection in the kitchen window. Home was the place to rest and lick her wounds while she thought and where to begin rebuilding her career.

It only took a few minutes on Google to find a locksmith who promised to change the locks this afternoon. The company asked if she wanted a surveillance service. It was something she hadn't considered before, but now thoughts about the flat being bugged by Gino bothered her, but if the locks were changed, she could organise that from Mundulla.

Her company phone beeped a message from Timothy reminding her to return the phone and computer. She ignored it. Michael, he was her answer. She took the card he had given her and walked to a nearby phone box to make the call.

'Hello.' Michael's wife answered.

'Hi, I need some advice about security.'

'We do security.'

'And I'm worried my home may be bugged; do you check for that kind of thing?' Sam asked.

'We do. We can offer a discreet sweep, or an obvious one?

'Can we meet and talk about what services you offer?'

'Sure, name a place and when it suits, but I'll need an hour or so.'

'How about Cafe Di-Milo in Rundle Mall, upstairs? Say one thirty in one of the back booths.' Her mood improved as she took control.

'How will I know you?'

'I'll text you a selfie. Do you have a mobile number?'

'Sure.'

Sam added the number to her phone.

***

The noise from car trailer made it hard to talk as Jeff wound his way through the Morchard hills and he waited until the road flattened out before speaking, 'what's with the trailer, Joe? I thought we were just going to clean up an old house, or something.'

'Laura wants us to pick up an old car at Wilson's. I told her about it before we found the homestead trashed and after your lot arrested all those bikies.'

'As I remember it, your one-man revenge mission destroyed twenty or more big motorbikes, a small truck and put the fear of God into more than one blackfella.'

'Funny, I thought I just created a diversion to rescue a girl who was being attacked.'

'Yeah, that fire in the horseshoe could be seen for miles,' Jeff grinned, his old boss, DI Harry Forbes had swanned in with a media circus to take over the investigation, only to miss catching the real culprits, 'but why does she want to bring it home now? Isn't there enough going on without adding something else to restore?'

'I think she wants to get my mind off all of the crap that happened last year.'

'Pretty hard for any of us to forget that,' he searched for the smoothest track on the road.

'Nah, I don't think she wants me to forget it, just distract me enough to deal with it, that's all.'

'The bloke's dead, Joe. He can't harm you or any of us now.'

'Yeah, I know, but something keeps nagging at me, you know. Something I can't see and yet it's right there where I can almost touch it. I don't know if I'm explaining it properly, but I'd like to know how Gordon-Sanders found me. And I don't believe that stuff about Jimmy Symes just looking him up on the internet either,' he looked out of the window as he recalled Vietnam and the evidence he gave at the Gordon-Sanders Court Martial years ago, 'anyway, he would have told the others, or me.'

'He's dead Joe, you have to let it go.'

'No mate, there's something more at work here, something a lot bigger than one crapped off American Lieutenant seeking revenge.'

'Like what?'

'I dunno, but whatever it is, it's big. I've pissed somebody off somewhere. I reckon it's personal, but I've searched my mind for months now and still can't work it out,' he stared at the hills hoping for an answer.

'The gold in the poem?' Jeff asked.

'Can't be. There's no gold out here. If there was, shepherds and prospectors would have found something by now. This land has been white settled for over a hundred and fifty years and nothing worthwhile has shown up anywhere. Our place has no mineral wealth.'

The Coomoroo road took them north-west, early sown oat crops emerging as rows of rich green against the red soil telling Joe he was home. Passing the gate to the sharefarmer's house he pointed at the crop, 'young Zach's just like his dad and got it in early. I reckon some farmers are as much born to the life, as learn it.'

'Probably comes from riding around in the tractor while still in nappies,' Jeff said, 'it's the whole nature nurture thing psychologists go on about.'

'You could be right, mate. You could very well be right, but the kid can farm. The place is tidy, the fence is old, but maintained. He'll be okay.'

Jeff heard the calm in the older man's voice, 'sounds like being home agrees with you.'

'I just like the country. Where we were in Britain it was all soggy fields and hedgerows. Look around you, the blue sky, white autumn clouds and the red dirt against the emerging crops. The place hasn't looked like this for seven years. I'm hoping this'll be the best harvest we've had. It'll put a bit of money back in the bank and you watch, come Christmas, there'll be new cars in the street. Women will get their farmhouses painted and new kitchens will go in all over the place. Yep, there'll be an air of optimism about the place after a couple of good rains. It's a great time to be alive.'

'That's what happens, then?' Jeff had noticed the fluctuation of the seasons in his job, but had never studied its effects on the population, 'is that why Brad asked if you're ready to make him an offer yet?' Jeff lifted his eyebrows, 'because he wants you to buy him out?'

'Something like that... and I'd like to, but I dunno? I reckon it'd take a bit of planning and I wouldn't want it to run the way he has. He's too reliant on the seasons and always hoping friends will pay on time.'

'So, what are you thinking then?'

'With the right plan, we'd restore classic and vintage machinery, rather than rely on repairs alone. You know, maybe use the internet to attract a broader clientele. I was thinking of all the old stuff we have taking up shed space and a team of craftsmen doing the same sort of work I've seen in England. It would not only bring in a quid if we sold it, you know, or maybe have a big auction when we've got a build-up of stock. I don't know if it would work, but at least it would be doing something different and hopefully keep a few people in work,' this was more words than Jeff had ever heard Joe say at the one time and he smiled at his enthusiasm, 'and maybe it would give kids an opportunity to stay here rather than migrate away to look for work in the city,' Joe's customary caution overrode eagerness and he pulled back, 'of course, it'd take time to build the business but, when I started thinking about Laura wanting to restore the barn and fill it with museum pieces... well, it would be a different way to make a dollar when we give the farm up.'

Jeff stayed quiet.

Joe wondered if he was boring him, 'penny for them,' he said.

'Oh, not much that makes sense. I hear your enthusiasm and remembered mine when we unearthed the old plane. Andy and I were gung-ho and full of plans, but the project has stalled. We're paying rent on hangar space we're not using and we're not committed enough to chase the maintenance work. It feels as if we're half pregnant. You know what I'm saying.'

'Shit Jeff, everyone gets the jitters when you start something new. It's natural, you know that.'

'Yeah, Andy does too, but he's not quite ready to toss his job at the moment. He has a fair amount of long service due and he's juggling everything around in his head. Really, he just needs a good kick up the bum but as his friend, I can't do it.'

'You're also his partner in an aviation business. You're the only one who can do it.'

'Yeah, I know. I've been thinking the same thing and if I don't say something soon then Tilly will. It'd be better coming from me,' he stared at the road, 'so what's really holding you back from making Brad an offer? You sound keen enough."

'Look, I can tie an exhaust up with wire and I can change tyres, but I'm no mechanic. How will I know if the people we employ know their jobs? If I...' he searched for words, 'if we do this, I want it done properly, you know. The business has to be sustainable, profitable and enjoyable. I'm nearly seventy-three, I should be slowing down and doing what all grey-haired men of my age do.'

'What, buy a caravan and annoy truck drivers,' Jeff grinned at Joe, he'd wanted to use that line from the moment he heard it and this was the time.

'Now there's a thought. No, I'm told to take it easy, I've already had one heart attack.'

'Yeah, but you've changed your diet, given up the smokes and have plenty to live for. Give it a go I say.'

'But what about skilled staff and all that?'

'What's Brad going to do? Would he stay, or leave town? He's got a few years left before he can retire.'

'Karen wants to live in Orroroo, so I guess they'd stay.'

'Why not buy part of the business, leave him with a share and keep him running it. If you ask him, I bet he'll say it's the money that's got him down. Tilly can draw up a business structure that would make it work. Talk to her about it. I'm a bit biased, but she's one smart cookie.'

'You reckon? She fell for you.'

'Like I said, Joe, she's damned clever,' Jeff's laugh drowned the road noise, 'is this the one?' he pointed to a gate on the left.

'Yep, I'll get the keys,' he dropped his hand into the boot surrounding the gear lever, pulled at the string with a single key dangled from it.

'Tilly?'

Jeff shrugged. 'She hates complication. What can you do?'

CHAPTER THIRTY NINE

Laura was in the kitchen, packing a hamper with enough food to feed a shearing team when she heard car doors slamming. Before she could pick up a towel to wipe her hands, Emily burst into the room and threw her arms around her.

'Mum said I could have the day off school so I can come out to see Jeff and Pop with you and have a picnic. Have you baked chocolate chip cookies, you know the ones I like with white and brown bits in them?'

Her words came with machinegun staccato. Laura bent her knees, and hugged her, 'I've made your favourites and I think they're Jeff's favourites too. Orange with chocolate chips, Jaffa biscuits I call them,' she looked up, acknowledged Tilly with a smile and stood up to greet her.

'Anything for me, Mum?' Tilly asked.

Laura winked at Emily, 'nope, just for Jeff and Em.'

'Nothing?'

'Well I've got scones with jam and whipped cream, oh and I have your favourite, shortbread.'

'Thanks, Ma...'

Tilly was anxious to get started, 'come on, let's get this lot into the car and I want to catch up with John for a tick before we go.'

John's police car stood out amongst the vehicles dotted along the main street and Tilly spotted him and Fiona enjoying the sun at a table on the footpath. The couple returned Tilly's greeting and John said, I'm glad you stropped, Tilly, because I wanted to ask if you'd heard from your friend, the mining company woman, I think her name is Sam.'

'That's why I stopped. I got a funny text from her the other day, but took no notice of it. I figured she'd defaulted back to witch, that's all. Now I'm not so sure,' she took out her phone and scrolled through the texts, 'why?'

'Oh, she and a suit from the city had a few words in the pub the other night, that's all.'

'I think the message is still on this,' she held up the phone, 'if you want to see it.'

'Nah, it's fine, text me a copy when you can. It's a bit strange that's all. Not often patrons from the pub call me when there's a stoush and it's just a bit strange they did it this time. Drinkers seemed to reckon he knew that Spoggy bloke, too. Said they thought whatever it was what they were arguing about, at least some of it was about him. Now that he's a bit belted and bruised, I'd like to know if she's okay,' he pushed under his hat with his fingers and scratched for a new thought, 'damned if I know. If it is linked to Spoggy clearing out, what does it mean and what was it that made him leave?'

Tilly held out her phone, screen facing toward him, 'this's what she sent, last Wednesday.'

'Rosie from the pub said she'd handed the guesthouse keys back early and paid the bill in full.'

'Are you worried about her?' she had noticed the concern in his voice.

'I don't like loose ends, everything happens for a reason and strangers threatening women in the pub is one of them. I'm a suspicious bloke and I reckon something's up.'

'Anything Tilly can do love?' Fiona didn't often comment on John's work, but sensed this was different.

'If you get a minute, text her and ask her to give me a call. Tell her there's no pressure, I just want to know she's okay,' he remembered the tone of the message, 'only if you feel comfortable with it though.'

'I spent a bit of time as a defender of criminals. I can talk to her. No worries,' she smiled and touched his arm.

'Well, I'd better go,' he said.

Fiona pushed her chair back and tapped her lips with a forefinger in farewell.

John smiled at his wife, tipped his hat and left.

Tilly and Fiona traded small talk for a few minutes before Tilly gave into Emily's impatience and said her goodbyes, seeing her mother headed for the driver's seat she called across the space between them, 'I can drive, Mum.'

'My car, my turn.' Laura winked at Fiona. It was good to be home and in charge of her own world again.

***

Joe fiddled with the chain and padlock but the key didn't work. He then noticed the lock and the key were different and asked Jeff to get the bolt-cutters from behind the passenger seat.

Jeff rummaged behind the seat for a couple of minutes, folding the back further forward to gain better access to where the bolt cutters lay below a steel box. The padlock wasn't under the hasp and Jeff lifted the lid to see an army issue 9mm automatic encased in foam rubber. He picked up the cutters and walked over to Joe, 'anything you want to tell me about the box under the seat?'

'Nope.'

'It's not locked.'

'And you looked?'

'The copper in me looked,' he said and paused,' plus I'm curious.'

'That's what got the cat killed,' Joe said, not looking up as he worked the cutters on the chain.

'Got a licence for it?'

'Not only that, but I'm cleared to use it.'

'Your old employer?'

'Never free of them. It's better you don't know.'

'I've been a copper too, Joe,' he reminded the older man.

'Yeah, but not anymore,' he turned and stared into Jeff's eyes, 'like I said, you don't want to know so just leave it, okay? I don't want to go into it with you or anyone else for that matter,' he tossed the bolt–cutters at Jeff's feet and took him by the shoulders, 'let it go. The last thing I want to do is make life harder for you and Tilly and Emily. Don't get any of your copper mates poking into it okay? It'll only bring a shitload of trouble.'

'Whoa... I'm on your side, Joe. I get the message loud and clear.'

'Good.'

Jeff walked away, unsure about Joe's outburst, spotting a padlock on the side of the track he picked it up and saw the shackle had been cut close to the toe, 'hey, look at this,' he held it up for Joe to see.

'That looks like a lock for this key but if it was Tilly, she had a key and wouldn't need to cut the lock.' The key slid into the barrel and Joe twisted. The broken shackle jumped out and fell between them.

Jeff picked up the pieces, 'Tilly said she'd changed all the locks last week.'

'What the hell's going on then? I can understand one of the neighbours cutting a link and replacing it with their own lock, but something's fishy about this and I don't like the feel of it,' Joe walked up and down the fence line. This wasn't a public road and it never had been, 'c'mon, we'll worry about it later. Never needed locks twenty years ago,' he mumbled to himself.

Jeff changed the subject, 'all the paddocks have names Joe, so what's the name of this one?'

'Millers.'

'Like in the poem?'

'Yeah, sad story. The credit squeeze in the sixties did it. When none of the Miller kids wanted to fight the banks to keep the place, the old people had to sell it in a mortgagee's auction and my old man was the winning bidder. He used to say it was the only way to get some of our land back,' Joe laughed, 'he might have been an unmitigated bastard and a complete and unreliable arsehole, but he let old man Miller and his wife stay on. They share-farmed here until Mr Miller died and she went into the Community Home not long after,' Joe pointed to the ridge, 'the house is just stones now, c'mon, we'll have a look around if you like.'

Jeff drove through the opening and waited while Joe wired the gate shut, he went over it again in his head. It didn't make any sense, there was nothing out here.

'I put everything back where I found it,' Jeff said, 'and you'd better lock that box, you wouldn't want Emily opening it.'

'Yeah, I know. Point taken and look, about back there, I'm sorry I was a bit short. I've been ordered to do some shitty stuff over the years and I wouldn't want anyone close to me have to do what's been asked of me,' he patted Jeff on the knee, 'I'm glad you're out of the coppers too. You don't need that kind of crap in your life.'

'Thanks, I'm getting used to it now, but I can't keep sponging off Tilly though, it's not me.'

'Don't worry... Tilly won't let you stay idle for too long. I'll bet she's mapping out your week off, as we speak.'

Jeff thought about the number of times he had been flying since he met Tilly. Joe was right, his days were different now, 'you want to come over and try the glider again one-day Joe?'

'No, but I don't want you to do less of it either. I haven't forgotten your desire to set that world record. It's important to you and I'll be buggered if I'll let you forget it either. You have to fight to reach your dreams, Jeff, no matter how far away they may seem.'

'I want to see Tilly happy, you know, support her for a while.'

'Just don't let her run over you, that's all. You make her happier than I've ever seen her and I reckon she does the same for you. All I want is for you both to share what Laura and I have. What Ted and your Mum had.'

Jeff turned to look at the track and beyond this to the old walls of the Miller's crumbled dreams, 'Joe, how did your family make it through when others like the Millers, Wilsons and Harris's didn't?' He spoke as he pulled of the track and parked by the remnants of stonewalled sheep yards.

'We were lucky and never spent more than we earned. Pop invested in stocks and shares, seemed to know when to buy and sell. It wasn't just luck though, we had some better country. Pop always worked on his asset to debt ratio, which meant he only ever borrowed an amount equal to a quarter of what he owned. If he didn't have the money, he didn't buy. When the hard times came, he had cash to buy farms when the banks foreclosed. Some people didn't like it, however the people whose places we bought never said a bad word against him because he took care of them. They were his friends. Dad and I worked on the same principal and so far, so good.'

Joe had the passenger door open before the engine died and walked over to the homestead. It overlooked a gum creek, where once a spring had trickled water into a rock pool which fed the house and garden. Mrs Miller had a Chinese gardener who helped her establish a grove of fruit and olive trees. Further up the hill a small cemetery defied the elements and marked the history of its inhabitants.

'What's with the old car in the scrub along the creek, Joe?'

'Shouldn't be anything down there, why?'

They moved toward it. A burnt-out Falcon ute was surrounded by spent shotgun shells and whoever dumped it had blasted every panel with shot, even the number plates were full of holes. However, it was the decapitated ribcage and dried out thighbones tangled in the rusty seat springs that caught Joe's attention, 'you'd better call O'Rourke, I think he needs to see this.'

Jeff was at his shoulder holding Joe back, 'don't bloody touch anything.'

'And don't tell me how to suck eggs. You might be a newly retired copper, but I'm not stupid either. Take the Cruiser to the top of the cutting, you should be able to get a phone signal there,' he sat back on his haunches, wishing he had a cigarette. Another burnt vehicle and what looked like another body. This was some kind of warning, it had to be. He watched Jeff pacing around on the rise, his right hand drawing circles in the air as he talked into the phone. He couldn't hear what was said, but by the way he jogged across to the Toyota then slammed the driver's door before speeding down the hill to him, that he was annoyed.

'I tell you Joe, we should have driven past and not said anything. All my time with the coppers and now they treat me like I'm a dickhead,' he picked up a stone and heaved it as far as he could, 'John's got the station phone diverted, so I was patched through to Pirie. Christ, I never liked that station much anyway, who do the bastards think they are, grilling me as if I'd committed murder. I even had to quote my old service number. In the end, I hung up and got on to Sarge at Pt Augusta and he radioed John who said he'd be here in an hour. He threw another stone. Shit I can't just sit around and wait.'

'So, you're not quite ready to give the force away? Something like this happens and you're ready to ride to the rescue,' he gave Jeff's shoulder a gentle push, 'I know how it gets in your blood,' he pointed to the ute, 'right now, you've got to act like you're in charge. Just remember to leave your old mates enough room to think they have it all under control.'

'Yeah, you're right. I'll take a few photos with the phone,' he pointed to the remains on the driver's seat of the Falcon, 'apart from the eagle and crow shit about the place, what do you think?'

'I think somebody's trying to frighten the crap out of me,' Joe took a slow survey of the area, 'and just maybe, it's working.'

CHAPTER FORTY

Waiting for John to arrive, Jeff searched for footprints, tyre tracks and anything out of place. He remembered his father once telling him not to look at what's in front of him, but look for what's not there. Ted's advice had often helped him to see things other coppers missed. His colleagues put it down to his being Aboriginal. Jeff knew different, but having white people think he had special powers, helped him to stand out by far more than just his skin colour.

Smeared along the top and down one side of the crumbling kitchen wall of the old house, he found what looked like blood. It was at knee height where a shotgun blast had peppered the remnants of plaster. A rusty stain and a line of ants added to the evidence.

He shifted a stick, poking at an ant's nest thinking back to the beginnings of Joe's trouble last year and wondering if this incident could be linked, then shook his head as if answering his own questions. They got the bloke who tried to murder Joe. He remembered Sergeant Doug Simpson and his forensic experiment of putting a cow's head on an ant nest and smiled. Police work was more than a job and he wondered if he could resist the pull of the force. Pushing these thoughts aside he continued to photograph the position and place of the bones that he assumed had been scattered by carrion. He was entering his findings into his smart-phone when John's car pulled up.

'Evenin' all,' John said, doing his best to parody the London Bobbies often seen on early television shows, 'and what 'ave we here then?'

'Not sure. Burnt out ute, with what could be human remains in the driver's seat. Blood and remnants of flesh on the wall, I'm not sure, though?'

'What is it you're not sure about?'

'Just a feeling that nothing is as it seems, but don't take any notice of me, probably blackfella intuition.'

'Pirie wanted in,' and as John spoke, he made a slow three hundred and sixty-degree scan of the horizon, 'but I told them it was closer to Port Augusta. Sarge and Cassidy are about an hour away.'

'We can go though?' Joe asked, 'Laura and Tilly are waiting for us.'

'No way, I need witness statements.'

'Here,' Jeff held up his phone, 'I'll send them to you.'

'Well before you do, walk me back down there,' he took a camera from the police car, then walked toward the wreck, taking care not to tread on a set of trail bike tracks.

'Anyone been out here on a bike, Joe?' John asked.

'Not that I know of.'

Looking around the scene and scratching their answers into his notebook. Although they had been blasted by pellets, he could still make out the raised numbers on utility's number plates and made a note of them too.

'I know this ute,' John said flipping back through the pages in his pad, 'yep, thought so, Spogg, or Spoggy is his name,' he looked in the cab, 'Jesus, what a mess.'

'It's all yours mate. We'll be over at the homestead if anyone needs us,' Jeff slapped John on the shoulder, 'come on, Joe.'

'What, you're leaving?' John asked.

'Yep, places to go, people to see,' Jeff was happy to leave. After Joe's earlier reaction, he wanted no part of it.

'See you later,' Joe shook John's hand, 'it seems we're on our way.'

'Yeah sure...' John was distracted, 'see-ya, Joe.'

'Better watch out, big blackfella magic out here, mate,' Jeff yelled in a thick accent, 'and it might be more than human, could be something else. Mooldarbie country, this.'

John was looking at the skeletal remains and took no notice of his friend.

'We'll be home tonight, if you want us,' Jeff said.

John waved acknowledgement as he continued to examine the scene before him.

Jeff eased the Toyota onto the track and they worked their way toward the well paddock.

'What was that about not being all human?' Joe asked.

'I reckon those ribs were from a pig, a big one too and the bones were all wrong and I found rough hair among the pellets in the plaster.'

'It'll piss John off when the penny drops,' Jeff said.

Joe wondered how long it would take the police officer to work it out. 'What about wasting police time?'

'We didn't. We reported a burnt-out ute with a skeleton in it. Besides, I'm not a doctor or a specialist in anatomy, are you? I'd love to see the face of the forensics officer when he gets here. That's if Sarge and the boys don't work it out first.'

'But why do that?'

'What?'

'Put a pig behind the wheel and torch it.'

'Cover up a murder somewhere else, or...' Jeff's mind cranked into gear, 'what if, after his belting, this Spoggy bloke wanted to disappear?'

'Yeah, I get that, but what's that got to do with us. That's what I can't get my head around. I don't even know the bloke,' he looked at his watch, 'look, rather than go across to Wilson's now, I think we'd better get back onto the main road and catch up with the girls. I don't want Laura thinking we've ploughed off the road or anything.'

'You point and I'll steer,' and he started to sing, Joe reached over and turned on the radio.

CHAPTER FORTY ONE

Laura and Tilly nattered while driving to the farm, in the back Emily put her iPod down to speak, 'Mum, you said Pop wanted to go to Wilson's, right?'

'That's what he said. Why?'

'Isn't that where you went with that Sam lady, Mum?'

'Whoa, what's all that about? Isn't she from the mining company? You've had dinner with her and now Emily says you've been out to Wilsons. When were you going to tell Dad about this?'

'Today,' Tilly turned in the seat to face her mother, 'jeeze Mum, what time have I had? Look I haven't seen you guys since Saturday and you were too spaced out with travel to take much in on the way home. It's the same old story. Sam's company RADOR wants our leases and she's the CEO. Since you left, I've been fending off requests to meet them and each time I've told them no. Then last week she shows up on my doorstep, we have words and she goes away.'

'And?'

'That night John thought Fiona could use some time without the kids, he said he'd take care of them if she wanted a night out. Well in Orroroo, all we've got is dinner at the pub.'

'Go on.'

'Anyway, I saw Sam alone at the bar in the lounge and so I asked her to join us for dinner.'

'And that's it? Laura asked.

'Not quite, I was thinking about Dad's maxim, you know. *Know your enemy better than you do your friends.* So, I asked if she wanted to come for a drive while I checked the waters. That was Wednesday. She looked at every ridge and gutter on the place, there was nothing to see.'

'But why take her onto the place. What are they looking for?'

'She didn't say and I didn't ask. They're one of the companies drilling into the coal seams on the Johnburgh Plain, so there's nothing new there. Everyone's known about the coal since the seventies. She knew all about Stockdale Exploration's activities, you know that mob that was chasing diamonds around Eurelia and anywhere they thought a kimberlite pipe might be. She did hint that RADOR's interest is gold.'

'Okay, but there's no gold bearing mineral around here,' Laura said.

'Pop's got gold bars though,' Emily added.

'Yes, because his Dad put them in the well,' Tilly said.

'But there must be a mine somewhere, Pop said gold comes from the ground, right?'

'Not on our place though.' Laura said.

Tilly started again, 'anyway, we lit a fire and grilled a couple of chops.'

'A chop picnic,' Laura laughed, sounds cosy.' In some ways, Tilly was the best friend she never had. Sure, there were the women at the bowls club and on school council, but with Joe, the farm and her job, Laura missed some of the friendships other people made. Her mind flicked to Elspeth and how great it had been chatting with her.

Laura turned the car off the road and onto the road leading to their almost rebuilt homestead. Stopping at the entrance, they walked to the stonework where Laura traced her fingers over the lettering announcing Wanooka's Well.

'This is nice. Look Em.'

Tilly had told Jake last week her parents would be coming for an inspection and he had landscaped the approach to welcome them. Clumps of lavender filled triangular beds edged with rocks from the creek. Two rows of saltbush would grow to form a hedge lined driveway to the house.

'Is it okay, Mum?

'Well Granny,' Emily asked, 'is it?'

Laura couldn't say anything, she tried, but her words would not come.

'Mum...'

'I'm fine love, it's just beautiful,' she looked at the solar panel behind the wall, 'and you've made sure the gates are automatic too.'

'I wanted you to feel safe. You know, if you ever decide to stay out here again.'

'I know, love. It might take a while, that's all.'

Tilly rubbed her mother's back, 'baby steps, Mum, baby steps.'

Laura continued through the gates and parked in the house yard as Joe and Jeff rattled up beside them. Joe and Laura had not been back to the house since they had found the gold bars in the well at Millers and the progress was obvious.

The stonemason was working on the north wall, the veranda flagstones were down, a pile of original floorboards poked out from under a tarpaulin and the original windows, now in pink undercoat, leaned against the dirty white of the shed wall.

Jake walked over to them, hand extended, 'Mr and Mrs Gillespie, Tilly, Jeff and oh no, I've forgotten your name. Must be Elsa is it, or no Freddie. Hang on, Georgina, that's it.'

'No silly, you know I'm Emily, you're just playing games, Mr Jake.'

'Joe and Laura, please, Jake,' Laura said, 'is it safe for us to look around?'

'Sure, let's go,' he walked them around the site showing the progress and introducing his team.

Joe stopped at the cellar, 'Tilly's idea?'

Jake nodded, 'it'll be a nice space when it's finished.'

Joe said nothing and Laura smiled. Emily reached for her hand and held it. While Laura listened to Jake's report she kept thinking to herself that, as promising as it all sounded, she had no desire to live here again.

Jeff ushered Tilly down the creek, away from the others, 'you didn't cut the lock on the eastern gate to Miller's and change it, did you?'

'Why would I do that? I replaced all of them with new master locks only last week.'

'Joe and I found a ute burnt out at Harris's.

'Wait, if I put new locks on Thursday, someone's cut and replaced it since then. Who and why?'

'Whoever dumped the ute I guess,' he waved a fly away from her face, 'then replaced it to keep people away, I suppose, or wanted to stall anyone from finding it.'

'Shit, a burnt-out ute, what kind?'

'A Falcon, fairly old, white or it used to be,' he looked at the hills behind the house, imagining the fear how trapped Joe must have felt here between the buildings, being peppered with bullets by gunmen, 'Joe thinks it's someone sending a message.'

'And what do you think?'

'I don't know. They tried to make it look like a murder.'

'Really?'

'Yeah, used a pig or something, maybe a big scrubber roo. John's waiting for Sarge and Darryl to meet him there now.'

'How's Dad?'

'Spooked,' lifting his hat he ran his hand through his hair, 'I'm worried about him. He snapped at me earlier over nothing at all.'

'That doesn't sound like Dad,' Tilly looked at the clouds and sighed, 'want me to tell mum?'

'Nope.'

'How about I talk to him?'

'No, I reckon he's trying to avoid talking about it, probably hoping it's nothing. Best just to let him work through it, I think.'

'Well what do I do then? Shit, Jeff it's important.'

He saw tears in her eyes and pulled her close, 'hey, it'll be okay, I promise. I'll talk to him again. He'll have a plan, he always does.'

'Yeah, he'll have a plan just like the one last year and that nearly killed both of you.'

'But it didn't. Tilly, he's tough. You've just got to remember that.'

Joe walked to the horse yards, they needed a tidy up. Emily came up behind him and took his hand. She was growing, becoming more knowledgeable and he knew that in a few years their relationship would change. She would need him less and he hated the thought he might lose her.

'Are you a bit sad Pop?'

'I'm fine Poppet.'

'You sure? You look sad.'

'I'm a bit worried I suppose. I hate seeing the house all smashed up still and I wonder if Granny'll want to live here when it's all finished.

'But you can live in town, right?'

'Yeah, we can live in town.'

'And I can see you every day then.'

He smiled at her, 'there is that, Poppet, there is that. Want to come for a walk?'

'Yep, where are we going?'

'Not far, I want to look at the place from the top of Wanooka's hill.'

'It'll take too long and besides lunch'll be ready soon.'

'That's okay, we can do it another day.' He was about to pick her up and swing her around but she had already darted off. This was another thing he wouldn't be able to do for much longer, she would be too grown up and his strength was leaving him.

'Race you back,' she called over her shoulder.

CHAPTER FORTY TWO

Waiting for plaster in the motorcycle tracks to dry, John watched another patrol car drift to a stop. Doug Simpson was first out, his years behind the desk showing in the way he put his hands on the small of his back and arched backwards. DI Cassidy walked around to the rear of the car. John watched him brushing the front of his shirt and assumed they had stopped along the road for something to eat. The thought of food made him hungry, he hadn't planned to be out here today.

'Plaster?' Darryl asked, 'I thought photos were all the go these days? 'they shook hands, 'How are you, John?'

John looked at his watch, 'I had to do something while I waited for you blokes.'

The senior raised his eyebrows at the detective and smiled, 'here we go again eh, John.'

'Yeah, but I dunno, Jeff says it could just be someone playing silly buggers. Anyway, I'll leave that to you, but we could all be on a wild goose chase.'

'Find the owner?' The senior sergeant asked.

'Registered to a Liam Le-Strange of Brahma Lodge, but a bloke calling himself Spoggy living in Orroroo has been driving it.'

'You said something about bones inside it?' Darryl said.

'Yeah, this way.'

They walked to the crime site and for the next ten minutes debated the need to involve forensics before the DI walked to the top of the hill and called Adelaide. He was told to count the number of ribs, a human skeleton has twelve pair. He allocated this task to his Senior Sergeant who counted fourteen, therefore it was not considered a homicide and forensics told them to manage the situation themselves.

'So, Jeff was right when he said it wasn't human,' John said.

'He could have saved us a lot of time if he told you why,' the DI snapped, 'but then he guessed I'd have called them anyway.'

The senior sergeant slapped dirt from his hands and said, 'there are two things I'd like to know. One, where's Spoggy now and why dump the car out here, and two, does any of this tie this in with the attack on Joe last year?' he slapped at some dirt on his pants, 'Christ, I thought we'd closed that case.'

'That's three things, Sarge,' the DI studied everything, searching for any hint that could link it to the Hammond murders, 'yeah, it's got to be about Joe, or the farm. Otherwise, why fake a murder on Gillespie country? There has to be a connection, but what is it?'

'Jeff said the padlock on the gate in was different, so whoever dumped the ute had to cut it. He thought it was strange, because Tilly had just replaced all of their padlocks last Thursday.'

'Where is it now?' Sarge asked.

'Still by the gate, I suppose?'

'We'll bag it on the way out, but I'm not hopeful,' the senior officer said, 'come on, we've done all we can here and we'll arrange for the wreck to be picked up,' he looked to his companion, delegating with a nod, okay?'

DI Cassidy organised for a patrol car to check out the Brahma Lodge address, the officers arriving there to find a fire crew on site and a forensic team on standby until it was safe to enter. He declared it a crime scene and directed the constables to run tape out and asked forensics to make it a priority.

A doorknock of the neighbourhood provided little information. The owner was often absent for months at a time. No one could offer a description and one neighbour thought the occupant lived alone. The mailbox overflowed with junk mail, but nothing to identify the owner.

Cassidy was annoyed at the senior constable's casual reporting and let him know it, instructing the uniform officers to intensify their search. There were too many coincidences to pass it off for the Salisbury branch to mishandle, he believed the fire to be arson and related to his case.

Within an hour, they reported a padlock to the shed door was unlocked and hanging in its hasp and the garage floor, being above ground level, was untouched by fire or water and covered with a centimetre of dust. Marks on the concrete showed that a larger car, possibly a Falcon or Commodore shod with wide tyres, had recently backed over a set of trailbike tyre tracks. They sent photos of their findings to the DI's phone. Forensics would offer a full report in a few days.

Simpson and Cassidy were only ten minutes out of Port Augusta when the detective's phone rang again. He answered and switched it to speaker so the senior could hear.

The young constable he had spoken to earlier offered more observations, 'I've been thinking, Sir, the shed floor looks suspicious. It's too new.'

'Constable what do you mean, too new?'

'Sir, this shed is over fifty years old. It's clad in rusty tin over crumbling joists yet there are splashes of new cement over the inside walls. The concrete floor's about a hundred and fifty millimetres thick and it finishes just inside the door, which is why water from the fire hoses couldn't wash the dust away. Why would anyone put a new floor in, without sloping it off, to get a car in or out?'

'Well, you tell me.'

'Well, I reckon at one time it was used by a mechanic, or someone who worked on cars. On the back wall, there's a shadow board above a bench. A few old spanners and screwdrivers still hang there, but no one has touched them for years, everything's covered in dust and cobwebs.'

'Spit it out son, what are you trying to say?'

'Well Sir, if you intended to use it for anything other than storage, you'd build a better and bigger shed in its place,' he tried to form his thoughts into coherent order, 'or I would anyway, and this is no man cave.'

'Get on with it?' Darryl had little patience for uniformed city coppers.

'It could be a great place to hide a body, Sir.'

'Are you winding me up, Constable?'

'No sir, but think about it. If this shed ever had a pit in it, and I'm betting it did, you'd have a readymade grave.'

'Constable, are you two taking the piss?'

'No, Sir'.'

'Good, now I want you two to doorknock everyone again. If no one's home, don't just leave a card and forget it, go back later if you have to. Check and double check everything. Tomorrow I'll bring a colleague and we'll be with you before nine in the morning.'

They turned right onto the highway, the traffic was light and Doug pushed the car up to the speed limit.

'In a hurry?' Cassidy asked.

'Lots to do and I want to leave on time tonight,' He looked back toward the ranges and rubbed a forefinger on his temple, 'tell me, we did get the right bloke, the American, who had it in for Joe Gillespie, didn't we?'

'Yeah... well I thought we did, evil bastard he was, too. Strange the way we found him though.'

'It was poison though, wasn't it? Not the Kadaicha Man or being sung to death like everyone talked about at the time, right?

'Yeah...' Cassidy screwed his face up, 'but, eating enough puffer fish to kill someone? I'm still trying to get my head around that.'

'You gunna tell Joe about this?'

'Well, no... the commissioner's still sitting on it. He doesn't want us digging any further because the prick was part of some prominent good old American family. It's crap, but he says he's waiting on the American Embassy and all the bullshit that goes with it,' he looked out the window and sighed, 'now I wish I'd left it to Harry Forbes and he'd have all this political crap to deal with.'

'Slippery bastard would only farm it out and it'd probably end up in your lap anyway.'

DI Cassidy was still staring out the window, 'yeah, you've been with the case from the beginning, what do you think?'

'Well,' he drew a deep breath and held it for a moment as if seeking an answer, 'I reckon Joe's in the shit. Somebody wants something from him and we don't know what it is, and I don't think Joe knows either.'

'Like what sort of something?' Darryl switched his stare to the back of the road train they were following. It revealed nothing.

'I don't know, but I reckon they originally thought if they could get Joe out of the way, then Laura and Tilly would cave. Trouble is, Joe's harder to kill than a three-headed snake,' he gazed back to the ranges and pictured the damaged homestead and the bodies on the road.

'He is that.'

'I'm worried, not only for Joe, but the others too. Think about it, if you can't murder him and his family stands strong, what do you do next?'

'What are you suggesting?'

'If I knew I'd tell you, but if it were me, I'd be making sure no one could get anywhere near my family.'

'You mean kidnap? Christ, I hadn't even let that cross my mind,' he typed instructions into the to-do list on his phone. There was much to do before going to Brahma Lodge and the site of the house fire.

'What's your next move?'

'Who do you think I should take with me tomorrow?'

'Angela, she's smart and she'll do what you ask.'

'She's just a kid.'

'Yeah, but you saw how she worked Joe's case last year. She knows more about it than anyone else and she'll do a double shift if you ask. Yep Angie would be my first choice.'

At the station, Sarge tossed the car keys to a junior officer. 'Give it a wash and vacuum and fill it up too, eh?' he pointed over his shoulder, 'the DI needs it tomorrow.'

Darryl looked for Angela. They had a lot to do before they went home.

CHAPTER FORTY THREE

A tall woman in a charcoal business suit and an ornate blue and gold hijab approached Sam. Her heels and bag matched the scarf and a scarab beetle brooch, fashioned from gold and diamonds, accented her left lapel. A discreet teak cross hung from a gold chain.

'Ms Lewis, Sam Lewis?' She asked. Sam nodded and shook the woman's hand, 'Helen Habib, may I sit down?'

'Yes, please do.' She opened her hand toward a chair. Michael's wife was not what she expected. They didn't match. He was of medium height, in his fifties and any visible hair that he had had long turned grey and his jacket buttons strained to meet across his girth. She was elegant with an air of purpose about her. Sam's eyes moved to the scarf and then dropped to her pendant.

Helen saw her companion's eyes move between the two. 'The scarf and the cross, let's get that out of the way first, so we can talk, okay?'

Her voice was melodic and rich, with a hint of accent, but Sam couldn't think from where.

'My family are Coptic Christians. I like the freedom of covering my hair. It makes me feel as if I've put on a suit of armour. Michael says it's my force-field, however, I find it makes the world easier to face at times. If it's unsettling, I'm happy to remove it.'

'No,' Sam waved the suggestion away. She could use her own force-field right now, 'I think it's lovely. I didn't...'

'Expect out of shape Aussie Mike to have a wife who looks like me?'

'Well yeah, I suppose,' Sam admired how forthright and confident this woman sounded.

'He's a wonderful father, a great husband and we share the same values. Our marriage may have been arranged, but I wouldn't swap him for the world. Now, that's enough about me. Let's get your problem sorted.'

The waiter arrived and took Helen's order, Sam asked for espresso.

'I bought the unit from my boss Charles Winkler who has also been my off again, on again boyfriend since I started working at Wagmin and I'm worried he may have hidden cameras or some kind of bugging devices there.'

'Why would you think that?'

'Out of the blue, they terminated my position today and over the past week I've found evidence that makes me distrust him.'

'What about selling, can that be a consideration?'

'Not at the moment,' she looked away, 'no.' She could feel everything she had worked toward slipping from her grasp, 'I just want to keep what's mine and it's important I feel safe in my own place, 'that, and I need to rescue my career,' her anger rose, yet somehow it hollowed her too, feeling vulnerable telling her story to a stranger. She forced her determination to replace her feelings of self-pity, 'and no jumped up bas...' she looked at Helen's cross and stopped, 'mongrel of a boss, is going to take any of that away from me.'

'That's the spirit,' Helen said.

Sam leant back to give the waiter room to set her coffee down. She told Helen about Gino appearing in the cottage bathroom and her fight with an unknown man, then finding her mail had been opened before she returned home.

Helen lifted the cup to her lips, the liquid was hot and she rested it back onto its saucer, 'you said you'd ordered a locksmith, when is he coming?'

'This afternoon, early.'

'Can you cancel?'

'I think so, why?'

'On the phone, you said you were going away for a few days. I suggest you act normally, pack everything that's personal or valuable and take it with you. Especially anything that has to do with your identity. Cancel the locksmith.'

'Again, why?'

'If someone is spying on you, it's an offence. When you know who it is, you can have them charged. Or let the matter go, it's up to you. I suggest that before we change the locks, we'll fit bogus surveillance cameras at the entrances and one in the living area. We want whoever it is to know they are dummies.' She took a brochure from her bag and passed it to Sam.

'Thanks.' She turned it over and put it alongside her coffee.

'Then, if someone is watching you, they'll relax. While we're there we'll check the house and if we find any transmitting devices, we'll patch in a loop to make your home look empty. When that's been done, we'll install a system you can monitor from your phone. It's the only way you'll know who's doing this.'

Sam picked up the brochure and looked for a fee structure.

'Once the loop is patched in,' Helen continued, 'we'll return before you come back and change the locks.'

Sam listened as Helen went over the costs, what was needed and how long it would take. She felt a shiver of doubt, it was not something she had thought about until now, 'and how do I know you're not a part of Gino's plan?'

'You don't,' Helen laughed, 'but I'm not working for your boss.'

'Gino was never my boss.'

'No, but you know what I mean,' Helen lifted her coffee, put the cup down and fished in her bag for a piece of paper, 'here's a number. Ask about us,'

Sam looked at it, she recognised the number. 'Someone dropped the ball with his security.'

'Not us. And I can assure you, Alex is not the man...'

Sam cut her off, 'yes, but the paper, the picture?'

'Our team has gone over that picture very carefully, it's a mock up, done to disgrace him. Politics isn't fair, Sam. The Premier replaced him the day the article came out, he didn't fall on his sword,' Helen stared at her hands and without thinking, straightened her engagement ring, 'he's a good man and the Premier was wrong. Anyway, the police are onto it now.'

'Will he sue?' Sam asked.

'Would you?'

'I'd think about the ramifications it would have on my career before doing anything.'

'That's wise,' she looked at her watch and stood up. Light from the window lit the diamonds in her brooch and it danced like fire across the white tablecloths, 'do you want some time to think about it?'

'Let's make it happen,' Sam said, 'but do it soon, can we?'

'We'll install the dummy cameras tonight. Michael will sweep your home for illegal devices and install our own. Now are you sure you're ready to leave it with us?'

Sam thought about her credit cards, Charles probably knew her passwords anyway. Fear of being found out this way gripped her, 'yes, I want you to do it, but how do I pay cash or credit card?'

'Problem?'

'No, I just realised I'll have to change all my passwords. God, it'll take forever.'

'Better than having your accounts stripped, or your reputation trashed,' she smiled at Sam, 'we'll see you through this, I promise. Oh, and we'll bill you.'

Sam fumbled in her bag, 'I have a spare key that does all doors.'

'Thanks, now how many of these are floating around with relatives or friends?'

'Only the one Charles has and I'll demand that back this afternoon.'

'Good, make a scene. We need them to think the cameras we put in are fakes.'

Sam stood and extended her hand. 'Thank you.'

Helen took it. 'You'll be fine. We'll take care of everything.' She turned and walked to the stairs.

Sam looked at the table, searching for a sign, anything to point her to a new start. There was nothing.

***

With the few things she needed in the boot of her car, Sam ran the back of her finger along its flanks and pondered how long she'd be able to keep it. It was a short drive to her office and she parked in the space reserved for Gino. His car was parked in the spot reserved for the CEO. She walked into the foyer and approached the security desk. Michael had finished his shift and the afternoon guard didn't recognise her.

'I'm here to return these.'

He looked at her card. 'Miss Lewis, I'll call someone down.'

The briefcase held her company laptop, phone, a few notebooks, her diary and an expense claim. She was tempted to delete the files on her phone and computer, but the company's boffins would recover it anyway.

'Thank you,' she said.

It took a few minutes for Charles and Gino to reach the foyer.

'Sam,' Charles held his hands out, 'last night I was about to call the police, we all thought you were missing. You hadn't called in and I was concerned something had happened. Timothy must have tried your phone a hundred times. I've had to ask Gino to step into your role.'

'Gino saw me in Orroroo,' she looked at Charles to gauge his reaction, there was nothing, 'he knew I wasn't due back until today, everyone did. I don't understand what all the fuss was about.'

'You know we needed someone on board to steer the ship, so to speak,' he held her shoulders and looked her up and down, 'you're okay?'

Sam shrugged his hands away and turned to Gino, 'just couldn't wait to take my office, eh? Congratulations,' it was difficult, but she kept the sneer out of her voice and offered him her hand. His grip hurt, but she squeezed until his surrendered.

'I'm sure you'll agree the package Charles and I have offered you is extremely generous,' Gino stayed expressionless, 'enough to help you to start again.'

She felt icicles coming from his smile, 'your offer is pathetic Gino and you know it. After what I've given to this company, what I've done for Charles both during and after hours,' she dropped the laptop bag onto the floor and kicked it with her foot, 'I expected much more than that little kiss on the cheek,' she tossed her mobile phone alongside the case, making sure it landed on the corner, snapping the back off of it. She beckoned him to step closer, 'my house key, you won't need it now.' She held her hand out.

'Gino,' Charles said it as an order and Gino passed her the key.

'What the...' Sam looked at Charles, grabbed his tie and pulled him down, 'why does this bastard have my key?'

'I gave it to him to check the flat when you hadn't shown up.'

She dropped the tie and span around to face Gino, 'so, you're the turd who went through my mail. You are a creep, a sneaky fucking creep.'

'Easy Tiger,' Charles said, 'he was just doing his job.'

Sam turned to Charles again, 'and you're no better,' her anger was on the rise and she enjoyed the feeling. Stepping so close she could almost touch him, she clenched her teeth and whispered, 'I want you to think about upping the ante, or we'll thrash it out through the courts,' she smiled coyly, 'oh and I'll call you in a few days for an update, Charlie.' She handed him the briefcase and he winced at the chill in her voice. It mirrored that of Gino's.

'It is generous, Sam... really.'

'It's your standard offer. Therefore, it's nowhere near good enough and you both know it. I'll give you a week.'

'Where will you be?'

'Looking for a job,' she lied.

'You signed a confidentiality clause.'

'I'll keep my word. We're done here.'

As Charles bent to retrieve the computer, Gino picked up the pieces of the phone, smiling at his boss, 'that went easier than I thought. Lunch?'

Charles' mind was elsewhere. If Gino had seen Sam in Orroroo and the team knew she would be in today, then why was he so anxious about her not returning calls, 'sure,' he said, whatever had happened could wait, Gino was still valuable.

CHAPTER FORTY FOUR

Sam parked in the hotel driveway. Enrico had her luggage waiting and walked it to the car, waving away her offer to help.

'I'm going to miss you, Miss Lewis.'

'Thank you, Enrico. I'll be back again, I promise.'

'How did your experiment turn out?'

'It wasn't what my old boss wanted.'

'Old boss?'

'Afraid so, sometimes the truth doesn't please the people who send you searching for it.'

'But it pleases you, yes?

'It pleases me, yes, but now I need to find a job.'

'No problem for smart people and I reckon you are, how you say it... a brainiac.'

'I hope you're right. Goodbye my friend.'

'Will you come back and see me, even if you only want a coffee. I want to know how you get on.'

'How I get on?'

'The experiment, you won't let it go, no way. I saw the colour of those little stones and I hope you find plenty.'

'Thank you.'

He opened the door for her and Sam promised to stop by for a coffee when she was in the neighbourhood next, knowing as she said it, it was extremely unlikely.

The little Mazda sports car reflected red in the windows of buildings and buses as she drove south along King William Street, before turning toward Greenhill Road and heading for the Adelaide Hills. Behind her the town hall bells chimed twelve o'clock and she found herself smiling at their sound. Were they calling her to return, or sending her on her way?

Swinging in to the service station before the Old Toll Gate to top up with petrol, the sun had broken through and after paying for her fuel, Sam folded the roof down and secured the tonneau. The car, purchased on a whim two years ago, had only been driven a few times, making today her day for loud music and top down travelling.

Driving in the slow lane and closing on a truck on an interstate run, she slapped the steering wheel in time to her favourite songs as she pushed on the clutch and flicked the gear lever to a lower ratio. The little Mazda's exhaust boomed until the noise of air rushing into the intake overcame it. She watched the truckie look down at her as she flew past, pulling the string to his air horn to answer her wave. Sun, speed and sporty, it was how her afternoon felt, a nice contrast to the morning she'd had.

At Tailem Bend she turned the music down and listened to the exhaust burble off the buildings. A police officer pointed a speed camera at her through the window of his patrol car and instinct made her lift off the accelerator and glance at the speedo. Relief swept over her. She was under the limit, relaxed and happy. She gave him a twinkle wave as she drew opposite. Tailem Bend wasn't much bigger than Mundulla and she wondered where he had come from originally and how long had he been stationed in this tin pot town as her small-town fears returned.

She thought about Mundulla and excuses for not going home seeded in her mind, the same reasons that made her escape the moment she was old enough to get away. By the time she reached Coonalpyn that thought had morphed into a strong argument. Common sense won the day as she told herself to stop being silly, she was just going home to catch up with her family, that's all and nothing could change her mind.

A song came on the radio and she remembered Gavin saying it was their song, always would be. Her memory wandered to the night of the cricket final when they slow danced on her mother's lawn, playing it over and over for hours. He should have been out on the booze with his mates, but he chose to spend the time with her. That night she didn't feel at all overweight or frumpy. He made her feel like a princess, his princess, and it didn't matter to him that it made Sasha jealous.

Small town girls can be bitches, but the coven from Sasha's private school were the worst, not that they treated any of the other girls much better. Sasha was the witch who did her best to make Sam feel insignificant whenever the chance arose.

At the slow down sign before Tintinara, the demons in her mind had once again morphed into reasons to turn around and she called home to offer up an excuse. Her mother was the one person who could see through any fabrication and she knew she would have to tell her the truth, that she just couldn't face Mundulla. She waited as the phone rang and was about to cancel the call when her mother answered.

'Hello, Lewis family.'

'Hi Mum it's me, I'm sorry I can't do this. As much as I need to see you, I can't come home.'

'Don't be so silly. Now, Samantha, you always do this. Where are you?'

'I'm just on the Adelaide side of Tintinara.'

'Good, your Dad is over there picking up stockfeed. If you can't come home, at least call into Cox Rural and see him. You know how much he misses you,' there was a pause and she waited for her daughter to speak, 'Sam, do you hear me.'

'Yes, but Dad will insist I come home and then he'll tell me how much you all need me. Mum, I'll weaken, you know I will. He'll talk about the farm, Simon and his family. I can't see him, Mum. He'll suck me in. He always does.'

'I know he will. I'm counting on it,' there was a smile in her mother's voice, 'look, come down the back road, no one needs to know you're in town. On second thoughts, what are you driving, yours or the company car?'

'Mine.'

'Even better, I'll put my face on. You can meet me at the pub and we'll have a couple of drinks. I'd love people to see me driving around in a jazzy little sports car., especially as I'll be sitting alongside my beautiful daughter, the mining magnate.'

'Not anymore Mum. They sacked me this morning, remember.'

'Oh yeah, sorry sweetheart. Look, come in the back way. You can hang out here until you're mended okay? But do drop in and see Dad first, do it for me. It won't take you long.'

'Yes Mum...' hearing her mother's voice had melted the reluctance of the morning. She smiled to herself, knowing when she decided to make the call this would be the result.

She drove into the rear of Cox Rural, where two men in their mid-twenties watched her intently. Sam Lewis wasn't fifteen and frumpy anymore and put a hint of swagger in her walk as she went to the side of the truck where her father was tying down his load.

'Hello Dad.'

'Sam...' he hugged her, lifting and swinging her around as if she were a small child, 'Mum said you were coming. Gawd, I'm that pleased to see you and I want to know everything. What you've found, where you're mining, everything.'

'He put her down. Gee it's good to see you,' he repeated himself several times as he pulled on a load strap and threaded into its winder, 'look you go on ahead. When Mum said you were coming, I thought you'd pull out again, but she said not this time and look, she was right,' he hugged her again.

The yard boys whistled when she opened the driver's door. She curtseyed and they whistled again. She thought of Helen's hijab and it made her wish she had brought a scarf to trail in the wind as she drove away. Something of an Isadora Duncan style gesture. Maybe not, Sam thought as she remembered the blue scarf that brought Isadora to her end.

With her spirits reinstated, she idled the Mazda out of the yard and onto the highway, the blokes whistling and whooping as she changed up into third gear. Well, at least the boys in Tinty liked her and it felt good.

CHAPTER FORTY FIVE

Joe could smell barbeque odours mixing with the eucalyptus of the gum trees in the creek below the homestead and he breathed deeply of his land. Laura and Emily were perched on a log that had been brought down by a flood years before. He sat on his haunches and leaned his back against a creek boulder and Tilly and Jeff lounged in the soft creek sand. A bushman's paradise he thought, as he watched the fat sizzle along the back of the lamb chop he had his eye on. Licking his fingers, he grabbed it from the wire mesh that served as a barbeque grill, slapping it onto a piece of bread he had slathered with margarine. The heat turned the fake butter to liquid that dribbled through his fingers and he gave it a good dusting of salt.

'Hey,' Laura called, 'easy with that salt and pull that fat away too. Remember what the doctor said, you're supposed to cut that stuff right out.'

Looking at Laura, he saw her eyes were fixed on the chop. Exaggerating his discontent, he tore the fat off with his teeth and flicked it toward Gip, 'happy?' he asked.

'Better,' she didn't want to be the family food police, but she wanted him to be around for a few years yet.

Joe watched his dog sniff the gooey morsel, then turn away, and he assumed it was too hot for her. Emily dropped a piece of bread and Gip was onto it.

Jeff rubbed the dog's head with the back of his hand and she lay down beside him and rested her head on his knee, 'that's the quickest she's moved all day,' he said.

Joe finished with his chop and lobbed the bone beside the fat he'd discarded earlier, 'there you go girl, get that inside you.' The dog lifted her head, looked at him, then nuzzled back into Jeff's lap followed his hand with his eyes as he reached for a sausage. When nothing came her way, she sat up and leaned against him, wriggling until she found the right position, eyes alert for anything he might drop.

Joe moved to pick out another chop.

'Here have this one,' Laura reached across and passed him one but with less margarine and, because she knew how much he enjoyed the flavour stored in that centimetre-wide line of temptation, she had removed the fat from the chop. She understood by the look on his face how much he thought he was giving up.

She threw the fat to Gip who sprang to her feet and picked it up between her teeth then shook it a few times before dropping it in a patch of grass under the shade. Here she licked, turning it over until she appeared satisfied it was cool enough, then gulped it and ambled back to lie beside Jeff again.

Emily's pool of scraps took the dog's interest and dropping a whole sausage when she thought no-one would notice, brought Gip to her side.

Joe set a sausage on a stone to cool and called his dog. 'Here, Gip, come on old girl, look what I've got for you,' he waved the sausage, her eyes followed, but she did not move, 'come on girl, good tucker this.' He put it down alongside him and Gip sauntered over, sniffed it and went back to lie beside Jeff. Every time Joe looked at his dog, she turned away, her eyes never meeting his.

Tilly wanted to ride with Jeff on the way to the Wilson place making Joe feel a little put out. The Toyota was his vehicle and today it seemed as though Jeff had commandeered his car, his daughter and his dog.

'Don't worry, Darling,' Laura said and rubbed his arm, 'you can ride with me, then you can tell me all about your morning and what it was you and Jeff talked about,' she didn't wait for him to answer, 'I asked Tilly if they'd set a date yet, but she went all coy on me. Did Jeff say anything to you?' She tipped the billy over the coals, they hissed their objection and turned grey. Using the side of her boot and pushing sand over it until the fire was safe.

'Didn't say a word,' Joe said. He whistled and looked for Gip, but she was waiting beside the Toyota's wheel watching every move Jeff made.

'I think she wants to ride with you,' he called.

Joe looked around for Emily, 'you can come with us if you want, Em.' he called.

'Nah, I'll squeeze in with Mum and Jeff, thanks.'

'Strike three and you're out,' Joe muttered.

'Sorry?'

'Nothing, just thinking aloud.'

Laura held back far enough from Jeff and Tilly to avoid their dust. She wondered about Joe, something had happened today and Jeff seemed distant too.

'You want to tell me about it?'

'About what?'

'Whatever's going on between you and Jeff, that's what,' she turned around to face him and as she did the car veered left.

'Watch what you're doing, woman. You nearly had us off the road.'

'Well, tell me what's wrong. What happened? I thought you were getting past this maudlin introspective business.'

'I thought I was too, but I dunno.'

'What don't you know? You're surrounded by people who love you, we have supportive neighbours and the season has opened up a cracker. You've got so much to be thankful for and you seemed to be getting back to the Joe Gillespie I knew, and now this.' She just stared at the road ahead.

Joe could see she was upset. He never wanted to make her cross, but sometimes these moods came on him before he knew it and he didn't know what to do about it, or even how to express how he felt and he knew it was the silences that worried her the most.

'It's not fair, Joe, not fair at all. If only you'd talk about what's going on.'

Joe didn't know how him feeling miserable could flare into an argument so fast. A lot of it had to do with him being a thinker while she was a talker and he wanted to assure her he was okay, but it took a couple of minutes more to compose his thoughts.

Laura waited.

'Look, I didn't mean to fire off at you, love, but sometimes I just need to process things in my own time before I can talk about it,' he took a deep breath, 'we found a burnt out Falcon ute out at Harris's and John thinks some bloke called Spoggy owns it. It's probably nothing to worry about, but someone tried to make it look like a murder and it set me thinking about last year.'

For twenty minutes, they went over everything he had seen and explaining it to Laura helped him rationalise it to an extent, 'I've got to say it's put the breeze up me a bit.'

'And I'm sorry too,' she reached across and rubbed his arm, 'it's just that I'm always afraid you'll slip back to like you were after the heart attack,' her memory flashed back to Joe's descent into the well and she chuckled, 'and for a while today, I would have willingly dropped you down the well again and left you there.'

Joe laughed, relieved at the banter, 'we won't be doing that for a long time, and when you do, it'll only be a couple of metres. Anyway, did Tilly tell you much about this Sam Lewis bloke?'

'He's a she,' Laura said.

'A woman?'

'Yes, and Tilly says she's quite nice, when she's not working.'

'Yeah, well I've been thinking about it. Maybe we should see what RADOR have to say.'

'You sure? That's a turnaround. What about all those reasons you gave us whenever we had an approach before? You know protection of the environment, protection of Aboriginal sites. Everything you've fought for, for years.'

'I know. Maybe I'm just getting old, or tired of fighting the bastards, but it can't hurt to listen to them,' he rubbed his forehead, just thinking about it was a pain, 'I know we'd need to go over every inch of their proposal, but Tilly has contacts and I've got confidence in her judgement.'

'It's a big shift for you, Joe.'

'It's just an idea at this stage, like me talking about buying Reardon's. I've got lots of ideas and no plans. He pointed to where the Toyota stopped ahead of them, Tilly was holding the gate and, in a few minutes, they would be at Wilsons dragging the Model T out of the dairy.

CHAPTER FORTY SIX

Lifting Gip off the Toyota's tray Jeff watched as she ran around sniffing at everything, passing on some, marking others. Joe resisted calling her, he had been away a while and knew it would take time for her to come around to him again. He squeezed Laura's hand, feeling better to be away from the reminders of the homestead. This place had its ghosts too but, so far, they had proved friendly.

'How do you want to do this Joe?' Jeff stood by the door untying the wire Joe had threaded through last year.

'We'll need to clear the dirt away first.'

'Or lift it off the hinges, they're only pinned,' Laura pointed out.

Joe studied the top of the door and the lintel, 'or we could do that,' he agreed.

Jeff eased a crow bar under the door at the hinge end and lifted, with no result.

'Nah, it's no good. Wait there until I get another bar,' Joe said, heading for his tool box.

Returning to the shed, he prised the door away from the lintel and, as Jeff lifted, the top hinge freed and then the bottom.

'Beauty, I'll give you a hand,' Joe offered.

The planks on the door were loose, the movement making it awkward to handle and Jeff called to Tilly to help them out.

Spider webs, dust and the settling of years were no match for the Gillespies and Joe and Tilly steadied the door as Jeff slid it across the dairy wall.

'Now, what do we have here?' Laura, who had been standing quietly and watching with interest, asked.

For most of the last century, dust and bird droppings had settled over the body work and, while the canvas roof had succumbed to its weight and collapsed long ago, the old car was as its last owners had left it.

Laura pulled a broom out of the Range Rover and followed Joe as he cleared a path into the milking shed. Jeff held a torch and surveyed the wheels and tyres. The wheels were sound, but the tyres had perished.

'She's still up on bricks Joe, What's your plan?'

'I'll get the jack,' Tilly said.

Joe leaned on a mud guard and gave a little push then started to cough in the dust flying from Laura's determined sweeping, 'will you stop with that broom. Jeeze woman, I can hardly breathe,' he coughed and barked orders at the same time, 'keep Emily back, Tilly, and if we use Laura's car to tow it, she'll soon rock off the blocks. Laura, do you want first steer.'

'No...'

'But it's your car. Are you sure?'

'You won't fool me with one of those old lines, Joe. No, I'm happy for you or Jeff to do the honours, thank you very much.'

Dark thoughts of the morning disappeared as Joe continued ownership of the task. 'Okay, here's what we'll do. Tilly, you bring the Range Rover around and we'll put a long rope between them then Jeff, if it runs forward too fast, jam that rock in front of the back wheel, and Laura, if you keep Emily and the dog out the way we'll be set to go,' with the rope tied Joe continued his instruction, 'now, Tilly, just take the strain and I'll tell you when.'

Not tempted to sit on a seat covered with dust and pigeon poop, Joe stood alongside, reaching forward to release the brake and putting the car in neutral, he took a firm grip on the steering wheel, 'righto.'

Dust flicked off the rope as it tightened and, in no time, the Model T was off the blocks and rolling into the sunlight, moving forward as the rope slackened, like a dog not wanting to leave its kennel, until the front wheels rocked up onto the mound of dirt and it retreated back into the gloom.

'Okay Tilly, this time go a bit further. You right over there Jeff?' Joe said.

'Still good here Joe.'

Tilly eased the car forward, this time the rope stretched and the old car emerged.

'Keep going, a bit more,' Jeff called.

Laura waved her broom slicing through the few cobwebs tying the old car to the shed.

'Well there you are, Lizzie. Pleased to meet you,' Laura said, as the others looked on, pleased with their effort. Jeff moved to drag the door back into place.

'Leave it mate, the birds can come in and clean a few webs out and we'll come back and fix it up later,' Joe said.

Jeff let the door rest on the ground then walked inside to put the bricks back against the wall. He bumped into something with his hip, reaching back to brush the dust off before trying to identify it. With his torch in his mouth, while clearing dirt off the front of it with both hands, he exposed the metal casing of a box like structure.

'Joe, did you know this was here?'

'What is it?' Joe asked, without turning to look at Jeff.

'Some kind of safe covered in crap and old bag or something. Hang on,' Jeff put his nose down inside his shirt as an improvised dust mask and slid the cover off. Dust flew everywhere as before and he bolted for fresher air.

'Pfwar, that's putrid,' he coughed and spluttered. Gip walked over to him, concerned, an action not lost on Joe. 'It's okay, old girl,' Jeff said and gave the dog a pat.

Tilly noticed her father was looking weary and intervened, 'come on we're all dirty now anyway, so while we wait for the dust to settle, you can show me these murals Dad. You've always said they were something special,' she grabbed a hammer, lever, and cordless drill and powered toward the house. She was already unwinding the screws that secured the corrugated iron over the front door before Joe caught up with her.

'Hold your horses, we'd better get Lizzie loaded first,' Joe said, digging around in the tool box for more ropes.

Laura was in the shed, her curiosity stronger than the dust that hung in the still air. 'I might want this safe to come too, Joe.' She said.

Joe slammed the toolbox lid. 'Well, who would have guessed,' he knew he was being sarcastic now, 'more bloody rubbish to rescue,' he didn't understand his mood and regretted the words as they left his mouth, 'sorry love, I'm all over the place today.'

'Joe, it's okay, really, I understand,' she rubbed his shoulders, 'we can leave everything and go home if you want. Tilly and Jeff can bring the trailer back.'

'No, I'm jumpy today. First it was Pop's office, then finding that ute, and now poking around in the old man's stuff,' he looked west toward the Flinders Ranges, as if seeking an answer to his moodiness in the clouds had formed a halo around Mary's Peak, 'I've never been good with any of the old man's junk. Too much shit happened out here when I was a kid and it's a box I've never wanted to kick open again,' he put his arms around her, 'when he wasn't in town, he spent a lot of time out here on the booze, or drifting around old mines and pissing it up with a bunch of his gold digging mates.'

'Tough memories, eh?'

'He let the place run to shit, you know that. I'm dodging bullets from the friggin' Vietcong and he's running this place into the ground and what for? Some bloody whim. I'd swear he was convinced he'd found Lasseter's Reef.'

She hoisted herself up onto the mudguard of the trailer and waited until he was ready to speak again.

'I don't know...' he looked around and ran his hand over his face, searching the horizon for something to focus on. Mount Mary's halo had gone. He shook his head in an action similar to a dog shaking dust from its coat, getting rid of things that made it uncomfortable.

'Come on, Love. I'm okay now, thanks.'

'Good to keep going?' she asked.

'Yep,' he waved his hand toward the house, 'let's get in and out of that mausoleum before it gets too dark,' he grabbed the spot light from the Toyota's toolbox and waved it at her, mimicking Jeff holding the torch in his mouth before morphing into Mick Dundee, 'now, this...' he said, 'this is a light.'

Laura laughed and resumed her broom duties, 'every house can use a sweep.'

Joe thought about the last time he had walked into this house, a few days after his father had died and he remembered his last hospital visit and his father's face as he lay dying, when the only thing he had asked was for him to read and burn the stack of papers by his chair. Returning to the Wilson homestead, Joe had seen the mess Les had left and, without touching anything, he had boarded the place up and left. Les was dead and that was that, another of his father's disasters consigned to memory. 'I should have just tossed a match in back then,' he said, 'and it would have saved us a bit of trouble now.'

'You said something.'

'Nothing important love, come on let's get this over with.'

When they reached the doorway, Joe and Laura could hear Emily shouting at spiders, wielding a stick and slashing at cobwebs while Tilly shushed her, calling for her to be careful. Jeff was leading the way through the house testing the floors as he went. Wilochra dust covered everything and the ceiling bowed under its weight.

The house was dark. Laura sensed Les' presence in every room and wondered how Joe was coping, finding him in the front room staring at his father's chair. The papers he had been asked to burn over forty years ago had fallen from the side-table and onto the floor and she was wondering whether Joe should look through them or leave them where they were when he picked them up and set them back on the table.

Laura rubbed his back, 'You okay?'

'Yeah, I'm fine. I've always hated coming in here. Whenever I came to check on him the old man would be full of booze and mean as sin,' he kicked at a lump on the floor, then reached down and picked it out of the dirt, 'with this resting on his knees,' he showed a double barrel shot gun to Laura and broke the breech, plucking two cartridges from their chambers, 'stupid, stupid, stupid... anyone could have tripped on this and blown their head off.'

'Jeeze Joe, you should have checked it when you came back to board the place up. You knew it was there and you have to lighten up on Les and let it go. This burden of hate is too heavy to carry around, even for you,' she grabbed him either side of his face and roughed up his jowls, 'he doesn't matter, Joe. Nothing does,' she stretched up onto her toes and kissed him, 'you're a good bloke and we're very lucky to have you. Now go and talk Tilly through the murals. I want to look at the portraits on the wall over there.'

'Sorry, Love, I don't know why it still gets me going, but it does. I promise I'll try to let it go.'

'Good, now just shine that light over here before you go.'

Joe waved the spotlight around the room to where Laura pointed at two candles and a box of matches on the mantelpiece, 'think it's safe to light them?' she asked.

'I'd have thought the rats and mice would have had them by now.'

She picked her way across the floor and pulled at the wick on the longest candle. She tried the matches but the head flew of the first one, 'damn, I thought it was too good to be true.'

'Keep trying, you'll get one eventually.'

On the third match the flame took and she managed to get a light, 'okay, I'm right now.'

He left her to it and found Tilly and Emily looking at the murals at the far end of the passage. Jeff had his back to them and was searching the room to their left, bumping the floor with a stick to make sure the boards were safe, stopping as he entered another room to call Tilly to look at a picture hanging over the mantle. 'Hey Tilly, come and tell me what you think?'

'What am I supposed to be looking at?'

'The painting above the fireplace, don't you reckon it looks out of place. The frame looks like it was pretty flash in its time,' he scoured the painting for a signature, 'well, look at this, it's signed Joe Gillespie. Here Em, have a look at your Pop's painting.' He lifted it down and headed outside for a better look, Emily at his heels.

Tilly was standing by the fireplace when Joe heard her scream, rushing into the room in time to see the tail of a snake disappear beneath the boards, Jeff not far behind.

'Aghh, I stood on it,' she said, her voice shaky.

'Gotcha, you're safe now,' Jeff was at Tilly's side hugging her, 'did it get you anywhere? Come on let's get you out into the light and I'll check you out.'

'Calm down,' Tilly told him, 'I just got a fright and probably the snake did too. I'm okay, really, I squealed and it's gone. It's probably lived undisturbed here for years. Now where's this painting.'

Joe felt Laura's hand on his shoulder.

'She doesn't need either of us as much now, does she?'

'Sometimes it feels as if everything's slipping away, and I miss her needing me. Silly I suppose, but I can't help it.' He shone his light at the hole the snake disappeared into.

'She still needs you Joe. She's just in love, that's all.'

Joe dropped onto his knees, playing the light into the gap between the floor and fireplace.

'Are you mad, what are you trying to do, coax the damn thing out again? Come on Joe, leave the bloody snake alone,' Laura wanted to get as far away from the reptile as she could, but her curiosity intensified and she knelt beside him, 'what are you looking at?'

Joe said nothing, but shone his light around the edge of the carpet square. He rolled an arm chair away and pulled corner of the rug back. 'There's a cellar, c'mon help me pull this back,' he waved her to the other side of the room.

'And what? Jump into a hole filled with snakes, I don't think so.'

'Come on. The snake is long gone. I thought I saw something shiny in there and I wondered what it was. Come on,' he coaxed again, 'it won't take long.'

She lifted a corner of the carpet, 'let's roll it, but do it slowly, I don't want to get any more dust in my lungs today.'

The carpet was fragile and as they rolled it back to the wall, it leaked silt into the air.

'Yep, just as I thought.' Joe twisted and pulled on the ring, flinging the trapdoor open, laying on his stomach as he lowered his head and shoulders into the cellar, leaving

Laura in a darkened room again. Light flickered through the cracks in the floor, casting spears of yellow along the walls and ceiling before Joe pulled himself out, rolled over onto his back and hauled up onto his haunches, 'here Love, give us a hand up, will you?' he panted and she held her hands out.

'We're not as young as we once were, so stop pushing yourself, okay?'

'The bloody place is empty. I thought he might have hidden it there.'

'Hidden what?'

'The gold, you know the stuff mentioned in his poem. I thought if he'd hidden it. It might still be down there, but no. Come on, we'd better load all this stuff and board the place up again.'

Emily wanted to keep the picture. She thought her Pop probably painted it when he was a boy, but because he was really old now, he'd forgotten it.

Tilly was not sure she wanted it in her house, but Jeff encouraged Emily and Joe agreed to clean it up for her.

After a lot of shuffling and shifting, everything fitted on the trailer and Joe tied the last rope over the safe. He found it hard to comprehend Laura's love for the junk, but knew she would have a plan.

'Hoarding is history,' she told him.

Again, he called to Gip, who looked the other way and sauntered over to sit by the door of the Landcruiser. Joe walked toward the Range Rover, waiting for Laura to climb in before opening the driver's door. He took a last look around and turned the key as Emily rapped on the window, wanting to ride home with them. He felt at peace for the first time today and smiled agreement.

Laura missed the action and her heart ached for his disappointments as she watched for change to write its way across his face, but he remained stoic as Emily enthused about Gidget, and she was proud of the way he encouraged their grandchild to tell him everything. Throughout the day, she could see her husband crumbling every time a complication presented, and needed a plan to get him through the black that dogged his mood. Before his heart attack last year, complications had been his specialty. He fixed stuff, people, places, things. It was what he did, who he was. She needed a plan and soon.

CHAPTER FORTY SEVEN

Gino relaxed in Sam's old office. He had changed her desk to the one he spotted in Prince Albert Antiques on Magill Road and the dealer found matching credenza in Melbourne he would deliver by the end of the following week. However, the chair would be a commission, so he would make do with a high-end modern unit for now. He liked the view, but thought the decor shabby. A decorator could give it an Edwardian feel, however, with the need for Charles to sign off on it first, he decided he could wait, it wouldn't do to get ahead of himself.

He ran a finger along the embossing of the inlay on his desk as he walked to the door and closed it. From the corner windows, he watched the street for a moment before closing the blinds and returning to his chair, where he lay back and clasped his hands behind his head. He closed his eyes and let success sweep over him for a few minutes. Today had turned out okay. Sam Lewis was gone from the company and out of Charles' life too. Now all he had to do was find Spoggy, he knew too much and Gino needed to be sure of his silence. He picked up the mobile phone he kept for these occasions and sent a text. Spoggy was always like a mouse to cheese on a trap, only this time it was his trap. For a few minutes, he pondered about ways to keep him quiet and decided to send him on a sea voyage, any worries he had about his snitch would be over soon.

***

In Mundulla Sam sat facing her mother, she looked at the tea set, fine bone china handed down from mother to daughter over four generations. Recycling before it became fashionable, she supposed.

'Tea tastes better from a proper pot eh, Mum,' she slurped, knowing her mother would tut-tut, but Penny Lewis said nothing, 'will I get this when you drop off the perch?' Her hand waved over the service.

'I'll leave it to whoever produces a direct in line granddaughter, I guess. Anyway, you'd only give it to Oxfam or something like that.' Two can play your game, her mother thought, and waited for her daughter to bite, but she changed the subject instead.

'Dad looks good.'

'He was rapt that you dropped in, we all wondered if you'd squib out again. Simon even wanted to take a wager on it,' she reached across the table and rubbed Samantha's hand, 'I hope you've learned that not everyone is out to get you. Mean kids grow up and they move on. All that rubbish from school is in the past and no-one could call you chubby now. You could be on the cover of Vogue if you wanted to.'

'Jeeze, Mum. You're laying it on a bit thick, now. I won't get out from under all of this bullshit, if you keep it up.'

'Yeah, but you didn't come home to ask about who gets the tea service and you didn't come back to wish Gavin well either. So what's up?'

'I got the sack, that's what's up, and I can't work out if I'm sad, angry, or hurt. I'm pissed off at Gino and even more so with Charles, but I knew what they were like when I took the job. I just don't think they ever saw me as more than an expendable commodity or took me seriously, and I really hate feeling like I've been used,' she stood up and paced the kitchen, 'do you know, Mum, just last week I was hell bent on destroying a nice family. I was prepared to dig up their farm to get Charles what he wanted. I thought I could show them I was tough, no bullshit, all business, but I'm not like Charles and Gino. They have no feelings for anyone and right now I hate them more than anything.'

'Hate's a pretty strong word.'

'It's the only word that's appropriate right now...' the conversation was going nowhere so Sam decided to lead into a less conflicted direction, 'oh, I just remembered I wanted to ask you about a caravan park in Orroroo I think we stayed in when I was a kid.'

'How could you remember that, you weren't much more than a baby, or maybe it was Gav who was the baby.'

'I went to see the reservoir while I was out there and it triggered a memory. I don't know why, but I remember water, a yellow speed boat and people having a picnic,' she waited for a moment, 'maybe I've seen a photo at some time, but the memory is real enough.'

'We were there off and on for about eighteen months, maybe more, when your dad ran a drilling rig. Ask him when he gets home, you know how much he likes to talk about the good old days,' she pushed a tray of homemade biscuits across the table, more out of habit than conscious thought.

Sam waved them aside, saying, 'Mum, how about we finish up and you can show me the farm. I don't think I've seen it properly in years.'

'Yes, and then my girl, we can show off around town in your racy little sports car, roof down, wind in our hair and watching the locals spin on their heel to look at us. It'll be great.

Later that evening Clive Lewis held the vial to the light and swirled the contents, while swiping buttered bread into the gravy from the remains of his roast lamb and stuffing it into his mouth with his free hand.

'So, from what I can see in here it's from the Pekina area. Not much out there other than road building minerals, looks like typical creek bed shit to me, nothing commercial anyway,' he chewed some more, 'how'd I do?'

'Hmm, not too bad, but if you look closer, there's a tiny garnet, or it could be a ruby, but that's about it. There were some blue chips and I'd hoped for sapphires, but it turned out to be bits of glass from a medicine bottle. I've searched the old records and scoured our own company's drilling surveys. If Joe Gillespie is sitting on a gold mine, he must be the goose that laid golden eggs, because I can't find a friggin' thing.'

'You're not in a mining camp now, you two. You'll use your manners at my table.'

'Sorry, Mum, I forget when Dad and I get going,' Sam lifted the wine bottle and her mother nodded.

'Sorry love,' Clive Lewis picked up his wife's hand and kissed it, 'it wasn't easy, was it?'

She smiled at him, 'well, it did set us with this place though.'

'Can either of you remember the Gillespies?' Sam asked.

'Joe Gillespie has a place out somewhere out on the Hammond to Quorn road. Yeah, I remember him, big man. His old man died and left the place in a hell of a mess,' Clive looked at Penny, 'you'd remember him, his wife was some sort of academic. Great people, but you're right. There's no gold out there.'

'I thought so,' Sam said.

'We never got onto their place though. We sunk holes all over the place in and around Eurelia and by the time we'd finished on one place, the paddock had more holes than a netting fence.'

'Yeah? Well when I went to give my boss that news, I lost my job and probably my reputation too,' she turned away to hide the emotion writing its way across her face.

Penny Lewis rubbed her daughter's hand again.

Sam leaned her head on her mother's shoulder, but after a second or two her anger returned and she straightened up, 'sorry, Mum, but stuff him. I made things happen for that company. It was my company, I was the boss and I worked my backside off to get that job,' she stared at the ceiling, 'the hours I invested just to please him and this is all the thanks I get,' she slapped her hand onto the table, 'and he can't even tell me himself but gets that piss-ant Gino to tell me he wants me gone,' she looked at her parents, 'then they added the ultimate humiliation in having security walk me out the door. I don't know whether to be angry or cry but, right at this moment, I just know I want to screw them over, big time.'

'Samantha.'

'Sorry, Mum I don't need to unload on you guys, but I have to talk to someone.'

In that instant Penny realised how much of her life Sam had put into this company and how losing close friends was part of the price she paid.

'We're here for you love, always will be... you remember that.'

Sam lifted her eyes to the ceiling, 'I know that Mum, I always have.'

Already onto his apple sponge and wanting to offer support, Clive pointed his spoon at her. 'Now look here Sam, I know you're not stupid, so what is it you're not telling them?' a grin split his face, 'if there is nothing on the Gillespie place, tell me what you found and where?'

'It's in this report,' she pushed a memory stick across the table, 'take a look later and tell me what you think.'

'Enough for now,' her mother tapped her spoon on the side of the bowl, 'you can do all of that tomorrow, tonight I want to hear about you,' she rubbed Sam's shoulder, 'not the business you're in and not the same one your dad wishes he was still in, but about you and you plans for the future.'

CHAPTER FORTY EIGHT

Darryl Cassidy stared past the young constable making notes on the incident board.

'Uniform tomorrow, Boss?' she asked without looking at him.

'Ah...' he was lost in thought, staring into the image of the dead face of Joe's attacker, 'sorry?'

Angela continued to post information from the Hammond Road murders on the board, 'what should I wear tomorrow? Uniform, or plain clothes.'

'Plain clothes, let's do our best to emulate our city cousins. We don't want them to brush us off as country hicks.'

She thought about the suit she had bought at the beginning of summer and hadn't worn yet, 'well, tomorrow, clothes will maketh the woman.'

'Yeah... okay,' still lost in his thoughts, he walked to the window and searched the streetscape as if seeking inspiration, then returned to gaze at the board.

'Boss,' Angela spoke louder to gain his attention, 'boss?'

He spoke without looking back, 'Ange, you're the computer whiz. Overlay the photo of those tyre tracks,' he tapped the board, 'and the ones near the gate where Jeff found the ute. Can you do that?'

'Yeah sure.'

'And the motorbike tracks in and around Joe's house when it was trashed. Can you get hold of the evidence photos from there?'

'Yeah, but Sir, there were hundreds of tracks out there. What am I looking for?'

'I want to know if that burnt-out wreck was either near the gate where the steer was killed, or at the farmhouse when it was trashed.'

'Care to share what you're thinking, Boss?'

'Not right now. It could all be a wild goose chase,' he went back to the pictures on the board, 'make a copy of anything interesting and bring it with you tomorrow. We'll see if my hunch matches the evidence.'

It was still dark when Cassidy arrived at his office the following day and, while he waited for Angela, he flipped through the file she had left on his desk the night before, plucking out several photos and spreading them along the credenza.

'Have you found them yet?' Angela swept into his office, ready for business she touched three photos with the point of her fingernail. 'It has to be the same bike. See, there's a chunk taken off the corner of the knobby tyre and look, there's a split or scratch running along the right-hand side.'

'How do you know it's the right side?'

'I checked with Sarge. He knows a bit about bikes,' she stood up and tugged at the hem of her jacket, 'want me to drive?'

'Uh, yeah sure,' he slid the photos into the folder and shoved them into his briefcase,' righto let's see what our city cousins have for us.'

In the passenger seat he reread the material in the file and wondered about the motorcycle and how it tied the three separate crime scenes together. He checked the photos of the burnt bike from the Hammond road murders against the tyre track photos. It was a different machine.

'Want to tell me about the tyre tracks?' Angela asked. They had travelled seventy kilometres south from Port Augusta and almost an hour of silence felt as if it were crushing her, 'boss?'

'Sorry, Ange, I'm trying to go over everything to see if I missed anything the first time around. I thought we had

301

Joe all tucked up safe and sound, but now I'm not sure. I reckon this has nothing to do with a fire fight in Vietnam,' he twisted in his seat 'sure, the bloke had a score to settle, but it goes deeper than that. This is about money, or land or something we haven't uncovered yet. What I don't want to do, is alert whoever it is that we're looking into them, or give Joe any grief if it turns out to be a wild goose chase.' He folded the file and sat it on the back seat. 'Give Rob a call and see where he is. If he's close, ask him to meet us at the next roadhouse.'

'No problems.'

'And tell him what we know and we can get some breakfast while he gives us his perspective.'

'That works for me, Sir.'

Senior Constable Rob Ackland had been with the traffic police for over six years, spending most of that time stationed in Port Augusta. He had been involved with Joe's case from the first day and, like Angela, he had a good eye for detail. His insight into what might be missing from the photo was invaluable. Cassidy wished Jeff Rankin was still with them, he saw detail most coppers would miss but he was pleased to see Rob waiting for them when they walked into the restaurant.

After they had ordered and sat down, Darryl opened the folder. He passed him a photo and spread the others along the table, 'look at the tracks. Are they all by the same bike?'

'Yep and they're all from different Gillespie crime scenes.'

'Christ, you've been talking to Sarge,' he looked at his companions, 'is there nothing you guys don't share?'

'Only our private life is off limits besides, as you'd said before, this is about the attempt on Joe Gillespie's life and everyone at the station had a role in that case.'

Angela looked at Cassidy, 'Sir, we all want to help. More than that though, we want keep it away from the city mob. This is a Port Augusta case and we feel obligated.'

Rob backed her up, 'look Sir, the way we found the American that night has haunted me ever since. No-one scares to death, or at least nobody I've ever heard of anyway. It never felt finished to me. I agree he was the bloke chasing Joe, but we all know Joe didn't do it, he was in no fit state to kill whatever his name was.'

'Gordon-Sanders,' Cassidy reminded him.

'Yeah, him. Well I know about the e-mails, the social media link and all that stuff, but why now?' he looked at the photo of a dead Gordon-Sanders sitting in a chair in front of a half-eaten meal, 'and he could have found Joe long before he did if he'd really wanted to. I reckon someone put him up to it and I'd be looking into his bank statements. How he funded the trip out here and who paid for the false documents, that sort of thing.'

'Are you questioning how I wrote up my investigation?'

'No Sir, I don't think we missed the boat on anything we had at the time, but I reckon we should roll a few more rocks over to sort the tadpoles from the snakes.'

'So, what you're really still saying is that I got it wrong,' the veins in his neck bulged as his temper rose. He was being unreasonable and he knew it. He needed to pull his head in and listen.

'No, that's not what I'm saying at all,' Rob noticed the red flush spreading across his senior officer's cheeks and tried to pull back on his comments, 'what I'm saying is that now we have a bit more evidence to prove this prick was put up to it.'

'Yeah, I'd go along with that, but still, my question is why?'

'I might be able to help with that, Sir,' Angela didn't want to betray a confidence, but finding who was behind this was more important, 'the word is that just before the Gillespies went to England, Joe found three gold ingots in a well and Jeff reckoned a poem Joe's old man wrote mentioned something about more treasure.'

'Anyone know how Joe's doing after this latest episode?' Rob asked.

'Andy phoned Jeff last night,' Angela said, 'and he told him Joe had come good for a while but the last few days he seems to be going back into his shell again. It seems he's worried someone was still out to get him.'

'Right, well we'd better make tracks and see what's what in the city.' Darryl picked up the folder and made his way to the door.

'Hey, Boss, it might be nothing, but the Adelaide traffic boys told me the copper in Port Wakefield found a burnt-out trail bike yesterday. It could be worth calling in.'

'Follow it up then,' he shook his hand, 'and let me know tomorrow,' he walked to the driver's side of the car, 'you can ride shotgun for a while, Ange.'

Pleasantries at the Salisbury Police Station over, Cassidy and Angela met up with the Senior Constable at the arson site, where he passed Cassidy a file, flipping the pages of his notebook as he went over the results of their second doorknock. The house had been vacant most of the time and a gardening service took care of the front and back yard once a fortnight. The letterbox had a no junk-mail notice on it and other mail was disposed of by the gardener.

A neighbour reported hearing a big single cylinder motor bike in the street late on Saturday night and the same person heard a car with a noisy exhaust idle past in the early hours of Monday morning, thinking it was hoons using their road to avoid the speed humps on the avenue a couple of blocks over.

Cassidy quizzed the officer, 'that's a comprehensive report, but I'd be interested your offsider's theories?'

'He should be back soon, Sir. He went to check with the owners of the takeaway places a few blocks away to ask if they'd seen anyone from this address lately.'

'Why?'

'We found a pizza box sticking out of a recycle bin and asked the people in the house if it was theirs. We know the family are Asian who speak little English and the box seemed out of place for what we knew of the family.'

'How would you know that?'

'We were called to a family violence matter there last year. Anyway, they denied the box was theirs, so he's gone to check.'

'Why did you think it was out of place?'

'The row was about keeping the family's traditions alive. The Grandfather had a cleaver and was chasing one of his granddaughters around the yard. A neighbour reported it and we attended. Apparently, he was furious at her for bringing something from McDonalds into the house,' Shannon shrugged, 'and it escalated.'

'That sounds fairly astute to me,' the DI said, passing the file to Angela, 'check the photos and see if you can find what I spotted. Then get Sarge to assemble the troops for a conference first thing tomorrow and ask him to call in John O'Rourke in too.'

'Sure Boss, anything else?'

'Not for now. He took Shannon's elbow, 'good work Senior, now let's have a look around.'

Angela looked at the photos while she waited for the phone to answer, her nail stabbing at a picture, 'you don't miss a trick, DI, this motorbike tyre is the same as the others.'

After finishing her first call, Angela phoned John O'Rourke in Orroroo and asked him to go to Spoggy's place and take photos of any tyre tracks he could find, particularly motorcycle tracks and any that might come from a high-powered Commodore or Falcon. She made a note in the file to check photos from the crime scene at the Hammond rail yards where they had found Gordon-Sanders' body, wondering if the same motorcycle been there.

Cassidy picked his way through the remains of a sixty's bungalow, there was nothing special about the house and its dated eighties decor. In the corner of what had once been the lounge room, the remains of a tube style television was out of place for this time and gave further evidence of the house's resistance to entering the twenty first century.

'What do you see, Shannon?' He asked.

'Looks old, like my grandparent's place before they moved into the nursing home. Old TV, kitchen is fifties I reckon, and the stove is from another age.' He wondered what Cassidy was getting at and hesitated. 'Drug lab?'

'Did forensics find anything to suggest that? Hydroponic system, pumps, plant material, crystal meth gear?'

'No, Sir.'

'Well speculate man, tell me what you're thinking.'

Cassidy read the senior constable's discomfort and backed off, he pointed in Angela's direction, 'look I know we're from the sticks, but we're used to working as a team. I want to know what you see, Senior, anything that can help with the case and you can rest assured I'm not going to bawl you out for giving me your opinion. Now, if you were in my position what would you be doing?'

'Okay to take some time, sir?'

'Sure.'

Angela saw the constable picking his way through the ruin to meet them.

'Sir?'

Darryl turned in reply, 'tell me about the pizza.'

The officer explained it had been picked up from the Polo Pizza outlet at Smithfield at eight twenty-five on Saturday night. The manager remembered the customer had called the order in from a phone box and he had had asked for a rego number as security because the caller wanted to pay cash on pick up. The registration matched the ute Spoggy had been using.

The DI passed the box back to the constable. 'Get that into forensics and have them run it against everyone in the system. If it was Spoggy, I'd like to know if he had company and... good work officer.' He walked back to the garage and turned to the senior, 'you might have laughed at the young bloke's theories yesterday, but now I want you to channel your inner Sherlock Holmes and tell me what you see.'

'There's a shadow board without many tools. It's pretty much as we said yesterday, car tyres in the dust that go over the knobblies from the motor bike, a Yamaha tool kit is open on the bench and there's a small battery charger alongside it. It's been moved recently and tracks on the bench and footprints show someone has stood in front of the car that was parked here. They've walked back and forth to the driver's door more than once,' he paused for breath, 'and there's a couple of early Monaro posters and a tune-up chart from nineteen seventy-nine.'

'Anything else?'

'Well the floor is as we said yesterday, it went in well after the shed was built. If you look at the headlight alignment board on the back wall, it's splashed with concrete and the vertical measurements are about a hundred and fifty mil short,' his confidence rose as he expanded his findings, 'there are no oil drops or marks on the floor, so whatever was parked here was in good nick mechanically and the tyre tracks are deep, so they could be almost new. There's only one set of foot prints leading from the door to the driver's side of the car, so we can be confident that the driver was the only one to enter the shed.'

'Righto, now that wasn't so hard was it. Don't ever discount your abilities, Senior. You could make a good bush detective one day,' he turned to Angela, 'can you think of anything before we go?'

'Not at the moment, Sir.'

'Sir?' the constable crouched by the door pointed to a mark in the concrete. It was a concreter's company stencil that had been defaced before the floor had hardened, 'we have a name.'

Angela took a photo of the mark before contacting the company to ask who paid for the work, while the other officers were ordered to tear up the floor to expose the old mechanic's pit. Cassidy walked to the north corner of the block where drooping branches of a pepper tree covered an iron construction. It could have been a chook run or a garden shed, leaning in dilapidation against the tree. He pulled at a warped pallet the served as a door. The place reeked from bird droppings that covered the concrete floor and he grappled with a grape vine that had invaded the wire netting before the tree overtook it all.

He pushed his sunglasses to the top of his head and his eyes adjusted to the dim interior, fixing his gaze on a mound in the rear corner.

Angela noticed the flash from the camera of his phone and watched him emerge, brushing pepper corns from his hair and pulling spider webs from his shirt.

'Getting back to nature, Boss?' She asked.

He answered with a grunt then told the senior constable to have forensics turn the shed over as well.

'What's the shed about, Sir?' Angela asked

'Probably nothing, but we want to show our city cousins that we're thorough,' he cleaned his sunglasses, 'how did you go with the company?'

'Good. They said it was a cash job invoiced to a Liam Le-Strange. Nothing special about the job other than the owner did the form work himself.'

'How long's it been down?'

'They did the job in November nineteen ninety-five.'

'A lot can happen in fifteen years.'

'Boss?'

'Just thinking out loud, Ange.' He turned to the Senior Constable, 'doorknock the area again. Check the shops too, find out who was living here before that floor went down. I want to know how many people have lived here, who they were and how they lived,' he passed him a card, 'email me with an update tonight and I'll phone tomorrow.'

CHAPTER FORTY NINE

Sam went with her father to shift the pivot irrigator. She knew it was a ploy to talk about mining and something she would rather do than grocery shopping with her mother. There was something about being on the farm that eased her mind, the rattle of tools on the tray of his four-wheel-drive was comforting and the incessant barking of the farm dogs riding in the back reminded her she was home.

'I've been thinking about the Gillespie place,' her father pointed for her to open the gate.

'Yeah?' Sam climbed out and waited until he drove through. There was no stock in the paddock so she left the gate open and ran back to the vehicle.

'I remembered something an old scratcher told me back in the seventies, reckoned he'd been done out of a claim, years before. He bragged about a reef that would make Lasseter envious.

'Scratcher?'

'Something my dad called people who scratched a living out of prospecting.'

'Where was this claim? And who was he?'

'I just knew him as Mad Charlie,' he eased the irrigator over the pivot point, 'here, jump out and pull the drawbar pin, eh,' he rocked the vehicle back and forward until he felt the pin loosen, 'then it would be a big help if you could give me a hand to set up.'

As they worked, Sam's father told her the scratcher had worked a claim at Waukaringa in the early days and asked Les Gillespie to back him. For years they combined to make the claim work and, like everyone else around there, they sent their ore to the battery in Peterborough. Rumour had it there'd been a card game at the Imperial Hotel the night it burnt down. Les Gillespie and Mad

Charlie were the last players standing and the stakes were high.

'Everything had been fine between Gillespie and the scratcher until the night of the pub fire in Orroroo. It was around September '69 and the licensee often promoted a card game to boost his takings. However, that night was a big one, a poker championship, something he wanted to become an annual event.'

'I can't see how that would have been legal,' Sam said.

'It wasn't, and his idea was scotched by the local copper and most of the town's wowsers, but he got around this by putting up stake money for the people who objected.'

'Yeah,' Sam knew her dad loved a story, but the mix of truth and fiction in his yarns could always be called into question.

'Two hundred dollars was a lot of money to most in the district, but Bert saw it as an investment that would pay dividends after the tournament. Five percent from each winning pot meant his plan couldn't fail and commercial travellers who were regulars at the hotel would soon spread the word.'

'So how did it work?'

'Bert capped the number of players at sixty and on the designated evening, thirty serious and twenty-six novice gamblers registered for the championship.'

'That many?'

'Yep, professional players deposited ten thousand dollar stakes, amateurs gamblers put up two thousand. Mug punters, for whom he had a waiting list, thrust their two hundred dollars at him.'

'You're making it up,' Sam said, 'that would never happen in a place like Orroroo.'

'You can scoff young lady, but I'm told at the gala dinner that night a red pyramid of notes built on the table as each gambler pressed forward to register their stake and before the soup arrived two hundred and ninety thousand lay before them. Bert and his wife stood behind the cash and as a photo was taken to record the occasion, Bert held up another ten grand.'

'A photo, really?'

'Yes,' Clive sounded indignant, 'I even had one somewhere.'

'Bet you can't find it now,' it felt good to laugh.

'It's in the wardrobe at the back of the motor-shed, I think.'

'That's lost then,' they both laughed this time.

'Anyway, he puts the ten thousand on the pyramid, declaring this the richest poker tournament in the State's history. After dessert, he puffed himself to full height and rapped on his glass. When he had the attention of the diners, he told them the games would begin at nine o'clock and asked the players to open the envelopes in front of them. He waited and they fidgeted. Each envelope held a card, a red number to tell them their table and the blue, their seating position. He wished them luck and said the match steward would call them at eight forty-five pm and the doors would close at nine until the first refreshment break at midnight.'

'It's a good story Dad.'

He passed her a couple of spanners and pointed at the toolbox. 'The mug punters took to their rooms where some tried to sleep while others flexed their fingers with a card deck and at eight fifty-five, the dinner gong sounded, and players were called to take their place at the tables.'

'And they had to stop at midnight?'

'Yes,' he rocked on a tyre and watched a wave of movement ripple along the irrigator's length, 'anyway, when tournament master called time, the gamblers returned to their rooms and the mug punters who'd lost went home to explain the unexplainable. Others sat outside in their cars and cried like babies. Only the winners were happy and twelve hours later those left in the tournament gathered again in the dining room, a scene more sombre than the night before.'

'How did anyone go to the loo?'

'They didn't, anyway it went on just like the night before until time was called. By then the room stank of cigarettes and the sweat of desperate men and the remaining players adjourned to their rooms for a shower and a change of clothes.'

'Dad, forty hours is a long time and even with scheduled breaks, how did the players rest?'

'It is a long time but think, everyone would be going over the other players' faces in their mind, trying to remember flinches, smiles, searching for anything that might indicate their next play.'

'But what has this to do with the Gillespies?'

'If you have some patience, I'll tell you,' he turned the key and started off again, 'Mad Charlie didn't like his last hand and called for a new deck. On the table, over two hundred and seventy thousand dollars in cash and bonds sat before them. Only four hours earlier he'd won the deed to the John Billings' farm. John sat in the corner drained, he couldn't go home. He had no home,' he waved his hands to emphasise the tragedy of it.

'Really?'

'Yeah, Bill Simpson had folded a broken man and the title to his engineering shop added to the pot. Together these two upstanding citizens owned only the clothes they stood in. Only Charlie, Les Gillespie, two other players and the dealer remained. There was still a lot to play for.'

'I'll bet there was.'

In the swing of the story, her father pressed on, 'Charlie reckoned he had a better gold find than the legendary Lasseter's Reef and pulled a map out of his jacket and put it into the pot. Les Gillespie called and raised with the deed to his own property and the two other players at the table folded and left. Everything to play for was now between the scratcher and the squatter.'

'So is that what I am Dad, a scratcher?'

He didn't answer and pressed on with his story, 'having matched and raised Charlie's bid, Les then drew three gold bars from his jacket pocket. The scratcher folded. He couldn't call or raise. He was out of options and Les had beat him.'

'And that's it?'

'Not quite, but yeah. Mad Charlie demanded to see the cards, but Les just laughed. I'd heard he was mean bastard, but mean enough to laugh when he turned over his hand, that's a whole new level of low. The bugger had nothing and he'd bluffed Charlie out of everything.'

'What do you mean?'

'Charlie had the better hand, but Les had more to bet. His only gamble was that Charlie had less to play with and it worked. Les Gillespie got everything and it pissed Charlie off.'

'I'd be pissed too.'

'That's how it works with poker, so be careful who you play with.'

'So, the guts of the story is, Charlie hated Les because he believed a Gillespie cheated him out of his,' she used her fingers to make speech marks, 'better than Lasseter's reef and their farm too.'

'Yep and that's why I never play cards.'

Sam loved her father's yarns but she dismissed it as a myth, something drillers in bush camps tell each other to pass time.

'Bigger find than Lasseter's, yeah?'

'So, the scratcher said.'

314

'Which we can't prove because neither has been found.'

'Yep.'

'So, the Gillespies have Mad Charlie's mine, if the map to its whereabouts didn't go up in the pub fire, and you believe that?'

'Nope,' he tightened the last clamp and straightened up and put his hands in the small of his back and stretched, 'the only bit I believe is that the pub burnt down.'

'So, you just told me a whopper to cheer me up?'

'You used to like my stories,' he feigned hurt.

'Of course I love your stories, but what I want to know is why Charles is so dammed positive the Gillespie land has gold on it.'

'I dunno love. Your former boss and Mad Charlie could be related, still carrying the grudge. Charlie told anyone who'd listen that Les had blown the entrance of his mine to stop people raiding it. He maintained there was an underground rift, or fissure, millions of years old running east west, on a line from Burra to Roxby, somewhere between the Walloway Hills South of Eurelia and as far to the north-west as Lake Torrens. If the reef does exist and is on Gillespie land, then it's probably on that line.'

'There's not much evidence on the surveys to support that.'

'Well, he was a bit of a crackpot. He reckoned if you knew where to look, you could grow gold.'

'Yeah?'

'So, he said. He also reckoned that the inter-plate fault line has smaller fissures, fault jogs he called them. Anyway, these lines can have several mini earthquakes a minute and if you know where they are, you can literally watch gold grow.'

'And you believe him?' She wondered if her father was winding her up with another yarn.

'Nope, and like you, I never found anything to substantiate his ravings,' he laughed.

'You bastard, Dad. You've sucked me in twice. I come down here for some respite and all you do is take the piss.'

He was falling over himself with laughter, 'Google it if you don't believe me. C'mon let's get Mum and take her to the pub for lunch.'

'Fault jogs?'

'Google   it.'

CHAPTER FIFTY

Gino read the headline in the Advertiser and smiled. All the dailies carried the same story, a surprise reshuffle with the Premier announcing a new cabinet. He spread the papers across his desk and waited for his boss to arrive.

'How did we go?' Charles walked in and spread his hands over the desk, scanning the headlines.

'We did okay,' Gino said, 'Pendlebury has Mines like we wanted and he gets Agriculture too.'

'Someone we can work with, good,' Charles felt a cloud lifting, 'I'm expecting a call from Hong Kong then you can brief me over lunch.'

'I'll make a restaurant booking.'

'Let's not get ahead of ourselves, a pub lunch will do us today.'

'Done.'

After he'd left the room, Gino looked at the spare phone. He had sent several texts to Spoggy over the past week and received no response. He deleted them, assuming the man had nothing to report and gone into sleep mode. Until something new happened, he had no reason to try again.

Timothy knocked at his door.

'Come in.'

'About the testing on Gillespies place, I've been going back over the documentation and the order is to sample soil to a depth of one metre and only to sample water from wells within a five-kilometre radius of the spill areas.'

'Shit, that's not what I applied for,' he scanned the skyline for a solution.

'What do you want me to do, Boss?'

'Keep it to yourself for now,' Gino picked up the phone, 'and get the crews out there today.'

'Yes sir.' Timothy wondered how he could send drillers onto an area without the proper authority, but followed the instruction.

At four o'clock Gino handed Timothy another set of documents.

'Check these, I think you'll find they authorise us to drill below the water table. And let me know when they start the holes?' he turned back toward his office, 'scan and email the documents to them now.'

Timothy was impressed with the way Gino managed to get what he needed and thought he should make it his business to follow his superior's lead.

***

Jeff Rankin studied the papers handed to him by the drilling crew chief. He knew enough about soil testing to know that a drilling rig was overkill to test for contamination. The crew chief was unhappy, pointed to the papers and argued that everything was in order, however he agreed to stop work until Tilly had been informed.

That afternoon, she applied for and won an injunction. There would be no more drilling on Wanooka's Well until their solicitors could verify the documents.

Jeff had waited while the drilling crew packed up, remaining until the last vehicle disappeared over the rise. He then photographed the mound of dirt and scooped some of the waste into a tin. To him it was just dirt, but he thought Joe might be interested. He wondered how deep they had reached and dropped a weighted string into the hole. It stopped at the three-metre mark, taking another photo for good measure.

Gillespie's lawyer assured them the injunction would hold RADOR off for a couple of months. If they countersued, he would apply to the court for time to prepare, which would tie the case up for months. Tilly had just wondered if her year could get any busier when Jake phoned, needing her onsite to qualify a few issues before fitting the windows and she realised the pressure was not going to let up anytime soon.

***

Joe overheard Laura on the phone, making arrangements for accommodation in the City. It had taken him by surprise until he remembered the reason they had left England earlier than planned. He had spent most of the last week absorbed in his own misery and giving her no space to tell him about her award, or what it meant to her. A sense of selfishness and despair threatened to overtake him, but he shook it off. Laura had always stood by him and he knew she wanted to share her honour with him.

'Time to buck up cobber,' he said to himself. Funny he thought, as the words came out, he had never used the statement before but had a vague memory of his mother saying these words when he needed a verbal foot in the backside.

Waiting for Laura to finish on the phone, he unwrapped the newspaper and turned it over, reading it from the sport pages forward as was his habit, but found nothing of interest. Flicking through from the front, he found an article on page six about depression. Any other time he would have passed over it, but he recognised things in the article he could relate to, that he had been experiencing for the past year. He wondered if this was his problem, but brushed the thought away. Depression happened to other people, not to tough blokes like him. He pushed the paper aside and went outside for some fresh air. That would do the trick.

Laura came outside, brushing dust from the picture Emily insisted they bring home from Wilson's. He had pulled a chair from the outdoor setting and faced the picture into the light so he could study it.

'I thought you didn't like it.'

'I don't,' he didn't look up as he spoke, changing the subject, 'are we booked in then?' He knew he was being abrupt. He wasn't himself and lately it seemed as if some other person had taken over.

'Yes, not that you seem interested.'

He felt the sting of her words and knew he deserved them. He searched for something positive to say but the best he could come up with was, 'good.'

'Good, just bloody good?' Her face dropped and she walked slowly back into the house.

He followed. She was in the kitchen waiting for the kettle to boil.

'Here I'll get that.'

'You don't have to do that, Joe,' the sadness in her voice deepened his guilt but, before he had a chance to respond, she continued, 'all I want from you is for you to recognise you've got issues that need to be dealt with. You've been through a lot and I understand that. I've tried to give you space to work it out on your own, but it's getting worse and it's wrecking both our lives.'

Joe listened as her sadness switched to anger borne of frustration and she let fly, understanding she needed to get it out of her system.

'And so, what if your bloody dog has taken a shine to Jeff. Emily gets a pony from Ted and Tilly is proving to you she can do your job.' She grabbed a tissue and after wiping her nose, continued. 'It's part of life Joe, and the minute you accept that you'll be much better off,' her face was flushed with the exertion from her words, her body tense, coiled like a snake ready to strike, 'well what about it Joe?

Are you going to get some help for this bloody black dog that's stalking you, or are you going to mope around and do nothing and let it kill you?' She softened her tone, 'me, I'm voting for help, but if you want to wither away in bitterness like your bloody father did, that's up to you. Just don't expect the rest of us to live in the shadow of your misery. Because we'll be moving on with our lives, enjoying the future.'

To answer her, he reached into his pocket and pulled the article from the paper and pointed to the helpline number, 'I thought I'd give this lot a ring when you were off the phone. You're right, I do need help to get through this.'

'Jeeze Joe, if you'd only said that in the first place I wouldn't have gone on my rant.'

'Better to get it out of your system though, clear the air, eh.'

'Yeah, well you can make the coffee now.'

'And you'd better tell me what the Governor has planned for you.'

Seeing Joe holding his hands out and beckoning, Laura leant into him, comforted by arms wrapping her in a hug of understanding.

Joining Laura and Joe along with other award recipients at the after party, Tilly and Jeff shared their table, while Ted took Emily back to their hotel after she started falling asleep during desert. Talk was lively and Laura shone as people from academia and other fields offered congratulations. Returning with drinks, Jeff found Joe in discussion with former police minister, Jack Pendlebury, about the need for an expansion of mining and how it would benefit their State. Jeff had always thought the bloke a grafter, when he was in charge of the police portfolio and had even less time for him now. Joe was being polite but, as Pendlebury pressed harder, Jeff took the minister by the arm and led him to one side explaining this was Laura's night and mining proposals could be discussed some other time. It did not pacify the politician, but he said his goodbyes and left.

Seeing opportunity in the moment, Joe excused himself and made for the men's room, slipping past Pendlebury and his cronies. Arching his back as he stepped up to the urinal, he sought relief from an overfull bladder, and then felt a presence on his right and another on his left. He hated the crowding, but ignored them and pressed on with his business. Midstream the man on his right took something from his suit jacket and dropped it into the piss tray. Joe took no notice, then the bloke on his left threw a piece of paper into the drain. It floated to rest on the first to the right in his line of vision and he saw they were photos. He watched the bloke on his right urinate on the picture, then another photo floated down and both men urinated on the images. In the filth before him, Joe saw a face he recognised. Emily in her school uniform. Struggling to comprehend, he zipped up and shifted his weight but before he could move again, a hand pushed his face against the wall and he struggled to maintain his balance.

'If we can't get at you one way, Gillespie. We'll just increase the pressure somewhere else. We'll get what we want in the end, always do.' He thought he recognised the voice behind him but drew a blank for the moment.

'For fuck's sake, I don't know what you want.' The pressure of his face against the wall made speech difficult.

Neither of the thugs holding him said anything.

'Oh, you know, Joe. You know.'

'I don't think so,' his words slurred under pressure to his head and shoulders, then the door opened and closed and the voice had gone.

The thug on his right shifted his stance and Joe waited, catching a glimpse of the second oaf moving to punch him, but Joe was quick. He spun out of the first assailant's grip and, gripped his ears from behind, smashing his face into the ledge above of the urinal. Before the second thug could land a punch, Joe spun around and unleashed a series of blows into the man's upper body. Now his anger drove him and as years of SAS training kicked in, Joe felt his depression lifting. He saw his reflection in the mirror, every inch a soldier.

He grabbed the first man by the throat, lifted him off his feet and ran him hard into the corner, his shoulder in the man's chest as he hit the wall and Joe felt the thug's lungs empty. He held him upright, feeling the man's larynx crush under his grasp before he relaxed his hold and the goon fell like a crumpled suit. 'I've had enough of this shit. Threaten me and I can handle it, but come after my family and all hell breaks loose.' Joe lifted him onto his feet and thrust him back against the hand basin. He smiled at the noise it made smashing down onto the tiles.

Turning swiftly, he grabbed his second assailant before he reached the door, dragging him back into the restroom and forcing him into a stall. He jammed the tattooed face into the toilet bowl and goon two let out a low moan as his forehead smashed onto the rim. Tightening his grip on the handful of hair, Joe lifted and bashed the face into the bowl again. Red blobs from the goon's nose and eyes streaked down the white porcelain. His face was in the water now and bubbles rose in his desperation to live.

'Who sent you?' Joe asked, pulling the thug's face out of the water.

'Fuck off.'

The man struggled, trying to stand. He was strong, but not strong enough to match Joe's fury and he held his face in the water until he went limp. Only then did he lift him out of the water and shake him back to consciousness.

'Again, who sent you?'

The head shook again and Joe smashed his face against the bowl once more.

'It doesn't finish here, prick,' the thug spluttered as his head went into the bowl again.

'You tell your boss that now he's started it, he'd better keep looking over his shoulder. Because when I find him, it'll be me who finishes this,' he lifted the face out of the toilet bowl again, 'you tell him that, got it?'

Gasping for air, the thug just shook his head and sucked deep.

'Understand?' Joe shook him enough to rattle his ears on the rim of the bowl.

'I'll tell him, you fuckhead.'

'That's Mr Fuckhead to you,' he shoved the thug's head into the bowl one more time, 'now wash your face, sludge.' Joe pressed the flush button and held him down until he went limp.

Keeping an eye on his victim, Joe started to stand, spinning around when the stall door moved to grab the shape behind him. Without looking he pushed it across the room until the shape's back was against the wall. Only when he heard the thud and looked at the face, did he realise it was Jeff.

'So, you've got everything under control in here then?' He said as Joe loosened his grip.

'Yep,' he patted Jeff's coat to smooth the creases. His soon to be son-in-law shrugged him off.

'All I wanted was to take a piss in peace,' Joe said, 'I guess these two fell over themselves getting out of my way.' He bent down and picked the photos out of the urinal drain.

'What's that?' Jeff asked.

Joe flicked the water off and turned them for Jeff to see, 'you better get over to security and grab all the vision from any of the cameras covering this area,' he said.

'What? I can't just go in and confiscate evidence.'

'Sure, you can, use your charm, pretend you're still a copper,' Joe smiled.

'And these two?'

'Best we leave them,' Joe dried the photos with toilet tissue and shoved them in his jacket pocket. I'll meet you back at the table,' he checked himself in the mirror for signs of the scuffle and finding only a few blood spots that would be difficult to see in the dim light of the venue, waved at the goons on the floor, saying, 'and not a word to the girls about this yet, okay?'

Jeff agreed, adding, 'good to have you back, Joe.'

Laura was talking to an associate from the university when Joe returned and Tilly appeared deep in conversation with an old colleague. He scanned the room, the crowd was thinning and with no obvious threats, only then did he sit down. Neither Laura nor Tilly looked up when Jeff returned to the table. He looked at his hands, then back at Joe and whispered, 'the tapes are gone.'

'How?'

'Dunno, the door had been forced and the control room was empty. I took photos, but unless we report it they're not much use,' he rolled his glass between his palms, 'did they say anything to you?'

'Someone wanted to scare me. I have my suspicions, but I don't know who it was. He stayed behind me so I didn't get a look at him. I remember the voice though; I just have to work out where I've heard it before.'

'So, do you know what they want?'

'I've got a fair idea'

'And?'

'They want us to lift the injunction.'

'And?'

'I need time to think,' Joe remembered Emily and Ted, 'phone your old man and tell him not to open the door to anyone before we get there.' He touched Laura's hand and nodded to the door and for the first time she noticed the wet marks on his suit and spots of blood on his shirt. She said her farewells quickly and asked Tilly to join her.

Jeff and Joe watched every shadow and every corner as they headed for the exit. Knowing how exposed they were, they hailed a cab to the hotel. Joe could return for the   car   later.

CHAPTER FIFTY ONE

Charles Winkler had stalled David Wang for over a week and knew the Hong Kong banker was nervous. Charles had brought in every other project they financed on budget and repaid the loans on time. This time he was late with reporting, development approval had stalled and Wang was threatening to quit funding the project.

Gino flicked through the latest prospectus; everything was in there. All they needed was to find a decent trace of quartz-sericite, or sericite-specularite, on the Gillespie place and the Minister would sign off on a new mine development. The injunction was a hurdle for now, but he knew how to get the Gillespies to revoke it. One way or another, they would accept RADOR's offer.

He flicked through information leaked by his contact in Queensland, where a scientific team pioneering new research methods, had discovered that trace minerals, including gold, were present in the leaves of gum trees. The study needed more testing, but Gino had a plan to collect leaf samples right across the Gillespie property, he only needed an excuse. If they couldn't drill under the guise of finding contamination, a project to collect vegetation might receive approval. He set Timothy to work drafting a new proposal to test the trees, scrub and grass in the contamination zones.

***

Back in the hotel after their premature exit from the awards party, Joe and Jeff had explained what had occurred. Ted felt helpless as he looked at the photo of himself, knowing he was a target, too. He had always walked his own path, but this was more than he could handle on his own and it felt as if someone had hollowed him out with a spoon. Tilly was concerned for Emily. Laura just wanted these people, whoever they were punished, and she was unhappy that Joe and Jeff appeared to revel in the challenge.

Once they were back in Orroroo, Laura set up a war room in the entertainment area of their cottage. Jeff had found a sheet of plate glass to use as an incident board and Joe promised to repaint the wall as he pressed pins through the photos and into the plasterboard, once they had finished.

'Dad, why don't we just report the incident to the police?' Tilly said.

'The bloke who warned me off...' Joe wavered, 'his voice sounded familiar, so until we work out who he is, I think it's better we plan our attack. For all we know he could be with the police.'

'Jeff?' Tilly knew the law and saw the danger of taking things into their own hands. The situation last year was different, because then they had worked with the police. What they were doing now was outside the law.

'We can't trust anyone at the moment, love,' he put his arm around her and squeezed, 'and I have to keep you and Emily safe.'

Joe slapped his forehead with the ball of his hand. 'Ted? I've roped you in and without even asking how you feel about it,' Joe looked at Laura, 'but, if any of you want us to involve the police, say now.'

'Nah, I figure if Jeff reckons we should stay under the radar for a while, then I'm in.' Ted said.

'I've never wavered, Joe. I trust you,' Laura said, 'I'm in.'

'Tilly?' Jeff bent in front of her and lifted her head so he could see her eyes. Eyes might be the mirror of the soul but they were also the mirror of Tilly's emotions.

'I'm in... for now,' she said, 'as long as you promise to keep Em safe.'

'We're gunna do our best love,' Joe said.

She spun around and lifted her eyes to meet his. 'This is not one of your bloody Vietnam War campaigns, Dad. This is about us, your family. You just make bloody sure nobody has to visit the cemetery so we can all be together.'

'I know it's about us, love. That's why I reckon we only have a few hours to work through this before we hear from the police, okay?' Joe reached for her, but she moved into Jeff's arms for support and then, after a minute, she stood back and picked up a whiteboard marker, 'okay let's go back to last year. What do we know?'

For the next hour, anything of importance found its place on an expanding list. Any event prior to finding the clay-panned steer in the well paddock was discounted as all agreed that was the first incident that had been more than just cattle theft. The covered boots, the gate lifted from its hinges, everything was different to the cattle stolen earlier in the year.

'I wish I had a copy of everything we had in Port Augusta,' Jeff said.

'Yeah, well what about Gordon-Sanders? I still don't get it,' Laura pointed to his picture, 'how did he find us? I know he hated you, Joe, but he'd resisted this urge to kill you for years so why then?'

'Yeah, good question, go on.'

'If it was only Joe they were after, why kill the steer?' Ted was pacing now, forming the shape of a pistol with his hand as he spoke, 'why not walk up and just shoot him? All this other stuff, the steer, them blokes murdered on the Hammond road and then Gordon-Sanders, killed by magic. None of it makes sense,' he ran a finger up and down his temple, as if massaging his thoughts to the surface, 'there's the murders, and now another attempt to intimidate Joe. Nope, I reckon this is bigger than one pissed off American's revenge.'

'It's all about mining,' Tilly said, 'RADOR want access. It's a dirty business at times, just look at some of the leaders of the industry.'

'Yeah, but even this is a bit Hollywood for a rogue mining group,' Laura said, 'RADOR is part of an even bigger company and I reckon the last thing they'd want is to be mixed up in murder.'

'I don't know anything about miners, but I know we are under resourced to deal with this on our own,' Jeff said, 'we can theorise and gather a few facts, but to be effective we need access to the police database. I tried to get in a minute ago and couldn't and now I'll probably have John down here in a minute to warn me off.'

Laura waved at the board. 'Well, if you reckon it's about mining, let's start there. Find out all we can about this Sam Lewis and her company,' she looked at her daughter, 'are you okay Tilly?'

'Not really.'

Joe felt hopeless, and sensed the support was shifting, 'yeah well while we're looking at RADOR, I think it's time we get to know who's who in their zoo,' he said, 'set up a meeting and ask them to call the dogs off. See what reaction we get.'

'What, you're going to give into them, Joe? What about the Aboriginal sites?' Laura picked up a magazine and slapped it against his chest, 'everything your family has preserved over three generations would be gone,' she walked off in the direction of the kitchen, 'I'm making tea.'

'Hey, I didn't say I was giving in, just suggesting we have a sit down. And as far as the sites go I reckon we have a secret weapon right here in the room, eh Ted.'

'Whatever it takes, Joe.' Ted wondered what Joe had in mind, but he was willing to agree.

From the kitchen, Laura saw Tilly move to the door and sensed her unease as her daughter waved her hand at the notes and photos. 'Look I take what I said back. I want to let the police know you were attacked in the toilet. All this stuff on the board, we don't have enough information. Are you going to call in your Canberra contacts?' Joe shook his head, 'and Jeff, what about you? Can you call on anyone now that you're out of the force?' Jeff shook his head too. 'Right, all I want is to keep Em safe,' by now Laura was alongside her and she put an arm around her mother, 'Mum, I love those galleries and fossil sites as much as you do, but I love my daughter more. I say we pack this up and let the cops do what's necessary.'

'Hey hang on a minute,' Joe wanted to rescue his operation.

'No Dad, I just want all of this to stop,' she was close to tears now, 'sometime this year, I want you to walk me down the aisle. I want you to be around long enough to dance at Em's wedding too. We can't do any of that if you've been killed trying to save the Well.'

Jeff walked over and pulled her into a hug and she fell against his chest, showing how vulnerable she felt. 'It's up to you, Joe,' he said.

They were interrupted by the sound crushing gravel as a car pulled up outside and Joe peered through the blind. 'Well now's the time to tell all I reckon, because it's John O'Rourke.'

Jeff held Tilly away from him and walked to the door, saying, 'Tilly, you better get Jonathon to give Sam Lewis a call eh? Try to set something up.'

Cassidy outlined the case to his team, his superiors had approved funding to solve this case and more officers were assigned. It was large operation and one he did not want to fail. Although he had never wanted to move from Port Augusta, solving a case like this would look good on his resume. He looked at his watch, no time now for the doctor's appointment his wife had made for him. They had a myriad of leads, but he needed to see a pattern if he was to prove his hunches.

'Angela, tyre tracks. What do we know?'

'Sir, we have one set of tracks that appear in every scene. At the windmill where Joe's steer was killed, by the road where Tamara Gibson was taken and at the Gillespie's farmhouse. These all came from the investigation into the attempt on Joe's life last year. We found several tracks at the railway yard where you found the dead American, but discounted them from the original enquiry believing they were from a similar bike used by him,' she walked to the incident board, 'now this set of photos are from the current case. The place where we found Spoggy's ute burnt out and, from the same paddock, tracks at the gate going in and coming out. These are from the shed behind Brahma Lodge. One set going over the car tracks and another, newer set, showing the car had driven over them.'

Cassidy motioned for her to sit down and asked the sarge to pass out a history of the case.

'We called it Kundela,' he said handing the files around, 'named because the locals were saying the bone had been pointed at this Gordon-Sanders bloke, the press went wild with outrageous headlines at the time,' he shifted his stance, 'anyway, have a read, there's stuff in there that has bearing on what we're doing today.'

Angela pointed to the incident boards, 'we know Spoggy is not this bloke's real name and he operates under at least one or more alias. Anything you hear, or find, no matter how small it is. Just let us know and we'll chase it down, right boss?'

'Right,' he was pleased with her enthusiasm. He appointed leaders and allotted tasks and, as the room cleared, he tapped O'Rourke's shoulder, 'John, I need to go over some stuff with you so hang around. Rob, that burnt out bike did belong to the tracks, so good work on that front. When you change over in Port Wakefield today, ask around. If it was Spoggy who dumped the bike there, then we want to know how he got back to Adelaide to pick up his car. Ask the local constable to make a few enquiries, who knows, he might have something for you by the time you get there.'

'No probs. I'll let Angela know and if I'm back on time, see you tonight,' he looked at his watch, 'I'd better go.'

The detective was on his way out of the room. He needed to talk to the constable at the Salisbury Police Station. More than that, Cassidy wanted to know why Jeff Rankin would be stupid enough to try and access the Police database. He had an explanation from John O'Rourke, but it was thin at best. He passed Simpson's desk, where O'Rourke was waiting, 'lunch in Orroroo. You, me and you too, Sarge. I want a sit down with our recently retired Jeff Rankin away from his fiancée and her family. Can you arrange it?'

'Done,' John said, 'is that it?'

'Yep, are you okay with that, Sarge?'

With a mouth full of biscuit, he could only nod.

'Good, I'll be ready to move at eleven.' He picked up the phone and postponed his doctor appointment.

CHAPTER FIFTY TWO

Tilly Gillespie called Jonathon Smythe-Simms and discussed setting up a meeting with RADOR to discover what the mining company was proposing.

Jonathon was cautious but, over a morning of endless e-mails, they framed a strategy. Before he could agree to a meeting, he informed RADOR they would have to provide written notice of their complete proposal, including timeframes and compensation. The Gillespies would need time to study the documents and seek expert evaluation of the proposal and only then could a meeting take place and it would be in his chambers.

Tilly felt that if the threats were coming from RADOR, this would relieve the pressure for now. Speaking against her parents was difficult, but a few days ago it seemed as if she was the only one in the room who could see the bigger picture. Her training, studying and practicing law, had provided those skills.

She had always involved herself with the grubbier side of the law and fought for the rights of petty criminals and those down the bottom end of the social ladder. Business law had never held an interest for her, but working with Jonathon rekindled her passion. After the call she felt a sense of accomplishment and pride, she had forgotten nothing. If there was to be no land to farm, she could always go back to law. But how would Jeff feel about his wife going back to her old trade? She thought about it for a while. It was something that might never happen and a discussion for another time.

Jeff was in the kitchen, 'do you want to go tell your folks what Colin told you?'

'Not yet,' she ran her hand through his hair, 'are you disappointed I quelled your fire for another gung-ho adventure with Dad?'

'A bit,' he put his arms around her and linked his fingers in the small of her back, pulling her into him, 'I heard you on the phone with Colin and the speed in which you flicked him e-mail after e-mail. Do you miss the law?'

'A bit.'

He heard the mimic in her words, 'a bit, a bloody bit. Don't give me that. I heard you and you revelled in the chance to go all badass lawyer again. I'd move for you, you know that.'

'And me for you, but we have other things to worry about for now, I reckon.'

'That we do. Better tell your folks then.'

'Yep.'

Before he could reply, his phone alerted him to an incoming text.

'What is it?' Tilly asked.

'The cavalry wants to talk to me. In John's office, one o'clock.' He showed her the text.

'They might offer you your old job back.'

'And they might want to arrest me for a hack attempt on their database, too,' his face changed colour as he imagined the worst, 'c'mon we'd better get down to your Mum's.'

***

Putting the phone down, Gino Di Massimo could not hide his smugness and when he entered his boss's office, Charles Winkler motioned for him to sit down at the desk. Charles was pacing, his left arm making circles as he tried to pacify the caller. The call ended and he tossed the mobile phone into his out tray. Gino centred it.

'Your day's going better than mine from the look of your face,' Charles said, 'what's going on?'

'The Gillespies want to talk. Their solicitor is sending a list today.'

'A list. What kind of list?'

'Just the usual, our assurances, offers, things like that.'

'We're not giving anything,' Charles said, 'that family…' he let the words die, there were a few things Gino didn't need to know.

'We won't have to. I still have a few friends in high places.'

'Yeah, but will they still be friends when the shit hits the fan.'

'It won't matter to us,' Gino said, 'we won't be the ones standing in front of it.' He laughed at his own joke.

***

The last thing John O'Rourke wanted was to spend the afternoon with his superiors, grilling a friend in his station. He had his own ideas about Spoggy and needed to chase those rabbits down their holes before he completed his report. Besides, he thought of Jeff as someone outside of the force he could talk with. For now, that had to wait. He phoned Fiona, letting her know he would have lunch in his office.

Jeff arrived a few minutes before Cassidy. It gave him time to tell John about the Gillespie's decision to talk with RADOR. He had told Tilly's parents the police were more likely to give him a dressing down rather than charge him, but he couldn't be sure. How things had transformed in the past year, he had spent little time flying, investigated a murder case, almost crashed the glider, left the police force and become engaged to the world's most beautiful woman. His life as a single man had certainly changed.

Cassidy sat in John's chair with Jeff opposite, Sarge had taken the spare seat and John leant against the filing cabinet. The room was too small for so many big men.

'Have some trouble in the city?' Cassidy asked.

'How do you mean?' Jeff went on the defensive, 'define trouble.'

'Joe Gillespie in a blood-spattered suit, you racing to the security office and two goons unconscious in the gents. I'd reckon that's trouble. Oh, and you all left in a hurry.'

'Is that right?'

'That and someone tried to access our database with your old password. Want to tell me what's going on?'

'Dunno, where'd the goons come from? They're your words, not mine.'

'Ease up Tiger,' Sarge butted in, 'we're on your side. Just tell the DI what happened at the hotel?'

'I noticed Joe was taking longer in the gents than I thought he should and I was concerned, you know, given he's already had one heart attack, but when I got there he had the situation under control,' Jeff pulled the family's photos out of the folder he had with him, 'he was taking a piss when these goons,' he used his fingers to show quotation marks, 'threw these into the drain. Silly bastards thought they could intimidate him, but Joe Gillespie's a lot tougher than that. When I got there one was down and he was trying to revive the other by splashing water on his face.'

'And the control room?'

'When I reached it, the door had been broken and the tape machines empty. Someone got there before me.'

'And the database.'

'I wanted to see if there was any record on the blokes who attacked Joe. Someone's been trying to kill him since last year and I wanted to find out who. In all honesty, you blokes haven't got too far with it.'

'So, do you want back in?'

'In brief, what, how and why?'

'Because we miss you,' Sarge unfolded his arms, 'and I reckon you miss us too, the job I mean, and besides, DI won't admit it, but he could use your help.'

'Steady on, Doug. I was getting around to that.'

For the next hour, Jeff went over everything he knew and that the family had decided to talk to the mining company in an effort to find out if the threat was coming from there. Doug thought it was a sound strategy.

'It won't be official and I can't offer you anything for your time immediately,' Darryl said, 'but if you come on as a consultant, we could get approval for that.'

'I'd have to talk with Tilly first. Call me tomorrow,' it was Jeff's turn to ask the questions, 'if you know everything about that night, then who was the third bloke who threatened Joe?'

'A third man?'

'Yep. Joe said he thought he knew the voice. It was familiar, as if he'd heard it somewhere before maybe on TV or the radio. He can't place him now, but I'm betting it'll come back to him soon.'

'I don't suppose you managed to get a photo of these blokes who attacked him?' Darryl studied his pen.

'You have them, or that's what you intimated.' Jeff said.

'Nope, just a couple of witness statements about a rumble in the toilets and a tip off to say it was Joe,' he clicked the pen, hoping as if by magic, it would write the answers to his questions.

'So, you have no clue then?'

'Nope, you?'

Jeff fumbled for his phone and shuffled through the options. He showed it to Sarge. 'Neck tattoos and one from the calf. I didn't have time for more.'

Sarge smiled, 'flick them through to Angela. John, do either of these blokes match the ones in Spoggy's description of the blokes who jumped him?'

John took the phone and scrolled through the screen. 'Nope, they were Asian, Chinese maybe.'

'Spoggy's a liar.' Sarge said.

The DI took the phone back and looked at the images of the crumpled shapes against the toilet wall. 'Joe did this?'

'Yep, didn't take him long either,' Jeff said.

Cassidy passed the phone to Sarge, who smiled and gave a little whistle as he checked each image. 'How's he holding up?'

'He's pissed off. Reckons we didn't finish the job last year and now he wants to do this on his own. So far, Tilly has counselled him otherwise,' Jeff stood and offered his hand to the others, 'but yeah, the rumble in Adelaide did him good. He's more like his old self and I wouldn't want to cross him right now.'

'Is he dangerous?' Darryl asked.

'It depends on who he's looking at,' he turned to walk out, 'best to leave him alone for a few days, eh.'

'Where is he now?'

'Checking on the renovations, they all are,' he made to tip his hat, 'call me tomorrow, yeah?'

***

The trip to Wanooka's Well had been broken by side trips to check on crop growth and recovering pastures. They had often talked about sowing more saltbush and returning part of the place to native grasses and Joe was keen to see how the indigenous plants were recovering after the drought. He was more engaged than he had been in a long time, something both women noticed.

Laura was mid paddock, teasing at the roots in a clump of wheat as she spoke to Tilly, 'the dust up in Adelaide did him good, Love. He's regained his power. Look at him, he's like an eagle ready soar again,' she squeezed her daughter's hand, 'you might have to let him take charge again, you know, bit by bit.'

'I'll try, but it won't be easy, I've become used to being boss.'

'But you have a wedding to plan.'

'Well, yeah I do have that.'

At the homestead, they found the windows installed and the veranda flagstones being re-laid. Jake's team had stayed on site for a few ten day stretches to get the place ready for second fix. With electricians due at the end of the week, Laura needed to mark where she wanted power points and switches located. For her it was becoming more exciting, any renovations she and Joe had done centred around painting the place. Jake pressed her for details, he wanted everything to be right. His reputation relied on pleasing his customers.

While Laura was busy inside, Joe walked around the sheds, his kelpie trotting behind him as if sensing the old Joe was back at last. He stopped at the place where they had been trapped last year, tapping a spot with his knuckle where winter rain had crept into one of the bullet holes and seeped behind the plaster and a clump crashed at his feet. Gip yelped and cowered behind him.

'It's okay girl,' he bent down and picked her up, cradling her like a baby, 'it gives me the creeps a bit too,' he rubbed her belly before setting her onto her paws, 'c'mon, let's check the horse yards, we might need them when everyone takes up riding again.'

Laura waved at him to catch his attention and he marched back toward the house.

'Have a look at this,' she pulled bubble wrap from the corner of her kitchen table, 'Jake's fixed it and now you can't even see where those bastards carved into it.'

Joe had worried the table had been scrapped. Or worse, that Laura would see the carving and relive the terror of the night they found it, but today she was excited, even planning how they would live in their home.

'Well I had to have it restored, as my gift to you,' Jake put his arm around her shoulders, 'when I told my mother what happened out here, she said unless the table was restored, you'd always be reminded of that night, Mum and some of her friends in Clare took up a collection. Some of the blokes' wives ran a street stall, the Clare Lions Club tossed in a few dollars and me and the boys made up the rest. We've enjoyed this project and wanted you to have something to remember us by.'

Laura reached up and kissed his cheek, too choked to speak.

'Thanks mate, it means a lot to both of us,' Joe said and stepped forward to hug him, an awkward man pat that both men pulled back from.

'Paintwork,' Jake changed the subject, 'have you thought about colours?'

'As a matter of fact, I have. I have spoken with your friend from the National Trust.' she fished around in her hand bag for her tablet, 'I thought we could try this.'

As Laura and Jake went through the rooms discussing ideas, Joe left them to it and walked toward the hill behind the house. He wanted to see the place where Gordon-Sanders had lain in wait for him. Remnants of police tape still hung in the trees. The sun had almost decomposed it, but it still marked the spot. He looked at the ground where the sniper had taken aim and found that the pock marks for his elbows had now filled with leaf litter. Joe pulled a branch from a bush and swept the area.

Laying down onto his belly, he settled into the gunman's position and simulated holding a rifle. Monty had chosen the place where he could see everything, the road into the homestead, the creek crossing where the second sniper lay in wait and the tank behind the horse yards.

Joe could see into the house from here and had a clear view of everything, the only blind spot had been between the sheds and he realised his good fortune in choosing to stop there. Any further and one of them would have had an easy shot. Gip nuzzled his face as if understanding.

'It wasn't our day to die, was it old girl?' He ruffled the dog's ears, talking his thoughts aloud, 'who was paying you, Monty?' then he stood and called Gip to race him to the top of the hill.'

The dog trotted ahead. It was a track they had walked many times and she sniffed and marked her territory as she went. A small grey kangaroo burst from under a bush and bounded a few meters, before stopping and staring back at them. Without stock on the place, the native wildlife was returning and snake and lizard tracks marked the powdered dust of kangaroo trails.

At the top of the hill he stood by the cairn that had been erected when the place was first settled. It had become custom for everyone who made it to the top to add a stone and Joe picked up a rock from the ground and placed it on top of one he and Emily put there the last time they had walked the hill. All around there were signs of new life. To the south, different shades of green looked like an emerald quilt, contrasting with the almost white roads that embroidered the edges. To the East he could make out the roof at Wilsons and the flat plain running south to Booleroo Centre that would be perfect for gliding. Something for Jeff in that, he thought.

Standing there and looking down on the work progressing on their buildings was a symbol of re-birth. Out of their problems had come the refurbishment Laura had pestered him about for years. All they had to do now, was to identify and eliminate whoever it is that's trying to harm him, then life would be good again.

CHAPTER FIFTY THREE

At three o'clock the DI brought his team together for another briefing. This investigation had his mind in a spin and he needed to break the information down. He felt Spoggy was a key, but a key to what?

'Angela, what have you got?' He asked.

'The team in Salisbury have door knocked and done a letterbox drop of the district. I'm still waiting for someone to get back to me and forensics will take the shed floor up next week.

'What! I asked them to get onto it yesterday,' he paced across the front of the incident boards,' Sarge, get onto whoever it takes. I want that floor up now,' he tapped the photo of the shed floor and then stood with his back to the room as he searched the boards, 'what more do we have?'

'The dogs in the backyard shed were greyhounds. Apparently, the old couple who lived there rescued dogs unwanted by their trainers, saved them from being shot.' an officer stepped forward and put photos on the board.

'I've got something,' Rob bounced into the room to place a couple of photos on the board under Spoggy's picture. 'CCTV captured this bloke in Port Wakefield buying a ticket to Adelaide on the Saturday, but he didn't board a bus until eighteen hours later. The driver dropped him at the servo at Bolivar. The picture's grainy, but for my money,' he tapped both photos, 'he's the same fella.'

'Anything on the bike to tie it to Spoggy?'

'Nothing in the way of prints. The bike's been out of rego for seven years. Last registered to a Peter Cook from Hamilton in Victoria and reported stolen five years ago.'

'Hamilton, remind me Sarge. Why does Hamilton sound familiar?'

Before the senior sergeant could answer, a constable pointed to the photos from Jeff Rankin's original board.

'The girl,' he blurted, 'Tamara Gibson, she came from Hamilton.'

'Follow it up, find a connection.'

'Will do Boss.'

'Get onto John O'Rourke, have him go back to Spoggy's place, paw over every inch of it if he has to. Tell him he's looking for anything that has a Hamilton connection. The other question is, does Spoggy here,' he slapped his pointer on the photo, 'have another alias?'

They were making progress, but it was slow. 'There's a connection and I'm willing to bet it's this,' he plucked the photo of the burnt motorcycle from the board, 'a trail-bike was ridden by the guy who picked her up. If that rider was Spoggy,' his pointer rested on the logo Dante's Disciples, 'the little bastard sold her to the bikies. They bloody knew each other,' his excitement rose, 'Sarge, get onto Hamilton see what you can find out,' he looked around the room, 'well that's it folks. I'll see you all back here at seven tomorrow morning.'

As the room emptied he felt pride swelling inside him, they were committed and eager, 'Angela, you're with me.'

The phone was ringing when Darryl reached his desk, he pointed and Angela picked up. She listened to the caller and held the phone out, 'Sir, for you.'

He mouthed his thanks, 'Constable?'

Angela waited until he finished the call, and then walked back to his desk. 'Sir?'

'Good work on the tyre tracks. You made the connection.'

'Anything come from that call?'

'They found a resident a couple of streets away who knew the Le-Stranges. The couple had a son that *wasn't the full quid*, her words not his, and they took in a nephew who was about the same age, hoping he'd be a positive influence on their boy. Twelve months later the parents

345

died from food poisoning after eating fish or mushrooms, she couldn't remember which, but she did remember the boys were away the weekend it happened. A neighbour had found the bodies and called it in. It seems the son became more independent and after about eighteen months, the nephew moved on. The son had learnt how to handle the money coming from the trust his parents had set up for him. She didn't think he worked and spent most of his time travelling.

'Nice.' Angela said.

'Not so sure about that. What do you think they called the son?'

'Liam?'

'Bingo, the very same.'

'And the cousin? Where's he?'

'That's your job,' he passed her his notes, 'the neighbour couldn't remember the name, but thought he came from the Coorong, or somewhere in the South-East. Get onto it before you go home and let me know what you find.'

'On it now.' She went to her computer and started tracking family connections.

The DI held a finger up indicating for Angela to wait as he answered a call. 'Well, guess what the nephew's name was?'

'Tom Clancy?' She shrugged, 'I don't know, who?'

'Peter bloody Cook, that's who.' He held his hand up for a high five, she obliged and smiled as he fist-pumped and danced his way around the desk. 'What are the chances, eh? I'll get Sarge to get onto the Hamilton cops. I want to know if he has a record. You check with children's services and see if they have anything on him.'

Hearing his name and the DI's raised voice, the Sarge walked in to investigate. 'Someone's happy?'

'Sure am and I've got another job for you but first, what've you got?'

'A mate with a backhoe can get into that shed in the morning, forensics will be there too. Excavation was the hold up.'

'How many favours did that cost you?'

'None, but a few blokes got to clear their slate with me,' he grinned, his station was excited and doing more than filling the cells with drunks, this was real police work.

***

John O'Rourke talked Jeff into searching Spoggy's rented farmhouse with him. Apart from a few tracks made by farm vehicles accessing the sheds and yards, the place was as it was when John was last there.

'What are we looking for?' Jeff asked.

'Beats me, anything that looks like it shouldn't be here. Everyone reckons you're the bloke with mystical powers, that's why I conned you into coming.'

'That, plus I'm bloody good company,' Jeff lifted the tape and pushed the garden gate open, 'simple living out here. Dad would love it.'

'Not you?'

'I like a bit of comfort when I'm not sleeping under the stars. I even put my place in Port Augusta on the market last week.'

'Committed, I like that. C'mon, the DI wants us to find something, anything.'

The contents of the cupboards were sparse, a few cans of home-brand tomato soup, baked beans, and canned meat. Enough cutlery for two, and a few plates that looked as if they came from an opportunity shop. Jeff noticed the dresser was out from the wall and marks in the dust around it looked recent.

He sniffed the air for clues, and then asked John to give him a hand to move the cupboard away from the wall, exposing an area where the floor had been cut away. Further investigation showed two loose boards covering a rough tool box.

'Gotcha, I know that smell, it's gun oil.'

John stood back as Jeff worked the box out and set it on the table. 'Is it empty?' He asked.

'Not quite, we have a rag and this,' he held up a 44 calibre bullet case.

'I thought it had to be a hand gun, a rifle wouldn't fit.'

'So where's the rest of it?'

'Rest of what?' John felt along the top of the dresser.

'Whatever it is that Spoggy was hiding. Where there's smoke there's fire as they say,' he shone his torch into the hole and searched the floor cavity, 'and a 44 needs a licence.'

'Either that, or it's hot,' John said, 'you know, until I heard he was tied to his steering wheel, I hadn't even noticed him.'

Jeff looked at him, 'he knew how to stay low.'

'Yeah, but what did he do for money? A bit of tractor driving won't feed you for long,' John pulled drawers from their runners and tipped their contents onto the table. A spider ran across his glove and toward his elbow. He brushed and slapped at it. When it fell to the floor, he stepped on it.

Jeff kept his smile to himself, 'so why was he here you think?'

'Running away, writing a book, or keeping tabs on someone.'

Yeah, but who?'

'Nothing here, let's do another room. Do you think those photos that Joe had came from, Spoggy?'

'Nah, we'd have noticed him hangin' around.'

John was still upending drawers. 'You reckon? He's already shown us he can keep out of sight. I'll bet if we can find a camera, computer or phone, it would prove those pictures came from him. Find a connection, bring him in.'

'If you can find him,' Jeff rifled through another drawer.

'Yeah, he's a cunning bastard. It won't be easy,' John said. The fridge was still running and he checked the freezer, 'he left a lot of beef behind. Do you reckon he's planning a return?'

'Nope, not the way he burnt the ute. That's our link, why burn it near the same place Joe's steer was butchered and, why replace the padlock?'

'Because he'd been there before,' John looked at the bags in the freezer, they were all dated the same night as the steer was killed. He showed the bag to Jeff. 'Coincidence?'

'A lot of coincidences are starting to stack up now,' Jeff checked a couple of bags, 'all of the dates are the same.'

'Shit, how could I miss that?'

'You didn't know what you were looking for. Maybe you should call this in before we poke around a bit more.'

Enthused by their find, the DI asked them to bag the evidence and he wanted pictures and anything that they could find for a DNA sample. A desk under the window of the living room offered promise, but they found no trace of paper, or a printer. A chewed pencil rattled in the back of a drawer, they bagged it too. Soiled bedding was rolled into a bag and the shower in the bathroom offered plenty for a DNA sample.

'You know, I reckon he was a loner,' Jeff said.

'Yeah, or maybe he just didn't like people.'

'No photos, no pets, a weirdo?'

'A weirdo with a gun. Let's get out of here.'

Jeff rolled the mattress onto its edge and something clunked as he slid it along the floor. 'Treasure?' He asked, pointing to a tear.

'Your turn, I've had enough of crawlies today.'

'Wuss,' he reached in and wriggled his fingers to reach the object. 'Eureka,' he held his find out to John. A 22 semi-automatic rifle gleamed in the sun that streamed through nicotine stained curtains, 'and a silencer too. Now, I'm sure that's not legal.'

John went back to the kitchen, 'let's find something to keep this frozen stuff in and get everything back to the Port, they can handle it now.'

'What about the sheds?'

John looked at his watch and then the western horizon. 'The light will be gone soon. We'll have to come back later.'

Jonathon briefed Tilly on his progress with RADOR. She felt it strange that Gino had replaced Sam Lewis. Big business could be fickle, but when they had met, Sam had seemed to be well in control of her world.

'Did they say why she left?'

'Only that the company had restructured, that her ideas didn't mesh with theirs and it was time for new direction. It seems kosher,' he said, 'I did ask if she was working somewhere else, just in conversation, and Gino said she was on gardening leave.'

'Gardening leave?' Tilly screwed her nose up, 'what the hell is that?'

'You know, when they pay you until the end of your contact. Until then you're not allowed to work for a competitor.'

'They're hiding something.'

Gillespie's Gold

'That's what I thought. I pressed for a contact number, saying you were friends. It didn't do any good though. He couldn't, or wouldn't say.'

'Not to worry, I have my sources.
She looked at the clock, time to collect Emily from school and call into the cottage to let her parents know of Jonathon's   progress.

CHAPTER FIFTY FOUR

Brad Reardon pushed a hand through his greying hair as he and the bank manager walked around the paint and panel shop. Dried grass poked between the back walls and the fences, everywhere in between had been cleared by the four sheep laying in the shade of an abandoned four-wheel-drive. A few wrecks rested in a line against the back of the used car yard fence. He had never used the second-hand yard seeing it as nothing more than useless real estate.

Two months ago, when a major customer declared themselves bankrupt, Brad had hoped for thirty cents in the dollar, but after the tax office and the first mortgage holders, there had been nothing left for creditors. Now he was in trouble and the banker had wanted him to cut his losses. His latest loan application would be approved, but only with more security and at a higher interest rate. The last thing they could afford was more interest.

'I can't do it to Karen, there's no way I'll put the house on the line.' He couldn't.

The banker tried to keep their mood upbeat. 'I've known you a long time now mate, and I know how much you've invested yourself into the business. If you can't find the security, maybe it's time to call it quits. Look, if it were me, I'd declare the business bankrupt and walk away. You're not fifty yet, you could always start again.'

'The house is freehold. If I did that, would we still keep our home?'

'I don't think so,' he shrugged, 'personal guarantees...' he rested his backside on the front tyre of a tractor, 'and I don't expect you'd have much to pay creditors either.'

'Just my debtors' ledger?'

'The bank's the first mortgagee. And there's the personal guarantees too, so the bank would take that too, I'm sorry.

'Sorry bullshit, what you're saying is, I'm fucked. Twenty years of slog down the drain. Have you got any good news?'

The banker held his hand out. 'Sorry,' he repeated as Brad slapped it away. 'Look Brad, I'm not supposed to warn you, but we've been friends for years. I don't think they'll move until the Regional Manager gets back next week. Get on the phone drag in what you can. Maybe you can stall us.'

'Stall you, be fucked. If I collect anything, I'll piss it up against the wall before pulling the trigger on the gun you've put to my head.'

'Don't shoot the messenger. I didn't beg you to borrow the money.'

'Maybe not, but you were always keen to extend the overdraft. Then when the financial world collapses, you make it my fault. Sell this off, your first loss is the best loss, you said. You and your regional manager trotted out every cliché in the book. I sold good stock for well below its real value, just to drag in your exorbitant bank fees. Penalty interest for this, extra interest for being overdrawn. You bastards ran me dry and you know it. Now, when the season is about to turn good, you decide to ruin me. Well fuck that, it's not gunna happen.'

'Brad...'

'No, just piss off, I need time to think.' He looked away just as Joe Gillespie padded toward them, his gait purposeful.

'G'day,' Joe greeted the men, ignoring the chill in the air, 'I was told I'd find you both here,' he turned the banker, 'sorry to interrupt, but I need a quick word with Brad.'

'Sure.'

Brad turned and shouted over his shoulder as Joe motioned for him to walk him away, 'I'm finished with this fucker and his piss-ant little bank.'

'I'll leave you to it then.' The banker was equally as keen to leave.

Joe put his hand, flat palm his chest to stop him, 'hang about for a bit, you might hear something of interest,' before easing Brad away, 'easy mate, we can fix this, but you've just got to trust me for a while, alright?'

'I don't see how but, okay.' Brad turned and walked away. He needed time to check his emotions.

Joe returned to the banker and walked him onto the street, well out of Brad's hearing, 'well, are the higher ups in the bank pleased now?'

'What do you mean?'

'Right through the drought you've done all you can to shake any money Brad had out of him and now it looks like you want to wring him like water from a wet rag,' the veins in Joe's neck stood out, 'are you taking any pleasure in destroying any pride the man has left?' He stared into the banker's eyes and could see the man was frightened.

'No, no, of course not.'

Joe thought he should ease up, but the man from the bank had it coming. 'Come on, tell me what's brought him to this? Is he a bad businessman, does he waste money, or is it something else?'

'Look Joe, I'm only the messenger,' the banker's words swelled and caught in his throat, 'Brad's always tried to pay his debt off but they've struggled from the day they bought the place. Before the drought, they were making headway,' he shook his head as if not understanding it himself. He had never expected to foreclose on anyone, let alone a popular bloke in a small town, 'but with the seasons and the interest rates,' he shrugged, 'it hasn't worked out.

'So how did he get in so deep, and what role did your bank play in this?'

'You know I can't answer that,' the banker shifted to stand on the higher part of the footpath, 'we let him ease over his overdraft limit time and time again. The penalties of doing that have conspired against him and if it wasn't for Karen, they'd be starving.'

'Without the debt, what's the business like?'

'He'd be in clover. Even with the droughts, the basics are sound. It's the overheads that are killing him.'

'Not saying I will, but after I've talked to him, I want to talk to you about buying his debt.'

'What, payout his loans?'

'No, I'll buy his debt from the bank. You work out what you'll take. I'll talk to Laura and Tilly and we'll make an offer.'

'And if we don't?'

'Brad will go under. The town will lose a business that employs three or four people and your bottom line will look like shit. At auction this place will make less than ten percent of what he owes you. His creditors go without, you become a pariah within the community and if we're really lucky, Brad won't top himself.'

'What do I tell my bosses?'

'Tell them you have an option to keep the place open, work from there. Sell them on the benefits of my offer. Paint a picture of disaster if you close him down. Your bank knows it needs businesses like his to stay open, because once it's gone, others in the town will follow and you'll lose to a competitor.'

'And if they still choose to foreclose.'

'I'll be the only one at the auction and buy the place for a song, you know that. Best we do it my way and leave Brad with a bit of dignity, okay?'

Brad Reardon watched the banker walk away and noticed the bounce in Joe's step as he walked back.

'What did you say to him?' Brad asked.

'A while back, you asked me if I was interested in buying the place. Well after our little chat over there, let's just say, things just cranked it up a notch. Where can we talk?'

'Karen's home. Anything we say, she should hear.'

'I'll get Laura and meet you over there as soon as we can.'

'Give us a bit of time to have a tub-up first.'

Joe shook his hand, 'we can do this mate.'

'I hope so.'

Earlier in the week Joe had discussed the buying Reardon's business with Laura, but they had not envisaged the turn of events before them. He mulled over possibilities while she fussed about getting herself ready to go to meet them.

They don't care what we look like, you know,' Joe spoke when he thought she'd taken long enough, 'they just want to hear what we have to say.'

'Don't panic, I'm not going out until I'm ready, never have, never will and you know that.'

'I'll be in the car.'

He sat behind the wheel knowing she would take longer because he tried to rush her. It was one of her ways. His mind drifted to the discussion ahead, he had said he wanted to buy, but it happened so quickly and making spur of the moment decisions was not something he was noted for.

***

Karen Reardon had a pot of tea, her best cloth and matching china on the table. She was house proud like most country women and eager to impress her guests. Brad had even taken time to shed the grime of the workshop and when they shook hands, Joe thought he detected a subtle scent of lavender.

Over the next couple of hours, they went over the company's books. Joe questioned the need for the number of ledger columns and Karen was able to show him how they depicted profit and loss for each segment of their business. The banker was right, every department showed profit. It was the interest compounding on high priced loans that was dragging their financial position down.

Satisfied all was as it should be, it was now between the　　　　Gillespies　　　　and　　　　the　　　　bank.

CHAPTER FIFTY FIVE

DI Cassidy picked up the package containing Spoggy's chewing gum that John O'Rourke had given to him, when they met at the scene of the burnt-out ute. He had meant to send it to forensics before, but pressures of the case had led him to forget it.

'Here, better get this off to Adelaide. It might help us identify whoever this Spoggy character really is,' he passed it to Angela, then looked at his watch, 'and call the troops together for a special briefing at,' he studied the board for an answer, 'say eleven. Yeah, I'll be right by then, make it eleven.' He screwed the lid off a bottle and shook a tablet into his hand, tossed it into his mouth and swallowed.

'Sure boss,' she had never seen him take anything before, 'are you okay Sir.'

'I'm fine Constable, just a bit of hypertension that's all.'

She looked at his profile, he may have been a bit on the heavy side, but he was not over weight. 'It's this case though, yeah?' she asked.

'Something like that, but not a word to the others, okay?'

'Sure, Sir, but you'd say if you were in trouble, wouldn't you?'

'I'm fine, now get that off to forensics.'

'Sir.'

He sat at his desk and sorted through the pile of notes left overnight. He looked at the one written with a red pen, *Harry Forbes*. It was obviously urgent and the time had been underlined by Sarge. He had little time for the media seeking cowboy, but knew he had to make this a priority and made the call.

'Harry Forbes.'

'Cassidy, Port Augusta, you called?'

'Yeah, I understand you're raking over my investigation into the death of the girl in the Flinders.'

'Have you found anything new?'

'Not much, you?'

'Well I think we may have found the bike that was used to abduct her,' Cassidy wanted to keep some information back, 'do you want to make a deal?'

'God no, I'm up to my neck in it and trying to retire. Take whatever you want, but be careful, yeah.'

'What do you mean be careful?'

'Like I said, make sure everything is done by the book, there are people watching you.'

'Who?'

'People with a lot at stake. People who want Joe Gillespie out of their way.'

'But his protection goes to all the way to the top.'

'Not this time, these guys are more local and, they have enough clout to ruin you.'

'Do you know why?'

Forbes didn't answer, but continued, 'just keep everything documented. This case has powerful eyes watching it.'

'Who?'

'I won't say, can't, but I just have an old copper's hunch that Joe's still in the shit. Oh, and your dead bloke in Hammond was a hired gun. I don't know who put the contract out, but it came from inside South Australia.'

'Can we meet?'

'No point, I've said all I'm going to,' he let out the sigh of one who'd been in the job too long, 'but good luck.' Cassidy felt his chest tighten again and thought about his last visit to the doctor before reaching for the phone to make an appointment for that afternoon. He searched the incident boards, knowing he had too much information and not enough knowledge. He wondered how Forbes knew the

American had been hired, a knowledge that added another layer of questions. Deciding the data should be divided onto more than three boards, he called Angela to create a fourth space and across the top of each investigation he wrote team names and those of its members. The *Kundela* team would go over everything from the attack on the Gillespies last year, team *Kadaicha*, would chase everything they could find about Spoggy, and the *Kangaroo* team would look into the goons who tossed photos into the urinal drain. The fourth board he left blank.

The doctor's rooms were quiet after the buzz of activity at the station, even the television was off. Cassidy looked at his watch, it was just after seven. He wondered how his wife would react if he failed to see the doctor as agreed, when a man around his own age walked in and sat in the seat across from him, lost in his thoughts he didn't hear him until he repeated his question.

'Whacha in for?' The man said.

'Sorry?'

'Whacha in for? I'm here to get my haemorrhoids looked at. Like him to lance 'em if he can. Bloody work related too.' He wriggled in the chair.

'Yeah me too, work related and a bloody big pain in the arse.'

'That's good, he gets to practice on you first,' His companion smiled as the DI was called in.

If only it were that simple he thought, as he shook hands with the doctor, explaining his symptoms while trying to ignore the discomfort of the blood pressure cuff around his arm.

'It's been a while since your last visit, Darryl.'

'I've got a lot on my plate right now and I've been getting some cramping across here,' he drew his finger across his breast.

'Pressure?'

'No, just a bit short of breath and I feel hot at the same time,' he was never comfortable speaking about himself, 'nothing really.'

'Your blood pressure's up a bit,' the doctor waved toward the scales. 'better check your weight while we're at it, just for the record.'

Darryl stood on the plate, then sat back down when instructed, waiting in silence as the doctor scribbled on the desk pad. Even he could do math in his head and this bloke had been to university.

'You've wacked on a couple of kilos since February last year,' he studied notes on the screen, 'we talked about exercise and diet then. What happened?'

'Work, I guess and if I'm honest I don't want to do more than the occasional game of golf and a bit of water skiing.'

'Right, we'll need to change that then?'

'I'll try to get in at least one game a week, maybe go to swimming training with the kids when time allows.'

'What's your handicap?'

'I'm getting older,' he tried to joke his way through.

'Not that, your golf game?' If the man had a sense of humour he was keeping it to himself.

'Oh, I usually break ninety on an eighteen-hole course.'

'Good, we've just lost one of our four to his career. You can make up the number. We tee off at seven thirty on Sundays and should get you home in time for lunch and that will be a light lunch. If you miss a round because of work, we fine each other two hundred dollars.'

'Two hundred?'

'Each.'

'But I haven't cleared it with...'

'Your wife called this morning, so there we go. A referral for a blood test, and a script to lower your blood pressure,' he opened a drawer and pulled a coloured note, 'and a complimentary green fee pass. See you Sunday.'

'Thanks.'

As he walked through the waiting area, his companion from before tugged his sleeve, 'How was it?'

'Stitched me up real good,' Cassidy smiled, lifting one leg a few centimetres and shaking it, 'all good.'

He stopped by the chemist on his way home and had the prescription filled and called into the station before heading home.

'You're supposed to be home,' Angela said.

'And you're supposed to be making dinner for lover-boy. What are you doing here?'

'I can't get my mind off some aspects of the case. I was going to leave when you did, but these came in,' she passed him two photos and a preliminary report.

'So the hunch paid off and we do have a body under the floor. Anything on the DNA?'

'Forensics will be a few days, but this was in the coroner's report into the Le-Strange couple's death.'

'Tetrodotoxin, found in the flesh of puffer fish,' he scanned through the papers in the report, 'but how?'

'Co-incidence, Sir?'

'I'll take this to read later,' he gathered the pages together, 'and no, I don't believe in coincidence. It could be a break through, though.'

'Night, Sir.'

He turned back as he reached the door, 'don't stay here too long, Andy always looks like he needs a good feed, so don't keep him waiting. We'll round up the gang in the morning and head across to the Gillespies in the afternoon. See you tomorrow.'

Joe shook the dust from the pile of papers Laura had rescued from his father's chair. Poetry, old letters written to his mother after she died, a few stories and a journal where he had begun writing his memoirs. He pushed it away, the last thing he wanted to do was drag up memories of his father's past.

'What's that? Laura asked as he pushed it too far and it slid off the bench.

Just rubbish. I'll burn it when the weather's right.'

'Here, let me see.'

Joe grunted as he leant over to pick it up. 'It's just more bullshit about who he was and what he did. He was full of it,' he passed it and the papers to her, 'you can give me a précised version later.'

As Laura read about her father-in law's life, she knew in today's more informed world, his mood and actions might be diagnosed as Post Traumatic Stress Disorder. The first half of the journal was stuffed with notes from his time in New Guinea during World War Two. She was about to mention this when he left the room.

Outside, Joe was cleaning the frame of the picture Emily insisted they bring home from Wilson's. He thought some bee's wax would reinvigorate the timber and prised the nails back to remove the backing and the sepia photo of a man seated with his wife standing alongside from behind the glass. He knew the picture well. It was his grandparents and he put it aside to show Laura later, knowing he would now have to find another frame for Emily's treasure.

Placing the painting face down on the bench, he noticed writing on the back of it. The print was faint, and he held it up to the light to try and decipher it. While the words didn't make sense, the image did and he pulled the dog-eared photocopy of the slate from his wallet and raced into the bathroom to hold the copy in front of the mirror so he could see its reflection. It was a map of an area north-east of Nackara, he knew it well, from when the family had leased a property there in the fifties and early sixties. When he turned the painting over and looked at the reflection, the words now made sense. Numbers pencilled in red indicated mining leases in the Waukaringa and Teetulpa areas. To the west, a number was ringed with red pen and Miller's Creek ran south east to north west along the southern line of a red triangle. An oval drawn in green pencil took in an area east of Olary and west to Baratta Station. To the South it reached Black Rock Peak.

'The cunning old bastard,' he spoke aloud.

'You said something?' Laura called.

'Yeah, take a look at this. I think we've found it.'

'Found what?'

'Les's gold.' It was a true eureka moment. His heart beat with excitement and he felt like yelling it from the roof top, but he knew full well the ramifications of sharing his knowledge.

'Where?' Laura was at his shoulder now.

'On a line between Teetulpa and Carrieton, just here,' he pointed the handle of the toothbrush at a number at the source of Millers Creek.

'What are you going on about?'

'I've always claimed the poem said Miller's Creep, right?'

'Yeah?'

'And what's the name of this creek?' he pointed to the map.

'Miller's Creek.'

'And what if I told you Les leased this area for fifteen years,' Joe drew lazy circles on the map with the handle of the toothbrush, 'I'd bet London to a brick, there's a ridgeline along that creek somewhere.'

'Who has the place now?'

'I don't know, but another bet would be that red brick wall in the cellar at Wilson's is hiding something.'

'Are you asking me to go on a picnic with you again?'

'It worked out okay the last time.'

'If we don't count the shoulder injury or you dangling from a winch bucket,' she laughed at him, 'but I can't tomorrow, I have a hair appointment.'

'Phone them and make you a new one.'

'Are you getting gold fever Joe Gillespie?'

'I might be.'

'Do you want to go tonight?'

His eyes widened and he drew her into a clinch and squeezed.

She patted his chest and laughed, 'tomorrow's soon enough. I'll phone the hairdresser in the morning, but you'd better find some snake repellent.'

'Oh yeah, I forgot about that.'

He went back to the records, searching for section and ordinance maps of the Millers Creek area. If he could find the co-ordinates he would be able to drive straight to the mine site.

It was after midnight when he found the lease numbers and realised some of the Millers Creek sites had lapsed. He used Emily's Trust account and bought a shelf company online, applied for a miner's permit and registered the leases and in a short while he had another new enterprise. It might be worthless but he hoped not.

Laura put an arm around his shoulders and kissed his cheek, 'I'm off to bed.'

'Yeah, I'll be there in a minute.'

'What's that she pointed to the screen?' Putting a hand over her mouth to stifle a yawn, 'Oh excuse me. Come on Joe, it's late.'

'That's the mine,' he said, circling the cursor over a slate ridge, 'I may have only been a kid, but I remember that place.'

'How?'

'It's where dad dug me out of the cave-in. C'mon, I'm done in too,' he closed down the computer and pushed his chair back, 'oh, and I just took out leases on it in Emily's Trust account.'

'You're supposed to tell Tilly, she's the other trustee.'

'Well she wasn't here to ask. Anyway, if nothing comes of it, she won't need to know.'

'You'll tell her in the morning.'

'Yeah course.'

'Joe?'

'In the morning, first thing.'

CHAPTER FIFTY SIX

Laura had reached for the telephone beside the bed before Joe had even recognised the noise. He looked across her shoulder to read the time, squinting to get a better focus. Eight-thirty. All the talk of gold mines and planning what they would do with Les's gold meant they had slept in. He rolled back onto his pillow and closed his eyes.

He listened to Laura agreeing to meet the caller at ten o'clock. They had plans, she should have put whoever it was, off. His mood darkened and threw the bedclothes back and headed for a shower. Running water always helped him think and as he stood there with steam clouding the shower glass, he thought about the papers beside Les's chair. If his father had left clues for him, why be so cryptic? Why not just say what was going on?

He lathered his hair and tried to remember their last conversation. He knew it had not ended well. Both men had lost their temper and words had been rough and heated. Les wanted him to know or understand something about the papers, but Joe had called it bullshit and asked why he should want it anyway. Les threw his urine bottle at him, telling him to burn the papers and board the place up.

Joe thought about it more deeply. Had Les handed him an olive branch during those last hours? If that was it, then the old bastard should have said so. For years Joe had tried to kindle affection into their relationship, but Les had been too wedded to the bottle and his wild ideas. Sure, he talked of some kind of quartz bearing reef and an Aladdin's cave of treasure, however, Joe had always believed it had been the booze talking.

He closed his eyes as he rinsed his hair, remembering the day an old bloke stopped him in the street, and tried to recall the meeting. Mad Charlie people called him, a drifter with yarns of prospecting and making a fortune from gold.

He had abused Joe for being a Gillespie and the son of a money grubbing cheat and muttered about Les dudding him out of a fortune.

Mad Charlie had been drunk outside Cash and Carry. When he saw Joe, he started yelling at him, saying how he had been duped by Les in a poker game. Charlie raised his fist to strike, but Joe caught it and spun him around forcing his head toward the gutter. A shearer's car with a waterbag on the bull bar was close enough for Joe to wrench it off and sloshed the contents over him in an effort to sober him up. Mad Charlie was mad alright, he kicked and squealed like a three-year-old.

Until now Joe had not given him another thought, but standing in the shower, he wondered what had happened to him.

He turned the taps off and reached for his towel. He could hear Laura still on the phone but, half way though his shave, she slid the door open and said, 'You better get your skates on. The bank wants to see you and the police from Port Augusta will be here at ten.' She wriggled past him, reached into the shower and turned the taps on until she had regulated the temperature

'Oi, you bumped me. Jeeze, now I've cut my chin.'

'Put a bit of tissue on it. You'll be right. And make the bed too, there's a love?'

'And what are you going to do while I manage all that?'

'Make myself ravishing and wait for breakfast. Toast will do today, thank you.'

'And our treasure hunt?'

'Oh, with the phone and everything, I'd forgotten,' she reached for a face washer and sped up her shower, 'leave the bed and be as quick as you can with the bank and then we'll be on our way.'

'You only want me for my fortune.'

***

Joe sat across from the banker, scanning the documents before him. He counted the properties held under mortgage and totalled their current value in his head, moving back to the overdraft, looking at the cash-flow for the past ten years. It wasn't the business that was bad, but someone had sold the Reardons loans that bordered on unethical. The core debt was not big, but it weighed on the business like an anchor.

'What do your superiors want?' Joe asked.

'Seventy percent.'

'They're dreaming. What will they take?'

'Fifty.'

'Ten is all they'll get at auction and you know it.'

'What can I do? My hands are tied.'

'Phone them now. Tell them I'll give you fifteen and settle today,' Joe interlinked his fingers, rested them behind his head and leaned back in the chair, 'it's your call.'

'How about twenty?'

'Try them on fifteen, first?' Joe liked having the upper hand. He stood up, 'I'll wait outside, but don't be long I have a meeting at ten.'

Joe could hear one side of a heated exchange and knew the bank manager was doing his best. The office went quiet and after a few minutes the banker opened the door, his face stiff and as grey as granite.

'Come in, Joe.'

'How much?'

'Round it to the closest thousand over fifteen percent. I argued for twelve and a half, but this is the best I can get,' his face broke into a smile bright enough to shame the dawn on a clear spring day, 'I don't know what you have planned Joe, but if you can keep Brad and Karen in town...'

Joe saw the strain on his face.

'I reckon they'll stay,' Joe stood up, 'don't say anything to them yet, but get the paperwork in place and Tilly will come in to finalise everything this arvo.'

'So, you'll tell Brad, then?'

'I'll tell him, but I have other business to take care of first,' Joe said. He was sure the bank would take his offer, but this turned out better than he had hoped. Today might be a lucky one.

Coming in through the back door, Joe looked at his toast. It was cold and Laura offered to make more, but he brushed her offer away. He dunked it in the tea she poured instead. Tilly and Jeff had arrived at the same time as the police and they were all waiting for him in the front room. Joe motioned for Tilly to come to the kitchen, telling her about his appointment with the bank and she agreed to take care of the documentation.

Only after completing business did Joe invite the others to join them in the kitchen, Laura served scones and Tilly had set a tea service in the middle of the table. Jeff raised his eyebrows at this out of character behaviour, she nodded toward her mother and mouthed, 'her idea'.

Cassidy reached for a scone and remembering his doctor's words, passed on it. Deciding he should have his tea black without sugar, he said. 'We wanted to talk to all of you today about the trouble you had last year and, ask if you've considered the possibility that it might still be connected to what's happening to you now.'

'It's crossed my mind', Laura said, 'and we started to go over everything after the incident in Adelaide. That's what we were doing when John came to ask Jeff why he tried to access the police database. Joe can fill in the gaps?'

Joe looked at the scones in front of him, decided they were off limits and joined Cassidy in a black tea. 'Well yeah, we were trying to link it all together, but decided you have more resources. So, if it wasn't the dead bloke in Hammond, who's out to get us?'

'Good question, but what I keep asking myself is, why?' The DI picked up his cup, 'what do you have that someone wants so badly they're prepared to go to any lengths to get it?' he leaned back in his chair, 'any thoughts?'

When no-one said anything, he leaned forward and put his cup down, stopping his gaze at each member of the Gillespie family. 'Here's the thing I don't understand, how does somebody find a bloke in America to come and kill you, Joe. Not just anyone, but some evil bastard with a grudge. And not just any grudge, but one that started in a Cambodian village and ended in a court martial only a few people knew about.' He put the crime scene photo of Gordon-Sanders sitting dead in his chair on the table in front of Joe.

Joe picked it up and looking at it replied. 'He doesn't look too healthy there,' he couldn't help it he smiled, 'evil as sin itself, the bastard.'

'ASIO granted me access to your file, Joe.'

'And?'

'Just me, no-one else gets a look,' Joe held the DI's gaze. This was the first time anyone's stare had ever made him feel this cold and he waited for Joe's reply.

'Best we keep it that way then?'

'I can do that,' he closed the folder and slipped it back into his briefcase, 'but what I can't do is protect you unless we find out who's behind the first attack. You agree?' He waited for Joe to answer and hoped he had thawed.

Joe was deliberate, still holding Cassidy's eye contact, he casually took a scone and without looking, layered it with jam and cream before putting the lot in his mouth. 'Well yeah, but we can only think it's this mining company,

RADOR. Our solicitor made a few calls, but the company's only been registered for a short while, so why, is anyone's guess,' he finished the scone and found he didn't enjoy it anyway and shrugged, 'and there's nothing on the place anyway.'

'We looked at that as a reason too. Our geologist contacts in Adelaide say the same thing. So, when I ask myself if this is about you refusing exploration on your land, I came up blank whichever way I look at it. For the moment, I'm going to dismiss that as a motive. Well, maybe not eliminate entirely, but make it less likely.'

Laura had listened enough and thought the DI was going in circles. 'Well, who is your prime suspect?'

Angela was taking notes and the detective waited for her to catch up. John O'Rourke opened his mouth and on DI Cassidy's signal, closed it again.

'There's evidence to suggest a bloke called Spoggy is behind it, but why he's singled you out and who he's working with is our conundrum. Is there anything you might know about this bloke that might give us a clue?'

Joe shook his head.

'Spoggy? I didn't even know the name before Joe told me about the burnt-out utility,' Laura said.

'You do actually, Mum,' Tilly said, 'remember the working bee to get Jeff's plane out of the barn. Dad asked who the bloke in the photo was, well that's him,' she turned to O'Rourke, 'do you know him John?'

'That's the one,' he said.

Cassidy's resolve weakened and he reached for a scone, slicing it with his butter knife.

'Sir,' Angela chastised.

'Oops, oh well too late to put it back now,' he slathered jam on each half. The spoon made a sucking sound as he dug it out of the whipped cream and dolloped it onto the jam, 'these are legendary, Laura, legendary.

Jeff's often told us they were good,' his mouth full of forbidden food, he said, 'it's okay Angela, I'll tell the wife tonight and take my punishment.'

Tilly scrolled through the images on her phone, 'there, leaning up against the barn wall, sort of blending into it, that's Spoggy,' she turned the screen to Joe and he dug in his shirt pocket for his glasses.

'Nope, the face doesn't ring any bells for me. He's not the kind of bloke you'd notice,' he took the phone and showed Laura, 'love?'

'Can't say I've ever seen him,' she shook her head, 'more tea anyone. What about you Darryl? Another scone?'

The detective patted his stomach. 'The doctor has me trying to reduce my cholesterol, best not,' he checked his notes again, 'how about the name, Peter Cook? Does that mean anything?'

Joe, Laura and Tilly shook their heads.

'How about Liam Le-Strange?'

'No, but that's a name that would stick in your mind,' Joe said, 'I read an article back in the seventies about a Le-Strange. I was interested professionally because he worked at the weapons research facility in Salisbury, but it was something about racing pigeons, or rescuing greyhounds, or something, nothing to do with us.'

Cassidy rubbed his forehead and squinted, feeling a headache coming on. Thinking fluid would help, he poured himself another tea and turned to Tilly, 'your Dad said you've spoken to RADOR, telling them you are willing to discuss their proposal, right?'

'Well not me personally, but our solicitor has our instruction.'

'And?'

'We asked for and gave them a list of discussion points,' she shrugged, 'and we're still waiting to hear from them.'

'They must be confident you'll comply.' He drew a folder from his briefcase.

'Why's that?' Joe asked.

'Because the prospectus released this week shows proposed drilling sites on your land. It describes the minerals they plan to extract and where they intend to put in an open cut mine. It'll ravage the place.' He passed it to Joe.

'This's bullshit. Tilly, call them now. I want to know if it's legit.' Joe stood up and paced around the table until Laura spoke up.

'Joe, for pity's sake sit down. The whole thing's probably just a scam. I don't want to be nursing you through another bout of misery.'

'I'm just pissed off,' he sat down again, 'we've signed nothing to give them cause to think they can come onto the land without permission. I'm still pissed that someone in the Ag Department gave them authority to test for contamination. They sent a drilling rig out to the well paddock. A bloody drilling rig, and for what? If they'd asked, I could've shown them where the water ran. A kilo of arsenic can kill a lot of animals, but it was in over a hundred thousand litres of water and ran a narrow stream into a large clay-pan so it was contained. Fuck, a good man with a shovel could get rid of it in a week. The bastards are just trying to backdoor us. We had to get an injunction to stop them drilling. Thankfully, now all they can do is collect vegetation and surface samples from the well paddock,' he slapped the bench, 'they haven't got permission to mine, drill, or do anything outside their testing brief.'

CHAPTER FIFTY SEVEN

Clive Lewis passed his daughter a stack of papers and a copy of the Adelaide Advertiser folded to expose the mining section, the warmth of the printer still in the papers. A quarter of the page was dedicated to RADOR, the newly appointed CEO, Gino Di Massimo and Charles Winkler. Sam received a mention and it was not favourable. She threw the paper on the floor and stared at the wad of papers that came with it.

'A prospectus, how?'

'Even an old driller like me knows how to surf the web. I downloaded it last night. It makes an interesting read, even if it is all bullshit.'

'Far out, Dad. Did you read what they said about me, the bastards, I could kill them.'

'Better to get even, that way they live to suffer longer.'

'Oh, I'll make them suffer Dad, don't you worry about that.'

'Call your friend, Tilly isn't it?' Ask her if she knows anything. I did a bit of digging and a friend in the mines department said the Gillespies took out an injunction to stop your lot drilling. They did get back onto the place, but only to take leaf and grass samples,' he pushed another paper in front of her, a summary of work done by a professor at Queensland University, 'you might want to read this too. I can manage a few days off if you want to go bush and maybe meet with the Gillespies. I'll ask your Mum too, she's met Laura before. What do you think?'

'Dad, I don't know.'

'Well I do and you've got nothing to lose.'

Sam spent the next few hours poring over the documents and could see the prospectus was pure fiction. She identified passages she had written for other proposals and knew the whole thing was nothing more than a cut and paste effort. The fact that Timothy had ripped documents and statistics from anywhere, just to get the proposal together was bad, but some of the research had been credited to her and that was taking it too far. She understood why he had done it, but the whole document was bogus and designed to mislead potential investors.

Fury building inside her, she knew there had to be a way to make this right. She picked up her phone and pressed Charles' number. It went straight to messages and every effort she made to contact her old firm to discuss the document met the same fate.

Picking up on father's earlier idea of taking a trip north, she phoned Tilly and set up the appointment. In the back of her mind was the faint chance she might bump into Jake while she was there, the perfect foil for her battered self-confidence and pride.

***

Tilly found her father sitting at the table in the outdoor area, poring over the slate drawing, an old section map, and a piece of brown paper that looked like a rough, hand drawn map. To one side, the papers Laura had rescued from the table beside Les' chair fluttered in the breeze under a magnifying glass used as a paperweight.

'I just had a call from Sam Lewis and she wants to catch up with us this week,' Tilly said, 'her parents are coming too. She said they know you from years ago, Clive and Penny Lewis. They worked for a team of drillers and lived in the caravan park for a while.'

'Maybe,' Joe worked the map, his finger following a creek line, 'we're a bit busy though. I've hardly had a minute with Brad and I need to get that sorted and I did promise your mum a picnic. What do you think, Laura?'

'Tell them it's okay to come this week, as long as we know when, and we'll work around them.'

'Jeeze you're a pushover. We could have put it off for a couple of months yet.'

'I know, but that would only gnaw away at you and I can't have that,' she forced a smile and he knew not to answer back, 'now what about that picnic, give me half an hour.'

'Good, I'll run Tilly back home then, because we'll need the Landcruiser today,' Joe grinned at his daughter, both knowing this was one way to get his ute back.

'I can walk,' Tilly said.

'It's no trouble, and I can see Brad for a couple of ticks on the way back.'

'See you later, Love,' Laura said as she turned to go inside, 'Dad'll drop it back tonight. You need it more than he does.'

Joe turned left at the police station and headed out the Erskine road.

'Whoa, where are you going?' Laura shouted over the rattling of the tools on the Toyota's tray as the wheels skimmed over the corrugations of the dirt road.

'It's a surprise.'

'What about Wilson's?'

'Wilson's will still be there tomorrow.'

'Is it somewhere I've been before?'

'Nope, not sure.'

'You?'

'Maybe, long time ago.'

'So, it's one of those aimless drives through station country, a picnic at a waterhole and home?'

'Nope.'

'What then?'

'You'll see when we get there.'

They travelled in silence for the next half hour and Laura was wondering just how much further they would go before he shared his secret when they passed Oak Downs Station, slowing to allow a group of emus to cross onto the road.

'Have you worked it out yet?'

'Worked what out?'

'Where Les got his gold from.'

'No, where?'

'About an hour that way,' he pointed north east, 'but it'll take us a bit longer to get there.

She looked around to get her bearings. 'Waukaringa? You could have said,' she slapped his arm, 'and we could have taken the bitumen road.'

'True, but this way we get to look around the country out this way too. How about we stop up ahead and boil the billy, eh?'

'And while we do, you can tell me more.'

'We might need to be a bit clever about this though, people out here probably protect their claims with vigour.'

'With guns, you mean?'

Joe just nodded.

After lunch, a relaxation of togetherness, they drove into the now deserted township of Waukaringa, where Joe stopped at the hotel and wandered around the back, looking around the yards. They walked through to the front bar and he rested his back against the fireplace, eyes closed.

'Yep, we're on the right track,' he said.

'Right track to where?' Laura was tired of this game and ready to go home. This morning she had thought they were going to Wilsons and now they were at this place beyond the black stump and none of it made sense. 'Come on Joe, either tell me what this is all about or we're heading home.'

'I'm just thinking about the day Dad dug me out of the dirt when he stopped here for a beer and I had a raspberry. I've got my bearings now, come on.'

Back at the car, he spread a section map across the bonnet. He picked up a piece of quartz to use a weight and studied it before handing it to his wife, 'here put this on the corner, and we'll keep it when we're finished here.'

'What were you looking at?'

'Gold is where you find it and I thought there was a fleck in that fault line,' he pointed to a line of dirt with his finger. We'll crack it with a hammer later.'

'Better to do it now then, while we're here.'

'You're right, we don't want to be accused of pilfering someone's claim.'

They put another rock in its place and went to the towbar where Joe rested it with the fault side down and raised the hammer.

'Wait,' Laura waved a plastic bag in front of him, 'we should try to contain what we can.'

He hit the stone twice. The was bag now full of holes and Laura cradled it in her palms while Joe put the hammer back, then spread the pieces onto the map and used the bigger chunks to keep the paper still.

'What've we got?'

'Sweet nothing I reckon,'

Her spirits dropped, 'I was hoping for something, anything, just one little fleck would do,' she moved to scrape it off the map, 'like they say, all the easy gold is gone.'

'Maybe, maybe not,' he pursed his lips and blew, holding his hand around the dust so it made a line on the paper. He licked his finger and dabbed it on the map, 'look, a fleck just for you my dear. Now what are you going to do with it?'

'It's hard to keep one little speck in anything. Would it be better to toss it away then?'

'There's a bottle over there with its lid on it, we could tip the dust in there and leave it in the tray, then wash it out when we get home.'

'Really, why?'

'It constitutes prospecting, doesn't it?' He winked and pointed to the map, 'now what do you see?'

'Miller's Creek,' Laura said.

'Yep, and that's where we're headed. We'll turn in off the Baratta road and drive along the creek bed for a few miles and it'll be on our left,' he put the folded map behind the seat, 'I remember Dad played cards that day with a couple of blokes while he had a few beers. I'm not sure if it was to brace his courage before he faced Mum, or to steady himself after what had happened.'

'Hang onto the latter, it's easier to carry,' she said as she clicked her seat belt home.

'I always thought that although the leases were marked Millers Creek, there'd been a typo on the papers when we renewed our licenses. It was only after I looked at the map behind the picture that I knew it was Millers Creek. The mine is up here a-ways and we still own the rights to it.'

'What about the stuff you said about people out here not being too friendly?'

'If anyone is working our claim, they're going to be really pissed off, so we'll ask a few directions and let the law deal with it. What I'm hoping is the old man set enough explosive to collapse the whole thing and hide it.'

'How the hell are we going to find it then?'

He tapped the side of his head knowingly, 'it's all in here girl, all in here.'

They tossed from side to side as Joe eased his way along the creek bed, Laura keeping watch on her side for any traces of a road or track that led off to the left.

Joe checked the GPS as he drove, he thought he knew the co-ordinates and they were almost far enough north, 'we should be up there soon. Otherwise we'll need to double back.'

'Joe,' Laura yelled, looking up to see a battered four-wheel-drive blocking their path.

Two men cradling rifles stood at one end, a mongrel, part Pitbull part German Pincer or Rottweiler strained at its lead. The slow growl felt like thunder and Laura supposed it was meant to. At the other end was a skeleton of a man no taller than the shoulder of the other two. His face was scared and looked like a chamois that had been left in the sun to dry. A hand rolled cigarette defied gravity as clung to his lower lip.

'Best you go now,' his voice sounded gravelly, like tyres on the creek bed.

'Can I ask where we are?' Joe did his best to sound lost, 'I sort of remember this creek from when I came here as a kid. My uncle bought some machinery from a bloke out this way and I wondered if there was anything left out here.

'Who was your uncle?' Chamois face asked.

'Ross Growden, he worked for Elders in Peterborough.'

'There's nothing out here now, mate. Like I said, you'd better go.'

'So, you're still working the mine then?' Joe pushed it.

'Look mate, there's a lot of country out here and it's full of holes and I'd hate to lose you both down one of them. I'm not a patient man and I've been good until now. Best you and your missus piss off.' He turned to the help, lifted his free hand, and they raised their rifles.

'We're going now,' Joe searched for and found reverse, looking over his shoulder as he backed away at speed while instructing Laura to keep her eye on the bloke on the right, 'he's the twitchy one. If his hand flinches, yell and dive under   the   dash.'

CHAPTER FIFTY EIGHT

DI Cassidy was in the office early staring at the incident boards. This case was beginning to block his ability to visualise, clogging his mind. He needed to take it back to the beginning and work it through from there and headed toward stationary to get evidence boxes to begin sorting. Walking past a vending machine, chocolate bars screamed at him and he dipped his hand into his pocket and fed gold coins into the machine, tossing and catching the apple he had picked up in the kitchen as he went. Satisfied with his prize he continued down to stationery. Losing weight and living longer could wait until tomorrow.

Back at the incident boards he marked each box using a formula he had seen on the BBC TV show, Top Gear. Moving a table in front of the boards, he arranged the chairs into lecture format. Next, he put the boxes onto the table and set them left to right so the labels, *What's Hot*, *Undecided*, and *What's Not*, would face the team when they arrived for the seven thirty briefing.

He looked at the chocolate bars and put them back in his pocket, satisfied they were there should he need them, went to his desk and started on the apple. The crisp freshness of it helped him think.

Now where was Spoggy?

He had checked with personnel and Jeff Rankin was still officially on long service leave. He picked up Jeff's file and shoved it in his drawer. 'Active is what you are Senior Constable Rankin and I'm bringing you into work today.' Jeff's intuition would be a big help. He picked up the phone to tell the newest member of his team he would now be getting paid.

When Jeff's phone rang, he and John were driving through Wilmington. He looked at John who just shrugged and stopped chatting. Showing him the caller's ID, Jeff listened to what the voice on the other end had to say before saying, 'well Boss, I'll need to be promoted if I'm going to withdraw my resignation, say to Detective Sergeant?'

'You wish. Let's get this case cleaned up and we'll talk about it then.'

'I'll need to talk it through with Tilly first before I can accept, and as I've already told you, I'll only be staying on until this is over.'

'Understood, we can talk more about that later, but for now, has anything happened with your soon to be father in law that I should know about?'

'It's all quiet over here. He's been looking at country out east, bought Brad Reardon's garage, and other than that they've kept to themselves.'

'Good, let's keep it that way. I'll see you at the briefing then.'

John O'Rourke flicked the indicator on and swung the patrol car left toward Horrocks Pass. 'Okay, what was that all about?'

'Getting paid. Cassidy wants to cancel my long service. It seems you blokes can't do without me. High five,' he raised his hand, John slapped it away, then swerved to miss a grey Kangaroo that lumbered across the road.

'Joe isn't worried about the photos in the piss drain then?' John asked.

'I think he's worried, but he copes by doing stuff. They both do and Tilly's the same. You'd never know it, but we're supposed to be getting married at the end of the year,' he looked out the window, 'and that's if I can ever pin her down to a date. She's been flat out with the restoration of the homestead and now Joe's bought the garage.'

'Everything getting to you, mate?'

'I'm glad of the distraction to tell the truth.'

'I saw them turn out the back road to Paratoo yesterday, do you know what they were doing there?'

'Picnic, they do this little fantasy treasure hunt thing. Joe says he knows where something is and they go looking for it,' he made circles around his ear with a finger, 'loopy or just getting older, I don't know, don't want to know.'

John pulled a folder from between his seat and the console and passed it to Jeff, 'well, it's time for you to get back into it I suppose?'

***

Tilly drove to her parent's cottage after taking Emily to school, finding them in the kitchen staring at the pictures on Laura's phone.

'Hello Darling. We hoped you might drop in this morning, because your father and I are going out soon and we wanted to tell you we do remember the Lewis's,' Laura stretched onto her toes to kiss her daughter's cheek, 'Clive and Penny. They camped in the caravan park. I don't know how she coped, what with a toddler and being pregnant at the same time.'

Joe twisted in his chair to greet her and she kissed his forehead as he asked, 'everything alright?'

'Just peachy, Dad,' she bent to study the faces on the phone's screen, 'who are they and why are they holding guns?'

'We met them out on our drive yesterday, about an hour after our picnic I suppose it was,' Joe expanded the screen and centred Chamois Face, 'he needs a bit of moisturiser, what do you reckon?'

'I reckon I ought to lock you two up for a while. Dad, will you stop finding trouble?' she rushed to the other side of the table and stretched over it until her nose was almost touching his, then lifted her eyes and stared at her mother, 'and you can stop encouraging him too.'

Both of them laughed at her and she dragged a chair out, flopped in, and dropped her head in her hands.

'We're only trying to make light of things, that's all,' Laura reached over and cupped Tilly's hands in hers, 'if we start to live in fear then the bastards win and we don't want that.'

Joe watched, feeling responsible for the pressure on his family.

'I dunno, Mum, Jeff just phoned to say his long service leave has been cancelled and they want him to cancel his resignation. Shit, they have plenty of coppers, I just want one,' her voice was tired, strained, 'can't we just stop all of this and go somewhere? Anywhere, away from the Well, Orroroo, bloody mining companies and people who want to peel a little bit more off of me, bit by bit, day by day.'

Laura stood up. 'Come on love, we'll get through. I'll make a cuppa and bring it outside, eh?' She looked at Joe and mouthed the words, 'take her outside and comfort her'.

'C'mon Tilly, better do as she says,' Joe pushed the door and held it as his daughter squeezed past, 'now tell your old dad everything. What's the trouble?' Even as he spoke he cringed, wanting to take the words back. Joe Gillespie didn't do treacle laden sentences.

'It's you Dad, you're the trouble. Someone takes pot-shots at you last year and what do you do? Let the police handle it? No not you, you fire up. You suck everyone around you into your vortex and we all go along willingly, because it's you.'

Laura could hear her from the kitchen and peered through the screen door. Joe saw her and motioned her to wait. She understood, best to let him handle this.

Gillespie's Gold

Tilly drew in a deep breath to compose herself. 'I thought we'd done with it after they found Gordon-Sanders. You were laid up in hospital, the bad guys were dead and we had our lives back. We were doing alright Dad. You asked me to step up and I did. I liked being you, ordering people about and making stuff happen. At the same time I was pissed off that you let me do everything while you wallowed around in a pool of pity, but I coped,' her sorrow and anger turned to frustration, she stood up and walked around, brushing leaves to the edge of the paving with her foot, 'how Mum has coped is beyond me.'

Joe watched her walk, picking dead leaves from the grapevine and crushing them in her hand. He wanted to say something, anything to make her feel better, but she held her hand up and continued, 'don't you dare say anything, because I'm not finished yet,' she walked some more, then turned and leant over the table, her arms spread to support her weight, her nose inches from his, 'Dad, I don't understand why you are out on this bizarre hunt for some mysterious gold mine. I don't care about Les Gillespie's gold. I don't care about Brad Reardon's bloody garage. You don't seem to comprehend the danger everyone's in. Jeff has only agreed to help, because I told him I wanted this over and done with once and for all.'

Inside, the phone rang and Joe turned to listen to Laura's side of the conversation, grateful for the break from Tilly's emotional outburst. However, she turned his face back to hers. He knew there was truth in her words, there were also contradictions and underlying this was the real issue, they were too much alike.

'Dad, look at me. I'm supposed to be preparing for you to walk me down the aisle in September. I want us to do everything we can to remove ourselves from the shit that's going on now. If we have to sell up, then we have to sell.

You know what, people have had worse and survived. We need to get over it.'

Tilly heard the door creak, 'it's okay Mum, I've said my piece, you can come out now and I know you've heard everything anyway.'

Laura put the tray down. 'That's as it may be love,' Laura smiled at the daughter they had raised to be independent and to speak her mind, 'but in all good debates, the other side has the right of reply and I think you should hear your Dad out. Joe?'

He wasn't ready. He wanted time to think. If he didn't, he might cry and blokes like him didn't show emotion that way. He took a deep breath and answered his daughter, 'I can't disagree with anything you say, Tilly. It has been hell for the last few months for all of you, and I know you want all this to finish, but it's not up to me. I'm only doing what I can to eliminate the threat and leave something other than a farm behind. What I've learnt in the last year is that I'm close to my use by date and I want to use my time to finish making my mark,' Laura putting her hand on his shoulder, gave him strength, 'not just to leave you and Em and Jeff better off, but look around, this town needs something. I thought if Mum's idea for a restoration centre and museum took off, it could be supported with a business restoring cars, trucks and machinery.'

Joe stood up, he knew most of these thoughts came from touring England with Bill and on the plane home he had wondered how it might work, now his head was clear, 'just think, making old new again. We can't wait for the Council and Government to take the lead, we can...'

Laura held her hand up, 'I think she's had enough, Joe. She could see Tilly had shut down and Joe's words were left hanging in the wind.

Sitting down, he made invisible circles around a knot in the table with his finger. He was ready to share and opened his mouth. Laura shook her head, the words dying on his tongue, he slouched back.

'Oh, before I forget, that was Clive Lewis on the phone, said they were coming tomorrow,' Laura put her arm around Tilly, 'anything you two want to get done will have to happen today. What have you got planned, love?'

Tilly felt better for getting her worries out into the open, and thrashing through her issues until she felt they understood, had eased her mind. 'I thought I'd hang around with you guys today. So, what are we doing?'

'I wanted to go to Wilson's, I haven't finished there yet,' Joe said, wondering whether Tilly had always been this quixotic, firing on all barrels one minute, acting as if everything was fine the next, and he hadn't noticed. Uncertain of what to say, he looked to Laura for confirmation and she smiled her approval.

'Good, Wilson's it is and you can tell me all of those plans again while I drive. We'll all fit in the front won't we Mum?'

'We'll squeeze in, but you'd better let him drive, he still thinks it's his ute.'

Watching Gip wander over and nuzzle Joe's hand. Laura thought it was all coming back together. The treasure hunt was still on.

CHAPTER FIFTY NINE

Cassidy called Jeff to the front of the room. 'Most of you know Senior Constable Jeff Rankin. He thought he'd be sunning himself on a beach somewhere, but I've asked him back to help out while we get onto sorting this out,' he waved his arm across the incident boards, 'Jeff, you can sit in, but as you're involved with the family, I'll ask you observe only.'

'I'm happy to leave if you like?' Jeff said.

'Just watch for now, okay? Sit up the back and keep Sarge company, give him a dig in the ribs if he starts snoring.'

A snigger rippled around the room and the DI was pleased with his joke. 'I want to conduct a bit of a straw-poll and you only get one vote. How many like Snickers,' he counted the hands and put the bar on the table, 'what about Cherry Ripe?' Four hands went up, 'and the Mars Bar?' he smiled, 'my favourite too.' He picked up the chocolate bars and put them in front of the boxes. 'Okay, today we're all playing for the Mars Bar and the game were playing is, Catch the Crim. I want you to study the boards and when you see something out of place, or irrelevant. Walk to the front, take it down and explain why it's not important. If the room agrees drop it in the *What's Not* box, same thing with the What's Hot board put your picture up, make your case and put a cross alongside your name on this piece of paper. Got it?' He held the paper and Mars bar aloft, 'the winner is the one with the most crosses and they get this chocolate. Got it?'

The room remained silent, uncomfortable with the new direction their DI was taking but, after he had asked the question for the third time, they could see he was losing patience and they responded as one. 'Got it.'

A constable broke the ice and walked to the front of the room where he plucked the picture of a burnt-out bikie camp, holding it up so all could see, 'this is not relevant to the investigation because these blokes are in custody and can't tell us anything.'

'Okay,' Cassidy asked, 'hot or not?' When the room remained silent he answered his own question. The game had got off to a slower start than he had anticipated. 'I'd say, not,' he said, 'the only thing is though, someone traded the girl to these animals. Put it in the not box, but keep the photos on Jeff's board up, eh?'

Another constable stepped up, 'the singing circle, sorry, but these women had nothing to do with the bloke in Hammond.'

He dropped it into the not box and put a cross by his name.

The meeting followed this procedure until they broke, their enthusiasm boosted by the interaction and sugar hit from the chocolate rewards. Cassidy felt it was more like a quiz show than policing, but it had worked. He checked his emails then prepared to walk around the block as his doctor suggested.

'What's with the walking, Sarge?' Jeff asked, nodding in the direction of the DI.

'High blood pressure. I reckon the doctor has scared shit out of him. A month ago, and he'd have scoffed all those bars in front of us.'

'So why am I here? If I'm not to participate, what does he want?'

'Another set of eyes. You know protocol, you can't have anything to do with the case so right now, he doesn't want you and Joe traipsing all over his investigation. Better to have you where he can control your movements,' Sarge shook his shoulder, 'anyway, where is Joe and what's he up too.'

'Dunno. Tilly has gone down there today to set things straight this morning. I'm waiting on a text,' he looked at the sky, it was a good day for soaring, 'you know I could be flying rather than sitting on my hands in here.'

'You could, but you wouldn't get paid. That's why he pulled rank and brought you in. Having you ride with John out to this Spoggy's place was one thing, but if we ask more of your time, this is his easiest way to compensate you,' he pushed a paper in front of him, 'here sign this, I've already filled out the form,'

'Hey wait, I haven't even read it, yet.'

'You sign and you get an acting detective sergeant's pay, so sign it, everything's done.'

'Yeah?'

'Just sign the paper and you're back to the rank you had before you left Adelaide. Pay office will take a couple of weeks to catch up, so welcome on board, Detective Sergeant Rankin.'

'I didn't think he'd cave,' Jeff said.

'He knows a good copper when he sees one and you can take over his day to day stuff while he gets on with the case in there, okay?'

'I'm fine with that, Sarge, but what have you got for me?'

'Nothing right now, but don't worry you can sit in on the circus in there until it breaks up. Just don't say anything.'

'Got it, I like the idea by the way.'

'He thought you might.'

When the group broke at one o'clock and the second round prizes allocated, the DI remained in the room, staring at the few remaining stick-it notes and photos on one board.

He took Spoggy's photo, renamed it Peter Cook, and put it into the middle of the board, then drew a short line with Tamara Gibson's photo off to the right and Joe Gillespie to the left. Coloured lines connected the clues and a legend in the top right corner indicated importance of the colour.

Jeff walked in and startled the detective when he touched him. 'Boss?'

'Jesus, Jeff don't creep up on a bloke, you could have given me a heart attack.'

Jeff laughed, 'you're a bit on edge today, Sir, but you called and I came. And thanks, it's good to get the rank back again'

'You're going to work for it though,' the DI opened a plastic container and Jeff watched as he took a carrot stick and snapped it off with his teeth, 'what do you see?'

'If I was on this case, Sir? I'd see a psychopath.'

'Me too, anything else?'

'The bullets in the dogs and the body in the pit match those of the rifle John and I recovered. The body was related to the dead couple, possibly the son.'

'Not possibly, definitely. Go on.'

'Gordon-Sanders died from eating puffer fish,' Jeff picked up the red marker, 'as did the dead boy's parents according to forensics. It would be interesting to know if he tried it on the dogs before he shot them?'

'Angela,' Cassidy's voice was piercing and she rushed into the room, a half-eaten sandwich in her hand, 'did forensics find any poison in the dogs?'

'I'll check, anything else?' Egg and lettuce spilled on the floor and she bent down and scraped it into a serviette.

'Find out if Hamilton has anything more on Cook.'

'On it now, Sir.'

'She should be able to finish her lunch first,' Jeff said.

'Wants to win the prize, I'd guess,' Darryl pointed to the spare Snickers, 'why did you ask about the dogs?'

'I wondered if he used them to test the method, or if he just shot them, or if he did the poisoning and persons unknown put the dogs down.'

'Persons unknown?' Cassidy raised his eyebrows, 'polishing up on your modern detective now, are you? I hadn't thought about it, but using a poison to kill is usually seen as a feminine method of killing. Men are more brutal, they'll use anything, happy to watch their victim die,' he stared at the photo of the two dead dogs, 'okay next?'

'It's also possible he's confused about his sexuality. His place wasn't anything like you'd expect for a single bloke's house,' Jeff stared at the board for a second, 'he couldn't take anything with him.'

'Why?'

Jeff moved closer to the board and tapped the photo of the rifle they'd found and the remains of the trail bike, 'he left the gun because he couldn't carry it on the bike without being noticed, so why would he take stuff like stick books?'

'And?'

'The ute at Joe's,' he stopped when Angela came back into the room.

'Sorry sir, Hamilton say Peter Cook's dead,' she put a photo on the board for comparison. Alongside a photo of the grave, 'tragic too, he was only twenty-four. Found him in his car after a fishing trip. He was a known drug user, so they put it down to an overdose. His father was prominent in the town and the station did him a favour.'

'Any friends?' Jeff asked.

'The contact said it happened so long ago and the staff has changed twice. The Senior Sergeant took early retirement and lives in Warrnambool. He could be worth a chat.'

'Thanks, finish your lunch and get the others back in here in fifteen minutes,' he turned back to Jeff, 'and you were saying?'

'I reckon he's left the ute out there to do two things, to stall us a bit and send a message to his employer.'

'Employer?'

'Think about it. He has no links to Joe, Tilly or Laura, so why cause all of this when he gets nothing out of it?' Jeff looked at the timeline still on one of the boards, 'and this,' he ran his finger along the timeline, 'when Joe was attacked, Spoggy had to be somewhere, doing something, or doing nothing, in the time between buying a ticket in Port Wakefield and lighting a fire in Brahma Lodge.'

'Yeah, that's what I thought. I want to divide this case into two. You can't go after the people threatening your family, but you can try to find our psychopath.'

'So, you didn't need all of that from me, just then?'

'Not really, but it's good to have confirmation. For now, we'll keep a space here for you, but you might want to work from John's station. There's not a lot of room, but he'd be around to do a bit of leg work and it'll help him with a promotion. I'll get everything duplicated before you leave and for now you can work on finding out who this Spoggy really is and, more importantly, where he is.'

'That sounds like a plan, can we use Angela as liaison?'

'Yeah, but don't pile too much onto her, use one of the young blokes for the phone work.'

'You getting soft?'

'Just find me Spoggy... before he kills again.'

***

Joe was driving, Laura pressed against him with Tilly squeezed between her and the door. Joe and Laura were on a mission, but they were wary of Tilly's mood sucking the joy from their adventure. 'So, what's on at Wilsons? You know Jeff and I would have fixed the dairy door over the weekend.'

Laura tapped the side of her nose, nodded toward Joe and winked. 'Treasure.' She said.

'What! Granddad's Gold?' It was a relief hearing Tilly laugh. 'You found it, where?'

'Shush,' her father bent down, squinted and looking both ways, whispered. 'where's Jeff?'

'Port Augusta, why?'

'We might need someone to bring the truck over? I'll tell you why later.'

'I can drive the truck,' Laura said.

'You might have to.'

'What time do you have to pick Emily up?'

Joe dodged a pot hole, 'the council should send a grader along here, it's been years.'

'Fiona will keep her until I get home. If Jeff gets home before me, he'll pick her up.'

Joe fished in his breast pocket and handed a yellow receipt to his daughter, 'that's what we're looking for and better still, I know where it is.'

Tilly looked at the paper, whistled and passed it to Laura.

'Indeed.' She said.

CHAPTER SIXTY

Joe handed out dust masks and rolled back the rug on the floor while Laura and Tilly put their safety glasses on, before opening the hatch to the cellar. When the dust settled, Joe lowered a ladder into the underground room. It was unusual for a house of this era to have internal access when most would have used an outside door. If it had not been for the snake, he would have missed the inside hatch completely.

Outside, the generator hummed easily at start up and Joe clipped the light to an extension cord. At least they could see now. Laura held the lamp while he descended and when he found solid ground she handed it down to him. He could see three of the walls had been hewn from the clay, the white lime wash turned pink from years of damp seeping in. Something crunched below his foot and he shone his light on the dried carcass of a python. Further into the room, a rocking chair in the corner seemed out of place and he knew the moment Laura saw it, it would have to be saved.

'Yeah it all seems fine down here. You can come down. Tilly bring a hammer with you. It's in...'

'I know Dad. I'll get it.'

'Joe,' Laura was at the edge of the opening, 'do you think one of us should keep watch?'

'Why?'

'I dunno, in case someone's watching.'

'Like who?'

'The people who are trying to frighten us.'

'If someone comes Gip'll bark her head off. You worry too much, girl.'

'Righto Dad, do you want me to come down?' Tilly was on the ladder. It seemed as if the scent of adventure had put her earlier fears to rest, her tiredness forgotten, 'oh, and I don't think Gip'll be much use, she's as deaf as a post these days. I startled her when I dropped the toolbox.'

'After the trouble yesterday, Mum's just a bit jumpy that's all,' Joe said.

'What trouble?' Tilly was coiled, ready to spring into another argument, 'see, it's like I was saying earlier, you too just can't help yourselves.' She tossed up between laughing and crying and laughing won.

'We were stopped by men with guns. It gives me the creeps to think about it,' Laura bent down and looked through the open trapdoor, 'they could be watching us now, Joe, I wouldn't trust the one with the dog for a second.'

'Dog, men with guns, where were you?' Tilly was in the cellar now.

'Waukaringa. It's a bit wild west out there now. Those blokes were working someone else's claim and didn't want anybody snooping around, that's all,' Joe said, took the hammer from her and started tapping the brick wall, changing the subject, 'Les didn't take long to knock this up. Whoa there!' Tilly stumbled and reached out to catch her balance, 'Mind all the boards, I reckon the water would have come in during a really wet winter.'

'Wet, deep, down there, my silent promise lies,' Tilly recited, feeling the pull of the chase for gold and understanding how people fell into the promise of riches, 'that's the line Dad, isn't it?'

'He thinks that's why Les stayed out here, shot gun on his knees, guarding his treasure like a spider at the edge of its web,' Laura said, 'I want all of this out of the way before the Lewis' get here and we talk to the mining company.'

'So, what happens next?' Tilly asked.

Joe had wriggled several bricks out of the wall and sat the light on the ledge of the opening. He looked into the cavity and urged her forward to look, 'we load that onto the Cruiser.'

Tilly whistled.

'C'mon,' he said, 'let's tear this wall down to get at it.'

'I'm coming down.' As Laura put her foot on the ladder, she slipped. Her hand caught the cord, the room went black in an instant and Tilly screamed. Laura thumped her ribs on the edge of the opening. 'Sorry, sorry, God that hurts.' Her feet made scuffling noises while she scrambled for grip. Sitting on the floor and her legs through the manhole she said, 'I may have to wait for a bit before I come down.'

Joe wished he was still smoking, at least he'd have a lighter in his pocket.

'Hang on and I'll get you some light,' Laura reconnected the cords and light streamed up through the hole.

Joe was at her side before she knew he'd climbed the ladder. 'Are you okay, love?'

'Just a bit of bruising, I hope,' she lifted one side of her shirt, 'here, you take a look.'

'You've got a fair-sized graze there. No broken skin though,' he touched it with the back of his hand.

'Ouch.'

'We'd better lock this up and get you into the town for an X-ray, you might have cracked a couple of ribs.'

'Not before we've loaded up. You and Tilly do what you have to and I'll keep watch.' She slumped into the kitchen chair Joe dragged into the room.

Tilly was now beside them lifted her mother's shirt, studying the marks and looking for any change in the contour of Laura's ribs. 'Dad's right Mum,' she pointed to the door, 'this can wait.'

'Sorry darling, but it can't,' Laura said, 'I'm not going to put up with your father bouncing around all over the place. I don't want him looking over his shoulder and rushing me to get better, just so he can come back here. We'll do this now and I'll go to hospital when we get home. Just don't make me laugh that's all.'

Joe helped her onto the veranda, dragged the rocking chair out of the cellar, dusted it off and insisted she sit. He took his rifle from behind the seat of the cruiser, checked it was loaded and sat it across her knees, slapping his hat on her head as a finishing touch.

'There ya go, Miss Kitty, you just sit there and keep them outlaws at bay, while we rescue the bullion. At the first sign of trouble, put a little lead their way,' he loved John Wayne and his impression of his hero made her laugh. He even walked away with Wayne's swagger.

'I told you not to do that,' she held her ribs, 'can I have your old man's shotgun too mister?' Laura had assumed the role, 'you know, just in case they rush us,' she turned her face up for a kiss. 'I'm serious, Joe, get the shotgun too and I'll feel better.'

When he descended into the cellar he found Tilly had most of the wall down and was piling the bricks in the corner, he started clearing the floor so they could walk without tripping. While they worked, he told her about yesterday's adventure and why he needed to drive around the Waukaringa Gold Fields.

'You said they were claim jumpers. How do you know that?' Tilly asked, passing him more bricks to make a path to the ladder, where he paused to listen for the soft sound of Laura humming each time he neared the trapdoor, 'because it's ours.'

'Ours? But we don't have a gold mine.'

'I'm afraid we do, missy, and I reckon they've been working it for a while too, following fool's gold all the way to the middle of the mine.'

'How do you figure that?' She was into the swing of it now handing him four bricks at a time.

'Just look through that hole you've made. There's a King's ransom piled there. The old man didn't mine that. Some of it yeah, but he traded too. Miners need cash and Les was willing to pay. It looks like he knew his stuff,' Joe stood up, put his hands in the middle of his back and stretched, 'do you reckon we ought to give the bank a ring and get this in their strongroom tonight.'

'Dad, slow down, I can't take it all in.'

Joe heard the seriousness in Tilly's voice and tried to match this with his explanation. 'Well, the Waukaringa mine is all part of Pictinco. We've been paying the fees without looking at the paperwork ever since Dad died. Those papers he'd left by the chair upstairs. It's all in there. I was so pigheaded I didn't want to think he had any nice in him. It seems I may have been wrong.'

'Oh, I'd never say you were pig headed, Dad.'

'I heard that Tilly Gillespie,' her mother's words Miss Kitty parody floated down into the cellar, 'you won't get to heaven telling lies.'

Joe fitted the last bricks into the path. 'I think we should move the bars from the cavity to the ladder and then onto the Cruiser. If I pass and you stack at the foot of the ladder, then I can lift them onto the edge of the hole, eh?'

'That works for me and I'll take them straight to the cruiser because I'm not sure this old floor will take the lot.'

'Okay, if we get going, we should be out of here in an hour or so.'

When they'd finished, they had forty-seven gold bars. Not much smaller than a house brick, they were cold to touch and several times the bars slipped in their hands. Joe held the last one under the light and looked for minting marks. 'These are unfinished, not like those in mint photos, they must be all the old man's work.'

'Not the fifty then?' Laura asked.

'Fraid not. I'll check again.'

'You do that. I don't want you leaving strays down there for others to find.' Laura said.

Tilly climbed down from the back of the four-wheel-drive and screwed up her nose at her mother, 'are you two finished yet? I've got to pick up Em and get Jeff's dinner on.'

'Righto, we'll be on our way,' Joe was puffing as he lifted the last brick into the light, 'bloody things weigh about ten kilos each I reckon.'

'Tasty.' Laura said as he gave her one to hold.

Joe lifted the ladder out of the cellar and shut the trapdoor, dust flying everywhere as he rolled the rug back. Once it settled, it was as if they had never been there. Tilly put a wool-bale down before stacking the gold behind the cab. Joe pulled the sides of the bale up to cover their find, loaded the generator and extension cord, and tied the ladder to the headboard. The load binder groaned as he secured their load.

'You're not finished yet,' Laura said, 'I want this chair strapped on too.'

'Well you would. Do you want me to strap you onto the back with it?'

'Thought I'd ride shotgun,' she drawled, waving the gun in Joe's direction.

In a single movement, he swiped the gun from her and broke the breech, 'I never thought I'd have to tell you not to point a gun at anyone,' his heart raced and although he regretted his tone, it had to be said, 'my God, you gave me a fright.'

'Sorry love,' firearm respect was an unwritten law for the Gillespies and in the excitement of the moment she had forgotten it, 'I just didn't think. Now let's get this lot home.'

'I'm sorry for snapping at you, too. I'll lash this on, help Tilly lock up and we're away.'

'It'll be nice to get home and have this looked at,' she said lifting her shirt to show a bruise that extended from under her shoulder to her belt.

Looking at Laura now and knowing that after all these years he was still captivated by her. Smart, sassy and as beautiful as the day they married. All he ever wanted to be her protector.

'All done, Tilly put the cordless drill in its case thanks. Ready?' She opened the door and slid into the middle seat.

'Home it is,' Joe helped Laura climb into her seat, 'Tilly, help your Mum with the belt while I get Gip.' The dog groaned and her legs searched for something solid as he set her down on the only clear spot on the tray and clipped her to the chain, sure footed once more, she stood with her back to the gold as if she were guarding it.

After ten minutes travelling Laura pointed, 'there's a rider coming in from the south,' her hand rested on the shot gun on her lap, 'should I reload?'

'Jeeze, Mum. You don't even know who it is and you're getting all trigger happy,' Tilly took the cartridges from her mother's hand.

'Well, it seems you can't be too careful round these parts,' Joe said, 'best we cover the gun for now. Don't want to send some innocent sod buster to the infirmary with a backside full of buck-shot.'

As the rider closed in they recognised him as Zach, their sharefarmer. Joe stopped and waited for him to reach them.

Zach turned the bike off.

'G'day, Joe, Tilly, Mrs Gillespie. I noticed the gate open again and decided to come in and have a look around. I didn't want any more of them old cars dumped out here,' he fished around in his jacket and pulled out a lighter and a cigarette. Joe's eyes followed his hands as Zach lit up and inhaled, smoke drifting from his mouth as he spoke, 'I found the padlock cut and the gate open the day you came home. I took a lock off my toolbox and locked it up again. Could you tell O'Rourke about it, because I haven't had time to get to town yet?'

'Yeah sure. How are things going okay with the sharecropping?'

'No bad,' he bent down to see past Joe and meet Tilly's gaze. 'although I might be a day late with my report this month, morning sickness and all that. Anyway, what have you guys been up to?'

'Mum wanted a few old keepsakes,' she jabbed a thumb her mother's way and smiled, 'as if she hasn't got enough already.'

Zach looked at the back of the Landcruiser, 'so I see,' he crushed the cigarette with his fingers and put it in his pocket, 'you'll tell John then?'

'Yep, you go on, we'll get the gate.' Joe waited for Zach's dust to clear before starting off. He turned to Laura as he selected first gear, 'and there you were, all ready to send him to the promised land too and him only a boy.'

'He's old enough to have that pretty young wife of his in the family way. We should call in one day and make sure she's okay.' Laura said to Tilly.

'Let's get the Lewis' out of the way first and Dad's got a million other things for me to do first,' she twisted the rear vision mirror and looked at the lines around her eyes, 'if I keep running around after you two I'll look like a hag on my wedding day. Jeff might turn and run with fright.' Tilly turned the mirror back and Joe corrected it.

CHAPTER SIXTY ONE

Back within mobile phone range, Tilly's phone beeped with a message from Jeff confirming he had been called back to work.

Laura saw her daughter's expression darken. 'Trouble?' she asked.

'I don't think this wedding will ever happen. Look,' Tilly turned the screen for her mother to see.

'Tilly love, we're carting around a king's ransom on the back of a bush ute, and I'm willing to bet all of it on seeing your Dad walk you down the aisle in September. What do you say Joe?'

'Yep and with our second grandchild due by July.'

'Hey wait, no. I already have a child and, anyway, that's something for Jeff and me to decide. No way Dad, I'm not having you lay that sort of pressure on us.'

Laura reached across to hi-five Joe, he touched her hand, 'what did she say when she was growing up, Joe?'

'She said she didn't want to have just one child. A home needs a big family was what she said,' Joe laughed, 'a husband who'd give her up to ten kids. That's what she used to say.'

Tilly joined in the silliness and the tension dropped. The three of them had not had a day alone on the farm together for years and today she felt their ties had strengthened again and knew she could cope.

'We didn't phone the bank,' Tilly whispered as she walked to her car, 'shall I do it now?'

'Nah, we'll leave it 'till tomorrow love. I'll unload the bricks later, okay?'

'Joe,' Laura thought about what he'd said. How could they leave their bounty on the back of the Toyota overnight?

'Before you go,' Joe called Tilly back, 'those papers you wanted me to sign, do you want to take them now?'

'Jeeze, Dad we had all day to work that out,' she was tired of the way he ebbed and flowed lately, not realising how erratic her own behaviour had been, 'c'mon then?' She slammed her door in a huff and followed her mother into the cottage.

'Settle down,' Joe said, 'I'm gunna leave the gold on the back of the 'cruiser tonight. I just don't want anyone thinking there's anything special on the back, that's all,' he passed her the envelope 'this has to go to them anyway. See you at the bank, say ten in the morning, eh?'

'I'd better go. See you tomorrow. Mum, I'll call you tonight after I know what Jeff is up to.'

'Ten it is then love,' Joe said, 'and then we'd better organise a meeting with Brad and Karren,' he rubbed a hand over his forehead looked at Laura suddenly feeling his age.

'It's time to get back on the horse, Dad. Enough of this, poor bugger me crap you wax and wane with. It's time to sit down with me and plan how we are going to handle all these projects you've got on the go now. Shit Dad, you've always been tough and smart enough to conquer anything,' she puffed herself up, swaggering around the room and imitating her father, 'Joe Gillespie isn't afraid of a little old death threat. There's too much to do, to worry about that,' she started to laugh, almost in hysteria, 'and after today, it looks like we can afford it.'

'Talk later,' Laura said and headed for a shower. She saw the red light blinking on their answering machine, pressed play and Elspeth's voice greeted her, 'Hello you two. I'll call later with terrific news. We can't wait to see you again. Oh, it's Elspeth this end.'

'You want to phone her now?' Joe asked.

'What I want now is a shower and to look at this bruise. If I think it's bad enough, I'll go to the doctor in the morning meanwhile, you can get something out of the freezer and start dinner. I don't care what, but you're cooking tonight. I'm happy if you only want to do baked beans, or something, surprise me.'

'I'm on it. I'll feed the animals and then us okay?'

'Sure, but I might need a hand to get undressed first though,' her voice was laboured she touched her side where she had fallen, 'and then again, I think I had better go to the hospital tonight. Something's not right here.'

***

With Emily in bed and the dishes done Jeff finally had time to talk to Tilly about his day and his promotion. Although she was excited by it, her mind was full of distraction. She needed to tell him about the truck load of gold that Joe had just left on the back of the Toyota. Then there was the pressure of the Lewis' being in town and her mother having a fall. A thousand things were crowding for space in her thoughts and she knew she wasn't dealing with any of them effectively.

She listened to him talk about Spoggy and how he and John had been charged with tracking this bloke down. She waited, maybe it was her legal training, maybe she was being polite, she didn't know. What she really wanted was for Jeff to shut up so they could talk about them. Their relationship had begun with her father's troubles and here they were, months later, still solving other people's problems. She sighed and hoped he hadn't heard it, but all she wanted was to find time to discuss their lives, their wedding and make their own plans.

'Are you right there, or am I boring you?'

'No, I'm sorry. I am listening.'

'But?'

'No, finish what you're saying.'

'I'm done, how about you tell me what's on your mind,' he reached for the remote, turned the TV off and put his arm around her, 'I just got a bit carried away, sorry.'

'Are we still getting married in September?'

'I hope so, that's the plan,' he looked at her drawn face,' isn't it?'

'Have you thought about who or how many you want to invite?

He said nothing.

She sat up and looked at him, 'Are we still doing this?'

'Where'd that come from?'

'I don't know? We just seem so busy that we've had no time for ourselves lately.'

'Well the answer is, yes we are still doing this. We have a date and as it falls after footy season, most of my mob will be able to make it,' he laughed at his own joke then stopped short when he saw she was in no mood for humour, 'I've made a list who I'd like to ask, but where do we cap the numbers do you reckon?'

'I'd like to elope, really.'

'We can do that.'

'Party in the creek?' Tilly found her laugh again.

'Big mob, my mob. Might move back in,' he was laughing too now.

'And where will we live?'

'What?'

'It's a fair question, because if you're stationed at Port Augusta, do we live there or do we live here?' she leant away from him so she could see his reaction, 'or, if Mum and Dad don't want to go back to the Well, do we move out there?'

'What, you reckon they'd go for that?'

'Why not?' She twisted her hair around her forefinger. 'Someone has to live there.'

'It's a lot to think about, I suppose I saw us living here, with me helping out, working for the company, not being one of the people who lived in a big place like that.'

'With what we found today, we could fix up the Wilson place and live there.' She waited for him to take the bait, but he missed it entirely.

'Wilson's, Joe once asked if it would be a good gliding area and then said something about a gliding school. After the last time I had him up in the air, I'd dismissed it. I can't see him learning to fly,' he paused as if only just hearing what she had said, 'hang on what did you say, what did you find?'

'On the back of the Toyota is about half a tonne of gold.'

'Half a...'

'That's what I said. Dad's starting to think his old man wasn't such a loser now.'

'Half a tonne, but that's....'

'A lot, even after the taxes are sorted.'

'And it's out in the street?'

'Not exactly, it's in the yard where he always parks it.'

They were interrupted by the doorbell, Jeff got up to see who it was and returned with Joe trailing Laura into the family room.

'We didn't want to disturb you, but we saw your light on when we came back from the hospital, so your father thought we'd call in and let you know what's going on.' Laura said.

Tilly picked up a tone in her voice that said she had argued against it, but Joe had pulled into the drive anyway.

'It's not your usual way to go home from the hospital, Dad?'

'Yes it is, well tonight anyway. I wanted to ask Jeff if he can help unload the Toyota tomorrow and wanted to know about his trip to the Port today, that's all.'

'Well first I want to hear how you are Mum. What did the hospital say?'

'Cracked ribs, not broken, bruising and contusions. I'll live. Nothing a good night's sleep won't fix,' she looked pointedly at Joe.

'I'm set to go love, just as soon as Jeff fills me in,' he caught the glares from both women, 'in brief will do.'

'Not much to tell Joe, I'm supposed to find this Spoggy while the others work on the threats against you.'

'I reckon that threat will go away after tomorrow.'

'Because?' Jeff said.

'Cause if it's okay with Tilly and you, we're going to invite the miners up for a little chat about exploration and such,' he tapped the side of his nose, 'I have a bit of a plan going around in my head, but it's not sorted yet.'

Behind him Laura mouthed the words, 'he's gone loopy.'

'Okay, we're on our way now. I'll see you tomorrow, Jeff.'

'What was all that about?' Jeff asked as they watched them back out of the drive. Tilly could only shrug, she was just about over trying to figure why her parents did anything   these   days.

CHAPTER SIXTY TWO

On the dot of ten, Joe backed the Toyota up to the front door of the bank, Jeff on one side and John O'Rourke on the other. The manager pushed the doors and locked them open while he and the staff ferried the gold into the strongroom. A small crowd gathered and John did his best to keep them back.

'Have you got enough insurance to cover this lot?' Joe asked the bank manager.

'I phoned Adelaide. They're sceptical that it is what you say it is, or how there could be so much of it. But yes, we can cover its loss,' he handed Joe a receipt, 'you can exchange it for cash once all our checks and balances are complete.'

'Fair enough. I'll just take a photo of it if that's okay?'

'It's your gold, Joe,' the manager grinned, 'you're not going to put it on social media I hope?'

'Hell no, but it makes a pretty picture and I hate to leave it all the same.'

'I would too,' the banker, spun the wheel to lock the vault.

'I'd better go,' Joe said, then turned to Jeff and John, 'I've got people to see and you've got a bird to catch.' They shook hands and he got into the Toyota.

'And he left all of that in the open last night?' John asked Jeff.

'Yep, but that's Joe and for the life of me, I don't know how I'm going to survive him.'

John took another look at the disappearing Toyota, 'another road-trip?'

***

With their treasure tucked into the vault, Joe was now ready to turn his attention to RADOR. He hoped that

411

speaking with Sam Lewis and her parents would give him some background on who he was dealing with.

Sam meantime had instructed her broker to sell her RADOR shares. She wanted to get her money out and now that Gino had released the prospectus, a frenzy of short selling made her interest more valuable. The share price was doubling every hour and selling her shares now would destabilise the market's confidence and cause ASIC to halt trading. Her broker sold the shares at three times their value. It may not have made her wealthy and it didn't feel right, but worrying could wait until after the meeting with the Gillespies.

Joe and Clive made easy conversation while Laura and Tilly made Penny feel at ease. Sam seemed introspective, only joining the conversation occasionally. Laura was happy to show the Lewis' over the barn and talked of her plans for it. Joe and Tilly didn't join the tour, she was on edge and walked around pulling at a lonely weed and dropping it over the pool fence, while Joe wished for the old familiar comfort of a cigarette.

'What do you think they want?' Tilly asked.

'Buggered if I know, if you saw that prospectus, her name's all over it and yet they still have no rights to prospect,' he opened the hood of the barbeque and lit the grill, 'he seems a decent enough bloke but I can't do any of this dance around shit. Keep an eye on this lot while I grab the grub.'

'There's a lot of work in those plans of Laura's, Joe.' The group returned with Clive in the lead.

'True, but I have to ask, what are you really doing here and what it is that you expect of us?'

'You're not one to beat around the bush, are you Mr Gillespie?' Sam had joined them and pulled a chair from the setting to sat down.

'Sam,' Penny Lewis had never witnessed her daughter in negotiation and was uncomfortable with her forthright speech.

'Call me Joe, Sam, and you're right, I'm not one to mince words. You came here for a reason. You no longer work for RADOR and yet your interest has doubled overnight. So what is it you want?'

Clive came to his daughter's defence, 'we wanted to...'

'I can fight my own battles, Dad,' she stood up, walked to where Joe was standing and turned so she could address everyone, 'I was shocked and washed out at being let go from the company I developed. They played me and won the battle. I know there's no gold here, in fact there is little chance of a commercial mining operation working on any of your properties, except for one,' she paused, looking from face to face, 'and that's the lease at Waukaringa.'

'Waukaringa? But when you came for a drive with me, you looked at every outcrop, ridge and creek we went past.' Tilly said.

'I was just confirming my suspicions. I didn't know why Charles was so intent on getting onto your land, but he was obsessed with it and I wanted to know why.'

'You want Waukaringa, well it's yours if I have any say.' Laura said.

'I know why Charles wanted our land. I've done some digging of my own. His name's Winkler, right?' Joe said.

'Yes'

'And his grandfather was a prospector?'

'Yes.'

'Mad Charlie, we called him, the grandfather this is. I guess the kid grew up with a big chip on his shoulder and he thinks I don't know about the ingots my old man stashed away. Ever held a forty-ounce bar of gold?'

'Well, no.'

'Clive, you look after this and I'll be back in a minute.'

413

Joe went inside while Tilly and Laura exchanged expressions.

'Can I do anything?' Penny asked, but before she could say more, or for Laura to answer, Joe was back. He held out two of the small bars they had found in the well.

'This is not what your Charles was looking for. I think his grandfather lost these in a poker game.'

'So, what was Charles looking for?' Clive asked.

Joe told them about the hoard Les had hidden and believed Mad Charlie would have known about it. They were partners, old Winkler would have known about his father's trading and about the Pictinco leases.

'Do you want revenge or success, Sam?'

'Joe...' Laura gave him her death stare.

'It's a fair question, love.'

'It's okay,' Sam said, 'I'll bet Mr Gillespie's just a big old pussy cat inside, but yeah. I want success more than revenge, it lasts longer.'

'Good, but making the bastards squirm a bit wouldn't hurt either, would it?'

'Where are you going with this Joe?' Clive wanted to protect his daughter, but sensed opportunity.

'I already have success and I'd like revenge, but most of all I'd like to live my life in peace,' Joe said, 'someone threatened harm to my family and it took a while, but now I know who it is. Proving it won't be necessary because with your help Sam, their lives will change and the public scrutiny will be so intense, it will become unbearable.'

'But how?'

'Friends in high places,' Joe raised his eyebrows and tapped the side of his nose, 'if we pull this off, I'll gift you the Pictinco shares. When I checked last, they were useless, less than a hundred bucks the lot.'

'You'd better get rid of those claim jumpers first though,' Laura said.

'Let's go for a drive. I want to show Clive around the place and why I didn't want anyone drilling holes in it.

Joe stopped the car a few meters from the edge of a water hole, where a circle of blackened stones made a crude hearth. 'People have eaten and camped here for thousands of years,' he pointed to the ring of rocks, 'those stones get washed away in times of flood, but the Adnyamathanha find them again and put them back. It's sacred, we call it Third Water. They have another name I can't pronounce. An old fella tried to teach me once, but after a while, he gave up.

'This whole place is sacred and we respect that,' Laura added, 'and now I think Joe wants to show Clive the artefacts in the cave, unfortunately we women can't go in. There are ancient taboos, so we'll have to do what women have done here for centuries.'

'Yeah,' Sam asked, 'what's that?'

'Dig yams and hunt goanna,' Tilly laughed.

Laura added, 'in other words, we make the tea.'

Emerging from the cave after their exploration, Clive helped Joe slide the stone back into its place and replace the wedges that held it. Joe chanted a few words and brushed all around the cave's entrance and the stone with a clump of smoking saltbush. 'We need to pay respect to the ancestors,' he said by way of explanation before putting out the herb and tossing it aside, 'c'mon, I'm ready for a cuppa.'

Penny wanted to know what her husband had seen, but held it in. She'd ask later.

Sam showed less restraint, 'well Dad, what's in there? Can you say?'

'Nope,' he held up his hand, a gash ran across the marriage line, 'silence sealed in blood.'

Joe lifted his hand, a similar line ran across it and he changed the subject, 'tell me Sam, what is it I need to know to about your old boss?'

Sam looked at her parents, Penny looked at Clive and he held his hand up for inspection, 'we're blood brothers now, I reckon it's okay to tell.'

'Look, Mr Gillespie, I need to be careful, I can't afford to ruin any chance of a career I may have left.'

'Or it could re-build it. We know this Gino bloke has put up a bogus prospectus and I'd bet they probably have a few pollies in their pocket too. However, we can't put it right without proof. Do you want to join an espionage operation?'

'Will James Bond be in it?' Sam felt her eyes brighten and then wondered about her choice of words.

'Only us, but we do have influence.'

Sam told them she had signed confidentiality agreements and couldn't comment about the company, or its financial position. The personnel were a different matter, office gossip was rife and there was no legal requirement to hold back her opinion. Over the next hour, she and the Gillespies discussed Gino and the connections he had to people in all tiers of government, she didn't know where, or who his spies were, but he had plenty.

Charles was more of a mystery, even though they had shared a relationship, he remained guarded. She was sure Gino held something over him, but she didn't know what it was. Everything she had learned screamed at her to keep those issues in confidence, but anger had driven her to unload and now she felt relieved, used and sad and angry, very bloody angry.

The women were silent on the drive home, in total contrast to Clive, who wanted to know about the Waukaringa leases, who Joe thought had been working the claim, and if he was serious about making the company over to Sam. Asking what Joe thought the chances were of it paying its way. They talked football, the price of sheep and new farming methods.

Too soon for Clive, they were home.

CHAPTER SIXTY THREE

After putting Emily to bed, Tilly told Jeff about their visit from the Lewis family, asking him to hold off on revealing anything to DI Cassidy until Joe gave the okay. He was reluctant, but agreed anyway.

'I'm chasing ghosts too,' he said, 'John and I went to Adelaide today, we interviewed everyone and still know no more than we did yesterday. Spoggy, or whatever name he is using now, doesn't seem to exist.'

'The job's going well then?' Tilly laughed.

'Yeah, real funny,' he laughed with her, 'anyway, what's happening with your Dad's find. Is it still in the bank?'

'No, their head office dispatched a truck within minutes of the deposit,' she shook her head, 'it's strange how it sat in an old house that anyone could have entered, for more years than we know, and it wasn't a problem. But the moment the bank has it, they send it to Adelaide. I suppose it got there okay.'

'It was a pretty sight though. Did Joe say what he's going to do with the money?'

'No, he's more concerned with finding the bloke who threatened him in Adelaide. Have you heard anything?'

'Nah, the boss has been out of the office all day. We have a meeting again tomorrow, we'll review everything I guess, and we'll go from there,' he took her hand, 'c'mon, it's a clear night let's go sit on the porch outside and count stars.'

'I'll grab a bottle of wine and the glasses,' she said, 'and then you and I can talk about our wedding plans.'

'And after that, I'll close my eyes while you're telling me exactly what our wedding night be.'

'Don't you start snoring then.'

'When?'

'Tonight, or on our wedding night?'

He walked to the veranda and waiting for Tilly while she loaded a tray with fruit, cheese and the wine, stared at the sky looking for answers.

'Hm, expecting a long night?' he asked while opening the door for her.

Putting the tray on the table, her tone was one of hurt and exasperation, 'well, we have lots to talk about.'

They were interrupted by a car driving around the corner, its headlights washing across the front of the house. It slowed and its light filtered through the hedge, making crazy patterns on the front of the house. A door opened and they heard it close, its lights remaining on.

'Stay still,' Jeff said, 'and maybe they won't see us.'

'Don't be ridiculous.'

The gate opened and closed and the form of a woman cast a long shadow as she walked along the path and past them, recognising her immediately Jeff called, 'is that you, Sam?'

Lost in her own world, Sam screamed in fright and dropped something as she jumped. 'Bloody hell, you startled the life out of me.'

'Sit down,' Tilly invited, pulling a spare chair closer to the table, curious as to the purpose of the visit at this unconventional hour, 'I'll get another glass. What brings you here so late anyway?'

'Sorry, I didn't want to trouble you, but when my folks took me to dinner tonight, Rosie from the pub gave me this,' she passed over the parcel she'd mailed to the pub containing Spoggy's broken phone, 'she said she was going to give it to the local copper next time he was in, but had forgotten about it until she saw me at dinner.'

'How did she know you'd sent it?' Jeff asked, standing to turn the veranda light on.

'Habit,' Sam shrugged and tapped the back of the bag, 'I put my name on it and she remembered me.'

'What's in there?' Tilly was back and filling another glass.

'A phone. I took it off this Spoggy bloke when he attacked me. It's buggered now though because I ran over it a couple of times before posting it.'

Jeff turned the package over and saw how it was addressed to just, 'Spoggy' and he smiled to himself, things were starting to make sense. 'Yeah, John told me about his little dilemma, but it seems as if he met his match when he tackled you.'

'He said he was working for Tilly. That's why I was so short with you on the phone that day. It was only after I'd looked at his call register and a few photos that I knew he was one of Gino's spies,' she looked at the stars, 'and believe me, Gino would not want anyone to know he was linked to him.'

'Are you okay?' Tilly noticed the quaver in Sam's voice and touched her arm in comfort.'

'Yeah, I'm okay,' she downed her drink and waved as she stood to leave, 'I'd better go, looks like you two had plans,' she stopped before closing the door and called to Jeff, 'I don't know if it helps, but I had the feeling he didn't like women much...'

Jeff's interest piqued, 'What makes you say that?'

'When he spoke to me it was nasty, vicious, almost as if he was settling an old score or something. It could be nothing, I might have even imagined it,' her voice sounded lighter now, 'enjoy your night.'

They watched the car reverse out from the kerb and head up the street before Jeff spoke, 'still want to count stars?'

'Like you're going to do that, now you've got another clue to think about.'

'You have my complete attention, now tell me about this wedding of ours?'

***

Laura woke to find the bed beside her empty and found Joe in the kitchen, running a glass of water. She put a hand in the middle of his back and made soothing circles. The glow from the digital clock on the stove read five minutes past two.

'It's five past two, Joe, are you okay? It's not like you to be heading for the Panadol in the middle of the night'

'I woke with a bit of headache again, that's all, they've been getting a bit more intense lately. C'mon back to bed and I'll make an appointment with the doctor tomorrow.'

Sensing a seriousness in his tone, she said, 'you can't say something like that and expect me to go back to sleep, Joe and I get the feeling there's more to this than you've let on so I'll make a cuppa and we can talk about it and then go to bed.'

'Aw it's nothing, I just need a referral to see a specialist, but I've got too much to do right now. C'mon, I promise I'll make the appointment in the morning, let's go to bed.'

Laura shook her head, trying to understand what it was she had missed, 'I'm sorry Joe, where did this come from? You say you need to see a specialist and then expect me to forget about it until morning. Why do you need a specialist? When did you think you'd get a referral?'

'Come on Laura, it's no big deal. I had a bit of a turn and collapsed when Bill and I were in London. It seems I've spent too much time in the sun and the doc found a spot that needed to be looked at.'

'A spot? Do you mean a Melanoma? Skin cancer? You have to have a cancer removed?' She wanted to cry and punch him at the same time, 'and you decided not to tell me and to just ignore it. Did you think it would just go away, or that I wouldn't find out?' She had been angry with him over the years, ropable sometimes, but she couldn't remember a time when she'd been this wild, an anger born from hurt and frustration.

He opened his mouth to speak, but she shut him down with an upheld hand, 'no, you don't, you just sit there and say nothing. We've never had secrets and this,' her hurt caused her to stumble for words, 'this is more than a secret and much, much worse, because it feels more like you've been lying to me.' She slumped forward and burst into tears, loud wracking sobs the like of which he'd never heard before and he resorted to banality, that affliction of males in the face of extreme emotion, 'I'll make the cuppa then, okay?'

She lifted her head, 'not bloody likely Joe, you'll stay right there and tell me everything. I want to know what doctor you saw, where you went and exactly what he said. Everything Joe, details. I want details.'

'There's not much to tell until I see the specialist and that's why I haven't said anything, although not talking about it has made it worse somehow, because my thinking goes into overdrive,' now he'd started talking it was as if he couldn't stop, 'when I'm in bed at night is the worst because then I imagine it's in my lungs, liver, everywhere, and what frightens me is the brain. I could handle losing a leg or something, but not if I'm going to wither and lose my mind. I don't know if I could handle that.' He had his head in his hands fighting tears of his own, 'and even worse, how could I put you through all of that, after the troubles of last year?'

Laura's natural pragmatism kicked in and she took control, 'well, the sooner we find out what it is we're dealing with the better. It may not be as bad as you think and cancer isn't the death sentence it once was,' she stood and filled the kettle, sitting back beside him and holding his hands in hers while it boiled, 'we can fight this Joe, whatever comes our way, chemo, radiation, diet, there's lots we can do but first we're going to find out what it is.'

He held up a flash-drive, 'the MRI I had in England doesn't look too good, that's why I've been moody and distant at times. The doctor told me to expect that. Then other times I feel invincible and I've been able to fool myself into believing the doc had it all wrong,' he stopped to regain his breath, 'Christ, I haven't known how to tell you. How do I put the people I love through this, I didn't want that? I think I'm dying love and there's nothing I can do about it except to make sure you're properly provided for.'

Laura made a fist, wanting the pain of fingernails cutting into her palms. Sobbing she fell into his arms and he held her until it eased. When she stopped, he scooped her up and took her to their room. Exhausted she succumbed to sleep while his mind swirled fixing a must do list.

CHAPTER SIXTY FOUR

Tossing the sheet back Sam waited for her eyes to adjust to the low light in her bedroom. The soft rumble of snore coming from her parent's room was not enough to take her mind off refuting RAYDOR's claims. Having someone attach her name to a bogus prospectus made her angry. She went outside, opening and closing the door quietly so as not to disturb her parents as this hour. Somewhere a dog was barking and she could hear an interstate truck pulling down through the gears as it made its way over the Morchard hills. There was dampness in the air, but she sat on the garden seat anyway. It simply didn't matter.

The more she thought about how Gino and Charles had used her, the angrier she became. She had seen both of them extract payback often and thought about how sweet a little of her getting her own back would taste. She wondered what was behind Charles' fixation on the Gillespie's property, knowing it had to be more than just the mining. As Joe had said at dinner, this was personal.

A cat brushed against her leg and began to purr. She bent down and slipped her hand under its belly, picked it up and sat it on her lap. And she sat for a long time, testing solutions out loud as the cat listened and purred. From the house next door, she heard a clock chime three. An hour of sitting in the garden with a neighbour's moggy on her lap and getting a wet backside, had been enough to formulate a plan in her mind.

'Righto Puss, you have to go. I've got things to do,' she lifted the cat down and went inside. She made a few notes on her phone and, after a quick change out of her wet clothes, she dropped into bed and soon fell into a deep sleep.

Her phone alarm woke her at six and she tiptoed to the bathroom and showered. Today her hair wasn't important and neither was her dress, but it was a great day for planning revenge. Setting her laptop on the kitchen table she began writing the rebuttal for use of her name in the RADOR prospectus. Her report should provide enough evidence for ASIC to charge Charles and Gino for falsifying their statements. Scanning the files, she came across a list of contacts and photos that matched the ones in the phone she took from the man who attacked her in Brambrick's Creek. Among these, she noted few short e-mails from Gino and reply texts to an unknown number she assumed to be one of the secret phones he kept.

The photos, some dating back as far as five years ago, were of greater interest. Many were of people and old buildings but she was drawn to one of a bloke and a girl on a trailbike. She knew the scenery, but couldn't place it. There were a few images of a group of bikies and she recognised their insignia as being from the same group as the one Joe and Laura rescued the girl from. This was the bloke Jeff had said he was looking for.

Although she had given Jeff Spoggy's phone, Sam knew it would take time to get anything out of it in a hurry. She copied all the information and forwarded it as an attachment to Tilly, marking it for Jeff's attention and sat back, satisfied with her effort. Gino would soon find himself on the end of some very difficult questions and she imagined him squirming, scrambling for answers. For her though, she had a report to write and she knew just the freelance journalist to contact. Matthew Naqvi was always on the lookout for stories of corruption and this one was a doozy.

**

In Adelaide, former Detective Inspector Harry Forbes looked at his watch and clicked his seat belt in. He reached across the console of their four-wheel-drive and squeezed his wife's hand, she looked at him and smiled.

'Ready,' she asked, 'I still can't believe you've done it.'

'I was born ready. Innamincka here we come.'

Harry had taken early retirement and they planned to see Australia while they were healthy enough to enjoy it. 'I'd like to stop in at Orroroo on our way and see if Jeff Rankin's around. Is that okay with you?'

'Sure, that's fine and we've got all the time in the world. It's been a while, is he stationed there now?'

'He's still at Port Augusta, but he's engaged to a girl from up there,' he looked at the camper in the rear vision mirror as it bumped out of the driveway, 'he actually resigned, but the DI in Port Augusta has dragged him back to help with a case.'

'We should stop in to a few of those wineries around Clare too,' she said squeezing his hand, smiling, making big eyes at him before suggesting, 'and pick up a few supplies before we hit the desert.'

'No worries,' he listened for any squeaks, or unusual sounds as they headed into the traffic, 'it'll give me a chance to check how the tinny's riding and retighten all the straps. We'll camp somewhere out of Hawker tonight, yes?'

She connected her iPod to the radio and scrolled through her play list. Their odyssey into retirement had begun.

CHAPTER SIXTY FIVE

Walking into the Orroroo Police Station office Jeff found John at his desk, the kettle boiling.

'Tea or coffee?' he asked, without turning around.

Jeff looked at the wall clock, 'tea, thanks,' he said, 'and I have a surprise for you.'

'What?' Sam's parcel hitting him on the chest and without thinking his arms wrapped around it. 'My ball,' he said and put it on the desk, 'okay, what is it?'

'Sam Lewis said she posted it to Spoggy after he attacked her,' Jeff took the cup and set it down. He sat across from John's chair, 'there's some photos and messages linking him to Gino Di Massimo. So now we have another connection and I reckon all of it ties back to Joe.'

'You're probably right.'

'And now I'll bet Darryl's going to think I'm too close to the case again and he'll want to pull me off of it.'

'Right again,' John was nodding.

'So how about we get someone to resurrect what they can from this, and we start digging deep into where Spoggy came from.'

'Okay, but what about the DI?'

'I'll tell him we have the phone and it's on its way to forensics, no lies there.'

'And us?'

'You'd better tell Fiona we're going to be late.'

It seemed like finding Spoggy in person might be easier than tracing his records. They knew he had changed his name more than once. The body in the pit and those of the greyhounds in Brahma Lodge, had been shot by the same gun they found in the mattress at the farmhouse. However, whether Spoggy pulled the trigger was just another question to join their many.

Jeff's phone beeped the arrival of a text message from Tilly, she was telling him to open his e-mail. He had just opened the laptop and turning it on when the office phone rang, John answered

'Just a minute,' he told the caller, 'Jeff's here, so I'll put you on speaker,'

'Juvenile Justice in Victoria came through last night. My contact would only give me the info if it was off the record, but she told me they did have a kid with multiple issues on their books between eighty-six and ninety-three, a Peter Crook. He didn't say what the sentence was for, just that he had an edge to him that workers described as 'creepy'. He was originally from Hamilton, and then went to stay with an Aunt in Adelaide, they lost track of him.'

'When?' John asked, adding. 'They haven't had contact since ninety-three?'

'Nope, but then they wouldn't have any contact once he reached eighteen, but the year does tie in with the time your bike owner died. It's a long shot but, when you've got nothing...'

'Did they give you an address?'

'Nope, they just thought it was one of the newer suburbs to the north.

Jeff was churning stuff over in his mind. 'Where did you say he was before, Hamilton?'

'He spent time in the usual places, Baltara, Turana and served a stint at Malmsbury Youth Detention Centre, between Melbourne and Bendigo, before he went to... hang on it's on a piece of paper here somewhere,' they heard him shuffling papers, 'Penshurst, an old bachelor with a dairy farm. The bloke got sick and this Peter Crook moved into a place in town when he started a pre-apprenticeship trial with a tractor firm. They had him for a month, before they said it wouldn't work. From there he went to Hamilton for about three months and that's when he dropped off the radar.'

'Have you talked to the people he worked for?' Jeff asked.

'Yeah, they thought he went to stay with a relative. I ran the name, Le-Strange past them, but they weren't sure. It didn't seem right to them.'

'Any prints, DNA, anything?'

'Nothing, the boss asked me to request a court order, but it'll take time.'

'Good work,' Jeff said, 'keep us posted.'

'See you soon, we'll be over there tomorrow in the afternoon.' John answered as he put the phone down.

'Crook, Cook, both Peter, what are the chances you think?' Jeff said.

'Better than good, now where is the nasty little bastard?'

Jeff's phone vibrated again, he ignored it and opened his e-mail. This time it rang, he looked at the caller's name. 'Tilly.' He walked outside to take the call.

Tilly sounded frantic, more agitated than he had ever heard her and he felt guilty for not reading her earlier texts.

'Can you come home for a bit?' He could tell she was trying to hold herself together, her voice breaking, 'I need you here,' she was half sobbing, half pleading with him.

'I'm walking home now,' he said, 'just hang on.' A million things ran through his mind as he ran, Emily being abducted, or had someone threatened her? He saw Laura's car in the drive and rushed through the door as Tilly burst into fresh flood of tears.

'It's Dad, he's taken off and Mum doesn't know where he is, or what he's doing. She thinks he might want to harm himself.'

'Whoa, back the truck up a bit,' Jeff rubbed a hand through his hair hoping to make some sense of what she was saying, 'he just found a truck load of gold. Why would he harm himself?'

'He's got cancer.' Laura spoke the words as three consecutive shots. Bang, bang, bang and he recoiled, 'and now there's enough gold to keep us in clover he thinks his job is done,' her comments bore no relation to her opening statement and he watched her pull and twist the sleeves of her jumper around her hands, 'he left us this,' she pushed a note across the table.

Jeff pulled out a chair and sat down. Tilly more flopped than sat and put an arm around her mother's shoulders, 'we'll find him, Mum.'

The note was damp and he suspected Laura had been crying for some time before reaching Tilly's place. It was scrunched up as if she had it in her hand as she drove. He recognised Joe's writing, but couldn't work out how Laura had jumped to the conclusion he intended harming himself. His police training led him to think that if Joe was going to do anything, it would be to eliminate the people trying to intimidate them.

'Laura, why do you think he's going to harm himself? The note just says he's trying to sort somethings out in his head. And he says not to worry, that all will be okay by the afternoon,' Jeff reached out and patted her hand in an effort to comfort, 'he'll bounce in here later wondering where everyone is and expect to see dinner on the table. You know what he's like.'

'He thinks he's got a brain tumour and he's going to do something stupid, I know it. He's thinking that by being out of the way we can all get on with our lives,' she stiffened and turned to Tilly, 'he's always said he wouldn't want us hovering around feeling sorry for him. He's going to do it. I know he will.'

Jeff looked at Tilly and back to Laura, 'how long have you known this?'

'He told me last night, he said it's why his mind has been all over the place and he wants to do something to make his mark, to be remembered for,' she looked at Tilly, 'I'm pretty hurt and disappointed he didn't say anything before now. He told me he'd had a bit of a turn in London and saw a doctor there,' she buried her head in her hands and cried. When she looked up again she said, 'and he's been carrying this around for a couple of months, not wanting to worry me.'

'So, what do we do?' Jeff said. 'Can you think of where he'd go?'

'Mum, is Gip with him?'

'I don't know,' She sniffed and then blew her nose. 'No, I mean yes, I think so. She wasn't at the front door when I left. So yes, he has the dog.'

Jeff looked at Tilly, 'well that's a positive sign then because he wouldn't let her fend for herself if he was going to suic...' he stopped, 'do anything silly, would he?'

'No way. Dad's like your old man when it comes to animals.'

'So, what's got you so worked up?'

'He left his mobile phone on top of the note, he never does that.'

'Unless he doesn't want big brother looking over his shoulder. Remember how he was in Adelaide last year when Harry Forbes was pressuring him. He had to leave his phone in the car so his old employer couldn't track him,' Jeff thought the words sounded plausible and wondered how Laura would take it.

'That's true, so what do we do now.'

'And he's not answering the CB?' Tilly asked her mother.

'I tried when I first found the note, not since.' She sounded tired.

Jeff turned to Tilly, 'take your mum home and stay with her. I'll let John know I'm taking today off. He's got stuff to do and we can pick it up again tomorrow.'

'Mum wants to drive out to the Well and I think she wants to look for him,' Tilly said, 'I don't want us to go on our own and, until Dad gets back, I don't want to leave her.'

'Can Fiona pick up Em?'

'I'll ask but I'm sure she can.'

'I'll come with you. We'll probably bump into Joe with a ute load of gold again,' Jeff stood and walked to the door, 'don't worry, we'll find him.'

CHAPTER SIXTY SIX

Charles Winkler swung his car into the underground carpark, winding around the piers toward the spot allocated for the General Manager. His tyres squealed as he stopped.

'Oi, you can't camp here, mate. This is a reserved parking space and you've taken up two places.'

He was out of the car, his head looking everywhere at once. 'Just pack up this fucking mess and piss off,' he pointed to the kelpie, 'and that bloody thing should be on a lead too,' his hand went in his pocket, 'I'm calling security.'

'I'm not sure that's a good idea,' the bushman had his hand on the pocket and with the other pushed a nine-millimetre Glock against Winkler's nose, 'when's your mate Gino coming in?'

'Jesus, what the fuck do you want? I don't know, he's out in the field for a couple of days.'

'So we'll talk here, will we?'

'Or my office?'

'Nah, I don't like crowds much. How about we get in your car and go somewhere quiet. I like sand hills, don't you? Nice and quiet. We'll drive out to Outer Harbour, where no-one can hear us talk,' he opened the rear passenger door and whistled, the old dog clambered in, 'I can't leave her here without water, that wouldn't be kind at all,' he kept the pistol trained on Winkler, 'now get in.'

'I'm going nowhere.'

'It's up to you, but you see I got some bad news the other day, really bad news, diagnosed with a brain tumour and I've probably got about six months to live. Only thing is though? The last four of those will be hell and I won't have the strength to do what I need to do,' Joe was playing the ocker and he could see Winkler was scared, 'so, after I told my wife I was dying last night, she knew I had nothing to lose. I even left her a note this morning telling her not to wait up,' the car was still running, 'put one hand on the wheel and click your belt on real careful, I don't want any nosey cops stopping us, just because you're breaking the law.'

Joe grabbed Winkler's phone and threw it across the carpark. 'Now, both hands on top of the wheel and drive slowly out Port Road, when I see the place I want, we'll walk into the dunes where only the wind will hear us.'

'Come on,' the words from Winkler's mouth sounded weak and he was pleading, 'I have a meeting to attend. Just put the gun down and nothing will happen. I only carry credit cards and a little bit of cash. I'll give you that and nothing will ever be said.'

'That's not the kind of words I'd have expected from the CEO of Wagmin,' Joe said, 'you have no idea who I am do you?' He took a voice recorder from his pocket and pushed record, 'I want this for my family,' he said, 'I want them to know you only died because you were stupid. I want them to understand why this is the only option I have left for you and your offsider,' he lowered his voice, 'After I'm finished with you, I'm so gunna love meeting your dirty tricks man.'

Charles stared out of the windscreen and said nothing.

Joe waved his empty hand in circles, 'you see, I want to make it so they no longer have to worry about him either.'

Charles stared at the road, not daring to look at the man holding him at gunpoint, who he was certain Joe Gillespie. He wanted to do something to attract attention, but could not think of anything other than dying at the hands of this madman. This was not what he had planned for their first meeting.

'All you have to do is tell me what I need to know,' Joe smiled as he tapped the barrel of gun against Charles left knee, 'and then we might toss a coin to see which way this thing ends, either way one or both of us will be dead come Christmas.'

Winkler had to be sure it was Joe Gillespie. 'Who are you?' The colour had drained from Charles' face and the knuckles on his hands were white, 'and what's all this about anyway?'

'Still haven't worked it out, eh? I thought the dog and the Toyota would have given it away,' Joe shifted in his seat and rested the gun on his lap so it was pointed at Charles groin, 'you got any kids Charles?'

'Me, kids... no.'

'Didn't think so, otherwise you'd know how pissed a man can get when his family's threatened, eh? You're Mad Charlie's grandson, that's right isn't it. Mad Charlie who used to bum around Orroroo, scamming a few bob out of old widows and pensioners to help him get his next stake. Always prospecting, never finding anything,' he dug the gun into Winkler's ribs, 'got any clues as to who I am yet?'

Charles wanted Joe to think he was ignorant, 'nope, look can't we turn around, there must be some misunderstanding. I run a multinational mining operation and people are probably looking for me by now.'

'Nah, I don't think so, I said I was your dad down from Nackara and we were going to meet for breakfast. The bloke in security said it was okay to park in your spot. Even said he'd look after old Gip for me, only thing is, I knew she'd sooner come with us.'

'I'll sack him.'

'No, you won't, you've got a date with destiny and I saw your Dad the other day, leather faced, angry and still working my leases too. You must know who I am by now and why it won't matter to anyone if I kill you?'

'You won't kill anyone old man. Yeah, I know who you are,' at the mention of his father, he lost his boardroom composure, 'I've hated you and every bloody Gillespie in the north for as long as I can remember because of your father,' Charles had venom to spit at Joe, 'my grandad told me he cheated us out of a claim that was every bit as good as the one Lasseter found,' it felt good to give this old prick a piece of his mind, 'your old man cheated at cards and we lost our claim,' he started to laugh, 'and the best bit is that you don't even know where it is.'

'Found a bit of spunk have you?' Joe pointed the gun just below Charles' crotch and pulled the trigger.

Charles dropped his hands and felt for his crotch, the car swerved out of its lane, Joe grabbed the steering wheel and held it steady.

Charles patted the hot fabric and looked at his fingers examining the red goo that covered them, 'you fucking idiot, you could have killed us.'

'It's not a big deal to me whether either of us lives or dies really,' Joe took his hand off the wheel, 'now concentrate.'

'On what?'

'Why I'm here.'

'So what...? Why are you here?' Charles was scrambling. 'What is it you want?'

'To put a stop to my family being harassed and threatened.' Joe checked and re-cocked the pistol. 'I know your old man. He was in the piss-house at my wife's award ceremony. So what I want to know is why that shits you lot off that much, that a woman who has had no interest in mining, or you, is recognised for her work, eh?' He pressed the gun into Charles hip. 'Want to know what I'm wondering now?'

'What...?'

'I just wondered if this nine-millimetre hollow point would take out your hip, bowel and right hip, or just the one hip and damage the bowel. I'd be kind of interested to know.'

'Don't be fucking stupid, you're not going to shoot me while the car's moving.'

'Like I said, I've got nothing to lose, but tell me, why my land Charlie, and why wait until now?' Joe gave a little snigger, 'and another thing I don't understand, is why anyone would take the risk to work my Waukaringa claim?'

'I know nothing about the claim being yours, old man, you're just talking shit.'

Joe reached over and knuckled his face and the car swerved a little, 'watch your mouth.'

'The bloody vehicles even had Wagmin markings on them, sure the stickers might have been removed, but you could still see where the logo had been. They were, or are your vehicles,' Joe pointed to a car park, 'turn off up here, we can walk into the sand hills.'

'It's broad daylight? Someone will see you.'

'Now you're starting to worry about my welfare, how touching,' Joe pointed to a quiet spot, 'stop the car here.'

'Are you gunna kill me here?'

'Your idea's a good one,' Joe looked around, 'there's nobody about. If you think about it, this is probably not a bad spot for it,' he rubbed his head and shifted the gun to his left hand, 'now take the keys out of the ignition real slow and put them on the console.'

Charles kept his eyes on Joe and did as he'd been told. 'Happy?'

'Nope. Did you hire the killers you sent after me last year, was that all your own work?'

'Fuck off.'

Joe flat slapped him again and Charles head crashed into the window.

'Gino set it up, I didn't know them.'

'What about the girl from Hamilton, did you arrange to trade her to the bikies as cover for them?'

'What girl? What bikies? No of course not. I signed off on a few extraneous expenses for Gino to pressure you, but no.'

Joe noticed the fog beginning to roll in, and he dug the pistol into Charles ribs.

'So, you didn't tell these American pricks where to find poor old Jimmy Symes either? You really are a piece of shit. There's been at least six, maybe seven murders, and it all comes back to you and your old man,' Joe laughed in disgust, 'and for what, a quartz reef that runs through our place. Oh yeah, I thought it was all bullshit at the time too. Even believed my old man was a drunken loser, but it's there.' He rubbed his fingers together under Charles nose.

The younger man went to grab his hand, but Joe smashed the butt of the pistol into his head.

'I've seen it and boy, does it sparkle. The quartz starts around Twiggy's old place just south of Morchard, dips underground to where Coomoroo Hill rises and doesn't come up again until you get to what we call Miller's. It follows a fault line all the way to Hawker and, at about twenty kilometres, a long jog runs off to the east toward the Nackara fault. Shit there must be some colour in there too.'

'Bullshit, all the reports say there's nothing there.'

'Enough to set a family up for life,' Joe had heard what Winkler said, but chose to ignore it, 'just think, people have been working their farms over all that gold and they still don't know it's there.'

Charles shifted in his seat, the windows were fogging and he could feel his heart racing, 'so, my Grandfather knew, my father knows, and now our prospectus has told the world where it is,' he sneered, 'It's only a matter of time before all that farming country will just be one big open pit.

Jobs will be created and I'll go into history as a hero,' he leaned toward Joe, 'and you'll go down as another sad old man, driven to murder because he couldn't make a living from the land.'

'I was just wondering, have you heard from your old dad since four o'clock this morning?'

'No, why?'

'Oh nothing, but I expect you'll meet him in hell. Joe took a silencer from the inside of his jacket and with practiced art, screwed it on. 'You should pick your battles better. You were never going to win this one,' he put his hand back in his pocket and drew out a cable tie, 'here, tie your left hand to the wheel.'

Charles did as Joe said. Joe picked up the recorder and switched it off, waving it so Charles could see, 'I don't need anyone to hear the shot, do I?' He picked up the keys and went to throw them into the sand, 'say hello to your old man and your grandfather for me.'

Joe lifting the gun was the last thing Charles saw before he closed his eyes.

Joe sliced the cable tie and put it in his pocket, slipped the car keys into Charles jacket pocket and looked around. There was no one in the park. He reached back and opened the car door, Gip slid out and looked for a post to sniff.

The street lights cast an eerie yellow glow in the mist by the time a man and his dog reached the bus stop. Joe looked at his watch as the bus stopped. 'Noon. Time to go home old girl, time to go home.'

CHAPTER SIXTY SEVEN

Harry Forbes stopped outside the engineering shop in Orroroo, checking the wheels on the camper before speaking to his wife, 'there's a coffee shop up the street love, I'll meet you there in about half an hour. He had seen the, *Out of Office* sign, on the door of the police station, and decided to drop his package off at Tilly's address. He knew she had a legal background and an unmarked brown file would make her curious. He scrawled Jeff's name on the front of it, shoved it into the letter box and walked back toward the shops. He spotted his wife in *The Store on Second*, Carol had a RM Williams western shirt in one hand and a kangaroo hide belt for him in the other.

'Anything take your eye?' He asked picking up a hat and sitting it on her head, 'an Akubra, maybe?'

She looked in the mirror, 'Kate out of McLeod's Daughters? What do you think?' She laughed, before turning to the assistant and pointing in her husband's direction, 'and we'll put it all on Harry's card,'

He pulled his wallet out, 'we're on holidays, so it's cash this time, I think.'

***

The diversionary run out to the homestead to check the progress of the renovations seemed to be working until Jeff noticed Laura look at her watch. 'Come on,' he said, 'let's leave Tilly and Jake to it while we take a walk to the top of the hill.'

'Do you think he's okay?'

'Who, Joe? Sure, look at how he was when we were tracking down that Gordon-Sanders animal. When Joe gets onto something like this he's as happy as a pig in poo.'

'I hope you're right, but I'm more worried about the cancer. He said last night he didn't want to go through chemo, that he won't fight it,' she plucked at a thistle, 'all these years of drought and now we have the best opening in years...' she tossed the weed aside, 'and there's a chance he won't see harvest.'

'When does he see the specialist?'

'I thought he'd see Dr Patel today and we'd go from there, but when Joe has a bee in his bonnet...'

He finished the sentence for her, 'we all do whatever Joe wants.'

They walked for another twenty minutes, it was cooler and Laura pulled her cardigan tight around her, looking back to the almost finished homestead, 'would you live in it?' She asked, pointing.

'In a heartbeat. Who wouldn't want this?' he held his arms out wide taking everything in, 'the last time I saw so much country I was flying. You have an awesome place here, Laura.'

'You're not afraid of ghosts, or the isolation then?' She felt a shiver and wondered if it was the cold air, or something else.

'Too much blackfella in me I suppose. I'm not frightened of emptiness, me.'

'And the girls?'

'Wherever Tilly and Em want to live, will always be my home,' he put his arm around her, 'whenever she's not with me, I feel as if half of me is missing. You know, I never thought it was possible to feel so empty as it is when we're away from each other. And when we're together, I feel complete. Even flying comes a poor second to being with those two. I love them.'

Laura smiled and nodded her approval before looking at her watch again. 'Three o'clock, I wonder where he is? We'd better get back.'

***

Joe drove into the cottage driveway and saw Laura's car was missing. He knew she would be peeved about his disappearance and he had beaten himself up all the way home from Adelaide. He tried telling himself she didn't need to know what he was going to do, but then she had always stood by him in the past. Joe had no option but to face the music when she got home. He went into the kitchen, made a cup of tea and phoned the solicitor. Jonathon was out of the office and Joe left a message with the receptionist for him to call back that evening. Sipping his tea, he mulled over the events of the morning, but nothing he had done to Charles bothered him, it was Laura he had to explain things to, and that woman was no push over.

***

Tilly slid into the driver's seat of the Range Rover and turned back to her mother, 'Jake said he'll be finished out here next week, his painters have only the detailing inside and floor coverings will be laid on Tuesday,' they both had bigger things on her mind, but went for the diversion anyway, 'they should have the landscaping done by Friday. Jack will be over from Wilmington to do a final check on the generator and all other electrical work. I have to arrange a tanker to come in and fill the bulk gas tank and we're ready to go. Exciting, yeah?'

'Sorry love, I don't know,' Laura looked out the window, 'drive back past Wilson's okay, I want to check that hanging tree.'

'Jeeze Mum, buck up a bit. There's no way Dad would do that to us. Think about the number of times he's stopped at that tree where his mum died and how it affected him? There is no way he's going to commit Hari Kari, it's not worth even thinking about. I'm more worried about his other announcement and the months ahead, so let's not be burying him too quickly.'

'Don't argue Tilly and just humour me please... I need to be sure.'

'You're the boss,' Tilly slammed the lever into drive and looked ahead.

'No, I'm not the boss. I'm just worried sick about your father and I know you are too.'

Jeff sat without saying a word, wondering what else the day would bring. After twenty minutes had passed, four gates had opened and closed without a word being spoken, each locked into their own thoughts. The car rocked and its wheels slipped on the bank as they drove down to the tree where old Mister Wilson had hung himself a century ago. Jeff opened his door and walked around looking at the ground for tracks.

'There hasn't been anything other than roos and a couple of emus here in the last couple of days. Want me to check the house?'

'Thanks Jeff, but I'm happy now. Tilly you're right, I was being silly. Take me home, I have to take this out on someone and it's not you two.'

'I can come down later Mum, to check up on you both.'

'It's all right love. I can see him now, sitting at the table and stewing because he hasn't told me where he was going and knowing I'll go crook. He'll have pushed his health concerns to the back of his mind and assume I've done the same. Don't you worry, we'll be okay.'

Joe's Cruiser was in the drive and Laura told Tilly to keep the car overnight.

Just the sight of the Joe's four-wheel-drive made Jeff feel a bit more relaxed, but he wondered what the old bugger had been up to today. There was a suspected serial killer to catch and he could do without any more distractions.

'They'll be all right, you do know that?' Jeff whispered to Tilly as he squeezed her hand. 'He can have another scan, find out what's really happening and get treatment. This disease is not the death sentence it once was.'

'I hope so,' Tilly had her thoughts on her daughter, 'I really don't fancy explaining this to Em.'

'She's been brought up around farm kids, spent time at both ends of an animal's life cycle. It won't be easy, but she'll cope if she has to, but for the moment,' he reached over and rubbed her knee, 'let's pick our girl up then I'm going to set about making dinner and you can take it easy for a bit.'

CHAPTER SIXTY EIGHT

DI Cassidy had spent another day chasing leads that went nowhere, and his team had expressed their frustration in different ways. He would prefer to be dragging a set of clubs around the golf course than walking to lose weight, but at least it gave him time to think. A lot of walkers would have a set of songs, motivational speeches or similar blasting into their ears while they pounded out their step count, not him. If he had to walk, he would rather hear the sounds of the birds at this time of day. It took him away from the drone of an office full of people and the endless urgency of a ringing phone.

His walk always took him from the station to the waterfront, across the old bridge down to the boat ramp, where he walked the length of the concrete five times and back to the station and his car. A month had passed since the last check up and, even if the scales were less than encouraging, his fitness had improved.

Arriving home, he flicked the television to the ABC. It wasn't his habit to watch the news, but with everyone out of the house, he grabbed a beer from the fridge and headed for the lounge. The bottle beading with condensation, he placed it on a coaster while he searched for a stubby holder. He knew he shouldn't, but a packet of crisps seemed to be shouting at him and he doubled back to get the pack, even though he knew this kind of before dinner snack was what led to all the walking anyway. He tore the packet, emptied the contents into a bowl and stuffed the paper into the bin.

A handful of chips crunched in his mouth as he flopped into his armchair and reached for his beer. The news was just starting and news anchor, Clancy Harrison opened with a cross to Outer Harbour where police were winding up their day's investigation of an alleged abduction of WAGMIN Resources CEO, Charles Winkler. Behind the reporter, SES volunteers were combing the sandscape. Deciding secret treats had no real attraction, he took a swig of beer and poured the remains into the kitchen sink, the chips rattled into the bin and he rinsed the bowl.

He reached for his phone and was still chewing when Angela answered, 'pick me up in an hour and tell Bob to meet us at work, okay?'

'Sir.' She wanted to say she had plans, but the job came first.

'Tell him to gather everything he can on this Winkler abduction. We might have found our link.'

He went back to the television, but all he saw was an empty carpark and a lonely reporter in front of a backdrop of foggy streetlamps. He turned it off went to shower wondering just what Joe had done now.

He heard a car stopping in the drive as he tucked in his shirt. Angela was early. He slung a tie over his shoulder, pulled a jacket from its hanger, scrawled a note for the family on the whiteboard and pulled the door behind him. This investigation would probably kill him because tonight, he knew would break his diet again, fast food on the way to Adelaide would probably add weeks to bringing his weight under control.

'What's up boss?' Angela seemed far too cheerful for someone he had dragged away from dinner with her fiancé.

'Charles Winkler. ABC News said police were investigating his abduction. I want to know why? We know where and we can speculate who.'

'Is he okay?'

'I'm hoping there's more information on that when we get into the office. Have you eaten?'

'Yes sir, Andy made risotto.'

'Nice.'

'Yeah, he keeps surprising me. I like it.'

'And how does he feel about you traipsing back to work at all hours?'

'If he minds, he doesn't say,' she shifted her hand to the top of the steering wheel, looking at her engagement ring as she spoke, 'are we ever going to solve this, Sir?'

'Sometimes I wonder,' he recalled Jeff calling in to say there was something he had to do today, 'did Jeff say what it was that kept him from coming in to work?'

'Only that there was bad news for the family and he needed a day to sort it.'

Darryl pulled out his phone and called, launching into questions before Jeff could speak. 'Are you okay mate? Is there anything you need to tell me, or have you been anywhere I should know about?'

Jeff didn't recognise the caller at first and his temper flared. 'Who the hell is this?' He looked at the screen, the name that appeared answering his question, 'Oh, it's you, Sir,' he took a long breath, 'why the questions?'

'I guess you've seen tonight's news. Were you in Adelaide today?'

'No, why?'

'How about you just answer my questions for now and then we'll talk about why?'

Angela sneaked a glance at Cassidy and could see the veins sticking out in his neck, she considered reminding him of his blood pressure, then thought better of it.

'Fair enough,' Jeff said, 'but then we get down to why you're on the edge a coronary, okay?' He waited for a reply, but nothing came. 'Joe told Laura last night he has a brain tumour. He's pissed off, she's a mess, and Tilly's no better. Once we have dinner out of the way we need to go through it all with Emily and I guess we'll go down and see if they're okay,' Jeff paused, 'it's been a shitty twenty-four hours. Now what's this all about?'

'I'm sorry to hear that but I have to ask, have you seen the news?'

'Not tonight, no.'

Darryl shifted in his seat, decided he'd said enough for the moment and finished the call.

Angela looked across the car. 'Sir you didn't think Jeff...'

'No, but I'm not sure who, or what at the moment, but we push people's buttons, even our own if we have to, it's what we do.'

'Even our own people?' she asked, pulling into his parking space.

'Especially our people,' he passed her a few coins, 'grab me a Snickers on your way the past the machine, thanks.' His diet was shot.

Jeff took a glass of wine out to Tilly, 'Em's homework is done, dishes are in the washer and I've just had a call from Darryl,' he sipped the last of the wine from his own glass, 'do you think it's safe to go down and see your folks yet? Em has school tomorrow.'

'Yeah okay, I need to see they're both okay and try to make some sense of it all. Dad has to sign some stuff anyway,' she picked up a pile of papers and drained her glass while she walked into the kitchen, 'okay young lady, we're off to see Pop and Granny now. Turn the TV off and put your dressing gown on.'

'Do I have to?'

'We won't be late and they'll want to see you.'

Emily shrugged, thudded the remote on the coffee table and put her gown on. Jeff could see she'd inherited attitude from her mother and grandmother. She would be a strong woman one day.

Pulling into her parent's drive they could hear raised voices, Laura's loud and Joe's apologetic. Emily slid out of her seat and was inside before Jeff and Tilly realised, standing between her grandparents before they had noticed their visitors.

She held her arms out and kissed Laura, then wrapped her arms around Joe and hugged him. 'What were you two yelling about?'

Joe put his best sorrowful face on and said, 'I went for a drive without telling Granny where I was going today. I was wrong and she was telling me how much I frightened her that's all.'

'Sometimes grownups annoy each other at times,' Laura said, and when you love them, you worry,' she went to the cupboard and took out a tin of biscuits, 'have you cleaned your teeth yet?'

Emily knew this tin, battered and from another age, was reserved for chocolate coated treats, 'not yet.'

Laura took the lid off and held it toward Emily, 'go on then,' she said.

'Mum?' she looked at her mother for approval.

'Yes, but only one, otherwise you won't sleep,' Tilly looked at her mother as she too, took a biscuit and mouthed the words, 'have you two finished?'

Laura nodded, 'look, we were going to phone and ask it was okay to come up, but now that you're here your father has something to tell Jeff,' she put the lid on the tin, 'do you want to watch the TV for a while Em?'

Tilly pulled some cups out of the cupboard, 'now Dad, you put the kettle on, and while Jeff makes tea you can explain to us why you couldn't tell me about this collapse you had in London,' she nodded at Jeff and he lined the cups up, 'is that why you've had everyone in a flat spin?'

Joe pulled a chair out and sat down. He took a few deep breaths. For the next ten minutes, he shared what he knew, speaking lightly but matter of fact, taking special care not to alarm Emily. Tilly thought her father seemed to shrink as he answered her questions and outlined his immediate future. She couldn't remember seeing him so sad, or drained of hope. The struggle to remain composed for Emily as she answered her questions was one of the hardest things she had faced as a mother. Returning home she watched Jeff take Emily inside, sat in the car and cried, knowing their hardest times were still ahead of them all.

CHAPTER SIXTY NINE

Clive Lewis walked through the house turning lights on. He lifted their bags onto the bed and started to unpack. Penny and Sam talking in the kitchen when the television news broke interrupted their discussion.

'Shh Mum,' Sam said, 'it's about Charles.'

The ABC Lateline News was starting and Charles Winkler was the lead story.

'WAGMIN Resources stocks have taken a dive on the New York Stock Exchange in response to CEO Charles Winkler's alleged abduction. Winkler was found wandering, disorientated, among sand hills at the Outer Harbour reserve earlier today. As of going to air, all requests to the company for a statement have been refused.'

The presenter went into a character profile of Charles and his rapid rise to the top of this multinational conglomerate. As a throwaway line they gave a short report on Wagmin Resources' subsidiary RADOR's entry onto the Adelaide Stock Exchange.

'You might have dodged a bullet there, love,' he put an arm around his daughter's shoulders, 'it would be interesting to know what's going on, eh?'

'Ninety seconds hardly tells us much though, does it?' She said and patted her briefcase, 'I might hold onto this for a few days until I know where Gino is and we see what shakes out.'

***

In Orroroo, Jeff had seen the opening headline for news report and was tapping on the window of Tilly's car.

'She looked up at him. 'What's wrong,' she asked, pushing the door open with her shoulder.

'You'd better see this,' Jeff cursed himself for the urgency in his words knowing it would startle her, 'a news report on the Winkler bloke,' he opened the door and helped her out, 'it sounds as if he may have gone troppo. His story doesn't make sense.'

Footage came through from the carpark at Outer Harbour. The news anchor cut across to a reporter in Adelaide's Light Square where a WAGMIN Resources sign on top of their office building threw a cobalt claim into the skyscape.

'I know RADOR was the company Sam worked for, but who or what is WAGMIN Resources?' Jeff asked.

'I've heard the name before, but I don't know, maybe Mum and Dad had some shares once. I'm not sure.'

'Any thoughts?'

'What are you suggesting?

'Not suggesting, just asking out loud I guess.'

'Let me see,' she grabbed her iPad, googled the mining company and scanned its home page, 'Les Gillespie and Charles Winkler registered the original company and another Charles Winkler, I guess it's the one who's in the news now, took the company to multinational status after opening up iron leases after 2002. During the GFC he soaked up as many struggling companies as he could. A new millennium share raider if you like.'

'Well there's one connection. All we need to work out is if it's that behind all the trouble with Joe,' he scratched his nose as he thought, 'do you still have shares or did Les sell them?'

'It doesn't say here. I'd have to look it up. Dad might know but I don't want to bother him now.'

'No, don't bother him now, I reckon it'll wait.'

'It's funny how they aren't giving any details about who abducted him.'

'They'd know more than they're saying, they always do, well mostly. I reckon a lot more will come out over the next few weeks. It could be they're creating a diversion for something that's happened in the business.'

Tilly stood up suddenly, 'not wanting to change the subject but I just remembered I saw something sticking out the back of the letterbox, when we drove in.'

'No probs, I'll get it,' he turned back to her, 'this is all going to work out okay, you'll see.'

Tilly just smiled.

Jeff took the package from the letter box and tugged at the brown paper on the parcel as he walked back to the house. A thought flashed into his mind about the threats made to Joe in Adelaide. He lifted the parcel and listened for ticking. A brown package, with his name scrawled in a script he didn't recognise, raised suspicion. This was not a package he was prepared to open without being sure. He carried it to the new garden patch they had made in the back yard, resting the package into the bed and piling spare bags of soil and mulch onto it.

'Where have you been?' Tilly asked, brushing a smudge of soil from his shirt when he eventually entered the house.

'It was a brown paper parcel with my name on it, no address or sender details, so I thought it's not a risk we needed to take tonight.'

'And where is it now?'

'In the garden. I packed those soil bags around it,' he smiled, 'we can worry about it tomorrow.'

'Where did you put it?'

'Why, what are you going to do?'

'I'll have get Em out of bed and go to Mum's. We can't stay here with a potential bomb in the backyard.

'I'm sure it will be fine but...'

'Well you can stay here if you want, but I'm going to the cottage.'

'It's safe.'

'And you know that, how?'

'Fair enough, I'll come too.'

'Well you bring Mum's car and that will be one job less for tomorrow.'

Jeff parked alongside Tilly's car opened the back door and lifted Emily out of her seat, she fell back to sleep before he reached the house. 'Shh,' he said to Laura who was now holding the door open. He put a finger to his lips as he carried Emily inside, 'I'll put her down in her room, okay?'

Laura nodded and turned to Tilly, 'what's going on?'

'I'll tell you when Jeff comes back.'

'Yeah, and when Jeff gets back your father can tell you just what he's been up to today. Seriously, I just want to knock some sense into him.'

Tilly hugged her mother in understanding, a silent acknowledgement of the long road, pitted with grief that lay ahead of them.

'Come on Mum, of course you can be upset. He should have told you he was going off on his own but,' she shrugged and they grinned at each other, 'that's dad isn't it?"

'Well, if he has to die, I hope he does it before he goes to gaol.'

'Whoa, back the truck up, Mum. Where is this talk coming from?'

'And what'll I do without him?'

'What do you mean, gaol?' Tilly was hearing questions without answers and answers to questions yet to be asked, lost in the maelstrom of her mother's words.

'On the news, Charles Winkler, he's not mad. That's where your father was today,' she pointed to the television, 'scaring shit out of bad guys.'

'Who's been scaring baddies?' Jeff was back.

'Into the lounge with Dad,' she pointed Jeff to the door, 'Mum, I'll bring the tea in.'

'You go in, Love,' Laura reached for a tissue and blew her nose, 'I'll be there in a minute.'

Jeff sat on the couch alongside Joe, who still had his eyes fixed on the television. 'Trouble?' He asked.

'Yeah, I've probably made an arse of myself,' Joe pointed at the screen. 'I caused that,' police tape flickered behind a spotty faced reporter, 'I figured if I've only got a few months to go and for the last few of those I'll be useless,' he passed his voice recorder to Jeff, 'everything he said is on that.' He wiped a hand over his eyes. 'It's not like I want to die, there's just nothing I can do to prevent it.'

'Yeah, but there's treatment, you know, chemo, radiation. There has to be something?'

'Nope, its gunna be up to you to look out for the girls from now on. I called my minders this afternoon, they'll protect me a bit, but I'm not going to make it to trial any way.'

'So, what's on the recorder?'

Joe gave Jeff a rundown of his day in Adelaide.

'Cassidy's not going to be pleased,' Jeff said.

'No, but now all he has to do is prove what's on this tape. Winkler might have been under duress at the time, but he knew the recorder was on. You can't enter it as evidence, but we've got the prick. Now I want that Gino bastard's head.'

'Be careful what you wish for, mate.

Laura put a cup in front of Joe, 'Tilly said something about a bomb'

'What's this about a bomb?' Joe turned to Jeff, 'where is it?'

'It may not be a bomb. It was a package. I didn't know what it was or who sent it and didn't want to open it in the house, that's all.'

'Smart.'

To Tilly, Joe sounded as blasé as Jeff. 'Dad... we could have been killed if it went off.'

'Do you know if it's a bomb?' Joe asked.

'It's a brown paper package with his name on it.' Tilly said.

'My imagination probably got the better of me, but I wanted to be sure. I'll take a look at it in the morning, it could be from John, but it doesn't look like his hand writing.'

'Or,' said Joe, 'I could do it tonight.'

'Have you got an early death wish old man?' Laura slapped his arm, 'you do talk some rot at times.'

'It's okay, I know this stuff.'

'True, but if it hasn't gone off by now, it can wait till morning and when you've done that, Jeff can arrest you,' the half joking tone in her voice showed some of her old humour had returned, 'now I'm off to bed. It's been a long day for all of us.'

Joe stood up and put the cup to his lips, sipped and put it down. 'I'm right behind you.'

Tilly put everything on a tray and took it to the kitchen. 'You go ahead, Jeff. I'll stay here for a while. Dad's going to need all the help he can get with this one.'

'He gave me this,' Jeff passed her the recorder, 'listen to it, it's not about the gold, this is personal.'

'Incriminating?'

'So he says, but I'm not interested in it, because the moment I hear anything, I'll be obliged to arrest him,' he ran a hand over his eyes, 'it'd be like putting the cuffs on my dad.'

'He's made a habit of crashing around like a bull in a china shop all his life and I guess he only wants these threats to finish. I'll get him the best legal help I can,' she took his hand and kissed it, 'you go to bed and I'll listen to this and make some calls. He won't spend a minute inside, I promise.'

'You reckon?'

'Getting crims off the hook was my speciality remember? Just leave it to your hotshot lawyer fiancée. I can do this.'

CHAPTER SEVENTY

Harry Forbes watched the last report on Lateline, churning it through his mind, pretending not to hear his wife telling him to come to bed. The police officer in him clung to the story like a bulldog on a bone then something inside him clicked and he reached for his phone.

He sat on the end of their bed, 'I have to make a call,' he waved his phone at her as a way of answering, 'I won't be long.'

'Yeah, I've heard that before,' she smiled at him, 'make your call and come to bed. You've retired remember.'

Jeff had settled into his bed and waiting for Tilly to come in when his phone rang. He snatched it before it woke Emily and answered with a whispered greeting.

'It's Harry. Did you get that parcel I left for you?'

'Harry who?'

'Forbes, how many bloody Harry's do you know?' He felt deflated, how could his old partner not remember his voice. 'Did you get my parcel?'

'What parcel?' Jeff wanted Harry to spill more than it seemed he wanted to.

'A brown paper package. I put it in your letter box, today.'

'Yeah, but without a sender's name on it and everything that's going on...'

'And what, you jumped to conclusions?' He started to laugh.

'No, I didn't want to take any chances so I buried it in a pile of bagged up soil until tomorrow,' Jeff felt annoyed with his former boss, but decided to hear his reasons for leaving an unmarked package, 'why not put your name on it.'

'It's pretty sensitive. Over the last three years, I've collected evidence of corruption within the current government. It's not confined to one party, or one group of politicians. What I do know is Winkler and his offsider Gino are behind some of it. With what I knew about the Gillespie case and the threats made to Joe I thought it might be useful.'

'Why not hand it on?'

'They'd bury it. You know I was put on the bikie task force because it was newsworthy and the minister needed to raise his profile. I can't trust anyone above my rank to carry it on and the junior ranks well, what can I say?'

'Where are you?'

'We were going to stay in Hawker, but got to looking around the shops in Orroroo and decided to stay here for a day or so. Carol wants to do the walk along the creek, check out the poem, the carvings and the big gum tree. You know all the touristy stuff.'

'Better drop around here for a cuppa and a chat tomorrow then, eh?'

'I'm on holidays.

'Then you and Carol have time to call in and visit an old friend. It won't take long. Come on, you know you want to. Let's say ten thirty at Tilly's. We all want to see you.'

'Yeah, I bet they do,' Harry stifled a laugh, 'ten thirty it is.'

Carol Forbes patted her husband's side of the bed. 'I heard half of that, so I guess tomorrow we're having morning tea with Jeff and his fiancée.'

'Sorry, I should've asked you first, but I'm so used to leaving police stuff at work. Something big is happening and I reckon Jeff is the only bloke I can trust to see it through.'

'Okay, but after tomorrow, you're to concentrate on having a holiday.'

Jeff lay there staring at the digital display on the clock well into the night. He could feel Tilly moving to the rhythm of her breathing and somewhere in the distance he heard a fox calling its cubs. A night bird gave a warning and then a chorus of other birds joined in.

His mind came back to Joe and to his first visit to Wanooka's Well after the steer was butchered. The homestead vandalised on the same weekend and a girl was sold to a bunch of bikies. How can so much happen to one family in such a short time, he wondered. He reached across to stroke Tilly's shoulder, he too was part of it now.

A rooster crowed and Jeff looked at the clock, why would a bloody rooster be going off now? It was only three thirty. Then he heard hens and more crowing, that fox must have got into a chook house somewhere. He held his breath and listened to pinpoint the direction the noise was coming from. He slipped out of bed and padded to the back door. The chooks settled down, he had missed his chance.

About to go back to Tilly, he heard a car at the top of Government Road. His interest piqued when he heard the engine switch off and the tyres roll toward him. He moved to the side of the house expecting to see headlights moving toward the tee junction north of Joe's cottage. There were no lights. Two doors opened and closed almost without a sound. He heard the familiar sound of a shot gun breech being broken and of cartridges plopping into their chambers. A bolt slid in and out of the breech of a rifle. As soft as the gun carriers trod, Jeff could hear them making their way toward the cottage. Fear fought for a place in his mind, but with all that had happened to this family, now was time to act as two shapes ducked into the shadows and heading for the cottage.

He retraced his steps quickly, a gentle shake and he had Tilly's attention.

'What why are you up?' She saw him hold a finger up to his lips encouraging her to stay quiet.

'Take Emily down into the cellar. I'll get Joe and tell your mum to do the same,' his whisper sounded like a shout inside his head, 'I'll send John a text and hope he hears it.'

'There's a landline down there, I can ring.'

'Yeah, let's do that. Don't turn any lights on until the door's shut,' he kissed her, 'I'll get your mum.'

Tilly smiled and made her way to Emily's room. Jeff woke Joe and told him about seeing the Toyota, with faded Wagmin logos roll down the street with its lights off.

'Charlie Winkler,' Joe said, 'you better go down with Tilly, love.' He kissed her cheek and rolled out of bed. As he shrugged on a shirt, he opened a drawer and took out his pistol and pushed it into Jeff's hand.

'Nah, I won't need it. I'll use Blackfella magic,' his smile and his eyes flashed, 'remember the Alamo.'

'That was America and everyone died.' Joe said.

'Good job we're on the winning side then, eh?'

They decided Joe would stay in the house and respond to whatever might happen and, with the girls were secure in the cellar, he turned on the passage light and made his way to the kitchen and filled the kettle.

Jeff grabbed a nulla-nulla from Laura's collection of aboriginal artefacts and the tins of ash and ochre make up. He thought about the woomera, but took a short spear instead. He swiped her laser pointer from the desk and sneaked outside. The Toyota tempted him, the keys were in the ignition and it would be easy to take it out of gear and let it roll downhill, but decided to leave that until later if it was needed. He could see the gunmen crouching in the shadow of the low shrubs.

Inside the house, Joe opened the drapes in the front room and turned on the desk light. It cast a shadow that made it look as if Joe was sitting there reading. Jeff moved closer to the shrubbery. One of the men raised his rifle and fired. Glass shattered and a moment later the veranda lights came on.

'Who's out there?' Joe was yelling. 'If it's one of you kids again, I'll kick your backside and drag your sorry arses up to the cop shop if you come around here again.'

'I don't think you'll be kicking anyone's arse anytime soon, Gillespie,' the voice was gravelled and slow, making Jeff want to swallow in sympathy, 'you don't get it, do you? Weeks ago, in Adelaide, I told you to give us what's ours, access even and no one would be hurt. But no, today you go and bully my kid, leaving him to think he's lost his mind. Come out into the light you bastard. I take you and everyone in there goes free.'

'So, Mad Charlie Winkler's little boy has decided to sneak out of the bush again, eh? Things haven't changed since Vietnam.'

'Wanna step into the light and continue this?'

'I want you to piss off back to your snake hole,' Joe searched for any sign of Jeff. He saw nothing.

'You were always a cocky, self-righteous, bastard Gillespie. All I want is what's rightfully ours.'

'Like what?'

'All the land, mining permits, everything.'

'Yeah, and how long have you been working my Waukaringa claim?'

'Yours?'

'Yes, mine,' Joe allowed anger to show in his voice, but it was slow, quiet and measured. 'I've been paying those leases for the last fifty years.'

'And you didn't even know, I s'pose?' There was a chuckle in Winkler's voice.

'I know now and that's what's important.'

'It's too late to worry about that, now I just want to see you suffer.'

Joe searched the bushes for any sign of Winkler, 'come out of the shadows, or are you still sneaking around like a mange ridden fox.'

'Piss off.'

'I want you and your cronies off of my claim before the police get involved.'

'It never was yours. Wagmin was a partnership between our fathers, it folded after your old man put his shares up as a stake in a poker game.'

'Maybe, but that was a poker game your old man lost,' Joe wanted more, 'Mad Charlie burnt the pub down in spite and you saw him do it, didn't you, you had to be sneaking around in the shadows somewhere,' Joe laughed, 'Mad Charlie Winkler. It's a good caption for scum like you.'

'Bullshit.' The voice was agitated. 'You're just like your old man. You think having money gives you the right to walk all over people and play god with their lives. Come outside.'

'You want to put your gun down first?'

'No, I don't want to put the gun down. I want to shoot you.'

'So, just like your boy you're soft and full of shit,' Joe laughed, 'just like in Nui Dat. Poor little Charlie Winkler, always sick or had an excuse, always hiding from the action. I was surprised to hear you'd been shot. Well not surprised, really. After all, didn't I get you off that charge, because the doctors determined the wound was self-inflicted.'

'That's right, bring up an accident and drop it all on me. You loved it didn't you, watching me squirm under a court martial.'

'I never enjoyed any part of the war, or what anyone had to do, but I wasn't surprised when they sent you home.

I was glad of it, in fact. I needed blokes I could rely on, not someone with a grudge and willing enough to shoot me in the back.'

'You had mates looking out for you.'

'Yep, but you weren't one of them. Is that why you told Gordon-Spencer who we were?'

'Yeah, Jimmy Symes got in touch, said he was dying and wanted to atone for his sins. Charles paid someone in the States to find Monty. I knew he'd want to settle his score with you, he was easy,' Winkler's sneer was almost a laugh, 'it took a while for Gino to find him, but when they did he just needed their fares paid. As I said, easy.'

'You know how he left Jimmy.'

'He told me.'

'No remorse?'

'Why? Monty did him a favour.'

'And the girl from Hamilton, the one your son gave to the bikies that all part of the plan?'

'You were on a string from the time you found the dead steer, remember, your granddaughter's pet. I knew you'd be like a dog with a bone after that.'

'I know you haven't got enough brains to wipe your arse,' Joe wanted to goad him out of the shadows, 'you're not smart enough to put all of this together, but I have to applaud those boys of Monty's. That was West Point genius. I knew from the moment I was in the crossfire that it was him. He was an arsehole, but it was a classic siege tactic.'

'That was me and the boys. Monty's men were waiting on the road.'

'Now that makes sense,' Joe whistled, 'and when they were hurt, you came along and murdered them?'

'Not guilty, your honour,' Winkler allowed a chuckle, 'Gino's had a bloke watching you for a couple of years and he was only too happy to do it.'

'And your kid, what trigger did he pull?'

'None,' Joe heard him snigger, 'there'll be a woman in Hong Kong to alibi him.'

'Chip off the old block eh? Just like you, any action in the jungle and you'd be AWOL with the Saigon girls,' Joe looked into the blackness and laughed, 'you know Winkler, I haven't spent a second thinking about you,' Joe kept looking for Jeff, 'want to know why?'

'You're not getting me to bite that easy, Gillespie.'

Joe wanted to make him angry enough to leave the shadows, 'because I thought the VD, or the drugs must have got you.'

'Not so lucky prick, and no thanks to you either. You could've signed my papers to send me home early, but no. You could have done on any number of times I'd been in hospital with malaria, but rather than sign me home, you always took another bloody mission and left the paperwork unsigned.

'Is that what this is about, another bloody poor little Private Charlie Winkler cop-out, and all because you wanted to go home,' Joe felt his voice rise like that of a Sergeant Major, 'well I've got news mate, we all did. There wasn't a man, woman, or child, who wanted to be there,' Joe fought to bring back a few of the horrors from that time and help his anger rise further, 'more than once we lost good blokes and why, because we were a man down, because you were hospitalised. Piss off, I've no more time left for you.'

Winkler felt his heart pound with anger, 'come outside, motherfucker.'

'Yeah and then what? I step into the light then you shoot me and disappear. Is that what you want?'

'Not until you make everything over to me. That's my plan.'

'And how do you propose we do that?'

'You got a hotshot lawyer in the family. Get her down here to do it.'

'When?'

'Now.'

'Piss off. I'm going back to bed.' Joe turned the inside lights off and closed the front door.

Charlie Winkler raised the shot gun and fired both barrels. A spear landed between his feet in answer.

Jeff felt a tap on his shoulder and turned, a row of shining teeth split the darkness.

'You gone all native again mate?' A male voice whispered. 'What's happening?'

'Did you toss the spear?' Jeff was confused, because he still held onto everything he'd taken from Laura's collection.

'Nope, must be black fella magic, I reckon,' he pointed and grinned, 'Kadaichi Man in them shadows, eh?'

CHAPTER SEVENTY ONE

Siege, shots fired, Gillespie House, Orroroo. DI Cassidy showed the message to his constable, 'better put your foot down, Ange. If it's Joe, he's going to be hard to contain. If it's someone else, I fear for them. After what we can assume from today, Joe will show no mercy.' He reached forward and flicked the emergency lights on.

'So, what do we sir?'

'I really don't know. I'll keep trying to get hold of John and you see if you can get Jeff to answer.'

Darryl Cassidy lifted the crime scene tape and walked across to Jeff, who had John's coat over his shoulders. 'What's all this? Have you gone traditional now mate?'

'Bloody John, won't let me inside the house.'

'You look like an old tracker, no wonder he wouldn't let you in. Go and get dressed and tell John I said it's okay if he tries to stop you.'

'Sir,' Jeff nodded and ducked under the tape.

'Detective Constable you saw nothing, clear.'

'Very,' Angela was surprised at the formal way he addressed her, 'oh, you'll find the letter on your desk when you get back there. Congratulations.' He smiled and then let it drop. 'Go into the house and see if everyone's okay. You know, do the detective thing.'

He turned to John O'Rourke, 'now tell me once again what's happened here and how come you turned rapid response back?'

'Your friends had it under control,' John pointed to a young aboriginal man and a man who looked like his grandfather, 'Jeff says you know Uncle Rupert?'

'Yeah, we go back a bit.'

'And Harry Forbes is in town. He talked to Jeff last night.'

'Oh, for fuck's sake.'

'No sweat, he's retired and on holidays,' John grinned, 'Jeff's planned a sit down and coffee with him for ten thirty.'

Darryl looked at his watch, 'good job I sent him in to get dressed then.'

Joe sat at one end of the table while Darryl leant against the kitchen bench and flipped through a summary of the witness statements.

'Were you in Adelaide yesterday, Joe?'

'What's it say there?'

'C'mon Joe, just tell me in your words, no bullshit and why?'

'Nothin' to lose by shaking the tree a bit,' he shifted in his chair and took a file from the sideboard, 'I needed to know we'd get them for sure this time, I don't want my family looking over their shoulder after I'm gone. You know, I was so burned up with hating my old man, I'd forgotten most of his past. Then after the attack in Adelaide, finding the gold and letters from him to me that I'd never bothered to read, I had it almost worked out,' he looked at the detective, 'call it providence, or whatever, but something made me go out to a claim that Winkler's old man and mine worked after the Second World War,' Joe watched as Cassidy thumbed through the doctor's report, 'that's when Laura and I were threatened at gunpoint by this Charlie Winkler. He didn't know who we were and Laura decided to record it all on one of those dash cam things that Tilly insisted we have,' he reached behind him again, 'here's the memory card, it's all on there.'

'Pity you don't have one for tonight and yesterday.'

Joe nodded at the display security screen, 'another one of Tilly's insistences, John has bagged it for forensics.'

'Want to tell me about yesterday?'

'Winkler's boy pissed me off. I'd guessed he was at the back of the whole thing and he told me as much during our chat.'

'It's his word against yours and now you've admitted you were there, it looks like he holds all the cards.'

'Maybe, maybe not.' Joe passed the recorder it across, 'you never know, this could be the winning hand.'

'You've got a lot riding on it.'

Joe smiled at him, 'it's the winning hand alright and that's all that matters.'

Angela walked in to the room and tapped her superior on the shoulder with her mobile phone. He ignored her.

'Sir,' she said.

'Okay Joe, stay there. I'll be back in soon,' he passed Joe's medical history file back to him, 'sorry to read about this, mate.'

DI Cassidy leant against the front fender of the police car while Angela walked across to where John sat on a wicker armchair in the shade of the veranda. They watched as their superior nodded to what the caller was saying.

'What's our next move?' she asked.

'It depends on what the boss tells us, I guess.'

'So, what was going on inside?'

'Joe laid everything out, not only last night, but yesterday too. Something of a vendetta going back to the sixties. I just don't get how someone can hold a grudge for that long?'

'Dunno, people don't always get what they want, or they blame someone else for their problems.'

The detective was back, 'Ange, finish what you have to do here. We're off to Adelaide,' he looked at his phone, 'I need to hear what Charles Winkler has to say. He's all lawyered up and that tells me he's hiding something.'

'So, now he's gone from victim to suspect?' John asked.

'Maybe, I need to look at all the security footage from the carpark, etcetera,' he walked toward the car, and then turned back to the cottage. 'I'll only be a minute,' he called back to Angela, 'warm it up and call your friends from Brahma Lodge, I want to see them this afternoon, too.'

'What's he doing now?'

She slapped John on the shoulder, 'taking charge I guess,' she opened the door and started the car, 'tell Tilly and Jeff I'll call when I get a chance, yeah?'

CHAPTER SEVENTY TWO

Sam Lewis received a message that David Wang wanted to speak with her. He was in Sydney and wanted a meeting in Adelaide the next day, if possible and to discuss RAYDOR and WAGMIN's future with her over dinner. He would email the questions he wanted to ask and give her time to prepare.

Before the end of the call she clarified, 'Mr Wang does know Charles has fired me?'

'Yes, Miss Lewis, it's Mr Wang's business to know.'

Sam set up her laptop on the kitchen table, making space where her mother was preparing vegetables for a stew. The message from David Wang was in her inbox when it opened.

'They want me to review the company's performance so I'm going to be in your way for a while, if that's okay with you and Dad, Mum.'

'No problems love, I've missed having you in the kitchen when I work. It's nice.'

***

Tilly's kitchen in Orroroo had a different atmosphere. It was quiet, tension filling the room.

'Carol and I planned to stay in Hawker last night,' Harry Forbes broke the silence, 'but once Carol started looking in that shop,' he grasped his mind for the name, 'the Store on Second, well the day got away from us. We stopped at the coffee shop, went to butchers for some saltbush lamb and to stock up on sausages. We booked into the caravan park, stopped at the top pub for a beer and saw a cow's ear sticking to a window frame with a knife. Well by the time we'd listened to the story behind it,' he shrugged, 'we decided to stay.

Jeff came in and tossed the package at Harry, 'what's so important, that you couldn't tell me over the phone?' he went to the sink and washed his hands, 'you frightened shit out of us.'

'Yeah, but from what I hear on the grapevine, that parcel might just have stopped Joe getting shot.'

'I don't think Joe would have been shot. I reckon he knew what he'd have to do to draw Winkler out.'

Tilly took Carol by the arm, 'c'mon, let's leave these two bulls bash it out, while you show me your camper.'

'No, it's fine really, I've never had anything to do with Harry's work. A little sharing now will do him good. Besides after hearing the rumours going around the town about what happened last night, I'd like to see what Harry has hidden from everyone.'

'Sure,' Harry pulled a hand full of eight by ten prints from the package, politicians with business men, politicians with criminals and criminals with business men. All were time and date stamped, complete with reference numbers, 'everything's in there,' he passed Jeff the ledger, 'when I saw the news with the reporter saying that Winkler was found wandering and rambling on about being abducted. I guessed Joe may have been involved.'

Jeff passed the file to Tilly and she flicked through the photos. 'This one,' she held a photo of Jack Pendlebury taking a package from a face she didn't recognise, 'who's this guy?' she flicked the photo over and read the back, 'Gino Di Massimo?'

'The one and only.'

Harry's smile was cold. Tilly went through the photos, 'there, that's Spoggy with him, and another one with both Spoggy and Gino with some bikies. What is this?'

'At first, I thought it was just about political corruption. Pendlebury is about as genuine as a three dollar note and most of the ministry are dirty. Until yesterday, I thought I'd need to let Jeff hang onto this until something broke. Last night it did and here we are.'

'So what do you want me to do?' Jeff asked.

'Wait until the time's right. Drop it all in Cassidy's lap and stand back. He's got a great record and, from what I can tell, he can't be bribed. He'll get the bastards.'

'Why not you, you were always hunting for a picture in the paper?' Jeff rubbed his forehead and wiped his hands on his shirt.

'Not anymore, I'm done with police work, I want to catch up with some old friends from the academy, but that's about it,' he clapped a hand on Jeff's shoulder, 'and you should give the coppers away too mate. Marry this girl and set that aeroplane record you were always yapping on about. Believe me there is more in life than getting to my age and worrying how to manage an ulcer.'

'This is all legit?' Jeff asked.

'Yep,' Harry looked at Tilly and smiled, this time it gave off warmth and genuineness, 'see Tilly, I may not be the big angry bastard as he's told you.'

'I can't remember if your name ever came up?' Tilly lied.

Harry smiled and said, 'touché,' feeling a little deflated, but knowing it was probably due. 'When we were pressing the bikies for information, we found out the bloke you know as Spoggy has had more names than you'd find in the New Testament. No one's been able to prove anything,' he tapped a manila envelope, 'but everything he's done since birth is in there.'

'Do you know where he is now?' Jeff's excitement built.

'Here, take this card. My contact in Juvenile Justice,' he held it longer than Jeff expected before he let go, 'lives in fear of him, but he does call her from time to time and she'll know,' he stood and motioned to Carol to follow, 'now we'll be off. There's a bloke I went through the academy with who runs camels on a place just east of here I want to catch up with.'

'Yeah, okay. I'll pass this along.'

The two men shook hands, 'think about leaving this to Cassidy and his team. Retire, spend time with your family and leave catching bad guys to someone else. You've always been too good for this,' he waved the back of his hand over the images.

Jeff didn't understand, 'why though? You said you wanted to see how far I could go.'

'Yeah, but then you had nothing worthwhile to lose. Now, you have a family and the opportunity to chase a dream,' he pulled Jeff into an awkward hug, 'you're too kind to women and children to not let the work affect you and that's a gift.'

Jeff pushed away, 'but you always said...'

'I've changed my mind, the job we do, have done, is too hard to keep it all together.'

Tilly looked at Carol, 'come on, let's leave these blokes to it. If Harry keeps this up he'll have Jeff blubbering and I, for one, don't need to see that.'

***

Angela tapped on the door of the interview room. Cassidy looked annoyed, but suspended the interview.

'Sir, there's a journalist at the desk.'

'You told him no comment?'

'I did, but he said it's not information he wants, it's what he has that's pertinent to our case.'

'Jeeze, constable, you're a detective now. Handle it.'

'Sorry sir, he says he'll only talk to the top,' she made italics with her fingers, 'he will only speak to you.'

'Shit. Show him into an interview room and tell him to wait.'

'He won't do that sir,' she passed him a card, 'he says he'll only talk to you in the carpark behind the Angas Hotel in ten minutes.'

'How will I know him?'

'I told him what you look like, and he's in a red Commodore. The plate number's on the back of the card.'

'Okay, and you can keep Lord Muck on his toes in there while I'm gone. The bastard thinks the world owes him. He only thinks it was Joe, but said it could have been anyone. I haven't got anything out of him about Spoggy or the bikies. It seems as if there's someone who frightens him more than Joe. Exploit that.'

'Hard arsed bitch, or feminine wiles?'

'I think he reckons he's God's gift to women, so you take the approach you think will work. We have enough to hold him. Lock him up if you like. It's up to you,' Cassidy grinned, 'I hope this meeting isn't a bloody set-up.'

Angela opened the door to the interview room, pulled the band from her ponytail and shook her head letting her hair loose to bounce on her shoulders. She smiled at Winkler, offered her hand and he took it. His grip was firm, his skin soft. He might look like he worked out, but he was not a man hardened by physical work. She sat down and took her time reading through the report in front of her. Twice she moved her head to give the impression she was loosening the tension in her neck, and then snapped the folder shut and slapped her hand onto it. 'Forensics say you spilt sauce onto the crutch of your suit,' it was as good a place to start as any and she spun the folder in circles with her right hand for effect, 'what's going on Charlie?'

'Charles please,' he winced, 'what do you mean?'

She looked at his lawyer and to the constable who had been part of the interview team before she entered the room, 'has, Mr Winkler been cautioned yet?'

'No Detective.'

'Best we do that now then.'

'Wait, what are you charging me with?'

'Let's start with extortion, conspiracy to murder, and we might chuck in perverting the course of justice too.'

He looked at his lawyer.

'I'd advise care Detective Constable. Mr Winkler has a lot of well-connected friends.'

'Read him his rights constable,' she said, 'then take him downstairs and charge him with conspiracy to commit murder, obtaining money by deception and anything else you can find in the file.'

Winkler turned to his solicitor, 'get me out of here Jones. They can't do this. I'm the CEO of Wagmin Resources, not some bloody two bit criminal to be trifled with.'

'I'll have you out in an hour Charles.'

Angela smiled at the solicitor, 'I wouldn't write cheques I couldn't cash, Mr Jones.'

CHAPTER SEVENTY THREE

DI Cassidy checked his firearm and, rather than keep it in the shoulder holster, held it in the pocket of his coat. For all he knew, Spoggy could be driving the red Commodore and even though he had doubts, Cassidy knew he had to do this alone.

'You wanted to see me?' The police officer stood by the driver's door, his gun hanging loose in his hand.

'Shit, Jesus Christ man, I came bearing information, not to have my head blown off.'

'Who are you?'

'Matthew Naqvi, investigative journalist.'

Darryl looked at the driver and watched the colour return to his face, matching this to the one on his Victorian driver's licence, 'you're a bit jumpy aren't you, Matthew?'

'Look, I'm going to break a huge story tomorrow and think I have information that will help your investigation.'

'Why?'

'Because I hate corruption and the bastards who facilitate it,' he opened the door, 'everything's on this,' he handed Cassidy a memory stick, 'and now I reckon we should find a quiet spot in the bar and you can buy me a drink.'

'Lock it up mate. I'll get the drinks.'

They found a table away from other patrons at the back of the room.

'You've got Winkler then?'

'I can't tell you that.'

'It's just that I saw him go in with his silk and only one of them has come out. There's enough on that little stick to keep him inside for a long time,' he took an envelope from his pocket and withdrew a proof for a front page, 'if Gino Di Massimo hasn't called me by ten tonight, this is page one tomorrow. I've been trying to call him since last Friday night. No answer. I have original copies of everything that's on that stick in a security deposit box. If you use it, I want the inside running on anything you release to the press. Deal?'

'I don't do deals, and you'd be best to know that.'

'I expected that. I just wanted to be sure who I was dealing with, that's all.'

'I passed?'

'You passed,' Matthew took a pull on his glass, 'it's my guess you're looking for Gino too. I've been to the marina at Glenelg where he moors his boat. It's not there and hasn't been seen for days. He likes fishing, but I don't think the Messina Maria would be something you'd spend a night on. Find the boat and you find Gino.' He passed Cassidy a photo.

'If we find the boat, I'll let you know, *eh*?'

Matthew put his drink down, 'I'll see you in papers then.'

'I don't think so.' Cassidy slipped the photo in his pocket and walked back to work.

He came in as Winkler was being booked and wondered which tactic Angela had employed as he moved to the incident room where she was addressing a crew thrown together from the different stations in the area.

'Okay troops, we have leads,' he took charge without introduction or greeting, 'in fact, that's one of the things we've always had too many of and now we are going fishing, not for clues, but a boat,' he held the picture aloft, 'this is the Messina Maria, white carvel hull with blue markings. Check every boat ramp, boat yard and marina. You know what to do.'

'Sir?' A constable tried to get his attention, 'I have John O'Rourke from Orroroo on the phone, he says it's important.'

'Christ, he could have called me on my mobile,' he turned to Angela, 'ask the chopper to sweep along the coast and out as far as the Marion Newtons Group. If Di Massimo is fishing, bring him in,' he looked at his phone and threw it to her, 'and get someone to charge this for me please.'

'John?' Darryl took the call, 'no, he can't resign and yes, he is off the case. You leave now and bring everything down here, but for Christ's sake don't show it to anyone,' Darryl thought for a moment, 'I'll meet you in the carpark across the road, plain clothes and come in your wife's car, okay?' He turned back to the group, 'okay I want everyone back in here at six o'clock. We'll debrief and then you can go home. Understood.'

A hand went up. 'Sir, I have an appointment at...' she saw the DI frown, 'no worries, I'll cancel.'

'Six it is then.'

***

Tilly wanted the air cleared before she found any more surprises, 'okay mister, you and I are going to write your resignation letter.'

'Come here,' his arms were out but she stood firm, 'whatever it is, we'll get through it and come out stronger. I love and value you, why would I want to destroy that. Harry made a good point this morning. I can't work this case, it's too close,' he smiled at her, 'I'll admit, I got a bit excited about being needed by the police again, but last night seeing Uncle Rupert made me realise there's more to life. You know, when I met you, a light went on for me, the kind of light that Mum and Dad had and what your parents share. The same light you and Em have, I'm not going anywhere near that off switch.'

'God you're a smooth-talker,' she put her arms around him and fell into his embrace, leaning against him for a few seconds before pulling back, 'come on let's hear what the crazies have to say for themselves. Somehow I've got to explain all this to Emily.'

'We'd better get down there then.'

Joe was talking to a group of Aboriginal men when Jeff and Tilly arrived. Jeff hadn't seen them all last night, but assumed someone had driven Uncle Rupert over here as he didn't drive. Behind the trees where the men were sitting there were three cars he couldn't identify as local, 'we'll be in soon, okay?'

Jeff shook hands with the group then addressed Joe, 'C'mon mate, the women are on the warpath.'

The group started to tease him in Adnyamathanha, Uncle Rupert clapped his hands together and their laughter stopped.

'See you later boys,' Joe waved and walked back to the cottage, Jeff by his side, 'I guess I've got some explaining to do.'

'You have.'

Tilly held the screen door for them as they passed through. 'Mum's in the kitchen and she won't say anything without you present. So Dad, it had better be good.'

Joe did his best to explain the headaches and the depression he had tried to hide from them. Tilly leaned back against the bench and stared at the letter from Joe's specialist in London, reading a line and turning it face down, then turning it up to read another line before putting it down again, as if she could only digest the information in small bites.

'But why didn't you tell anyone? Why not tell Mum at least? It isn't fair. What would have happened if one of those bullets had hit you last night?' she threw the letter in the air out of frustration, 'do you want to end your life with me resenting you because of what I don't know?' Jeff went to stand, 'no, you don't, Jeff. You just stay there.'

'Tilly love?'

'No Mum, I don't need comfort from you right now. I want Dad to get it all out. No more secrets, no more hiding behind my father was a bastard, either Dad. I've read his letters to your mum. He might have been a screw up, but he loved you in his own way,' she watched Joe stand and her anger turned to grief, 'what am I going to do without you and how do I going to explain all this to Emily?' She was openly crying now from sadness and hopelessness. Joe moved closer, pulling a couple of tissues from the box by the sink and passing them to her. She nodded a thank you and dabbed at her eyes. 'Oh Dad, I don't want to lose you.'

'I know love,' he folded his arms around her and she felt his protection once more before pushing him away, 'and don't do that. Don't make me feel protected when I'm vulnerable. Don't make me need you more than I can bear, because in six months or so, this will all be gone and how will I get those reassuring hugs then? Who will dry my eyes and tell me everything will be okay then, Dad... who?'

Joe went to say something.

Tilly shushed him, 'and don't tell me I'll have Jeff and Mum and Emily, or Ted. I want them in different ways, but I need you. I need the man who came for me in the middle of the night when my world was upside down. I want the man who taught me everything is possible. I want the strength to get back on the horse when it tossed me off. All the things I am, is part of you and if you die without a fight, without a second opinion, well I'll feel diminished.'

'Have you finished now?' Her mother's words were soft, but Tilly knew she was ready to step in and defend Joe.

Jeff stayed quiet.

Joe wrapped his arms around her again and this time she didn't resist. They stayed that way until she cried herself out and he felt the time was right for further explanation.

'I'm sorry about what's happened, I just wanted to draw these people out into the open. I knew that voice in Adelaide and when your mum and I saw him at Waukaringa, but I couldn't quite place him. Then I saw the faded Wagmin signs and it came to me, and after I'd looked through all of the old man's stuff from the house at Wilson's, I knew who was behind everything. The Winkler's have been behind this from the get-go. None of this is about gold. It's about a grudge, a falling out over a bloody card game.'

Laura again came to his rescue. 'We only heard part of it in the cellar, you should tell her the rest of the story love.'

'Mad Charlie bet his half of the mining company and Dad matched it with the farm. Charlie was holding three aces and a pair of threes. Dad never looked at his hand, it just sat on the table until all he had left to bet with was the farm. It was a massive pot and, in the end, it was just the two partners, Dad and Charlie. Dad still hadn't looked or taken a card for the whole hand, then he bet the farm and called,' Joe paused and looked at the faces soaking up the story, 'Charlie smiled and reached for the pot but the dealer held him back.'

'And we know this how?' Tilly asked.

'It's all in the letters. Apparently, Charlie turned Dad's cards over, first a ten of spades, then an ace of spades, a king rolled over next, same suite. He couldn't turn the rest of the cards so the dealer did it to reveal the queen and jack of spades.'

'I don't understand cards,' Tilly said.

'Les's hand out scored Charlie's,' Jeff wanted to know more, 'so that's where he got the gold?'

'Yeah some of it, but even though the old man could be spiteful he gave the deeds back to the other business men and farmers who'd lost everything to the cards. Oh, I'm sure he kept the cash, but it was his spite in not returning Charlie's share that brought all this upon us.'

'I get that, but why didn't he?' Tilly asked.

'Probably because he was a controlling bastard,' Laura added, 'or maybe he just wanted rid of Mad Charlie.'

'So Wagmin resources is that the same company?' Tilly asked.

'No, I don't think Les and Charlie registered anything, it's just that their names appear on the mining right.'

'Okay, so now all I have to do is keep you out of gaol until you die then?' Tilly tried to bring some lightness into the room.

Joe raised his eyebrows and smiled at her, taking her cue, 'yep, that's about it.'

Jeff was still trying to get his head around it all and understand what Joe was saying, 'Yeah, but you had half a tonne of gold in smelted bars out there. Where did that come from?'

Joe put his cup down, 'My father was cunning. He traded anything and everything. Thinking back now, it probably explains why he was always in the pub, buying and selling, wheeling and dealing and building bullion. The mine probably provided half or more of it. Some of that's at the back of Charlie Junior's grudge, but even as kids we didn't get on and I didn't see him until Vietnam. They never should have sent him, he didn't cope and I didn't help. I thought he was a malingerer, a lazy bastard.'

'And the boy, Charles?' Laura said.

'Don't know, don't care,' he stood and went to the sink, 'now it's time for lunch I reckon. Laura's shout.'

'Why's it my shout?'

'Cause you're married to the happiest man in the world,' he picked through the notes in her purse, 'and you have   the   money.'

CHAPTER SEVENTY THREE

Cassidy sat outside the Superintendent's office, fanning his face with the folder the reporter had given him, wondering if the super could be trusted. He had only met her once before, on a flying trip to meet the country personnel in her charge, and that had not been long enough to form an opinion one way or the other. If he thought anything at all it was that she appeared to be overly political and scheming. While some of the information would help with his case, he didn't have the skills or desire to wage a war with politicians. Superintendent Salma Akbar could allocate that.

'Come in come in, take a seat,' she waved toward a pair of chairs placed either side of a glass coffee table near the corner, 'can I get you tea or coffee?'

'No thanks Ma'am.'

'I can call down and have it sent up.'

'No thanks, but I do need to show you this. I can use some of the information, but the rest of it is sensitive and to be honest I'm not equipped to deal with it.' He passed her the folder.

Cassidy waited while his superior tutted and nodded as she read the documents before her, 'I knew they were crooked. You can't do what he's done on a ministerial salary. How long have you known this,' she turned the card over and reached for her glasses, 'Matthew, how do you say his last name?'

'Naqvi, Ma'am.'

'Oh yes, Nack-vi,' she smiled at him, 'and what do you want from me?'

'Well I want to clear this case I'm on now and palm the glory over to someone who'll get the corrupt bastards,' he tapped the file, 'Naqvi says his paper is going front page with it tomorrow. I phoned the editor and they confirmed it so I thought you needed a heads up.'

'Tomorrow?'

'That's what he said.'

'How long have I known you, Cassidy?'

He looked at his watch, 'less than ten minutes ma'am.'

'And the case you're working is?'

'The Gillespie case, Ma'am.'

'Operation Kundela, some sort of feud come family grievance if I remember. Where are you up with that?'

'We've made arrests, but still have two suspects to find.'

'Better you'd get on with it then, detective. E-mail a report to my secretary tonight. I'm going upstairs to walk on eggshells.'

'Tread carefully ma'am.'

'Thanks,' she stood, opened the door and ushered him out, 'catch me a killer, okay?' It sounded like a cliché, but she had used the same catchcry for years.

Angela met Cassidy as he exited the lift and they walked back to their temporary offices. 'Sir, the chopper has found the Messina Maria anchored close to the place you suggested. They say it has signs of a struggle on board,' she passed him a salad roll, 'the water police and a dive crew are underway now.'

He opened the roll and searched for any sign of meat, 'is this all they had? And why the divers?'

'Sir, a red HSV Commodore was left at the marina three nights ago, registered to Liam Strange of Brahma Lodge. So I asked them, at your request, to bring it in for forensics to go over it,' she put her cup on the corner of a desk, sat down, and leant back in the chair to study the incident board, 'and what do we do about Joe Gillespie because, whatever happens, he's still going to die,' she popped the plastic top from her coffee and stirred in two sugars, 'can we prove he abducted anyone?'

'No, we have no witnesses and there is no security footage from the car park. We know he left Orroroo and returned after fuelling up at Clare. The security company says their system was hacked and the cameras were down for over twenty-four hours. It's not something they'd expect and they're trying to trace the origin, but it's probably someone working the dark web.'

'So, it's his word against theirs.'

'That's about it,' he sipped his coffee and grimaced, 'did you get any more sugar with these?'

'Sorry, Sir. I had yours.'

They sat in silence and scoured the board for inspiration. Angela's phone rang and she answered, listened and ended the call.

'John's just parked, Sir.'

'Right, I'm on my way.'

'Want me to come too?'

'No bloody way, you're likely to take my drink away,' he smiled at her, 'you hold the fort here, I want to see what he has and then decide who, if anyone, should see it. Find a good photo of Gino Di Massimo and Spoggy and get them circulated. They're starting to annoy me, big time.'

Darryl motioned John to the table in the corner, 'have you had lunch?' he asked.

'No not yet. I came as quick as I could.'

'Here order me a schnitty with chips and bring back a beer, light,' he passed over a pair of fifty dollar notes, 'and get something for yourself, my shout.'

'Done.' John passed over the file before making his way to the counter.

'Did you look in it?'

'No, Jeff reckoned the less anyone sees of that the better.'

'He's probably right,' the DI opened the file and noted it had similar information to that of the reporter, but the fingers of corruption in this one were longer. He looked for reference to Superintendent Akbar, there was nothing.

'There we go,' John put the drinks down and gave Cassidy his change, 'and your receipt.'

'Thanks.'

'You might as well look at this, most of it will be in the paper tomorrow anyway.'

John sipped his orange juice as he read, 'God, no wonder Jeff wanted to drop it.'

'How long have you been a copper?' he asked John.

'About twenty years.'

'Do you like it?'

'Yes, I do.'

'And you never wanted to move to the city.'

'Once upon a time, but not now.'

'Good, because when we hand this over, it may make promotion impossible for you.'

'More money would be nice, but I like the country, it's peaceful and safe out there,' John played with a coaster, 'why?'

Darryl passed him a photo, 'this is your old sergeant, isn't it?'

'Yeah, but what are you driving at?'

'Here, this bloke, he's passing him money, wouldn't say?'

'So? He's always played the ponies.'

'Concentrate on the kid copper driving the car in the background. That's you, isn't it?'

'Yeah,' John felt his face redden as his anger built, 'and if you look hard enough you'll find where I made a report. Every time I saw something I made a report and nothing was done.'

'Did you keep copies?'

'Absolutely.'

'Good, we might need them,' the older officer leaned back for the waiter to put is meal down. He waited until they were alone, held his palms up and said, 'a bloody Caesar Salad?'

'Yep, you don't want to fatten a thoroughbred.'

Cassidy chose to ignore the comment. 'So you knew he was bent?'

'Everyone did. I had my guts kicked out more than once after I put in a report. I took a country post to get away from it, met Fiona and realised there was more to life than the politics of city police work.'

'Will you make a statement?'

'If I can keep my pension.'

'You'll keep your pension,' he picked up a chip from the side of his plate and dipped it in the runny egg yolk of John's salad, 'Jeff is finished with the force too I guess.'

'He told me Joe was dying and I reckon he'll have to take up the slack until they adjust.'

'Have you ever looked at his record?'

'Nope, but it's similar to mine. He was lucky when he got to Harry Forbes though.'

'How do you mean?'

'Harry might have pushed the boat out a bit, but he never went across the line according to Jeff.'

The DI sipped his beer, set it down and wiped his top lip with the napkin, 'do you want to go home, or look at what we're doing inside?'

'If I never have to go in there again, that will be fine with me, but I'll do what it takes to solve this case.'

'You go home mate, we have this and thanks for the file.'

'Are you going to be okay Sir?'

'I'm fine, and you take care, okay?'

'Sir,' John stood finished his juice and pushed his plate in, 'I should have ordered the squid, too much dressing for me.'

Cassidy watched him walk past the rows of poker machines. When he was out of sight, he dipped another chip in the runny egg, finished his meal and left a five-dollar tip.

Superintendent Akbar sat at her desk, the contents of both folders scattered across its surface, 'you really are a harbinger of bad news, Cassidy. There's a team out at Pendlebury's now. Christ, I hope we can sort through this.'

'All my team wants is for you to make it right, Ma'am. One of my team told me he's raised this over and over, only to have his guts kicked in by these old bastards. I want your word that he didn't take that kicking in vain.'

'It's a bloody mess. I don't know what parliament is going to do about their problems, but I assure you he'll get justice,' she stood and looked out the window, 'how did you come by the second file again?'

'I can't tell you ma'am.'

'You'd better catch me a killer then.'

'Pulling in the net now, Ma'am and it's full of killers.'

CHAPTER SEVENTY FOUR

Sam put the phone down. She could not believe what she'd just heard and ran outside to tell her mother, finding her in the garden, a basket of vegetables at her feet.

'Done with your phone call then?' She asked.

'I've been offered a job.'

'That's good dear, where?'

'Still in Adelaide. That was David Wang. He told me the board has dismissed Charles and Gino is going too, whenever they find him. Where's Dad?'

Her mother's spirits sank. She hated mining and was sorry Sam was so hooked on the industry, but she kept her feelings to herself as she answered, 'down the shed, love.'

'Get your best dress on Mum, we're going to party until the morning. I don't want to tell Dad till we get there, okay. I just wanted to tell you first. Woo-hoo, I'm back in the game, apparently. Mr Wang wants to meet me tomorrow and I want you to come too.'

'Why me, I thought you'd...'

'What, want Dad? Not this time. This is about a steady and strong influence to guide me through the negotiations and help me check the fine print, to make sure I'm not blinded by all the glitter and unicorns. I should you tell you more often that I need you. I'll try to do better.' She kissed her mother's cheek and walked toward the shed.

'Well what about that, Penny Lewis, she loves you. Better get cleaned up then.' Penny didn't talk out loud often, but with what Sam had said, tonight she felt as if she moved on air.

'What-cha-doin-Dad?' Clive hadn't heard that for a while.

'Well, look out, Cyclone Sam is home.'

'I'm taking your wife to diner, want to come too?' She watched him tap his hip pocket. 'It's okay Dad, this one's on me,' she climbed the saddle rail and straddled a pony saddle from her youth, 'do you reckon Simon's wife would let the kids stay up on a school night?'

'Dunno, ask her,' he helped her down 'I remember you riding that pony for hours. Poor old Honey I had to do it though, love. She was in agony and a bullet was the quickest way, I never knew the wedge it would put between us.'

'It's okay, Dad. God, I loved that horse, she listened to all my secrets and never asked for anything in return,' she brushed her sadness aside, 'it was a lesson I needed to learn, but it was hard at the time.'

'Just give them a call, Sam. You know you have to give love to get love, you just have to offer it first, Honey taught you that. Remember how wild that horse was when it came here, but you took a snow country brumby and within a month she let you put a halter on. Be gentle, ask nicely, she is as frightened about building a relationship as you are.'

'You do it for me Dad, please?'

'Sam.' He pulled his phone out and scrolled through the contact list. 'You can get past this Sam. You have to.'

'Thanks Dad.'

Clive sat on the end of the table, Penny at his side, on the right Sam moved in alongside her sister-in-law, Chelsea, exchanging small talk until dinner came. Sam felt as if she was pulling answers from Chelsea, as if they were trapped behind a sieve.

'So, Sis, what are we celebrating, a new man in your life?' Simon asked.

Chelsea shushed him.

'Nah, something's up, she hasn't come home for years, now here we are and she's paying. What's up Sam?'

'Simon?'

'No Chelsea, don't shush me, I want to know.'

Sam stood up, 'I just had some news I wanted to share. Simon's right, I've always pulled out of the family stuff, never felt I fitted in. I'd love to have my brother's confidence, Chelsea's style or Mum's ability to feed the nation with a tin of sardines and half a loaf of bread,' she looked down at her hands, 'but I'm too much like Dad, pigheaded, and I'll bulldoze through to get the job done. I'm not good with people, so don't expect a steady relationship and kids from me for a while. I'm still trying to learn that,' she picked up a glass and filled it, 'I want to propose a toast. I'd like to thank my family for letting me chase my dream. Dad, I understand yellow fever, you get it in your system and it lurks there until someone like me comes along and says drill a test hole, then the imagination soars and the dream takes hold. To Mum, who is always there with a steady hand sailing HMAS Lewis through stormy seas, and to Simon, a mate to all my boy crushes, football champion and all round smartarse, you don't know how much I miss you at times, big brother,' she sipped and refilled the glass, 'and I'm sorry I've taken longer to get to you Chelsea, the sister I'd always wanted and never took the time to get to know and I promise to do better, and,' she drew out the word to stress the importance of what she was about to say, 'last but not least, the little Lewis generation, I love following the pictures and stuff your mum puts on Facebook.'

'So, Sam just what are you saying?'

'I'm saying I love and need every one of you and I got another job today,' she splashed more wine into her glass, 'to the Lewis's.'

'Hang on a minute, what did you say?' Clive shook his head hoping to find some clarity, 'you have a new job?'

'If I want it, I'm going to borrow Mum for a few days while I go over the contracts. If it looks worthwhile, I'll sell the unit and the Mazda and put a deposit on that small farm just south of Simon and Chelsea's. I might even get a horse too, what do you think Dad?' She sat down and received reciprocal toasts with a contentment and sense of belonging she had never known before.

***

Angela passed Cassidy a coffee as he looked at his watch. It was almost six.

'We'll get this over quickly, reset the team for tomorrow and be in our own beds tonight, deal?' he raised the paper cup to her, 'and thanks.'

'That sounds good Sir, it seems ages since we left home.'

He set the coffee down, put his hands in the small of his back and stretched, 'okay, what do you know from what we see before us?'

'Well, that Joe Gillespie is hard to kill?'

'That joke's been done. Concentrate, what do you see?'

'Other than the Gillespies, the mining company and Winkler names show up the most.'

'Go on,'

'Take the stuff we know about Spoggy away and treat him as a gun for hire, then it's these guys we're after,' she stabbed the photos as if trying to trap a fly, 'Gino, and the Winkler Charlies.'

The team began to file in.

'Sir,' a uniformed sergeant put a photo of a medium sized Willow cooler on the board, 'it comes from the back of the HSV and it's not unusual I'd say, but on the inside...' he held another photo up and Gino's blue eyes looked out at them from the inside of the cooler.'

His partner stepped up. She had to reach on tip toes to move her photo to the top of the board, 'I raise your lifeless Australian-Italian enforcer with a copy of his killer putting the cooler in the boot of the HSV.'

'How can you be sure detective?'

'The closed circuit video shows the car arriving and the owner or driver get out and take the cooler from the boot. He loads it onto the stern of Gino's boat. The vision is grainy but you can see both faces, Spoggy and Di Massimo.'

'How did Di Massimo get to his boat?' Cassidy was impressed.

'Silvertop Taxis, he always uses them to go there during a weekend.'

'Weekend?' Darryl shuffled his files through his files, 'How old is this vision?'

'We have everything from Friday morning until the car was found.'

'And no sign of Spoggy since?'

She shook her head. 'No sir.'

'Any trace of a phone?'

'No sir, but we have people searching Di Massimo's homes and offices now.'

The DI's phone rang and he passed it to Angela who made notes of the conversation.

'And?' he asked, 'what else have you got?'

Another of the team joined them. 'Well, if it's show and tell,' he said, putting up a photo of the boat's deck, 'that mark below the seabird droppings is blood and most of it is bovine blood. He added another under water shot to the board, 'and here we have what appears to be the rest of the remains that belong with the head. If you look closely you can see the anchor rope threaded through his belt. Forensics need more time, but they say it's likely he was shot while crouching over and away from the shooter.

Without internal organs, or lungs, or a stomach full of gas, the anchor would have held him there for ages.'

Cassidy noticed Salma Akbar enter the room as Angela showed him the phone.

'Find a printer and get it up on the board. The rest of you chat among yourselves for a minute,' he waited for the super to walk over.

'You didn't have to stop for me,' she said.

'I didn't, the police divers have found something worrying.'

Angela came back into the room and put another photo on the board, moving others out of the way to make room, 'the rope on the anchor shows someone has tried to cut it. The weather's been good with little tide movement. We might have caught a break, Sir.'

'And the next photo, Angela?'

'This is pretty grainy and we'll have more once the team is on shore, but it shows what appears to be a bone yard. The divers passed it off as animal bones until they found these,' a picture of two skulls half covered in silt and marine detritus lay on the sea bed.'

'Has anyone got anything to add?' Cassidy asked the assembled officers.

A murmur of no went through the crowd and no-one came forward.

'Okay, that's it for today then and I'll issue instructions by text tomorrow. Well done all of you and thanks for pulling together so quickly. The Superintendent and I appreciate it.'

'You're wasted as a bush copper you know, that was impressive,' Salma Akbar studied the board, 'but DI Cassidy, you certainly know how to open Pandora's box when you set your mind to it.'

'Not me Ma'am, I only play the cards I'm dealt.'

'Remind me not to get into a game of poker with you then.'

'That's not my problem, I've got enough on my plate. I just want to catch Spoggy, he's the priority of this team now,' he thought about the briefs to be prepared, 'I'm going to have to pinch time from somewhere to make this case stick. Now I'm sorry Ma'am, but I'm off home now, I have a family who don't see enough of me these days.'

'I understand, good work today.'

'I'd like to think it was me, but if the truth be told it was serendipitous the way it all fell into place.'

'You do have to be in the right place though, don't you?'

'There is that Ma'am, there is that.'

CHAPTER SEVENTY FIVE

Angela walked toward the passenger seat but the DI handed her the keys. She opened the door then stood back and stretched before settling in behind the wheel.

'Are you all right Ange?'

'Sure, just stiff. I do want to find out how Tilly is doing, though.'

'I'll send her a text. Is she in your phone?'

'Yes.'

'What shall I say?'

'Say I'm driving, that I'm still working and I'll try to call tomorrow.'

'Getting hard, is it?'

'Yeah, when your friend's father goes rogue and then people are trying to kill everyone. I'd say it takes a toll. It's been going on for nearly twelve months now.

'If it's hard on us, how do you think the Gillespies are travelling?'

'That's why I'm worried Sir,' she watched him fumble with the message then noted the petrol gauge was below where she liked it to be, 'we'll need to refuel at Port Wakefield Sir.'

'Good, we can get food and a coffee, then you can sleep and I'll drive from there.'

'That sounds good, sleep well.'

She pushed through the traffic, it was easing now and she was pleased to see Adelaide grow smaller in the mirror. Twenty minutes to the North of Adelaide, Cassidy's phone rang and she pushed the Bluetooth button.

'DI Cassidy's phone.'

'Hello Angela, it's Salma Akbar, the Superintendent.'

'Ma'am.'

'Is the DI with you?'

'Yes, Ma'am, he's napping at the moment.'

'How far out are you?'

'By the Raceway at Virginia.'

'Can you turn around and come back to headquarters?

'Yes Ma'am.'

'I know you'll be late home, but it's important and I think you'll both want to see this.'

'We're on our way back now,' Cassidy had his head back and his mouth open.'

'Don't wake him yet, I'll see you when you get back here Angela.'

'Thank you, Ma'am.'

He continued to snore until they parked and Angela turned the engine off, 'what are we here already?'

'No Sir, we've been called back.'

'Damned mobile phones, who?'

'The super, Sir.'

'Why?'

'I don't know, she didn't say.'

'Right-o then, let's go and face the music.'

'And dance,'

'Wouldn't that be nice, detective.'

Salma Akbar had changed clothes since they last saw her and now looked more gym junkie than the Superintendent. 'Sit down the pair of you, I know you must be tired,' she put a couple of photos in front of them, 'the divers found this one further into the bone yard. Similar fate, shot from underneath and tied to an old cast iron plough wheel.'

Darryl picked up the photo and passed it Angela, 'Spoggy.'

She nodded in agreement.

'And for the interesting bit,' Helen Akbar turned the laptop so they could see the screen.

'I can see Spoggy's car,' Darryl said and leant forward to study the screen.

'Wait for it, now.'

'A scuba diver, he carries the cooler to the car and puts it in the boot. Wait when was this?'

'Before first light this morning. Now we don't have the face in this shot, but see here, his hand keeps slipping on the key. Now he takes a glove off to open the boot, in goes the cooler with Di Massimo's head, then he uses his arm to push the boot shut and goes to the water's edge. In a minute, you'll see one of Glenelg's patrols head toward the bridge. He must panic and throws the keys, missing the marina. There, you can see one of our blokes chalk a tyre and the frogman is away.'

'Jeeze that's a relief we found Spoggy or whoever he is,' Cassidy felt the tension starting to drain away and he listed in his chair.

'That's not the best bit DI. The Frogman is Hans Schmidt.'

'Who?'

'You know Sir, the slimy politician from Clare. God botherer by efficiency.'

'How?'

'A witness saw the keys of the Commodore on the tarp covering the boat next to his and called it in. I think you two caught more than one killer today and deserve to be filled in. I've arranged for the Ministerial chopper to fly you home.'

'Really?'

'Sweet.' Cassidy said.

'There's no-one there to use it until after dawn tomorrow anyway. Come on I'll drive and tell you about the raids we've planned for tomorrow. Well done you two.

It was after two pm when Angela made it into work the following day, Cassidy had phoned in to let them know he was taking the day off.

'I see you did okay in Adelaide yesterday,' Sarge pointed to the news streaming from the National Broadcaster, 'you got them then, Spoggy and the Winkler bloke,' Angela smiled at the station's father figure, 'a different time, a different place and I'd hug you,' he said.

'And I'd want you to,' the words had to work their way around the lump in her throat, 'thanks, Sarge,' she blew him a kiss that he pretended to catch and tuck it into his pocket.

The biggest arrangement of yellow roses she had ever seen hid the top of her desk. She knew they weren't from Andy, he wouldn't be caught dead ordering flowers, let alone going into a florist. She pulled on the silk ribbon and watched the loop in the bow disappear. Only her name was on the envelope, written in a woman's hand and in ink, not ball point. It had to be Tilly. She looked at the clock and made a mental note to call her. The card was scented, and read,

'Angela, yours is a bright and rising star, please make an effort to stay in touch, we can all use a friend in high places now and then. Kind regards, Salma Akbar'

'Well done girl,' a constable walking past high fived her, 'and because you got noticed, I've phoned Andy and told him it's his turn to buy first drinks tonight.'

After everyone had finished congratulating her, only the Sarge stood at her desk, 'here let me carry these out to your car for you. You don't need to be here and I want you to have a good rest and come in late tomorrow. The DI won't mind.'

'Thanks, I am tired.'

Tilly lay in Jeff's arms staring at the stars. 'A penny for your thoughts?'

'I was thinking with your Dad's health, the Winklers locked up, the homestead finished and with me out of work maybe we should bring our plans forward.'

'I think that's a good idea and it will give us all something positive to focus on.'

CHAPTER SEVENTY SIX

The waiting room felt cold and more than once Laura rubbed her hands over her arms, listening to the ordinariness of a brush cutter working outside above the noise of North Adelaide traffic. She looked at the clock and checked her watch, they were keeping time. The clatter of designer nails tapped across a keyboard and the murmur of the receptionist's voice, too low to make sense of anything.

Joe was standing in front of her and looking at the empty passage way, 'they said ten o'clock and we were the first appointment,' he picked the envelope off the chair alongside of her and dropped into it as if he were a sack of flour, 'when I say, I'm going to be somewhere at a given time, I make bloody sure I'm there. This is bullshit, it's quarter to eleven,' he stood up. 'I'll tell that girl to get him on the phone so as I can give him a piece of my mind.'

'And how will that get you seen any faster?'

'Well what do you suggest?'

'Sit there and read a magazine or something and wait.'

He thumbed through a stack of magazines, found an old edition of TIME, and sat down. He had just started reading an article on ecological farming techniques when he was called.

'Joe, Mr Joe Gillespie?'

Laura stood up, 'Joe,' he didn't respond immediately, 'Joe, the doctor.' She kicked his foot and he lifted his head.

'This way please.'

For five minutes the doctor explained the reason for their wait. He had spent a good part of the morning conferring via Skype with the doctor Joe had seen in England.

'Joe, Mrs Gillespie I'm not sure how to explain things, I have your MRI results from yesterday, remember the one where we used the contrast, and they appear the same as those without the dye that Dr Patel ordered a few weeks ago,' he moved the computer screen so they all could see it. The cursor circled an area of Joe's brain, 'this is the scan from King's in London, no contrast, and you can see there,' he pointed, 'is a white mass that looks to be about the size of a golf ball. Now if I show you yesterday's results, the golf ball has disappeared and, looking back to the one Dr Patel ordered, there is no mass.'

'So, what's it mean, doctor. Does Joe need more tests?'

'Not in the short term. I have no explanation for what has occurred but for now, I think we can let everyone get back to life as normal. I'll order another scan for six months and we'll take it from there.'

'Yeah sounds fine,' Joe was eager to get out of the place, 'c'mon love we have taken up enough of this man's time.'

'Are you a spiritual man Mr Gillespie?'

'Not particularly, Why?'

'These things happen from time to time and in some of these cases the patient and their families put it down to miracles, to faith, I wondered if that's how you see it?'

'I'm a bit too pragmatic for that, no I don't think so.'

'And you, Mrs Gillespie?'

'No, although I understand the universe is filled with things we can't explain,' her mind wandered back to the previous year, the Adnyamathanha, her sighting of a Kadaichi Man and Tilly's brush with the Mar'rallang, the women singing, 'maybe, anything's possible isn't it?'

Joe stood and reached for the doctor's hand, 'well I'm not going to question anything. I'm alive and I'll be alive for longer than I expected so thanks doc, I'll see you in six months.'

The doctor didn't respond, instead shifted his attention back to Laura, 'you said maybe, Mrs Gillespie.

Now I read the papers and watch the television. I saw Joe, I'm sorry, it is okay to call you Joe, I hope? I've been doing it since yesterday.'

'Yeah, no worries,' he folded his hands behind his head and stretched his frame as tall as he could.

The specialist spoke to Laura in reference to her own work, showing genuine interest in her replies to his questions about her discoveries and theories, but this visit was about Joe and she was as eager as he was to leave and to discuss this change of events in private, but the doctor hadn't finished, 'like I was saying, I follow interesting things and last year's sightings of the Kadaichi Man piqued an interest. You see, in my thirties, I spent a lot of my time in the bush working as a remote doctor. I'm convinced there's still a lot we can learn from these ancient customs and beliefs.'

Joe offered his hand for the second time and surprised himself by agreeing, 'me too,' he said.

The doctor took his hand, 'okay Joe, I'll let you go now,' he broke away and offered his hand to Laura, 'I'm glad to have met you, Mrs Gillespie.'

'Thank you, see you in six months then.'

'All the best Joe.'

Joe didn't answer, just nodded and turned to the door. Laura couldn't tell if he was deep in thought or sulking because of the attention the doctor had paid to her. 'You know Joe, you're a grumpy old bugger at the best of times, but I'm glad you're going to be around for a few years yet. You haven't finished half the jobs I've got for you.'

In the formal wear hire company in Rundle Mall, Jeff looked at another suit Tilly had pulled from the rack and screwed his nose up. He knew she wanted a simple wedding with only a few guests, as they'd both agreed on, but Laura saw it differently. To her, the wedding was an excuse for a party and the way the invitation list was growing they might be better advertising it as an open house.

'We might go traditional instead,' he said.

'Mum would freak. So I think we'll stay with the good old fashioned, you in a suit and me in a gown kind of do,' she pulled another suit from the rack and showed it to him.

'Yeah, no...look, how about a compromise? We can slip down to Percy Street, pick up some moleskins, nice boots, fitted shirt and a jacket. I know Dad and Joe would sooner have that than parade around in these monkey suits,' he passed the latest offering back to the saleswoman, 'do you want us feeling like that?'

'If I have to do the whole, look like a meringue thing, why don't you?' Tilly heard the huff in her voice and drew back, 'sorry, I didn't mean to bite, it's your wedding too.'

'Yeah, but when we first talked about it we wanted more of,' he used his fingers to make quotation marks, 'a *Little House on the Prairie* than a *Gone with the Wind* production I thought?'

'That's true. I think Mum got carried away with her lavish plans. I'd be happier in something other than white too and I think I need to rein her in. It's just that I haven't wanted to upset her with all she has on her plate and the diversion has been good for her too. Come on let's drive out to RM Williams and then I'll gather the courage to tell mum I've changed my idea about the dress,' she took his hand, 'and you can stand in front of me to catch any flack that she throws our way, deal?'

He looked at his watch, 'what time are we supposed to meet them?'

'Dad wanted lunch in the Casino at one o'clock, that's if the specialist hasn't held him over for more tests. Don't worry Mum would phone if there was anything wrong.'

'Shall we look for something for you now, or go to Prospect?'

'I'm not having you there when I pick out a dress. It's bad luck and besides, Mum would kill me.

'And you won't want the stuff us blokes wear to clash with the bridesmaids.'

'Matron of honour and junior bridesmaid. Fiona will want something she can wear again and Em will grow out of hers in no time. You can show me what you like and I'll tell you if it's okay. Brides have worked this way for generations.'

'And in Adnyamathanha tradition, the man tells the bride what she will or won't wear.'

'I think I'll check with Mum before I fall for any old line like that. Come on let's find the car,' she laughed at him, 'and don't think I'm silly enough to fall for any old ochre and feathers line either.'

Knowing Joe was okay, Laura felt their troubles were behind them, but Joe still seemed distant.

'Okay, what's going on in that mind of yours now? You're like a cat who's just realised it's lost eight lives.'

'It's nothing about me love. Just processing what he told us and it's made me think, that's all.'

'Care to share?' she waited for him to open the car door for her.

'Well yeah, kinda,' but he didn't expand on this as he waited for her to settle before he shutting her door and walking around to the driver's side and kept his silence as he started the engine and moved the gear selector to reverse.

'Now would be a good time, Joe.'

He moved the lever back into park and turned the motor off. 'All of the old man's gold,' he looked at her, 'there's a lot of money there, isn't there?'

507

'More than we could ever want.'

'So, if we were to set some of it aside to use and the rest could go into a trust or something, what do you think?'

'I think you might just be the best man I know, but have you thought what kind of trust you'd like to set up.'

'Well, first I thought we could quarantine seventy percent of it for some sort of trust and the rest we can call discretionary funds.'

'You've always talked about a farmer's hall of fame. That would be good.'

'And you once told me an interpretive centre was something you would do if we ever won the lottery.'

'But Joe we were just talking, dreaming, none of it was serious.'

'It's money we didn't know about and it's like winning the lottery. Let's just think about it for now, what do you think?'

'Yes, I think that's the best thing to do and now we'd better get cracking, Tilly will be waiting and I have no idea what she wants for a wedding dress so let's go.

CHAPTER SEVENTY SEVEN

Over lunch, they celebrated Joe's good news and, for Tilly, the past week had morphed into a distant, surreal time that she couldn't be sure had happened at all, then Joe and Jeff left the women to seek out a suitable wedding dress. Although Laura had argued suits would be a better option, Joe liked the RM Williams outfitters idea and that's where they headed, until Joe came up with a plan of his own.

'I have a few things I want to show you,' he tapped the side of his nose, 'I talked to Bill the other night and he suggested we should visit a few aviation museums and I reckon we could just about squeeze in the one at Port Adelaide.'

'Yeah, I'm up for that, but we have to be home in time to pick Emily up and Tilly will kill me if I screw that up. It's the first time I get to have her on my own and I want to be sure that when the girls get home tomorrow, Emily says I passed the test.'

'Yeah, just a quick visit, then we'll go back to the outfitters, grab a catalogue and head home. Anyway, Bill said they have a Gypsy Moth out there that's worth a look.'

'Font of knowledge, old Bill.' Jeff was laughing at him and Joe knew it.

'Can't hurt to look, what say we give it an hour. I'll even let you drive.'

'Not the Range Rover?'

'You want to drive or not?

'Chuck me the keys, then,' Jeff grinned, only three people had ever driven Laura's car and now he would be the fourth.

They exited the Grosvenor carpark and turned left towards Port Adelaide, 'so, no tumour then?'

'The doctor told us it was gone and who am I to argue,' Joe pulled the sun-visor down to reveal the courtesy mirror and checked his image.

'The tumour would be on the inside Joe,' Jeff laughed, 'I doubt if you'd see it.'

'Don't be an arse, I know that.'

'How do you feel though, you know, after all that's happened?'

'I thought I was going to die and it scared the shit out of me. Not so much the dying, but it got me thinking what if there is an afterlife?'

'What?'

'What if there is an afterlife, you know, heaven or hell or something we don't know about. If there's not, there's going to be a lot of dead pissed off people roaming around out there just waiting for their opportunity to exact vengeance.'

'I'd jump on the Christian boat if that's the case, they offer redemption.'

'Any room at the inn, yeah?' Joe turned and watched the tail of a Qantas jet on its approach to the airport.

'I don't know of an innkeeper in either heaven or on Earth who'd refuse you mate. Anyway, what's brought this on?'

'I've never given any thought to my mortality much and it's something Laura said before lunch,' he shifted in his seat and flicked the visor up, 'she said I looked like a cat with only one life left. I guess it made me think about my mortality.'

'Jesus Joe.'

'You reckon he's the answer?'

'I don't know, our mob has more superstitions than most, but I reckon you're over analysing it. Sure, the road's been rough, but go back to the stuff you said to us when we were four goals down at three quarter time in the Grand

Final,' Jeff turned to look at Joe, 'you told us we could only be beaten by ourselves, we just had to want it bad enough and what happened after that?'

'You towelled them.'

'And?'

'I don't know, what?'

'Some of us went on to greater things because we believed in ourselves. That didn't come from nature, Joe. That came from someone showing us that it was within us. You taught us to believe anything was possible Joe, anything.'

'Yeah?'

'So it seems to me that you need a little bit of that same talk now. Want me to recite it?'

'After all these years?'

'Okay, go on then.'

'Nah, just kidding, I can't remember a bloody word of it.' Jeff lied.

After spending an hour at the museum and getting the curator's contact details, they headed home. Joe pushed his seat back and reclined it, the sun was in his eyes so he returned it to upright. As they passed Gawler, he studied the various hangers and sailplanes at the gliding club.

'Have you two thought about where you want to live yet?' Joe asked.

'We haven't had time to discuss it much, why?

'I just wondered that's all,' Joe lay his head back, 'keep the shiny side up mate, I'm going to check my eyelids for cracks for a while.'

'No worries.'

'And stay under the limit, Laura gets really pissed if she finds a ticket in the mail.'

Jeff smiled and set the cruise control. He looked over at Joe and heard the murmur of a snore before reaching across to tune the radio.

'She doesn't like anyone fiddling with the stations either.'

Jeff put his hand back on the wheel.

At home without Laura, Joe, rattled through the bookcase, pulling and prodding several books along every shelf, but nothing took his eye. Pushing the last book back he heard something slip behind the case and the volume refused to go back where it came from. He unloaded the shelf until he located the culprit, he'd seen it before. Neville Shute's, *A Town Like Alice,* this time he opened the cover, the pages were creased with edges worn thin from reading. The dedication intrigued him. It was from Les to Joe's mother, '*A guide to a dream for my Dream and only we can make it happen.'*

Joe had refused Jeff's offer to stay for dinner and wanted to settle down to baked beans on toast, now he had something to read while the ads interrupted the football on TV. As he poured the beans into a bowl the phone rang, it was Elspeth. She and Bill had put their home on the market and were emigrating to Australia.

Joe felt a smile form and as he listened, a hundred scenarios played in his mind. She asked if Laura was home, because she wanted to share the news with Laura first. Joe promised Laura would phone her the following day. When he finished the call, he felt torn between sadness and joy, he wanted to quiz Bill on a few things about Jeff's old aircraft and hearing his voice always lifted his spirits too. The cottage seemed to grow when he was home alone, he looked at his watch and changed the channel on the television. He wanted to make sure he was sitting in front of the screen at the first bounce.

Taking a mug from the cupboard, he emptied a can of baked beans into it, cracked two eggs on top of the beans, pricked their yolks and set them in the microwave. With bread in the toaster he had two minutes to heat the beans and spread some toast. A cup of tea and he would be set. While he waited, he thought back to Elspeth and wondered if he should phone Laura and get her to call England. Deciding it would tie him up in conversation as the game started he thought sending Laura a text would be a better option. As he fumbled his way through the text message he smelt burning. His toast black, he pulled it out of the toaster and went back to the text. The bell went off on the microwave and his meal was ready. As Joe corrected and retyped his text his dinner went cold, he could hear the football starting as he buttered new toast, balanced everything along his arm and set himself in front of the TV. Satisfied with the message he pressed send and slid the phone onto the side table.

Joe had a spoonful of egg and beans ready to follow the toast into his mouth as he watched the umpire hold the ball aloft and as the ball hit the ground Joe took a mouthful of beans. The phone rang in the kitchen and he set his meal aside to answer it. Laura wanted to know what he had said to Elspeth before she called her.

Before Joe got back to his meal his tea was cold. The eggs had gone hard, but he had eaten worse and decided they would do. During the next advertisement break he opened the book and started to read, by half time in the football the phone rang again. Joe slapped the book onto the side table snatched up his cup and bowl and headed for the kitchen.

Another call from Laura. 'I've just got off the phone from England, Love. I said it would be okay for Bill and Elspeth to stay in the cottage while they looked for somewhere to live.'

'And us?' Joe liked them, but wondered how four adults would go in the same house for an extended period.

'I thought we'd be back at the Well by then.'

Joe smiled, he was ready to have a bit of space around him again. 'Are you sure you want to?'

'Yeah, there's lots to do before then though?' she waited for Joe to say something, the line was quiet for a minute or more, 'are you still there, Joe?'

'Yeah.'

'What's going on?'

'Nothing, just thinking, I've got a number of things to work through that's all.'

'You're not going all maudlin on me again?'

'No...'

She heard the determination in his tone. 'And?'

'And how Bill might help Jeff out with the old plane, that's all.'

'Good, Elspeth said he had a few ideas and would send you an e-mail with some things to talk to Jeff about. He's not home today, but you should call him tomorrow night.'

'Okay, well I'll get back to the footy.'

'Are you rushing me off Joe Gillespie?'

'No,' Joe knew Laura was wanting to talk and so they did for the next thirty-five minutes.

'Tilly's off the phone now, gotta go,' Laura said.

'Just like that?'

'I love you, old man.'

'And I love you too,' Joe smiled and remembered how when they first started calling each other, how the silent pauses would drag out without either of them being first to say goodnight and hang up. Tonight, the phone went dead without a pause.

The game was lost by the time he got back to his chair, so he turned off the TV and continued to read. The book was a classic and more engaging than when he had read it in college. He heard a rooster crow and looked at his watch, it was five o'clock in the morning. He would read another chapter and go to bed.

When he did manage to drag himself to the bedroom the sun was up, but he slept until the alarm raised him at ten o'clock. There was much to do.

At one o'clock Joe parked at the top of Tank Hill look out. The farmland was a picture of promise, the creeks now drawn with lines of new green regrowth. The view took in the Oladdie Hills to the north west, the Black Rock Range to the east and, if he used his binoculars, he could see the back roads and tracks that took him over the Morchard hills to Wanooka's Well, his home. He imagined the old homestead at Wilsons and the number of people the station had supported in the old days. Erskine to the east, where he could see the remains of stone farm houses abandoned during times of depression and hardship. Since the turn of the twentieth century the population had fallen by over seventy five percent.

Although it saddened him now, Joe had an idea how to reverse the trend and it could all start at Wilson's.

CHAPTER SEVENTY SEVEN

Tilly and Jonathon Smythe-Simms sat opposite David Wang, Sam Lewis, and the Wagmin Resources legal team. The meeting had the feel of a cold war negotiation with all friendships suspended until a resolution was found. Tilly insisted the matter be dealt with before her wedding and had determined that Joe would be a liability to reaching a suitable settlement.

Jonathon was the first to speak, 'welcome everyone, before you is our proposition seeking compensation on behalf of my client, Mr Joseph Gillespie,' he clicked the projector's remote and a photo of Joe flashed on the screen, 'in an effort to frighten my client into allowing your company and its affiliates onto Gillespie land, your CEO,' a picture of Charles Winkler in handcuffs and prison greens replaced Joe on the screen, 'set out to threaten maim, or murder my client.'

David Wang raised his hand, 'we agree this happened and we are prepared to accept that the company has a responsibility to compensate the family, so put your number forward and we'll negotiate from there.'

'Sir,' one of the legal team passed Wang a piece of paper, 'we cannot acquiesce or admit anything, to do so will put the company in peril.'

'Sorry Graham, these people have a strong case and a wish to settle outside of a court case. I'm in favour of that.'

'But sir, we could keep this going for years and I'm sure Ms Gillespie and her counsel know that, which is why they wish to make a deal.'

'Any other time I'd agree with you, but my business is banking and if Wagmin wanted to fight this then we would need to review our lending criteria,' he nodded toward Sam, 'as it is, Charles and his cronies have all but drained the company's reserves. I've made my decision and Ms Lewis is charged with restructuring the company. Now Ms Gillespie, let's make a deal.'

For the next five hours David Wang and Tilly Gillespie negotiated over the minutiae of the agreement, while Jonathon and Wagmin's legal team made notes to ensure integrity of the electronic recording

Joe didn't want money, but a trust fund set up to rebuild or restore the numerous mining sites dotted throughout the Flinders Ranges and to repurpose these as historic tourist venues. Tilly and Jonathon negotiated, David and Sam argued their company's point of view and by three o'clock an agreement had been reached.

A précis of the agreement was sent to Wagmin public relations department to be reworded as a press release announcing a new beginning of responsible mine management at the scheduled press conference and photo call. Sam's time to shine had arrived and, as she referred questions to David Wang, Tilly leaned over to him and said, 'she's good.'

'And someone with the integrity to match her ethics too, but this is a tough business.' He was well pleased with his choice.

'And?'

'And I'll support her until her wings are strong enough for her to soar on her own. I'll wager it won't take her long.'

'You're a good man Mr Wang,' Tilly said.

David just smiled and took a few questions and used the opportunity to outline his vision for the Wagmin Mining Trust.

After the meeting, Tilly guided Jonathon away from the crowd and into the street, 'My parents will be proud of our achievement today, thank you.'

'It wasn't much really. I think David Wang and his company would have done anything to keep this quiet. In the end, we gave them an opportunity to bury the corruption Winkler and his mate created and rebrand them as responsible,' he opened the driver's door of her car, 'how's the progress with those wedding plans?'

'Getting bigger by the day. Jeff's side are wanting us to include something to acknowledge his aboriginal heritage, Mum is inviting a cast of thousands and Dad wants another grandchild. I'm glad we've finished with all this mining crap, so I can get on with it.'

'If you ever need someone to shoot the breeze with, or feel a need to come back to the law, you let me know okay.'

'Thanks, Mum's been shopping up a storm and said to pick her up from the Uni. I'd better go and get her before Adelaide is devoid of stuff to sell,' Tilly slid in and pulled the belt over her shoulder, 'see you in September,' she said and closed the door.

Jonathon watched until he lost sight of her. As he walked to his own car, his phone rang. It was Sam Lewis offering him the role of managing Wagmin Legal Department, he told her he would need to think about it. The traffic seemed to carry him along and soon Jonathon was singing to the drive time playlist Smooth FM piped across the airwaves. Their move to Adelaide had been a positive one.

Laura was with Professor Thomas when Tilly found her. She smiled, it must have been a productive discussion because Laura only had a small group of parcels and yet Tilly could see she was beaming.

'Okay, I'm ready for home,' Laura thanked him, picked up her parcels and passed them to Tilly, 'see you in September,' she said to him.

'What was all that about?' Tilly asked her mother as they walked to the car.

'Just business, darling. Nothing to worry about. You have enough on your plate with the wedding.'

'What are you scheming, you haven't asked the university choir to perform? Mum you're not making a big production out of this, are you?' Tilly was starting to speed up causing Laura to almost run.

'No... What do you take me for?'

'Well then what were you doing?'

'Just asking for all my research work to be saved onto the electronic register.'

'That's it.'

'Fraid so, now let's get home to your father and the others.'

'Those are my others, Mum and very significant others at that.'

Laura smiled to herself, Tilly had taken the bait and now it was time to rest her eyes on the way home.

Tilly left the bags on the front veranda and said she would see her father the next day. It felt good to back away from the cottage and go home.

'You there, Joe?' Laura called as she pushed the door open and shouldered her way through, 'be a love and put my bags in the bedroom.' there was no answer, 'Joe...' Laura decided to manage the bags herself and look for him later. On the bench, she picked up the copy of *A Town Like Alice* and a note on the fridge said he was in his grandfather's office and she whispered to herself. 'Just what are you up to, Joe Gillespie?'

She found him at his grandfather's desk, so captivated by his mother's journal he had not heard her until she was standing close behind him. She put a hand on his shoulder, the ancient office chair spun around and his knees caught her, almost knocking her over in the process, 'Shit woman, you frightened the life outta me.' She bent down to kiss him.

'What's going on, love?'

'Catching up with the ghosts from my childhood,' she stood alongside him, moving a few strands of hair aside and kiss the bald spot on the top of his head. He put his arm out and wrapped it around her waist, 'don't worry, they're friendly.'

'I've never been worried by ghosts, Joe. They were your demons.'

'Demons of my own making.' He felt her kiss him again.

'Yep.'

'I should have read this stuff after Dad died no, thinking about it, I probably should have taken more of an interest before he died,' he passed her a journal, 'this is Mum's diary, I came looking for it after finding some notes she'd made in a book I was reading.'

'A Town Like Alice?' Laura raised her eyebrows, 'it's not like you to be caught up in a novel, Joe?'

'Pfft,' he waved as if swatting the statement aside, 'seems she knew about all that gold and between them they were planning to do something special with it. Have a read and let me know what you think.'

'Okay, then how about dinner at the pub. I think we could both do with a decent meal.'

CHAPTER SEVENTY EIGHT

Arriving home from the pub Joe and Laura didn't want to sleep, instead sat up talking for what seemed like hours. Life was giving them a fresh start and now they could afford to work on new dreams, different to those they had forty years ago. Tilly was settled, Emily had taken to Jeff, they had financial security and although most of their generation had planned a retirement of travel, they had different desires.

'Laura rolled up onto her elbow and kissed his cheek, 'big plans love, but do-able,' she kissed him again, 'Good night.'

He rolled over and propped up on one arm and returned the compliment, 'night, love,' he held his lips on hers longer than usual and felt her smile, 'thanks.'

'For what?'

'Being you.'

She laughed at him, 'go to sleep, Joe. I'll see you in the morning.'

It took ages and he felt her breathing as she slept, he knew she was smiling when he too dropped into sleep.

That night Joe slept the easiest he had for years, Jeff and Tilly were getting on with their life, Bill and Elspeth had settled into the town, the workshop was full of tradesmen repairing and restoring vintage vehicles, and tourists and students pouring through Laura's barn.

When Laura woke next morning, Joe was laughing and talking in his sleep. She slipped out of bed, eased into her dressing gown and went to the kitchen. As she waited for the kettle to boil, she read the notes Joe had made while reading *A Town Like Alice*. He had roughed out a plan to regenerate his home town and now with the gold find, they could afford it.

'We can do this Joe, we can do this, Joe.' she said to herself, 'we can do this.'

About the Author

Born in Orroroo South Australia, Terry ran a successful motor business until joining AGCO Massey Ferguson in 1996 and going on to work in sales and marketing roles within the tractor and machinery industry. Diagnosed with muscular dystrophy in 2012 he decided to change focus and put those skills into fiction writing.

Today he lives in Melbourne and travels Australia seeking locations, characters, and plots for his next novel.

Acknowledgements

Writers are a strange lot, we sit in front of a blank screen shuffling letters into words, only to backspace and replace them with others, editing and proof reading as we type. When satisfied and if we belong to a writing group, as I did at the time Gillespie's Gold first started becoming more than an idea. With as much trepidation as hope, we e-mail it to our colleagues to critique.

My friends at Wordsmiths of Melton have invested a lot of themselves in Gillespie's Gold. Offering advice on flow, if there is too much tell and how to fix a boring storyline. My time in the room at our library in Melton, is a sanctuary of ideas, as much as it is a cauldron of critique. To my friends who offered help with this story, I would not have reached this point without you.

Every good manuscript needs a steady hand who will guide the author through the editing process and Merlene Fawdry has stepped into that role once again. I can't think of enough ways to thank Merlene for taking my words and making them glow. Merlene, you are who I turn to whenever words are hard to find, or if I am sliding away from the plot. It's your encouragement and support that brings us to this result, a crafted yarn for everyone to enjoy.

To my wife Ruth, I thank you for understanding my needs. It's not easy being ignored for weeks on end as someone you love, goes to their computer day after day, living an almost hermit existence, only coming out of their cave when they want to be fed and watered. When the writing is finished, you are then coerced into reading a rough first draft and later proof reading numerous rewrites until I'm satisfied. You are my inspiration and without your encouragement, I doubt I could do this.

To those people who have been kind enough to buy my books, investing your time reading a yarn that has floated around in my mind until it eventually escapes onto the page, thank you.

The story lives because of you, through you and beyond us. Who knows, someday other generations may find entertainment in our stories too.

Other Titles by Terry L Probert

KUNDELA

The theft of a prized steer, trashing of the farmhouse, an abduction and rape of a young woman upturns the lives of the Gillespie family.

Set in the beautiful Flinders Ranges during drought, Joe's raid on the bikie camp, clashes with the political ambitions of the police minister and clouding the judgement of the head of South Australia's Bikie Squad causing their case to implode.

Interference by ASIO complicates the police investigation causing Joe to divulge his past, breaking the Official Secrets Act and the pressure of him being hunted leads to a mid-air heart attack.

DI Cassidy believes Joe is responsible for three unexplained bodies found on the roadside, their faces and hands blown away by shotgun blasts. However, Senior Constable Rankin s not as sure, but his attraction to Tilly Joe's daughter complicates his involvement in the case. Bush forensics by a senior policeman bring an unexpected result. While modern aboriginal women in traditional dress sit in a circle around a large flat stone in a Port Augusta park. In the centre, dry bones shaped to form kundelas point to the effigy of a man. They are singing Joe's attacker to death.

KUNDELA won a COMMENDED in the 2013 Christina Stead Awards

VOSS The Price of Innocence

When a series of murders are linked to Detective
Inspector Voss, he is stood down from active duty. With
the aid of Eddie, a homeless man who lives in Voss's
front garden, he leads his former colleagues into the
seedy world of Canberra's porn industry and uncovers
corruption at the highest places. In the process, he's
forced to face some unknown and unwelcome truths
concerning one of the victims – his ex-wife. *The Price of
Innocence,* is a fast-paced crime mystery that will keep
the reader guessing until the very last pages

www.ingramcontent.com/pod-product-compliance
Lightning Source LLC
Chambersburg PA
CBHW020537120726
47903CB00001B/16